Lurid Curse

His Name Was Augustin
Book V

C.L. Carhart

LURID CURSE

Book 5 of *His Name Was Augustin* series

Copyright © C.L. Carhart 2022

First edition: March 2022

This is a work of fiction. Names, places, characters, and events are fictitious or are used fictitiously. Any similarity to real persons, living or dead, is coincidental.

ISBN: 978-1-954807-08-2 (paperback)

ISBN: 978-1-954807-09-9 (eBook)

https://www.clcarhart.com

Edited by Elizabeth Johnson

Cover Design © J. L. Wilson Designs | https://jlwilsondesigns.com

For Mommy
who reads murder mysteries
and taught me to conquer adversity

Other Books by C.L. Carhart

His Name Was Augustin [Complete Series]

Arcane Gateway, Book I
Mystic Passage, Book II
Astral Fantasia, Book III
Cryptic Pathway, Book IV
Numinous Fortune, Book VI

Brief Pronunciation Guide

Augustin – Au-GUS-tin
Bayerisch – BEYE-rish (eye is pronounced like eyeball)
Bayern – BEYE-urn (eye is pronounced like eyeball)
Dane – DAH-nuh
Eihalbe – EYE-hahl-buh (eye is pronounced like eyeball)
Freia/Freya – FREYE-yuh (eye is pronounced like eyeball)
Isar – EE-zahr
Muniche – MYOO-nih-khuh
Swanhilde – Swan-HIL-duh
Thaden – TODD-n
Torstein – TOR-stein (stein is pronounced like a beer stein)
Traudl – TROW-dool (trow is pronounced like cow)
Üwe – EW-vuh
Vreni – FRAY-nee
Wuotan – VOH-tahn

You can find a full pronunciation guide and translations at the end of this book.

Table of Contents

Prologue

Before I commence writing the most convoluted book of all—rampant with the greatest glories and deepest distresses—I must record, with a patient smile, a snippet of Augustin's remarks about Book IV. He finished reading it some time ago. A bit of business lately called me away from my inexperienced chronicling, and I return to this writing desk that has occupied too many hours of the past year at the dawning of the next.

A snowstorm whirls outside the window now, rustling my papers. I shoot one glance at the calendar, its vellum glowing blue in the candlelight, and I shake my head as I wonder how long it shall be before I consider my tale complete. Augustin insists that my son deserves to read my entire life story, but as I look ahead to this particular book, I cringe at the memory of its events. Max experienced many of them himself, so when he reaches this volume he might wish to breeze through and avoid its tragedies.

To Max, I say, please read on for a look at your mother's heart during the brief time we spent together. Too much lies beyond what we can see, and thus I return now to history.

As I recall, Augustin eyed me with an expression somewhere between satisfaction and pity when he finished inspecting Book IV. His fiery blue eyes alight with a dark humor, he said, "You certainly have always been a hopeless case, Swanie. Married to your Keyholder here, at the end, as we had wished—" he tapped the final page of my work with one finger, the sound seeming to echo off of the stone walls around us "—and yet you persisted in your whims, promising inglorious wishes that your fettered heart would not allow you to keep."

I scoffed at his criticism, turning around on the stool to look up at him where he stood over me, frowning at the last paragraph I had written. And I reminded him with a bit of smugness that I need not answer to him for my fantasies, and that he ought to be grateful for them. "What would it be for us now, if I had chosen to banish all thoughts of you into the past?"

"It would be a misfortune for you, for then you would have no professional critic here to mend your grammar." He smirked at me, his teeth a brilliant white.

I pouted at him and made a dismissive gesture with one hand, suggesting that he leave me in peace if he had no positive judgments to impart. But he went on to inform me of a few pressing matters, asserting that I abandon my pursuits until a more favorable time.

So I laid my pen and paper aside with some regret, snuffing the candles and trailing Augustin as he quitted the chamber. He paused just outside the door, waiting for me to come to his side so we could descend the staircase beyond together. And I asked him if he had any advice regarding Book V, which in some ways would be the bane of my account.

"I can plead only that you cease writing these scenes of lugubrious farewells," Augustin replied after a moment's consideration. "They grieve my heart, Swanhilde, dredging up a lake of sorrow, memories that I rue." His eyes burned into mine as we progressed down the stairs. His right arm wrapped snake-like around my waist, a thousand ghosts seeming to haunt his visage.

I sighed, knowing that he referred to the severance of our heart-bond. "Unfortunately, there are more partings that I have yet to address."

"I trust that they shall not damper the dawning of the sun," Augustin hinted, and I assured him, with a confident smile, that they would not . . . .

Chapter One:
The Patriarchy

Upon my return to München, I discovered that my new roles of businesswoman, wife, and Lady of the local Teuton community rendered me thoroughly busy, with hardly a moment to spare for my own pursuits. I had to shadow my father at the office on weekdays, and was afforded the title of his personal assistant. Along with doggedly honing my skills at the responsibilities of my position, it seemed like I would never finish meeting the highest officials of Süddeutsche Getriebe. I already knew my Onkel Derek, but the others had remained on the fringes of my childhood. Many of them reminded me of my noble peers in medieval Muniche—wealthy snobs who cared only about money and power. The world of high-end business had not changed much throughout the centuries, it seemed.

I spent the evenings with Hans, my faithful Keyholder, who worked with me to redesign my rooms and the spare office on the second floor of the Thaden house. We agreed to expand and refurnish the bedroom, and transform the office into a private parlor for our use. Once the contractors began the renovations, I would move temporarily into one of the guest rooms on the third floor; and I assured my husband that he could spend the nights there with me if he wished it.

Hans joined me in our spiritual dream world every night, the magical bonds of our city drawing us ever closer. Oftentimes, we discussed what had happened during our workdays, how we had to navigate separate spheres of the corporate world. We also shared some of our personal concerns and triumphs as we drifted above the roofs of München, Hans' fiery element shrouding my heart in serenity. My husband admitted that it was a relief to have me home, that he felt a sense of satisfaction rising from our city's spirit at the nearness of its *Leitalra*.

"Though I've held the keys for three decades now, I don't think I'll ever stop learning about the mysticism that binds us," he told me one night as we strolled along the path of the Isar, the moonlight casting argentine slivers upon the river's surface. He held the heart of my soul in his hands as we walked, his aura relaxing my spirit, like it always did. "I felt restless when you were away at college, as though a piece of my heart had broken away to roam the world alone. It scratched at my contentment, though I'd never admit it to my peers."

I slowed my pace and looked at my husband's spirit, silently marveling at the magnificence of his black fire. It blended his robes into the summer night and rose from his head in obsidian waves. The pale skin of his face glowed with youth and gratitude as his elemental eyes gazed down at my heart, beating softly in his hands.

When we met in our dreams, it was easy to forget that Hans was fifty-six years old, a man with decades of experience upon his shoulders. Truthfully, I, too, was much older than I appeared—for I had spent twenty-two years in the eleventh century, a time far different from the modern day. Although my physical body was that of a youthful maiden, my mind bore burdens similar to Hans'.

"I'm glad to be home, too," I murmured at length, a renewed notion of belonging swelling within me. "I know this is where I belong, in spite of . . . ."

I stopped myself before I spoke further. If I wanted to continue reveling in the peace that my Keyholder offered, I needed to funnel my repressed yearnings away, into the darkest corner of my mind. I adored Hans, and I trusted him to treat me well as both his wife and his Lady. But sometimes it was hard to ignore the life I had left behind—the poignant love of a Cursed One, a dead man doomed to wander the earth in search of what he could not regain.

Hans' lips brushed my heart, and I groaned softly at the intimacy of his gesture. "It's my duty to heal the wounds your past left upon you, my precious ice princess," he said, his voice low and husky. "I'll do all that's in my power to ensure that you never regret your choice."

"Choice," I repeated with a scornful snicker, my gaze upon the Thalkirchner Bridge in the distance. "I wasn't aware that I had a choice."

I recalled my elderly mentor Bertha Lohr, the previous Lady of Muniche. On her deathbed, she had urged me to seize what life gave me and make it beautiful. But I had never expected to be bound to a fated mate and raised up as the Teutonic symbol of my city. *And I never expected to be ripped away from my one true love in the process,* I thought, my muses a thousand years in the past.

"You could easily have chosen to follow your Black Priest into the depths of hell," Hans answered. He cleared his throat over the words 'Black Priest,' an odd sound for a spirit to make. I shot him a suspicious look as he placed my heart inside his robes, safe and protected beneath his elemental sway. Hans caught my gaze, and his thin lips twisted into a simper. "You know it's true. I'm still astonished that you picked me over him."

My Keyholder looked embarrassed, and he ran one hand through the sable fires of his hair. But I just raised my eyebrows at him as I sensed his wavering emotions. He did not imagine himself worthy of my love. He knew that Augustin had more to offer me as a Cursed One, my advocate before Wuotan, my city's immortal avenger.

"You're forgetting that even Black Priests haven't found a way to break the bonds of a Teuton city," I said. "That means even if I did take a quick jaunt to the past in hopes of enjoying a few rounds of elemental sex, my stupid heart would tell me I want Prince Otto. And I don't want him at all, not now, not then, not ever."

Hans shook his head a few times, his focus on the bridge rather than me. "I guess I should feel honored that you'd choose me over the famed Prince of Teuton history." He dove into the sky before I could reply, so I propelled my spirit to follow him into the atmosphere.

"As long as you don't curse me with your blood and abandon me to Wuotan, you're a far better man than he could ever be," I declared as I drifted to the edge of a cirrus cloud where Hans had halted. He grinned and held out a hand in invitation to dance. And the two of us whirled together in a graceful gambol of black fire and ice, with the city lights of München decorating the ground far below.

Dreams such as that invigorated my spirit, granting me the optimism to tackle each new day, the hope that Hans and I could use our authority to guide the Teutons in our community toward the path of light. I had already begun to work on lesson plans for the children, to introduce them to the histories no longer taught in schools. Under my watch, every young Teuton in München would learn to wield their elemental magic, to speak and read our ancient dialect, and to look deeper into our cherished stories and divulge the cryptic secrets. I wanted the youth to recognize their gifts and their faults, to treat others respectfully whether Teuton or outsider, to rise above any vestiges of victimhood.

But I had a fair number of cultural norms to push against in my quest to create a better world for my own people. Hans had advised me that a Teuton Lady's influence tended to increase over time; and therefore, I ought not to attempt any rash changes. Although he agreed with my desire to promote equality amongst our people, he suspected that some of the priests on the Teuton Council of München would not readily fall in line. He arranged for us to meet them in our official stance as the married Lady and Keyholder on the last Saturday in June, for he averred that it was time to make our intentions known as a couple.

On the Friday before Hans and I were to meet the council, I mentioned our rendezvous to my father. For the past two years, I had kept my status as *Leitalra* under wraps to protect him, since he had shunned all Teutonic magic after my mother died in childbirth. Recently, Hans and I had told him the truth about our relationship, and I also gave him a rundown of my experiences in the eleventh century. At first, my father responded with foreseeable dismay, but he had come to terms with the situation during our recent family vacation.

As his chauffer drove us home from work, I confessed that I was nervous to confront those five priests in such a manner, for Hans had said that I should present my plans for community improvement. "I'm scared that Herr Dantzler might try to stop me, if he gets wind of what I'm going to do," I noted, shuddering at the memory of the Old One on the council. He put forth a grandfatherly air, but I knew not how he would react to my radical ideas.

"And what exactly are you going to do?" my father asked, leaning back in his seat and favoring me with an encouraging look. His gray eyes sparked just a bit with elemental energy, his brown hair slicked perfectly even after a full day in the office.

"Teach the kids that men and women are equal," I said with a careless shrug, though that concept tended to be outlandish to those entrenched in old Teutonic traditions. "That a girl shouldn't offer her heart to the first man who asks for it. That people need to respect fairies and nature as much as they respect human beings. Who knows, I might even teach them blood control."

"Hmm. Might not be wise to go that far. It'd lead to more suicides."

"Good point. Guess I'll save that part for the older teens." I smiled at my father, pleased that he seemed to approve of my plans. Hans had once told me that my father distrusted a lot of Teutonic customs for good reason, and I had a strong suspicion that he found much of it repressive and antiquated. Eventually I hoped to uncover more of his motivations there, especially since he and my cousin Beth were madly in love. Neither of them had disclosed whether she intended to take the risk of obtaining Teutonic magic through the blood-transfer.

"If those priests give you any trouble, threaten to take away their Teuton blood," my father suggested as we reached the Thaden grounds. He said it bluntly, and I giggled, thinking that he was being facetious.

Hans and I talked about what we would say to the council when we met in our dreams that night. He promised to take the flack if any of them complained that we had sealed our bond in a Teutonic wedding back in December of 2001. Technically, we should have invited the entire council to the ceremony, along with their wives—but we had married in secret in my backyard, our ritual hardly one for the history books. We had not started our relationship off on the right foot, according to our people's customs; but Hans suspected that we could smooth things over by inviting all of the Teuton families in München to our church wedding. We planned to hold that one on May 3rd of 2003, and afterward the two of us would embark on a private honeymoon.

On Saturday afternoon, I stood at Hans' right side in the Teutonic meeting place outside the city, his strong hand wrapped protectively around mine, while he addressed the five priests before us. I only half-listened to what he said, as I allowed my gaze and my spirit to stalk the clearing in silent observation. It was a hot summer day, so I had dressed down for the occasion; I wore jean shorts and a tube top, my mid-length black hair braided and pinned to the back of my head. My Keyholder, meanwhile, wore the standard set of priestly robes with the five keys of München hanging from his belt. I sensed significant heat radiating from his body. Hopefully his fire shielded him from the sweltering sunshine.

We stood toward the center of the clearing, with the trail to the parking area behind us and the light green waters of the Isar before us. No one had bothered to light a fire in the pit off to the left. None of those gathered had brought any offerings along, like they had the first time I met the council after Muniche's spirit bound my heart in the summer of 2000. Instead, the five priests stood in a semicircle around us, clad in black robes and staring us down in silent judgment.

Rudi, the helpful man who had officiated our wedding, interjected a couple phrases of support for Hans and me, saying that the way we chose to handle our relationship was our prerogative, not anyone else's. I exchanged a brief look of thanks with him, relieved at his easy support. He had always been very kind to my elderly predecessor, and it seemed like nothing would change for him now that Muniche's spirit had taken residence in a much younger maiden.

The other four men did not appear quite as accommodating. The youngest, Jürgen, looked as though the neck of his robes was choking him; he did not speak, but he often scratched at his goatee, and wisps of smoke rose occasionally from his close-cropped hair. Warren, the tall priest with light brown hair, cleared his throat every few minutes and pointedly did not look at Hans or me; he kept his focus on the notes he took on a small pad of paper. Oskar, the short bald priest, looked from Hans to me and back again, his lips pursed as his eyes zeroed in on our clasped hands. I wondered whether he was jealous or simply shocked.

Herr Dantzler, the stout older head of the council, bobbed his head up and down when Hans finished speaking, his earth-tinted eyes looking rather askance at my casual outfit. "Well, well. It is good to hear that you and Swanhilde have consummated your bond, *Leitaeri*," he said in a gravelly tone. "It has been far too long since our city's leaders have come together for the good of our people." Some of the other priests muttered in agreement, and then the gray-haired man added, "I trust that we can expect a few children from you in years to come?"

I had to actively restrain myself from rolling my eyes, and I shifted my gaze toward the Isar behind the row of priests. *Damn Teuton men are always offspring obsessed, no matter what era it is. They think all women are good for is having kids.* I worked to keep my discomfiture to myself as Hans replied succinctly that we had agreed to try for two children. All of the council members—even Rudi—sounded thrilled by this. I even heard Warren say, "Ach, thank God!"

Then Herr Dantzler turned his gaze upon me and said, "Please accept my hearty congratulations on your wedding, *Leitalra*. Your readiness to seize your duties breathes new life into the Teuton community. You may recall that the late Lady Muniche gave generously to those in need all the years of her life, and that she trained the youth in both their magic and Teutonic traditions. Can we expect the same from you, dear Swanhilde?"

The older man's face appeared friendly, but I sensed the eyes of every priest in the clearing boring down upon me. All of my intentions began drifting away from me like balloons escaping into the sky, and my mouth went dry as my veins cooled with ice.

Can I really stand here and tell these men that I plan to teach young girls to stand up for themselves? That we need to be more accommodating to spouses trying to escape intimate partner violence? That it's okay if a girl doesn't want to have kids, or if a boy doesn't want to become a Keyholder?

Hans' hand squeezed mine in support, and I opened my mouth, trying to figure out where to start.

But before I could find the right words to say, Herr Dantzler's eyes widened in apparent horror, and I heard several gasps from the other priests encircling us. My ice froze my skin in an automatic defensive response, and I shot a glance to the left, to my Keyholder's face. A tight smile crept across his lips, and his eyes closed for a second before opening in a flat black—the color of his element.

My icy spirit recognized that someone had intruded upon our gathering, an unanticipated interloper. I sidled closer to Hans and endeavored to extend my spirit just enough to identify this new presence without being obvious

—something I was not particularly skilled at doing. The eyes of all five of the priests before us were veiled by their elements, and I sensed an energetic tightness in the air, along with an erratic breeze stemming from Oskar—the whirlwind.

A moment later, I heard a chuckle in my brain, the voice of a spirit that was not unknown to me. And Herr Dantzler gaped like a fish as he stared over my head toward the man who had entered the clearing in spirit form. His jaw moved back and forth before he managed to splutter a greeting.

"Herr . . . Herr Max von Thaden. What a pleasure . . . to see you here."

Chapter Two:
A Strong Ally

Taken off guard, I kept my focus on the priests before me, though I wanted to turn around and look upon my father in spiritual form. He had shown me the power of his energy earlier this month, but I did not realize that he knew how to separate his spirit from his body. *Pappi knows a lot more Teutonic magic than he lets on. What would a Teuton of energy look like? Intimidating, judging from the reactions of the council members.*

I knew that I needed to appear unsurprised, as though my father's intrusion was welcome and planned. But my heart pounded swiftly as the five priests stood silent, waiting for my father—or perhaps my Keyholder—to answer Herr Dantzler's salutation. My element crept into my eyes, blurring my vision behind my glasses; I needed to put them in my pocket. But my arms had frozen solid.

Greetings, gentlemen. My father spoke at last, his mental voice poised and cool, practiced elegance. *I trust that each of you has expressed a willingness to support our new* Leitalra *as she takes up her appointed role among us?*

A rock dropped into my gut. "Swanie was just about to address that very subject," Hans said, his right hand still clasping mine protectively. He had switched from the Bayerisch dialect to Teutonica, mimicking my father. A sense of formality descended upon our gathering.

Is that so? My father sounded guarded now, and I sensed his potent element drawing closer to my right side. *Why don't you tell them what you told me in the car yesterday, Swanie?*

He offered the suggestion in dialect, and I suspected that he spoke it to me alone. I flexed the fingers of my free hand—their icy coating clinked them against each other—and reached up to remove my glasses. As I tucked them into a pocket of my shorts, I directed my eyes toward my father's spirit.

He hovered just centimeters from my right side. His robes were a glorious amalgamation of energy's translucence, the vibrant hues of lightning, and swaths of dark energy's shadow. A halo of electricity encompassed his hair, and his eyes sparked with a brilliance I could hardly withstand, even with icy vision. He nodded once at me and added, *Don't fear them. Muniche is on your side.*

A sense of certainty pervaded my spirit as I recognized the inherent power I held in this moment. My Keyholder of black fire stood at my left side, and a man of pulsing energy stood at my right. Muniche's spirit urged me forward, to take hold of her authority once and for all. None could challenge me now.

"To answer your question, Herr Dantzler, one of my primary goals as Muniche's Lady is to dismantle the outdated prejudices that have held the Teuton people back," I began, speaking Bayerisch even though I could have easily recited my entire discourse in Teutonica. When I had first returned from the Middle Ages, Hans told me that I spoke Teutonica with a weird accent; and I did not need these priests to freak out about something that ridiculous.

Before any of the men before me could protest, I pressed on. "Rudi and a few other people have mentioned the importance of preserving Teutonic heritage, ensuring our people's magic doesn't die out." I met Rudi's gaze for a second and caught his look of interest. "The primary way our people have done that has been to elevate Teutons of high blood, and indoctrinate the young to believe that they ought to seek a partner with the purest blood possible.

"If you look at our situation rationally, that concept is antiquated. We all know that women of high Teuton blood have a difficult time in childbirth. It would be smarter to include more people of lower blood levels in our celebrations, in our peer groups. That way, those who can't grasp their magic could partner with those of eighty-five percent or higher, especially the ones without destructive elements. Then, we could increase our numbers over time in ways aside from childbirth, and broaden the gene pool in the process."

I paused to catch my breath, surprised that I had managed to speak on that issue without pushback. I looked at each priest on the council in turn, reading hesitation, astonishment, and reflection in their expressions. *Am I really the first person to think of this? Have the Teuton people been stooped in eugenics all this time, after the outside world moved on?*

"The other thing I'd like to do is give a platform to Teuton women, especially the ones who've been abused by their partners," I went on before I lost my nerve. Herr Dantzler's countenance darkened at the subject, so I said, "Our culture can't progress if we don't recognize that men and women aren't perfect, and that priests are taught a type of sorcery that can shackle a woman into spiritual slavery. I have nothing against the heart-bond when used out of love, but some men use it for sin. And I'm not going to stand by and watch Teuton children grow up in broken homes due to a master's cruelty."

I stand by my daughter in this, my father declared, as several of the priests shuffled from one foot to the other. Warren scratched down several things in his notebook, while Rudi and Jürgen averted their attention from me to my father. *I know exactly what priests are taught on the subject of heart-bonds, and much of it is despicable. I will personally fund any efforts the* Leitalra *chooses to take in her quest to bring true liberty to our people.*

A scoffing sound rattled in the air, and I shifted my gaze to the priest who stood nearest to Hans, at the far end of his comrade's semicircle. "Your daughter has lofty goals, Herr von Thaden, but what will come of them if she takes after her mother in due course, I wonder?" The smoky gray eyes of the youngest priest on München's council regarded my father's spirit in what appeared to be scorn.

I opened my mouth to give the man a piece of my mind, but Hans' spiritual hands tightened around my heart in silent caution. I shot him a pointed look, and my father spoke again before my Keyholder deigned to acknowledge me. *Jürgen Peninger, correct?*

My father's mental voice held immense implications as he mentioned the name of Jürgen's employer and mused about the young priest's position therein. Jürgen took a step back and stared at my father's spirit with an arch look. To his credit, he stifled any further criticisms he may have entertained.

By the time Hans and I parted ways with the council, Rudi and Oskar had pledged their assistance to my cause. Herr Dantzler had conceded that he would share my concerns with the three current priests-in-training. After realizing that I did not know any of them personally, I proposed that my Keyholder and I meet with them to test their motivations. "No one should be taught how to create the heart-bond unless he respects men and women equally," I said.

As I rode home in the passenger seat of Hans' BMW, he held his peace for a while, the songs from the latest Tristania album providing background noise. I sang along with most of the songs, feeling satisfied with myself for the first time in a long time. I had not backed down before the council; the priestly guardians of my city must come to terms with a more inclusive society.

"You'll want to get in touch with your friend Ina," Hans said after the song "Deadlocked" had ended. I turned the music down and looked at my husband, who had halted the car at a traffic light. "She's nearly done organizing her affairs after her husband's death last year. I'm pretty sure she's back in München."

"Was she able to get custody of Lea?" I asked, recalling Ina's love for her stepdaughter.

"You'll have to ask her about that. She's had some legal struggles."

I frowned, wondering whether her husband's parents had come into the equation in a negative way. They had raised an abuser, so my opinion of them was not particularly positive. "Ina will probably want to get involved with whatever we end up doing to help Teuton women. Maybe we could start a shelter for victims of domestic violence, both Teuton and outsider. There's enough of that going on in this world."

"That's not a bad idea. We could likely get our church involved, along with some of the local charities and trade schools. Help oppressed spouses and children learn to provide for themselves."

"Yes! Exactly!" I exclaimed, pleased at Hans' interest. When he turned his car onto Thaden grounds, I noted that we would need a lot of help to accomplish such things, especially since my occupation took up most of my time and headspace. My husband smiled as he said that we had enough contacts to bring our plans to fruition, and that I could plant some seeds at our church wedding the next year.

I entered the house through the doors onto the back deck, having walked through the back gardens from the employees' garage. I took the time to admire the grounds-keeper's skills as I passed through a lane of blooming shrubs, and my thoughts drifted back to my father's appearance at the forest clearing. When I had told him of my upcoming meeting with the council, he had given no hint that he planned to follow me there as a spirit. It was high time for me to find out exactly how much Teutonic magic my father actually knew.

Upon entering the house, I cast my icy senses forth, seeking his presence. He was in the family room, so I headed that direction after calling a greeting to our cook, Gregor. The savory scent of pizza wound its way out of the kitchen as I passed by. It would be a good meal tonight, and I hoped Hans would come to share it with my father and me.

My father lay sprawled on a couch in the family room, clad in a T-shirt and shorts, his fingers cradling a bottle of Radler, my fuzzy gray cat Thunar stretched out upon his chest. I saw an extra bottle sitting on a side table, so I went to retrieve it. It was hot outside, and although my father had spent a fortune to add a central AC system to our aged house, I could use some hydration after my experience with the council. I took a sip and smiled at the refreshing flavors of beer mingled with lemonade, then my eyes locked with my father's.

"I sensed you coming a kilometer away," he said, his gray eyes enhanced by his energy's sparks. "For someone who was bound to a Cursed One for two decades, you're not very subtle."

The energy pervading the room spoke softly to my ice, welcoming me home. I shook my head at my father and flopped onto a nearby chair, kicking my sandals off as I enjoyed some more Radler. "So says the man who kept his energy bottled up inside for most of my life," I rejoined.

My father snickered and ran a hand through his dark hair. "I'll admit that it's nice to show off some of this stuff at long last." He drained his bottle and took a second to pet Thunar, who purred in response and flexed five of his claws. "Beth's been breaking down the walls I built one brick at a time. Even if you hadn't become *Leitalra*, I couldn't have hidden my magic from you for much longer."

I studied him from behind my glasses, having held my element back from my eyes, though it flowed in traces through my blood. He appeared relaxed as he stroked my cat's fur from head to tail, the fingers of his left hand toying absently with his empty bottle, his gaze directed toward the double doors to the sunroom. They were shut against the summer heat, and he murmured in an offhand tone, "Damn Föhn has been like a desert today."

"Just how much Teutonic magic do you know?" I asked him point blank, brushing off his comment about the weather.

He turned his head to face me where I lounged in the chair. "I planned to attempt the initiation just two weeks after your Mutti passed away. I never did it, and never will, but I'm no novice." He set the bottle onto the floor and turned his palm upward. To my surprise, a natural-looking flame appeared above it. "I can manipulate my element and its derivatives in every known way, and call on nature's vitality to enhance my own."

The flame vanished, and his eyes held mine darkly. "I can uncover specifics from a Teuton's blood, and control its flow with precision." I sensed a tingling in my toes as he spoke, as he drained the blood from my capillaries. I sat up straight in the chair and narrowed my eyes at my father, picturing the vessels in my mind and seizing the blood magic inherent in my spirit. The entirety of my circulatory system arose in my imagination, and I wiggled my toes, preparing myself to rebuff any further attempts to alter my blood flow.

"I can sense the spirit of the River Isar in her waters, and the fatal potential held within the dusky spurge. And I can summon our demon lord by the power of my element . . . and demand his reasons for taking her from me . . . and saddling her son with an incurable sickness." My father's visage contorted into something that resembled a livid tiger, and I sensed his energy prickling in the air.

Dread swallowed me in its jaws as I choked out the words, "Did you . . . did he . . . answer you?" I did not know whether he meant that he had actually spoken with Wuotan, or that he simply knew how to do so.

My father sighed and fingered the lip of his empty bottle, where it sat on the floor beside the couch. "He wants you, Swanie," he said at length, giving me a look that wavered between defiance and dismay. "There's a reason I tried to spare you from this. He's had his sights on you since you were a child."

I put a hand to my throat, the truth of the matter coalescing before my eyes. "It's because I lured Augustin away from him, taught him love . . . and Wuotan . . . wanted to stop me before I ever found the Torstein."

"You'll have to consider your steps very carefully," my father warned, "for our demon lord prefers Teutons to wallow in the fleeting thrills of magic. He knows what you did in the past, and now that you've finished, he'll expect payment."

My mouth had gone dry, and I felt as though specters watched us from every shadow on the walls. "A fairy I knew in the past told me that the price of Wuotan's sorcery is death," I remembered, shivering as I drew my knees up to my chest and wrapped my arms around them. "Would Wuotan try to kill the Lady of a city?"

"I don't know, Swanie. That conversation happened a long time ago, and he didn't say whether he wanted you dead . . . or something worse." My father stared at me, his forehead wrinkled in concern.

"Have you told Hans?" I asked, sending a silent call to him through our bond. We needed to discuss this at dinner as a group. I had no plans to cow before some vague threat from a demon. The Teutons of München needed to progress into the modern era, whether Wuotan agreed or not.

"We talked about that at Ocean City," my father replied. Thunar jumped to the floor after a methodical stretch, leaving my father free to sit up. He did so and groaned as he stretched his own back in similar fashion. "You may need more than Muniche's legions to protect you as you work toward your goals. If God doesn't let Wuotan harm you, he might default to subtler methods. Like inciting the priests of the council to thwart your plans."

I made a face and climbed to my feet, stretching while taking one final swig from my bottle of Radler. "I'm glad you're not a Teuton priest, Pappi," I told him as we turned for the pantry to recycle our glass. "The only priest who has ever been open with me about this stuff is Augustin."

"Guess I'd make a good Cursed One, then," my father joked, and I gave a weak laugh in response, my thoughts mired in potential catastrophes. He slipped an arm around my waist when we entered the hallway and murmured, "Don't worry about the priests on the council, or any of the others who gripe about your intentions. None of them want to face the financial repercussions if they come down on Max von Thaden's daughter."

Chapter Three

Divergent Perspectives

The mood at dinner was subdued. Hans and my father did most of the talking, shifting from Bayerisch to Teutonica when the topic of time travel arose. I admitted that I had gotten lax about the multiple warnings I received regarding the cost of Wuotan's sorcery. I felt sure that he had directed Muniche's spirit to bind me as *Leitalra* to break my connection with Augustin; and I knew that my first child—Augustin's child—had died at Wuotan's hands. But as yet, I had noticed no direct threat to my own life. When the demon had possessed Augustin on that lurid night in the eleventh century, he held the power to send me to the future, not eternity.

Neither my father nor my husband knew that tale, and I preferred to keep it that way. It was better for them to imagine my past lover as simply a fallen man, rather than a demon's host.

My father mentioned at one point that I ought to keep up with my prayers and other expressions of faith. "Having God on your side would be your most valuable asset, since He sets the boundaries for demons and their ilk," he said over his glass of dark beer.

Hans murmured in agreement, and I started thinking out loud. "I wonder if that's why Freia had such a peaceful home life. She was honestly the most faithful Christian I've ever known, and it showed in her actions along with her prayers."

"Immortal allies make the greatest difference when we're fighting forces beyond this world," Hans said as he favored me with a grave expression. "I do think that your plans to help others are excellent, since Wuotan avoids the path of light. If we promote peace and acceptance among our own people, there will be fewer resources for Wuotan to tap, if he plots to harm you."

"I don't think Wuotan has as strong a grip on his Black Priests as he wants to believe," I recognized, my thoughts having turned to that summer night when the fairy led me to the Torstein. "I nearly fell to my death in the Leutasch Gorge four years ago . . . but a Black Priest swept me to safety in an elemental storm. Do you think it was Günter?" I met my Keyholder's eyes as I chewed on my final piece of pizza. Who was that mysterious entity who had mocked me but saved me anyway, before vanishing into the forest?

"Wait a minute. Are you saying there was a Black Priest involved when you found the Torstein?" My father looked from Hans' face to mine, his upper lip curled in distaste.

"Possibly, though we're not sure of that." Hans came to my rescue, but then cleared his throat and pulled the rug out from beneath me. "So, Swanie didn't tell you how she found the stone, eh? Your daughter's been frolicking into danger for a good many years." He smirked as he took a sip from his own glass, and my father spluttered, his gray eyes boring into mine in silent reproach.

That night, I decided to sleep in Hans' cottage for the first time since our Teutonic marriage; for while he and his boss believed that we could outwit Wuotan as long as we chose good over evil, a sense of nervousness tingled on the edges of my spirit. I did not want to spend the night alone on the third floor of the Thaden house, fabricating devils around every corner. So I packed my toiletries and a few outfits into my backpack and struck out for the group of huts at the back of our property, my ice grasping the twilight's serenity as I walked.

Hans and I shared a warm round of intimacy before I settled into the empty side of his twin bed, the tight quarters awakening unwanted memories of the years I had spent with Joel. "This'll be a lot more convenient once they finish our suite," I remarked, looking toward the darkened ceiling above. Hans' cottage was small, his bedroom even more so—and it had no air conditioning. The scent of peonies outside his window filtered in, along with the feathery breeze of night.

"You could have invited me to your room for this," Hans pointed out in a sultry tone. He lay upon the blankets at my side, and he ran the fingers of his right hand down my bare thigh in a sensual fashion.

I tried to force my lips to smile, but I could not clear my head of the subjects we had covered at dinner. "I needed to get away from the house. I'm really starting to think I've been dodging bullets my whole life somehow, after what Pappi said about Wuotan. He's the reason I nearly died trying to get the Torstein, the reason I got raped, the reason I became Lady Muniche, the reason Augustin broke our bond. For all I know, he might be the reason Beth died right after we went to the past. It's such a mess, and I don't know what to make of it."

Hans sighed as I shut my eyes, trying to lose myself in his touch, in the sense of security I felt in our bond. My Keyholder and my father had both pledged to protect me as far as they could, but I could no longer count on my undead advocate to shield me from Wuotan's machinations. I could lead the Teutons of München down the path of light, but could I evade the cost of my mistakes forever?

"Your Pappi was correct when he said that your faith in God is your greatest defense," my husband said, his hand having found its rightful place over my heart, merging with his spiritual hands to swathe me in tranquility. "A demon's schemes don't always come to fruition. We know what happened to Lucifer in the garden."

"I'm trying to figure out *why* Wuotan hates me so much," I murmured, his rationale still escaping me. "So I found the Torstein and traveled to the past three times. Big deal. It's not like I changed anything or challenged him directly when I did it. Is Augustin really *that* important to him, or is it something more?" I could not grasp why a demon would care so strongly about a human's fate.

"I guess we'll have to wait and see." Hans did not sound as upset about the situation as I felt. We kissed goodnight, his confidence soothing me to a degree.

As the summer progressed, I spent what little free time I had working on lesson plans for the children, editing some of Bertha Lohr's notes to reflect a more modern viewpoint. I sat down with Hans, Rudi, and Üwe several times to lay out plans for a new shelter for domestic violence victims. Rudi nailed down potential locations, and Üwe worked on fresh nature paintings to decorate the walls once we got it up and running. He and his business partner even offered to give our future clients the opportunity for art therapy, if they wished it.

Hans and I codified our marriage by German law at the registry office in mid-August, with my father and Sebastian as witnesses. Sebastian was enthusiastic about our marriage, since I had spilled the story of our stolen kiss to him three summers before. Though as an outsider he did not know the intricacies of Teutonic magic, I simply told him that Hans and I were fated mates now, which was good enough for him. He jokingly asked whether he could expect to hear us howling at the moon every now and then, for he enjoyed reading werewolf novels. My husband answered that he ought to watch for fairies on his walk home each day. Sebastian laughed heartily, unaware that Hans referenced our local *Eihalbe*.

I caught up with Ina at the end of September, having invited her to share a snack and tea in the sunroom one Saturday afternoon. My friend's face glimmered with a mixture of anticipation and exhaustion when I met her at my front door and gathered her into an embrace. She wore a jean jacket and matching capris, her straight black hair pulled back in a braid similar to mine, her full lips and striking eyes highlighted with skillfully applied makeup. She carried a frayed purse and a fresh loaf of walnut bread, and she apologized on her way into the house that she could stay for only two hours at most.

While we sat together on the settee in the sunroom, enjoying her bread and a snack tray Gregor had prepared, Ina told me that her life had gone crazy since Walfrid's death the previous September. She discovered that her late husband was not as rich as he had tried to appear, for he had merely rented their house in Berlin and gambled away a fair amount of his money. "I know how to stretch my funds, thank goodness, and I've had help from unexpected places. I'm supposed to get some sort of stipend from Walfrid's employer, but that hasn't come through yet."

Walfrid had been a victim of the terrorist attack on September 11th, and the first anniversary of his passing had occurred just two weeks prior. I studied my friend's face as I nibbled on some buttered bread, trying to see beyond her outer façade. "Ina, I'm so sorry. My offer of one of the suites upstairs still stands, if you're looking for somewhere to stay."

Ina shook her head slowly, her dark blue eyes gazing vacantly at the unlit lantern and the putto statue across from us. "I've stayed with a lot of different people since I sold Walfrid's stuff and moved out of Berlin. I'm hoping to find my own place now that things have gotten settled with Lea." I saw her wince when she spoke her stepdaughter's name, and her shoulders sagged.

"Hans mentioned that you had some custody issues."

Ina made a face. "Walfrid's parents wanted sole custody, since he never allowed me to adopt her. His father's just as bad as he was, so I couldn't let that happen. Thankfully, Ada's mother got involved, and she's a firebrand. You'd love her. She and the Weisses get Lea every other week, and I have her on the last weekend of every month. It's hardly enough time for her to get to know her sister."

I struggled to keep up with her explanation. "Ada was Lea's mother, right?"

"Yeah. Honestly, I have no clue how Ada ended up with Walfrid, considering how liberated her mother is. He probably bound her heart without her consent, just like he did with me. It makes me sick every time I see a Teuton woman bound to a priest. I know how they twist the mind, stifle magic, weaken the will." Ina gave me a side eye and took a sip of tea.

"It's not like that with Hans and me," I rushed to say, though I wondered if Ina would believe me. "If the city bonds aren't built around mutual love and respect, the Teuton community here will suffer and decline. Hans has held the keys long enough to know that, and he's never used his fire to hurt me."

"But how often does he bleed you?" Ina questioned, shifting on the settee to look directly at me.

My eyebrows came together as I met my friend's gaze. "He hasn't bled me once yet, actually. He told me he doesn't like the taste of blood." That was one thing Hans and I had in common.

Ina raised her eyebrows and took up several pieces of cheese from our snack tray. "That's interesting. Walfrid bled me every single night whether I liked it or not. He claimed it would help me depend on him more, but all it did was mess up my brain and make me weak. I'm actually surprised I survived giving birth to Alison, even with my element's help. That jerk bled me *twice* when I was in labor, when the nurses weren't in the room. Pretty sure he wanted me dead."

My stomach clenched, and I nearly choked on my tea. I set the cup on the table before it spilled, and worked to keep my ice at bay. It lurked on the fringes of my veins, cooling my skin. "What did your Mutti think of that?" I asked. Ina's mother had been present for Alison's birth.

Ina wrinkled her nose. "Walfrid convinced her that he did it to help me, that my blood pressure was up again." She rolled her eyes. "I haven't talked to her once since I got back in town. She believes everything we're taught about Teuton priests and heart-bonds, how it's all beautiful and protective. I know better now. I've told Marga she needs to keep her heart to herself, and stay away from freaks who want to beat and shock you while you're strapped to a cross."

I blinked at Ina, utterly repulsed. "So Walfrid was into sadism *and* spiritual abuse. Gross. I know some women like that stuff, but—"

"Anyone who likes it doesn't know her worth. No one should give up her independence just to be with a guy. Doesn't matter how rich he is. I'm done with that stuff. Done. I'm raising Alison to *know* her worth, to love herself, and I'm going to try to do the same for Lea." Ina lifted her chin as her eyes blazed with victory.

I reached out to clasp her hand in both of mine, and my ice entwined with her air in spiritual amity. "That's something I want to do, now that I'm Muniche's Lady." I told her about my plans to establish a shelter and rehabilitation program for people who had suffered domestic violence. Ina's eyes lit up with excitement, and we exchanged ideas of how to get the word out to the Teuton community once the facility opened.

For the rest of 2002, I found myself hampered in business duties. My father had to take four separate trips, two to other countries; and now that I was training to succeed him, he required my attendance at such events. I got to know my father better as we bustled here and there, and at one point he confessed that he and Beth would likely get married in the next year or two. Beth had told me over ICQ that she planned to move to München in time for my church wedding in May, and I could hardly wait to have my best friend close by once more.

My father refused to come clean with me about how he and Beth intended to handle her low level of Teutonic blood. Her father—my mother's younger brother, Jens— was a Teuton of mist. But Beth's mother, my Aunt Linda, was full-blooded American with British, French, and Native ancestry. Therefore, my dearest cousin could not sense her element at all, the wonders of Teutonic magic wholly out of her reach—unless she took part in the blood-transfer, the deadliest Teuton ritual performed in the modern era.

After Beth had admitted that she was seeing my father, she told me that unless she attempted the blood-transfer, her only chance to gain Teuton blood was through elemental sex. But my father's element was energy, and I felt certain that he could not safely meld with an outsider's empty spirit without electrocuting the person in question. Every time I brought it up to Beth on ICQ, she simply typed, *Don't worry about it. We've got it under control.*

I silently prayed that Beth could be satisfied to be like her mother, observing Teutonic magic from the outside. But I knew from past experience that few found contentment with such a fate. I advised Hans on several occasions to read up on the blood-transfer before Beth moved in, just in case. He claimed that he had performed that ritual four times, and that one of the participants had died in each case. My Keyholder was not particularly skilled at the devil's duties.

My father and I took a three week break from work for the winter holidays. He flew to New Jersey to spend the first week with Beth and her family, while I endeavored to catch up on my friends' lives and current events among the Teuton community. Erika came home from Vienna for a few days, and we met for dinner at a brewery close to my house on the Friday before Christmas.

Erika had bundled herself in a thick coat, hat, and gloves, while I just threw a leather jacket over my sweater, leaving my hands and hair open to winter's chill. Once we sat across from each other at a small booth and ordered glasses of holiday Glühwein, Erika favored me with a keen grin, her hazel eyes dancing as she tugged her gloves off her hands. "So, Swanie, have I got news for you."

A moment later, I was staring at her right hand splayed on the table before us. A glittering emerald ringed with yellow diamonds sat prominently on her ring finger—the place where Germans display their wedding rings. I gasped and shifted my gaze to my friend's face. "She asked, and you said yes!"

Crimson bloomed upon Erika's cheeks, but her eyes glimmered with joy. "She did, and it took me *completely* by surprise. We'd just gotten off a roller coaster at the Prater, one of those really crazy ones, you know? We were both screaming and clinging to each other the whole time, and then as we're staggering off, she says, 'I don't want to face death with anyone else for the rest of my life.' And she pulls this ring out of her purse and I just . . . well, I started crying," she confessed, tears welling in her eyes.

"Oh Erika, I'm *so* happy for you!" I exclaimed, picturing her standing proudly beside Iliana, the creative partner she dearly loved.

Our drinks came, and Erika blotted her tears, hues of watery blue having altered the hazel of her irises. "I mean, I've known that she's the one for years now, but I wanted her to take the lead. It's such a big decision, a big choice to make. Her ring's a ruby, since red's her favorite color. And by the way . . . ."

Erika paused to blow on her wine, the fragrance of cinnamon enveloping us in its cloud as her jubilant eyes met mine. "We might . . . just *might* . . . be moving to München next year, at least for a while." She mentioned the name of a successful fashion designer and said that Iliana had applied for an apprenticeship.

My heart seemed about to burst with happiness for my friend, and we spent a long time discussing the possibilities of such an arrangement. Erika had her invitation to my church wedding, and she said that she and Iliana would be there for sure. Over a thousand people were set to attend thus far, and I had fittings for several possible dresses on Monday morning.

"Hans hired wedding planners to handle everything, and it's a darn good thing, because I think half the Teutons in München are coming, along with most of my coworkers," I related.

After we finished our meal, we conversed about my plans to help the Teuton community, particularly women who had been misused by priests. I noted that Ina seemed pretty much anti-heart-bond thanks to Walfrid, and Erika responded that she understood her feelings there. "I found the spell to create the heart-bond in the old version of *Der Weg*," she said, referencing the standard tome of Teutonic history and culture. "I don't know about you, but *I* think if someone's going to make the heart-bond, they should offer *their* heart in return. I take Iliana's heart, and she takes mine. That way the relationship is equal, with both partners protecting their beloved's heart."

I frowned at that concept, uncertainty stirring within me. "Huh. That might be . . . a little too out there for me." I tried to imagine myself cradling Augustin's sinful heart in my spiritual hands, tucking it away beneath my icy robes. *That'd be a bit too much responsibility for me,* I thought.

"You've spent your whole life doe-eyed by priestly power, so you wouldn't appreciate the appeal. It's about time I let you in on a little secret." Erika winked at me and made her way out of her coat, revealing a V-necked sweater underneath. She glanced around to ensure no waiters or customers were paying attention to us, and then pulled her neckline down to show part of her bra—and two scars arching upward from her heart.

My eyes bugged, and my ice veiled my vision in blue. "You did the blood-transfer!" I gasped in a low voice, vivid memories of infernal torment in Wuotan's bloody river resurfacing in my brain. I knew that Iliana wanted Teuton blood so that she and Erika would be true equals, but my nervousness about such prospects had migrated to the back burner.

Earlier fears erupted in my mind, and I hissed, "*What did Günter demand in return?*"

Erika chuckled and waved a hand at me carelessly. "Cool down, Swanie. We didn't ask him. Üwe did it for us for free."

I muttered a few curses in Bayerisch as a massive weight lifted off of me. "I might need to hug that man the next time I see him."

"Üwe's a gem. And Iliana got the same element as your medieval squeeze. Blue fire." Erika wiggled her eyebrows at me and said, "I, like, *totally* get the lure. Blue fire is freaking sexy." I blinked at my friend for a second; and then both of us dissolved into a puddle of laughter, memories of sizzling cobalt scratching at my joy.

At the New Year's festival, I made my rounds from one group of my people to the next, the frosty air heavy with anticipation for the fireworks displays. From the meeting place on the banks of the Isar, we always had an exceptional view of several shows in München itself, along with the nearby neighborhoods. Many people congratulated me on my marriage to Hans, and some pledged to attend the ceremony at Alter Peter in May.

Some of the other women who were married to priests offered advice both humorous and disconcerting. Eva Peninger, wife to Jürgen on the council, told me that she always had to disengage the smoke alarm whenever she got in bed with her husband; she hinted that I might need to be aware of that myself, since Hans' fire had the potential to exude smoke. Ada Dantzler reminded me to guide my Keyholder well, that priests needed their wives' faithful support. And one elderly woman I had never met before informed me that if I had trouble keeping my neck from looking like I had married a vampire, the leaves from silver oak trees could heal the scars from lingering bite marks.

At one point, I found Ina at the food tables, compiling one plate of fondue and another of Lebkuchen stars. I grabbed a plate myself and asked her how things were going, as I pricked a nugget of bread to dip into the cheese bowl.

"As good as it can be when I'm chasing two little fairies around. Lea's here until Sunday." Ina beamed as a toddler scampered her way, tugging the hand of a much smaller child who seemed wholly entranced by the bonfire at the river's edge. She gaped at it with a wide-eyed stare and dragged her feet.

"Lebkuchen, Mutti?" the older one inquired once she had pulled her quarry to the table. Lea's eyes sparkled in the firelight, and her countenance appeared wise beyond her four years.

Before Ina could hand her stepdaughter the plate of cookies, a deeper voice repeated Lea's query. "Lebkuchen, Mutti?"

I looked up from the two children and saw that Fonsi had joined us, a jaunty grin on his face as he reached out to tweak Ina's braid. She thrust the plateful of treats at him and said in a flirtatious tone, "Thought you'd be more interested in fondue, but if not, that's more for me!"

Fonsi winked at her and lifted Alison onto his shoulders. "Hey, Swanie," he greeted before turning his attention back to Lea. "Come on, let's go eat these by the bonfire. Your sister seems to have an affinity for it."

"What's uh-finty?" Lea demanded as they left us behind.

Ina chuckled and turned toward the fire herself, affection evident in her dark blue eyes. "Fonsi's really good with kids. When he's around, I almost believe that I could take a chance on a man again."

Ina and Fonsi had dated off and on since they were in high school together. I remembered how devastated he had been when Walfrid came into the picture. I swallowed a bite of savory fondue and heard myself saying, "You know Fonsi would do the *Virstohran* for you." He had told me that at the May festival in 2000, after he witnessed Walfrid abusing Ina. Fonsi loved her enough to avenge her blood by rite of Teutonic law—something far afield from the German legal system.

"I know he would," Ina said when we neared the fire, preparing to find a place for ourselves among those gathered there. She lowered her voice to confide in my ear, "I saw it in his blood."

Chapter Four:

Official Union

The day of my church wedding with Hans dawned pale and gray, though the cloud cover broke into sparse puffs of cumulus by afternoon. The early months of 2003 had chugged past like an unstoppable freight train with each dress fitting, client meeting, and rehearsal leading toward my predestined fate. Swanhilde Rolande Meissner von Thaden, Lady to the Keyholder of München, wife to a Teuton priest thirty-three years her senior. Nearly two thousand people would bear witness to the finalization of our vows, and in the aftermath I may hardly remember the lighthearted maiden I used to be.

A wielder of the keys to time's gateway. A partner to a Black Priest I loved more than life—the man who had relinquished his name and his freedom to spare me from medieval justice. A woman who could choose to love whom she wanted.

That woman was gone, and my heart sensed it deep inside. Although Hans had agreed not to have the blackened wall and scratched balcony door replaced, during the renovation of what was now our private bedroom suite, I saw the pain in his eyes whenever he caught me looking at those imperfections. We would embark on a month-long honeymoon following our wedding, and Hans had already told me that he planned to drink my blood for the first time at some point during our travels. When he did, I knew what he would see.

I loved Hans very much. His steady support during the past year and a half had deepened my trust in him, while Muniche's bonds augmented the desire I felt on his behalf. He was not bad at sex, nor was he bad at emotional tenderness. But I still saw Augustin's light blue eyes in my mind each night before sleep took me, still recalled his wise counsel, his vicious vengeance, his stern fidelity even when his demon master tortured him on account of his love. I had no choice but to build a happy and healthy family with my Keyholder, but my muses would belong forever to a dead man bound for hell.

Strangely enough, I found myself reminiscing on my parents' wedding as I progressed down the main aisle of Alter Peter. Vierne's Final, Symphony 5 rang in the nave while I passed row after row of smiling faces and affected gasps. The onlookers doubtless reacted to my dress, which had cost a fortune—pearly satin with diamond-sprinkled veils and a train that stretched three meters behind me.

But I saw none of the faces, discerned none of the whispered phrases; for I kept seeing my mother as she had looked during my first trip to the past—gorgeous and blissful, awaiting her marriage with my father, her chosen love. This very song had played just before she walked the aisle, her favorite organ piece.

And now, I took the same steps in a different church, to the high altar where my fated mate stood clad in a black tux with the keys of Muniche hanging from a golden chain around his neck. That chain and those keys seemed to symbolize the demise of my agency, of my individuality, the very things I wished to champion before my people. A hypocrite without choice, without freedom.

We women never have the choices men have, and it doesn't matter. Bertha Lohr's final advice surfaced in my brain while I ascended the high altar, preparing to stand dignified at my Keyholder's side, to exchange vows of love and loyalty until death. *All that matters is what you do with the situations that are given to you. You can accept them and make them beautiful, or you can pine away your entire life about something you can't change.*

It was up to me to welcome this destiny, to make it beautiful, to use my position for good. My yearnings for Augustin must remain in the darkest corners of my heart, locked away until the tide turned . . . until he uncovered a way to break Muniche's bonds. For now, I was Hans' Lady, *Leitalra* of the grandest Teuton city in Bavaria, a woman who could effect change among her people.

No pressure, I thought to myself as I clasped hands with my master and looked into his gaze. I saw the fire simmering deep inside his dark blue eyes, and I smiled a real smile while my icy spirit reached out to his. Black fire's warmth blazed through me, welcoming, accepting . . . and I spoke the vows to Hans with confidence, Muniche's spirit expanding her elation to everyone in the nave, to the entire city.

The reception was set to take place at an aged hall on an island of the Isar. About a third of the wedding guests were slated to attend. Hans and I climbed into my father's Rolls so his chauffeur could drive us there, and I laughingly refused Üwe's invitations to ride with him instead. As Hans' best man, the jovial artist might try to kidnap me to hit up the pubs before the celebrations began, and I had no wish to abide by that particular German tradition. I wanted to appreciate the meal, the dances, and the conversations before I clouded my brain with alcohol.

"This'll be a short trip," Hans remarked after Thomas managed to pull the car away from our crowd of guests. My husband's expression implied that he had already had enough of the limelight.

"Pretty sure we're supposed to make out the entire time," I said, trying to gear myself up for the reception. This was the only privacy Hans and I would get until we left for our honeymoon, which would likely be hours from now.

"Oh really?" Hans met my gaze, dark fire smoldering in his irises.

"Well, that's what we did in the eleventh century. Couldn't get Joel off of me during the carriage ride back to the estate." I cringed at the memory. At least Freia had married the love of her life that day.

"You and your medieval habits," Hans chided before grabbing me in a bear hug, his lips claiming mine in a wondrous clash of fire and ice.

As Thomas dropped us off outside the hall, I asked Hans to not let go of my hand until we sat down at our appointed table. A fair number of people were already there, and I did not want Üwe to snag me good-naturedly before the party commenced. Luckily, we had gotten all of the professional photos taken before and during the wedding, so only personal cameras flashed at us as we marched toward our first official outing as Herr and Frau Meissner von Thaden.

The food was spectacular, as were the drinks. The hired DJ sailed through my requested playlist with finesse—my favorite metal anthems transitioned into familiar pop and rock both German and American. I felt like I barely had a chance to enjoy the ravioli in truffle sauce on my plate, for a steady stream of well-wishers seemed to flow before our table offering congratulations, advice, and anecdotes. Beth, my maid-of-honor, came to my rescue on a few occasions. She sat at my right side and worked hard to engage with the guests in German only. Just two weeks earlier, she had moved into the Thaden house, and perfecting her German was one of her first priorities.

After the massive wedding cake had been cut and enjoyed by all, the DJ announced that it was time to open the dance floor. Only Hans and my father could dance with me for free; any other interested parties must pay a fee that started at five Euros. My father had declared during the planning stage that I should demand a much higher price, but I wanted my friends to get their fair chance before our wealthier contacts monopolized my time. I exchanged loaded looks with many of them—Beth, Ina, Erika, Vreni,

Marga, and my cousins—as I rose to my feet and took my father's hand, allowing him to lead me to the dance floor.

The two of us cut the floor with elegance as the song "I Hope You Dance" played over the speakers. I tapped into the nearly-forgotten skills I had learned in ballet as a young child, though my feet could not quite match what they had done before my brother's death. But my father guided me expertly, and tears dampened my eyes by the time the song had ended. It was one of his favorites, and while I appreciated its inspirational message, I had not quite managed to shove aside my memories of a lover long gone.

My father and I returned to our table as Hans stood to retrieve his elderly mother for a short, slow dance. I had never met Johanna Meissner until that day. She was no taller than me and just as slim, with silver curls and eyes that matched her son's, though her bifocals obscured that fact. She seemed in good health and quite grateful to be dancing with her son, while I stood to the side and thought of what Hans had said about his mother after we first sealed our bond. Johanna had been the wife of a Teuton priest who passed away some forty years ago, but she had never remarried.

Did Hans' father create the heart-bond with Johanna, or did he leave her free? Does she still think of him so much later, or has she managed to move on with time? Will I be ever be able to leave Augustin to his era and cloak myself in my own, maybe after Hans and I have a child or two? Will this empty space in my heart ever fade away, maybe from the magic of Muniche's spirit?

By the time my husband approached me for our first dance, my brain was thoroughly embroiled in questions that might never be answered. He murmured something sultry in my ear as he led me to the dance floor, and the triumphant tones of Nightwish's "Ever Dream" surged from the speakers.

It had taken me far too long to find a love song to share with Hans for our dance, because I had sung nearly all the ballads I knew to Augustin in the eleventh century. And I should not think of him while clasped in Hans' arms, turning a symphonic metal song into a ballroom serenade. No, I should not.

Thankfully, Nightwish had put out another album in 2002, one stuffed with songs that Augustin would never know. Thus, "Ever Dream" was for Hans and me.

Toward the end of our dance, Hans informed me in a quiet voice that I was his dream come true, that he had always imagined how incredible it would be to claim an ice princess for himself. And I worked to hide my uncertainty as I replied that fire would always be my favorite element, and that the darkness inherent in his flames stirred my soul. Hans responded by pulling me against him and pressing a seductive kiss to my lips. "I'm not sure I can stay here until everyone leaves," he muttered in my ear as the spectators showered us with applause.

German tradition required the bride and groom to remain at their reception until all other guests had gone. I was unsure whether I could put up with the crowd that long, myself. So I winked at him and whispered back, "Why don't we sneak out around eight? We can pretend we have to hit the bathroom, and meet up at your car."

"Deal." Hans nodded once in determination and then passed me off to my cousin Beth, the first person to pay the fee to dance with me.

The music transitioned to a popular song by Aerosmith, so my cousin and I danced in a casual style as more people joined us on the floor. "You look like your thoughts are miles away," Beth noted after a few seconds. She looked concerned.

I felt myself blushing and shrugged, trying to pull the standard mask back over my face, since my true sentiments were apparently peeking out. "It's a lot to take in. The Keyholder's wife," I said in a neutral tone.

"The most powerful Teuton woman in München," she supplied, giving me a supportive nudge.

I rolled my eyes toward the ceiling in an attempt to lose myself in the lights painting their colors against the stone.

"Don't remind me. Maybe I can pretend *this* is all a dream, that I can travel somewhere else later on tonight."

Beth wrapped an arm around me. "No matter what you do, make sure you come back at the end of the month like you're supposed to. Max and I have our own vacation to take in a couple months, and you'll have to cover for him at work while we're gone."

I heaved a sigh. "Beth, honestly, you're not helping. Just let me dream while I'm here, lost among a group of people who'll hardly remember today's events." Alcohol had flowed liberally already, and it was about time for me to imbibe.

My cousin seemed to read my mind, for when the song changed, she let go of me and slipped away to snag a pair of champagne flutes from a tray. She handed one to me, and I downed it without tasting it. "I might need something stronger," I said.

Before Beth could answer, Sebastian appeared before me with a bow, his silver tie standing out against his dark suit coat. So I smiled primly at him and got rid of the empty glass before joining him in a goofy jig as "All Star" by Smash Mouth played over the speakers.

Eventually, I managed to consume enough alcohol to swathe my brain in a haze. I lost track of what songs played, of what unknown guests appeared to dance with the bride. At some point, the CEO of one of the largest industries in München corralled me into a rather sloppy waltz; he was more buzzed than me. "So you and the accountant, eh?" he asked through a rather wet cough. I barely managed to nod my head before he added, "You like *older* men, I see. That's quite all right with me . . . quite all right. I could show you a few things if Hans doesn't put out."

He grinned at me and proceeded to belch; the man was in his sixties. I knew that he would not behave this way if he were sober, so I discreetly detached myself from him and snagged Marga from near a punch bowl. "Free dance." I muttered the name of the presumptuous CEO and said that I needed a diversion.

"What are you going to do, toss ice crystals at him?" Marga positioned herself between me and the offending man, her stocky frame hiding me from the crowd. "He might be wasted enough not to notice."

"Nah . . . getting out of here in a few," I said, shooting a glance at the nearest clock as I chugged a glass of punch. I knew it was spiked with vodka, my father's staple. It looked like the clock's hands read seven thirty-five.

"You throw a good party, just like your Pappi," Marga commented. She had retrieved a cheese-stuffed date from a tray carried by one of the waiters, and she chewed it slowly, relishing its flavors. "That's one thing I miss about living in your house."

"Yeah, food's good," I managed to reply. I vaguely saw someone heading my way from the dance floor; it might have been Trudi or Traudl. My ice had confined itself within, a common result of drunkenness. Everything was blurry now, for I had not worn glasses or contacts for the ceremonies. Instead, I had kept a thin sheen of blue over my eyes, except during the photoshoot. My irises were gray, not blue, and they must look that way for posterity.

"Swanie, are you totally, *completely* sure you're doing the right thing, being with Hans this way?" Marga leaned in close and lowered her voice, her blue eyes searching my face. "Ina told me what Walfrid did to her with the heart-bond, and I'm, like, worried for you."

A hand clapped down on my right shoulder before I could piece together a response, and Traudl's voice cut through the haze. "Come on, Swanie, let's get back out there. He's playing the good stuff now."

I drifted vaguely along the dance floor as some sort of metal song played—it might have been Stratovarius or Amorphis—safe under my cousins' watchful gaze. Maybe this destiny of mine was not so bad after all. Hans was a good man, no matter what Marga might think. He was known amongst the business leaders in München, just like my father was . . . he could help secure the Thaden family's financial position . . . and help me find my way in the

Teuton community . . . to help the women whose masters had failed them.

My Keyholder would not fail me. The sturdy bonds pulsing around my heart seemed indicative of that. I was his chosen responsibility, his city personified, his chosen fate, his dream come true.

And when he gathered me into his arms away from the fray, making some sort of excuse to the crowd, the hesitant part of me began to fold at long last.

His dream come true.

Chapter Five

Not Quite Paradise

The first portion of our honeymoon passed in glorious fashion. Hans drove us to a snug cabin on the banks of a crystal clear lake deep in the Bavarian forest. Owned as a vacation home by Oskar on the council, it was off the beaten path and provided a bucolic privacy that both of us craved. Although Hans and I both spent workdays steeped in humanity's throngs, we longed for peace and solitude, a restful retreat to recharge from the corporate world. After our rooms had been renovated in the Thaden house, we both agreed to maintain his cottage as it was, rather than open it to other employees or guests. That way we could escape the main house whenever the activity there grew too oppressive.

My husband and I took long hikes through the forests and mountains, and explored the lake by boat and in spirit form. Its waters were too chilly to swim in early May, but I conjured ice from it nearly every day, creating artistic sculptures for my fiery Keyholder to admire and dissolve with his heat. We cooked our dinners over black flames beside the lake whenever the weather permitted. And as I gazed into Hans' mysterious fires, their shades ranging from smoky gray to obsidian's depths, my rational mind gradually recognized that I should count myself lucky.

God may not have seen fit to grant me my chosen love, Augustin; but that made perfect sense, for my medieval partner had forsaken God for His antithesis. He had staunchly refused to acknowledge my pleas for him to repent, to change his ways. In fact, he preferred to double down into sin, sacrificing our enemies like a heathen, making ominous deals with his demon master as though they were on equal ground. Augustin loved me, but he had turned his back on God. And I knew that marriages worked best when both parties worshipped the same entity.

Perhaps God had known that I would never forsake Augustin without some outside force driving it—Muniche. I had fallen into the hands of a man with decades of experience, a deep-seated loyalty to my city, an element that whispered to my inmost desires, an accomplished businessman, a Christian. After my persistent defiance, I deserved much worse.

Hans and I bathed in intimacy multiple times each day, trying out new ways and new places to draw us together into sexual ecstasy. His prowess surprised me, truth to be told, for I had wrongly assumed that men cooled down as they aged. But he took me in the shower, in the Jacuzzi on the back deck, on the couch, on the expansive king bed—and even taught me some things Augustin had not. He often called me "ice princess" in the throes of passion, uttering the name in Teutonica, in Bayerisch, in German . . . his groans were incredibly sensual. At one point, I asked him what elements he had screwed in his lifetime.

"More than you," he answered, casually resting on the bed after a round of sex that had coated the wooden head-board in ice and set black flames upon the scented candles around the room.

"I've had blue fire, black fire, and wind," I reminded him, my ice coursing through my veins in a latent manner, soothing the ache from my husband's heat.

Hans chuckled in a wicked manner and said, "I've had ice, stone, yellow fire, wintry wind, and smoke. Worst one is smoke. Gets stuck in the lungs."

I started laughing, but now I had a lot of weird encounters to contemplate. "You got around before taking the keys," I commented.

"Hmm. Most young Teuton men do. They like to test the waters, so to speak, find out which element melds best with their own." Hans had closed his eyes and placed his hands beneath his head, his countenance not appearing apologetic about his carnal exploits.

I rolled to my left side to eye my husband curiously. "Have you ever had it with an outsider?" I asked, remembering Augustin's views on that subject. *It is best followed by murder.*

"Only once," Hans answered, his black eyebrows scrunching at the subject.

"Boring?"

He turned his head toward me and met my gaze with a sly look. "It takes effort to keep an element chained in the throes of passion. I don't recommend it."

During our second week at the cabin, a batch of stormy weather descended and lingered for a while. As a Teuton of ice, I had no problem with dancing and exploring the outdoors in the rain, but Hans preferred to remain inside and enjoy the cabin's comforts—the Jacuzzi, the tabletop games, and the TV.

I informed him on the third day, as sheets of rain pelted the roof, that his distaste for precipitation reminded me of Augustin on the night when we watched the Teuton army retreat into Muniche for their last stand. He had hidden beneath his priestly cloak while the clouds poured their relief onto the parched ground. "I'm starting to think fiery Teutons have an irrational fear of water from the sky. You're okay with lakes, rivers, and oceans; but make the sky wet, and you all freak out," I said while lying on the couch.

"A sense of foreboding accompanies the rain," Hans stated, his eyes drifting from the television to me. He retrieved the remote and switched the TV off, then went on, "Fiery Teutons who've been trained to manipulate other elements usually have the greatest trouble with derivatives of water. They grapple with the magic in our blood, in our spirit. 'You have no power over me . . . I will consume you,' they seem to murmur in words beyond our comprehension."

The way my husband spoke prompted me to shiver all over, my desire awakening anew, though we had already mated in the shower that morning. "That's . . . a massive turn-on . . . *Leitaeri*," I told him in a breathy voice. He had risen from the recliner to stretch, black fire darkening his irises.

I watched him approach me, and I shifted my hips a bit to loosen my shorts. *Always ready for more,* I thought to myself, though my period had started several days prior. We had found creative ways to avoid staining the cabin's furnishings.

My Keyholder's knees cracked as he knelt before me, his eyes shifting from mine to my lips, which were parted and ready to receive him. But instead of kissing me, one of his hands reached out to stroke my hair, to brush its strands away from my face. I shut my eyes to concentrate on his touch, but then he said something that brought me up short. "All the better for you, my lovely Lady, for a woman should be relaxed and yearning when her master bleeds her."

My eyelids shot open, ice veiling my vision in blue as I stared at the man bending over me, his eyes fixated on my neck now, tracing the line of my carotid artery. "*What?*"

"Swanie, I may not like the taste of blood, but you ought to know that when a priest bleeds his woman, it's a very intimate act. It's something we ought to share, to enhance the beauty of our relationship." My neck was bare before him, and his warm fingers traced my artery seductively. I could sense the blood pounding there—he had augmented its flow. My heartbeat sped beneath his influence.

"But . . . wait." I could not organize my thoughts, and a cascade of emotions had pounded me to the ocean's floor.

You knew he'd bleed you eventually, Swanie, I reminded myself, trying to pull my element back into my spirit. It had coated the whole of my skin and extended my finger-nails into claws.

Hans smiled down at me, and I detected a warning in the curve of his lips. "I wouldn't advise you to fight me, darling," he crooned, his free hand taking hold of my right wrist, though as yet I had not struck out at him. I sensed his fire seeping into my spirit, driving my ice back.

"What exactly are you going to look for?" I demanded, not happy about the prospect of my secrets open to Hans' judgment. I had no intentions of fighting my Keyholder, for I had experienced the power of his sway already. I had no chance against him unless I wanted to actually hurt him, and I loved Hans too much to do such a thing.

"I'll look for what I wish to see," Hans replied, his face just centimeters from mine now, his spiritual hands having directed my heart to drop its defenses. The icy sheen had vanished from my vision, and I stared into Hans' dark blue eyes in silence as he murmured, "I wish to truly know this woman who embodies my city." Then he bent his head to my neck, and his teeth pierced my flesh.

A soft cry of pain broke from my lips, and my body shuddered before lying limp, permitting my master to see all that I kept to myself. My eyes remained open the entire time as I gazed toward the beams of the ceiling, the electric chandelier at the center of the cabin's parlor; the sound of the rain seemed to fade into the distance; and after about forty seconds, Hans released me.

I focused on the artery out of habit, slowing the flow and calling the platelets to seal the wound. Since Augustin had taught me the nuances of blood control long ago, my subconscious did most of the work for me. I suspected that Hans tapped into his own Teutonic magic to aid my efforts, but he had paced to the window, his back turned to me. Tracing the fingers of my left hand along the thin scabs that now ornamented my neck, I deemed it healed enough for the time being, although the flesh was still tender.

I pushed myself into a sitting position on the couch and turned my attention to my Keyholder. He stood with his right hand pressed to the glass just over his head, his left hand against his hip. He seemed to breathe very deliberately, as though he struggled against the urge to vomit. Hopefully he would snatch the nearby trash can if his stomach could not handle my blood.

The silence stretched long; Hans appeared more like a statue than a man. Nervousness roiled in my gut as I wondered what exactly he had seen. There were enough horrors in my past to give even the strongest man pause . . . but I suspected that he had probed my inner longings for Augustin. Had he just now learned that his wife had imagined herself with someone far different, when we spoke our vows before a vast crowd of witnesses less than two weeks prior?

I knew I should bring that up, but I chickened out. "There's a trash can over there, you know, if you need to puke." My voice wavered, and I tried valiantly to gather my courage. "I can go get some soda or ice cream, if you—"

Hans made a slicing motion with his left hand before clenching it at his side and turning slowly to face me. His face looked haunted, his eyes shadowed like a man who had just stared death in the eye. My offerings of help died in my throat, and my ice trickled into my blood as it sensed Hans' agitation. He stood still, about a meter away from where I sat, and he shook his head once, twice, lines of anguish sketching their patterns across his forehead.

"Swanie." He said my name at last, and it sounded like a croak. He cleared his throat and gripped the bridge of his nose, his visage contorting into an awful expression. "What . . . the *hell* . . . did you see . . . in that beast?"

I opened my mouth, but no words came out. *He looked for Augustin's worst attributes. That figures. Similar to his medieval predecessor, Prince Otto. Do all Keyholders despise Cursed Ones?*

Hans glared at me, his eyes as black as pitch. "That man *tore* your child from you, chained you to the ground, spilled his death into you over and over again . . . broke your bones

. . . sliced you like an animal upon the altar to the final point, that point where the only thing left to do was extract your heart . . . left you broken and forsaken for nine whole *months* . . . and you *love* him. I saw it. You love *this* man, the one who'd drag you to hell if God loosened his grip on you."

When Hans paused for breath, I lifted my chin at him and said, "You drank my blood for over half a minute, and *that's* what you decided to look for. Same as Prince Otto, the bastard who cursed Muniche's blood. Let's lay out all of Augustin's sins instead of acknowledging the good he's done." I crossed my arms.

"The good he's done," Hans repeated, disgust dripping from his tone. He ruffed his hair until it resembled flames, though I noticed that he kept his element restricted, except where it flecked his eyes.

"I had never imagined you to be the type of woman to cast yourself into the arms of an abuser, to wave off his murders, to ignore the fact that he obviously sees women as *property*, not as human beings. You're trying to plant resources for battered women, while well-nigh worshipping a Black Priest who discards them like garbage!"

I blinked at Hans, horrified that he had managed to twist what he saw in my blood to such an extreme. "I don't *worship* Augustin," I snapped at him, climbing to my feet and marching forward to stare him straight in the eye. "I made a choice to love that man after seeing the depths of his love for me in *his* blood, not like you bothered to see that part. And you obviously didn't bother to notice that Augustin tortured me that night because Wuotan possessed him. He didn't do that of his own free will."

Hans shook his head again, appearing weary now. "You stand here defending the man who told me he needed to leave you behind, to accept the demonic destiny before him. He chose the devil over you the moment he severed your bond, and if you continue to cling to his memory, you'll only bring pain on yourself, on both of us. The Teuton people in our city need you, Swanie . . . and I need you. Please let him go . . . open your eyes and see."

My husband's expression looked pained as he reached out to brush a stray lock of black hair away from my cheek, his warm fingers lingering on my skin. Moisture welled in the corners of my eyes, and I wondered whether I really believed what Hans was trying to say—or if I understood it only due to the bonds of Muniche. I sensed his hands stroking the heart of my soul, imparting his love and yearning to me, his desire to see us both succeed, to wholeheartedly grasp our duties.

"I love you, Swanie," he murmured in a husky voice, leaning down to touch his forehead to mine. "And I've seen the threads of pain that man left in your heart. I would never, ever use my fire against you as he did. And I would never guide your heart toward the path to hell. You are safe with me, lovely ice princess, safe to be strong or weak, to rejoice or mourn."

Hans enfolded me in his arms as the tears leaked free from my eyes, sobs contracting my chest at the true state of things. Augustin had indeed left me behind, returned to the past to follow Wuotan's lead. His memory of my love would not fade, he had promised . . . he would complete his vengeance on our enemies and then seek a way to free my heart, to bring me back to him.

But would my path back to him require that I abandon my responsibility to the Teuton people? Would his demon master twist his love for me into odium, into an urge to transform me into something I'm not? I knew Augustin could not withstand Wuotan's torments indefinitely; I had experienced the results once already. How long would eternity's gates remain closed to him?

After sobbing on Hans' T-shirt for a good long while, as his hands gently soothed my sorrow, I managed to gasp out my desperate wish. "If only . . . if only . . . God . . . would hear my prayer . . . for Augustin's soul. I've prayed so much . . . and he still . . . he won't . . . ." I sniffed, unable to speak the words that would lay the final nail in Augustin's coffin. *He won't turn from evil.*

"God's ways are not our ways," Hans reminded me quietly, "and the records of the Cursed Ones are jealously guarded. Some of them may turn to God, but their master doubtless wouldn't want it known if they did."

My Keyholder had a fair point, and I grasped that tiny strand of hope like a desperate lifeline. It was not too late for Augustin until hell's gates closed behind him. And I still had Prince Otto's Song of Time solidified in my musician's memory. It was time for me to lean into this fate of mine, to work with Hans for the good of our people, to build a family with him, to stand as an example of how fulfilling an honest partnership could be.

After I had left a strong legacy here, I could summon time's gateway again, to see whether my cursed lover had kept his promise. Until then, I must seek to evade the fatal cost of Wuotan's sorcery.

Chapter Six:
Deep-Seated Prejudice

Upon our return to München, Hans and I dove back into our corporate duties with renewed energy. My father had me spend time with the managers of different departments —production, purchasing, sales, engineering, quality, and human resources—so I could get a clearer picture of each division's role in Süddeutsche Getriebe. He and Beth were about to take a three-week vacation in August, and he emphasized that he did not want to have to worry about work during his absence. "Don't make any major investments or other decisions without talking to Derek first," he instructed me, referring to his brother-in-law, the CFO.

In what little downtime I had, my husband and I finalized my lesson plans for the local Teuton children. Bertha Lohr had been too ill to teach anyone in the final months of her life, so many of the youth had not gotten proper instruction on their gifts for almost four years. I planned to invite groups of every gender to the Thaden house once per month for instruction, dividing them by age. Hans noted that I would likely meet some opposition since I wanted to train everyone together, particularly the older teens. "Most young men who wish to study for the priesthood begin the path in their mid to late teen years, at least the ones who live in a place with a wealth of priestly mentors," he said.

"Then that's exactly when they need to have classes with their female peers, so I can emphasize the importance of respect and consent," I rejoined. "If any of them show a thirst for power and control, we can order München's priests not to train them."

Hans appeared pensive at that concept, but he muttered, "They'd probably go somewhere else to learn if they're desperate enough."

"Sounds like we'll need to have a heart-to-heart with all of the Teuton Ladies and Keyholders," I proposed, wondering just how many Teuton cities existed in Germany and Austria. I had read the list before, but I had never taken a count. "Let them know that it's time to enforce consequences for those who twist Teutonic magic into something it shouldn't be."

On the last Saturday in July, a group of friends and I got together for dinner at a beer garden on the banks of the Isar. It was the first time I had seen any of them since my wedding, and this time, I wanted to catch up on their lives instead of drowning myself in alcohol. I hardly got the chance to chat with them on ICQ nowadays, since I passed most evenings relaxing with Beth or brainstorming with my husband. Beth was in full preparation mode now, anticipating her romantic holiday with my father—her fiancé. He had proposed to her at my reception, and she had floated on cloud nine ever since.

My cousin Traudl sat beside me at our table, her straight black hair cropped short, a NY ball cap shielding her eyes from the brilliant sun. I had fallen out of touch with her and her twin sister, Trudi, when I went to college in the U.S., and she had reached new heights in her career as an auto mechanic in recent months. The two of us chatted for about five minutes before our other friends arrived, Traudl's eyes shining with victory as she told me of a recent promotion. "Within a few years, I should have enough money set aside to start my own repair shop," she said. "And we've been thinking about renting a space on the edges of the city, with an attached suite for Trudi's massage parlor. She'll offer her clients a discount if they get their oil changed while she works her magic on their tense muscles."

"That's seriously genius," I said. "That way people will have something to do while they're waiting for their car to get fixed. And something soothing at that."

"We're going into business together, no questions asked. We've wanted to do it for years, since we first learned our elements. My shop can help us stay afloat while Trudi raises a family. I can be the cool aunt with all the tools."

Traudl grinned, and Marga arrived before I could press her for details. She pulled out the chair across from mine and situated herself, remarking that the U-Bahn was full of tourists that day. "They all seem to think I know the lines like the back of my hand. A guy from Spain had a one-way ticket to the Ostbahnhoff and wanted to know whether he was on the right train. He was flirting with me by the time I got off." Marga snickered and ordered a Radler, her brown curls draping her shoulders in wild ornamentation.

Once the waitress departed, Traudl leaned forward and placed her chin on her fist. "Was he cute? Did you get his number?" she asked.

"Ah, I've seen better. A college freshman at best, and I'm no cougar." Marga combed her fingers through her hair while holding a scrunchie in her teeth, her blue eyes scanning those seated at the tables around us.

I could not stifle a snort of disbelief; Marga was only twenty-five. "Vreni's coming," she said, rising halfway from her chair to wave in her direction.

As always, Vreni was dressed in style, her figure prompting several heads to turn as she approached our table. Her bleached blond hair was pulled back from her face in a silvery clip, emphasizing the jeweled earrings she wore; her red top resembled something I had seen on a British celebrity in one of the tabloids. "Hey Swanie," she greeted me first as she took the seat beside Marga; we had attended a private high school together. "Traudl, Marga. Has everyone ordered yet?"

"Just the drinks. Wanted to wait until we were all here," I answered, turning my attention to the menu. I was thinking about Jägerschnitzel with Spätzle.

We talked about our respective careers while enjoying our beverages. Marga said that her job in medical billing kept her busy, and that she had started taking note of which codes were used for labor and delivery. "I've been watching to see if any Teuton mothers or infants don't survive childbirth at my hospital," she stated, her expression that of someone who had opened a crypt for the first time. Vreni gasped, my forehead wrinkled, and Traudl's eyes widened.

"Well, how bad *is* it?" my cousin asked, pulling her mug of Weißbier toward her chest, as though seeking preemptive comfort.

"I've only been at this for two years, so keep that in mind. Counting only the viable infants, thirty-two have passed, and only six mothers." Marga held up six fingers for emphasis and finished, "I check the records in the library every time a mother passes away. So far, five out of the six were Teutons. It's harder to keep track of the babies, but I did see one whose father was a friend of my Pappi."

I winced at the figures she quoted, rethinking my plans to have two of Hans' children all over again. "Guess I'd better get at it as soon as I hit eighty-two percent," Vreni commented, her eyebrows crimped in thought.

"You sure that'll be high enough?" Marga questioned, giving Vreni a major side-eye. "You don't want your kids to end up like me, kicked to the curb by all the guys in town thanks to one stupid wannabe priest."

I looked from Vreni to Marga, unhappy with the direction of this discussion. Vreni was not a full Teuton yet; her blood had tested at seventy-five percent when she was born. Thanks to her boyfriend Stefan, her blood level had climbed steadily for the past five years through elemental sex. Although she sensed the magic of fire dormant in her spirit, she would not be able to invoke it until her blood reached eighty-five percent. She had told me several summers before that she and Stefan wanted children, and I knew that it hurt her to wait.

Marga, on the other hand, had blood at the lowest level possible for Teutonic magic: eighty-five percent. She claimed the element of earth but had trouble seizing it for most of her life; I had helped her improve her skills two years ago. But she had a terrible experience with a former beau who argued that her blood was just below the Teuton level. Apparently, the jerk had spread his tale far and wide before disappearing like the stereotypical outlaw.

"Serious question. How much did Bertha—my predecessor—emphasize the importance of finding a guy with high Teuton blood?" I looked from my cousin's face to Marga's. Vreni had not trained with us since she could not grasp her fire.

"I can't remember, but I know she mentioned it a few times," Traudl said.

"Ina got really deep down that rabbit hole," Marga put in. "She's had her eyes on Fonsi since we were kids."

I shook my head and met Vreni's gaze. "It's going to take me years to break that mentality. The priests on the council looked like deer caught in headlights when I told them it'd be smarter to tell Teutons with non-destructive elements to match themselves with Teutonic people like you."

"Sex doesn't awaken Teutonic magic overnight, though," Vreni said, a trace of unhappiness passing over her face. "Most young people don't have the patience to wait years for it to happen."

"It'd happen a lot faster if you . . . uh . . . ." My voice trailed off as I realized what I was about to say, and I felt my cheeks flush. *Augustin told me that you can get an extra point of Teuton blood right away if you have anal sex.*

"Oh shit, Swanie's into the kinky stuff!" Marga crowed, pressing her hands to her mouth in feigned horror. "Never expected that from you after what you had to put up with from—"

"We're in public!" I hissed, gesturing wildly at Marga before she spilled the beans about my time travels to everyone at the table. Marga and Erika were the only girlfriends of mine who knew that story.

"I'm just not comfortable with that stuff, even though Stefan's brought it up a few times." Vreni came to my rescue, her expression contorted into a delicate cringe. Our food arrived moments later, prompting the focus to change.

Vreni talked a little about her corporate pursuits; she worked as her father's assistant at a local pharmaceutical company. Stefan had a lucrative position in the research department there, and Vreni planned to be a stay-at-home mom after she and her boyfriend had children. My three friends tossed a few potential baby names around as I chewed on my Schnitzel, my attention drifting into my own mind, my own past. I thought of my oldest daughter, Cammie, starting a legacy for herself in Eisenwald, along with my other four eleventh century children. *I'll never know their stories now that I left Augustin behind, not unless I go back there someday.*

"So how many kids are you going to have with Hans?" Marga inquired, her voice pulling me back to the present. I looked up from my plate and saw what may have been anxiety lurking in her blue eyes. "I know he'll make you have some even if you don't want to, since you have to be an example as the Lady."

I frowned at my friend, unsure why she insisted upon defaulting to the worst about my Keyholder. "Hans and I have agreed to try for two kids. We *agreed*. He's not forcing me into anything, and you need to stop assuming that."

"The heart-bond just grosses me out. Walfrid used it to force Ina into S&M when she didn't consent." Marga did a parody of vomiting. Vreni curled her upper lip at the young woman beside her, appearing as frustrated as I felt.

"In the end, it comes down to the man and the woman," Traudl said. "Some girls love the idea of being submissive to a man, and they can look for a guy who's into that stuff. Other guys—even Teuton priests—would rather treat their wives or girlfriends like partners, equals. I think the point is, you need to train the youth in discernment and how to set the boundaries they want, Swanie."

"That's it, a voice of reason." Vreni raised her glass to my cousin, and Marga rolled her eyes. My cousin proceeded to inform us that Trudi was pregnant, and that she had struggled with nausea and exhaustion for the past few weeks.

"Crackers," I heard myself saying as Marga and Vreni erupted into joyful congratulations. Traudl tilted her head at me, and I realized that I had spoken the word in Teutonica. I repeated myself in Bayerisch and suggested mint as well. "It helps with the aftertaste. But Trudi should be fine by the fourth month."

"And how would you know?" Traudl narrowed her eyes and glanced at my abdomen. "Are you pregnant too?"

My brain was back in the eleventh century, recalling that I had vomited the most while carrying Marelda and Erika—my first and eighth children. "Not yet," I said quickly, "but I've been doing some research so I'm ready when it happens." I caught Marga's knowing look, but thankfully she kept silent this time.

After we had finished our food, the four of us sat chatting and sipping our drinks until the sky above began to trend toward twilight. I learned that Ina and her daughter shared an apartment with Marga currently, but that she planned to move in with Fonsi before year's end. That explained why Marga had closed herself off to the concept of heart-bonds and relationships with Teuton priests. She had gone on several dates with outsiders recently but complained that they were just as shallow as Teuton young men.

"You could always message that guy *Idealismus* from the Teuton forum," I noted, thinking back to the days before I had become Lady Muniche, when I had to field advances from an odd variety of young men. "He's an artist, and he likes metal music. Pretty sure he's still single." I used my lunch hour at work to catch up on posts there; at this point, Hans was the primary moderator.

"He's in Regensburg, right?" I nodded, and Marga made a face. "I don't think I can do the long-distance thing. Besides, what does he even look like?"

"You could always go to a New Year's festival in another city," Traudl said. "That's how my parents met, in Salzburg."

Marga still seemed disgruntled by the time we parted ways, promising to stay in contact as much as we could, to meet up at the Oktoberfest for sure. And as I retrieved my Ghibli from the street and turned it south toward the Thaden house, I ruminated on the deep-seated prejudices of the Teuton people, how destructive they could be to one caught in the cross hairs.

Maybe I should start a new topic on the forum declaring that it's time to welcome those with lower blood status into our ranks, and stop hiding the truth about spells that can be used to enslave. Erika may have had a point, when she said it's best for partners to guard each other's hearts. If we don't want Teutonic magic to go extinct, we need to wield it correctly and offer it to those just below the threshold for elemental control.

I started a topic to that effect when I returned home, and asked my husband to keep a close eye on it and promote respectful discussion. "Of course you have to open that can of worms right when Beth and my boss are about to go on vacation," Hans chided, his spiritual hands giving the heart of my soul a tolerant squeeze.

I stifled the groan his actions brewed and responded, "The kids are going to find out about my can of worms in early September, so it's only fair to tell the adults first." On the second Sunday of that month, Hans and I would hold our first class on Teutonic magic and traditions—for the twelve-through-fourteen age group.

While my father and Beth were on vacation, I barely had a minute to think about their itinerary. Both had kept it entirely under wraps, although I suspected that they planned to explore the Alps, since Beth had packed sturdy clothing and footwear along with hiking staples like granola bars and Landjäger. But when they returned home on the fourth Saturday of August, I found myself facing a plot twist I had not anticipated.

Hans and I were cuddling on the couch in our private parlor after a steamy round of sex, my Ocean City blanket draped over our nakedness as his hands stroked my back. I had my eyes closed to concentrate on the warmth of his touch, my heart throbbing in steady bliss at the proximity of its master guardian. When Hans stirred and spoke, my spirit hesitated to relinquish its reverie. "I do believe that your Pappi has returned."

My husband reached for his pair of discarded shorts as I tugged the blanket more tightly around my body, turning my gaze toward the door to the hall. My ice detected my father's energy—along with something else, a wispy breath of spirit.

And they stepped into the parlor together, my father's right arm holding Beth against his side as he said in Teutonica, "We seek a Teuton priest to conduct our wedding, *Leitaeri*. Would you do the honors?"

Chapter Seven

Unknown Sorcery

I found myself utterly unable to speak as Beth stood just a few strides from where I sat on the couch with the Ocean City blanket tucked beneath my armpits, abruptly feeling like I had passed into another dimension entirely. My icy spirit sensed the chill that comprised my cousin's once-empty aura—familiar, but not a replica. My ice represented frozen water's solid foundation, thoroughly bonded, protective and a contender. Beth's element enveloped her spirit in a misty cloud, with the lightness that held frozen water in the atmosphere just a bit longer than in its natural form.

She was snow.

And my ice-heightened vision zeroed in on the tanned skin of her chest. She wore a lavender halter top that left little to the imagination—and her flesh sported no scars. None. No lines, faint or stark, that indicated her violent induction into the realm of Teutonic magic.

She had not done the blood-transfer. But she was a Teuton now. And that meant . . . but my father's element was energy . . . destructive . . . he could not give Beth Teuton blood through elemental sex. Yet Beth had always been committed to purity, to monogamy, to waiting until marriage. And my father had just asked Hans to officiate their Teutonic wedding.

What had they done?

Hans and my father exchanged a few phrases while my brain floundered in turmoil; I heard none of it. But somehow I sensed that my husband was not surprised at all by this turn of events. He had known it was coming and had not seen fit to tell me.

My horror, confusion, and disenchantment found shape at last: petulance. *So all this time, Beth and Pappi plotted to do something awful so she could have Teuton blood. What'd he do, hire a male prostitute to repeatedly screw her ass? She was at forty-something percent before this . . . it would take a lot of sex to get her to eighty-five percent. Some "vacation." I hope her intestines still work. Does she have hemorrhoids now or what?*

Suddenly, I felt Hans' hands upon my bare shoulders, a latent brush of fire against my deranged ice. "You and Beth should go talk it over," he murmured in my left ear, his spiritual hands imparting a touch of calm to my pattering heart. I managed to tear my eyes from my cousin to meet his gaze, and the ends of Hans' thin lips curved into a tight smile. "Don't forget your panties," he added, too quietly for our company to hear.

My eyes traveled down Hans' bare chest to his cloth shorts, which he had frantically thrown on without underwear, my mind desperately working to find my reason in a sizzling heap of emotion. *Talk it over with Beth? A little too late now, isn't it? She already screwed some dude who's not her husband over and over just to get what she's always wanted . . . and my Pappi told her she didn't need Teuton blood to please him. What in the world was she thinking?!*

Somehow I managed to grab my underwear from the floor and stumble out of the parlor behind my cousin, who had detached herself from my father's grasp. She muttered something about how Sebastian had brought her bags upstairs to her room and that she had asked him to bring us tea and a snack tray. "That was ten, fifteen minutes ago? It's probably already there," she said as she headed for the back staircase.

I still could not put my whirling thoughts into words, but I took the time to study Beth's appearance while following her to the third floor. She wore jean shorts and flip flops, her tanned legs and arms appearing as healthy as they always did, as if she had enjoyed a hiking holiday after all. She walked steadily, showing no obvious signs of rectal injury, and I noticed no bruises or other wounds on her neck. *How long has she been a Teuton? They were gone for three weeks. Did she do this at the start of their vacation and spend the rest of the time recovering?*

Before I knew it, I found myself seated in a chair with maroon upholstery, a cup of herbal tea in my hands, its heat clashing against my spirit's frostiness. My eyes looked blankly at Beth, who had settled upon the bed, the bags she had taken on her journey pushed against its foot. She blew on her tea in silence for a second, then met my gaze and said, "You might as well just spill all your questions, Swanie. I'm ready for it."

"When you first started falling for my Pappi, you told me that he didn't want you to taint your blood," were the first words that left my lips. I narrowed my eyes at her as I took a sip of tea, my ice coursing thickly through my veins.

Beth's brown eyebrows wrinkled, and she looked away, toward the table that held the teapot, a tray of vegetables with dip, and a crystal bowl of chocolates. "I didn't do it for him," she said, a twinge of defensiveness in her tone. "I've wanted to be a Teuton since you showed me your ice when we were teenagers. You know that. So no, Max didn't force me into anything, if that's what you're thinking."

I felt as though my lungs had frozen solid. Breathing took conscious effort; I set my teacup onto the table beside me and thrust my hands beneath my thighs. The blanket had begun to slip down my chest, revealing the top two scars from my blood-transfer with Freia. "You didn't do the blood-transfer," I said in a flat voice.

"No. You always told me that was the most dangerous way to gain Teuton blood. You said you have to be in cahoots with Wuotan to survive it."

I did not appreciate how Beth cast my own admonitions back at me. She was right. I had spent nearly a decade of my life begging her *not* to offer her blood to Wuotan's burning river. So instead . . . . "I thought you were all about purity, but apparently you decided to plant your butt on some Teuton's cock."

I glared at my cousin and attempted to rein in my irritation, reaching out to take up a handful of carrot sticks and cucumbers. That was the part that felt like a betrayal. Beth had reproached me for offering my virginity to Augustin before we married in the past; she had planned to wait for a wedding ring before she sealed the deal with my father. But here she was, a proud Teuton who got it through elemental sex. *And not with my father's energy.*

"Max and I got married at the registry office before we . . . uh, before." This declaration brought me up short, and I stared at Beth, one carrot half-crunched in my mouth. A blush bloomed on her cheeks as she admitted, "We kind of did it on the sly, I know. Just grabbed a couple people who worked there to witness. We're going to have a real wedding later, in Jersey so my mom's family can come."

I blinked at her, my confusion deeply entrenched. She sported a platinum band on the ring finger of her right hand; I had not noticed it before. "So you and my Pappi got married and then spent the next three weeks . . . but it can't be. His element is energy. It would electrocute you."

Beth sighed and arose from the bed, taking up a plate to fill it with veggies. "I don't actually remember how it happened," she said, glancing at me out of the corner of her eye as she spooned some dip onto her plate. My eyes widened, and then she added, "They put me under anesthesia for it."

A piece of cucumber nearly dropped down my windpipe. I coughed, beating my chest with my right fist, the Ocean City blanket bunching up around my hips. "You . . . *what . . . they?!*" I could hardly get the words out, and I grabbed a napkin to dab my eyes. I had never once heard anyone mention a way to gain Teuton blood that involved anesthesia. What the *hell* had Beth done?

"Are you okay?" she queried, her expression worried.

I held up one finger as I finished coughing, then took a few sips of tea to clear any lingering traces of cucumber. I stared daggers at my cousin over the rim of the teacup, silently demanding the full explanation that she seemed hesitant to share. Beth eyed me for a few moments before retaking her seat on the bed, folding her legs and retrieving a stick of celery from her plate. And then she told me a story so insane that I could merely sit and gawk at her, the tea and food forgotten.

"After we got married, Max drove us into the mountains, to the Black Castle. Günter's domain. Apparently he has some sort of medical background. He pretty much has all of the resources of a standard hospital. I saw some of it, and it shocked me . . . but the point is, during his exile he's uncovered a way to safely awaken the element of a non-Teuton . . . using some sort of device to channel the energy away, so it doesn't cause a heart attack or electrocution. It was like something from Mary Shelley's *Frankenstein*, to be honest." Beth tittered, blushing anew.

My jaw quivered as my brain began to put two and two together. Beth and my father had gone to Günter Setzer—my era's Black Priest—and made a deal that would grant her Teuton blood. And to do it, the mad Cursed One had anesthetized her, attached her to some freaky machine, and repeatedly . . . .

"You . . . *fucked* . . . Günter Setzer?" I ogled my cousin in abject horror.

"Well . . . it was more like the other way around. I don't remember any of it."

A tormented squeak burst from my throat, and my fingers balled into icy fists. "You, the person who's been a faithful Christian all this time, *you* decided to let a *Black Priest* fuck you so you could gain Teuton blood?!"

"Swanie—"

"*What* did you give him in return?!" I shouted, my voice having risen at least an octave. *Teuton blood comes at the highest price. Sex—even sex times fifty—wouldn't be enough to pay it.*

"That's . . . kind of . . . in process," Beth answered, her eyes dropping to the vegetables on her plate.

"Not a child. You didn't offer him a *child*, did you?" The possible meanings of the phrase *in process* infused my blood with true terror.

"*No!*" Beth exclaimed, her brown eyes condemning my assumption. "He and Max hashed it out for four days before they came to an agreement. Max gave him a semen sample for his . . . business." My cousin cringed at the word and then said, "He's given me a different task to do that's between us. And it doesn't involve magic of any kind, dark or light. It's more . . . research related."

I slumped against the back of the chair, my emotional hurricane draining what remained of my strength. I heaved a sigh and muttered a few curse words in Bayerisch, then grabbed a handful of chocolates. "So now I have to spend the rest of my life worrying about what Günter might do to you if you don't pay your debt. I already have Hans' pledge hanging over me, even though he swears that he won't curse any children we have. I almost wish my Pappi had hired a male prostitute to screw you instead, one of water to keep things lubricated."

Beth laughed. "My anus was sore for a while, even with all the precautions Günter took. He made us stay at the castle for an extra three days, to make sure my digestive system still worked. He's done it before, apparently, but never to someone with blood as low as mine was."

She seemed lighthearted about the situation, ready to laugh at the absurdity of what she had undergone. So I did my best to follow her example, turning it over in my mind while I chewed on a chocolate with strawberry crème filling. "Just how low was your blood, anyway?"

"It was forty-seven percent when Max tested it before we left." That tidbit brought my head up again. My father, the man who had spurned Teutonic magic for most of my life, had tested my cousin's blood for her. "Now it's eighty-five percent," Beth finished, pure joy evident upon her countenance.

"When I woke up from the anesthesia, I sensed it all around me, permeating my spirit. The wintry cold. At first I thought I was ice like you, but Günter identified it as snow right away. He said he detected it when we showed up at his front door."

"Like Augustin with Freia," I murmured, recalling that he saw the light in Freia's spirit when her blood was a mere fifteen percent Teutonic. Maybe that was a talent priests in league with Wuotan learned to hone.

"I had hoped you'd be happy for me," Beth said in a tone that tugged at my heartstrings. When I met her gaze, I saw moisture dampening her eyes. "I've wanted to be like you for years, to not have to sit back and let you take all the heat for the darker things you know. I want to dance in the spiritual realm with you at the first snowfall, see the magic of the silver oak, and help oppressed Teuton women take back their agency."

"I could use all the help I can get with that last part," I told her, gratitude washing through me at last, conquering what remained of my doubts. "Maybe you should come to the classes I'm going to start teaching next month, give your unspoken support. You might learn a thing or two, unless my Pappi has set you on the path to the priesthood. Did he teach you blood control yet?" I grinned.

"No, but I seriously need to learn how to do that!"

Beth exulted about her newfound magic for several minutes, while I wound the blanket back around my torso and poured myself a fresh cup of tea. She seemed wholly thrilled by her new status, and she said that my father had helped her with the basics of how to invoke her snow. She had not yet fully grasped it but suspected that it would be easier come winter. She already felt an amity toward streams and lakes—she and my father had spent a week at an Alpine hut after leaving the Black Castle behind.

"Now that I'm a Teuton, I can honestly say that it would have cheated Max, if I'd stayed the outsider that I was,"

Beth mused, balancing a celery stick between her fingers. She looked toward the window as she spoke, her expression pensive. "He'd have had to stifle his energy anytime we had sex, and that's just cheap. It's a rush to get in bed with him, by the way." She gave me a naughty look.

I held up a restraining hand. "You can keep the details to yourself. But are you actually going to sleep in *this* room, now that you're his wife?"

Beth scoffed. "Heck, no! I just have to get my stuff sorted, and then move it all into his rooms. He's already shuffled his things around so there'll be space for both of us."

After we had talked about various aspects of the new world that had opened its doors to Beth—she intended to join the Teuton forum and get to know all of my girlfriends—I broached the subject that had gnawed at my peace, since she revealed exactly what she had done to become one of my people. "So. Günter Setzer."

Beth giggled and rolled onto her stomach on the bed, having finished with both the snacks and her tea. "What about him?"

Curiosity churned within me. "Is he energy, too?"

"Nah, he's lightning like your friend Rudi." She winked at me.

"What's he look like?"

"He has a six pack," Beth responded immediately, "and he kind of reminds me of James Bond, you know? Short black hair slicked back from his forehead. Dark blue eyes similar to Hans'. Tall, broad shoulders, strong fingers, smelled like a mountaintop during a lightning storm. When I met him, I understood what makes Black Priests attractive. They may be dead, and they may have sinister gifts, but . . . wow." Beth fanned her face with one hand and snickered.

"And he screwed you, so that's something you can brag about. 'I had sex with the dead and lived to tell about it.'" My cousin shrieked with laughter as old memories rose to the surface: Augustin's solid chest, broad shoulders, thick neck, elegant hair, sky blue eyes that held the depths of eternity. *I promise to love you, to cherish you, to remain faithful to you as your wife for all of eternity.*

And yet here I was, playing a role with Hans Meissner. The familiar pain clawed at my heart, and I endeavored to push it aside as I addressed my cousin once more. "So you were with Günter for about a week."

"Yep."

"Did you happen to . . . see the evidence of what he does . . . with Teuton women and children?" I asked, the topic provoking my stomach to roil. Hans had said that the man bred and sold Teutons, his nefarious business.

Beth sighed and propped her chin onto her fists as she met my gaze. "What he does is breed women of lower blood status to produce children of eighty-five percent or higher. He keeps them in a separate wing of the castle, and he didn't let either of us meet any of them. He wasn't up front about how he lures them in, either, so I think there's something funny going on there. But he doesn't flat out 'sell' the babies. He adopts them out to Teuton parents who've struggled to have kids."

My lips parted in surprise, for my cousin seemed all too ready to forgive the Black Priest's immoral practice. "Hans told me he sells them."

"Adoption costs money, no matter how you slice it. Whether you do it through government programs, private programs, or international programs. Does that mean those kids are sold, too?" Beth raised her eyebrows at me.

I cocked my head at her. "What'd he do, convince you to justify his crimes?"

"Haven't you done the same every time *your* Black Priest slays someone on the heathen altar?"

"Touché." I rubbed my forehead, thinking that might be another gift Wuotan offered his servants—persuasion. "But what woman would agree to be used for that purpose? Bearing children that she'll never see grow up."

"I guess in some ways it's like being a surrogate mom. But I'm not sure all of them consent. Max told me to stop asking him about it, so I think that's the dark part of his business, actually. Not the adoption, but how he gets the mothers."

"More reason to train young Teutons to seek partners of lower blood status," I grumbled, the fires of my resolution stoked hot. Günter would have fewer mothers to reap once I had finished promoting inclusion.

Beth and I chatted for a while longer about the classes I planned to teach to the local Teuton children. I ran through a list of topics to cover—the uniqueness of each Teutonic element, the need for greater acceptance of those with lower blood status to strengthen our community, the importance of treating *Eihalbae* and nature itself respectfully.

"I think I might sit in on a few of your classes," my cousin said, her countenance pensive. "Max has taught me a lot already, but there's just so much, so many things I've yet to grasp. Maybe working with the kids can help me get better at summoning my snow."

The first classes for the children were a major success. The youngest ones proved especially enthusiastic about the pointers I taught. Several of the kids declared that they would find every silver oak around München and offer elemental gifts to the fairies. All of them listened with rapt attention when I related the true reasons why the Teuton people fell to the Saxons in the eleventh century, and many denounced the prejudices that had led to our defeat. One young man of air breathed a sigh of relief when I told the older teens that if they claimed an element that was not destructive, they ought to seek out a partner who wished to seize the magic beyond their reach.

When that particular class prepared to depart, the young man hung back, his hands stuffed in his pockets while he waited for the others to file away. Then he looked at me from beneath his thick brown brows and said, "Thank you so much for bringing that up about Teutonic people, Lady Muniche. There's a girl I like at school. We've gone out a few times . . . but her blood's at seventy-eight percent. I've always been scared my Mutti won't approve."

"Well, if your Mutti gives you any grief about it, tell her to come speak with me," I urged him with an encouraging smile. "There's more than one way to make sure our people don't die out."

Hans congratulated me on the wisdom with which I handled the sensitive topics, saying that those moments were when the experience I had gained during my twenty-two years in the past shone brightly from my aura. We often finished such days with fervent intimacy, Muniche's spirit augmenting our passion. It came as no surprise to me when I missed my period at the beginning of November. My Keyholder and I would soon welcome our first child.

Chapter Eight:
Lingering Shadows

During the first months of my pregnancy, several contentions occurred that sent my thoughts back into darker environs. For one thing, my cousin Trudi struggled with her health as her own pregnancy progressed, saddled with preeclampsia and water retention. As a young woman who had always claimed a stellar figure, her weight gain saddled her with a cumbersome burden, her tears flowing whenever we talked on the phone. She told me in December that she had been plagued with nightmares, awful ones where Wuotan tried to drag her into a crypt to give birth in mephitic shadow.

Trudi's experience brought back memories of the Teuton noblewomen I had known in the eleventh century who had not survived their labor. Alvira Adler and Dorli Ahloch had both complained of nightmares involving demons before they had passed away at childbed, so there might be some connection there. I shared my concerns with Hans, who brushed it off. He said that pregnant women were often plagued by nightmares and that the surefire way of solving that problem was to use a heartbond to guide them to the realm of dreams each night.

I faced no troubles in the first months, myself, not even morning sickness. This prompted me to suspect that my child was a boy, for girls had always given me more trouble in the past. Hans asserted that I must hire a doctor to keep tabs on my condition, for he did not wish to lose me or the child due to unforeseen circumstances. I did not share his opinion and dragged my feet on the issue, doing research on local midwives and doulas instead. No matter what my husband might think, I planned to have my child at home, apart from the sterile formality of the hospital.

Erika and Iliana married in a Teutonic wedding on Christmas Day. German law did not yet recognize gay marriage, but Teutonic law could be bent at the hands of a willing priest. Üwe conducted the ritual for them at the meeting place beside the Isar. Although the two lovers had faced a fair amount of criticism from the older Teuton priests in München, Hans put his foot down at my insistence. He declared that if the marriage scar appeared upon their wrists, then their union was blessed by the elements and therefore legitimate.

Erika looked striking in a cerulean gown plunging from her shoulders like the waves of the sea, her red hair dusted with matching sparkles, her poise strong and triumphant. Iliana wore a dress that she had designed herself, with a midnight bodice and a skirt patterned with sapphire flames. She had added flecks of blue to her dark hair, woven into an intricate braid that fell to the middle of her back.

I stood beneath the linden boughs to observe the ceremony, a long wool coat protecting me from winter's chill, though I hardly needed it. My Keyholder stood beside me in the robes of the Teuton priest, his visage solemn, his dark gray hair silvery beneath the moonlight. The clearing was quite crowded; Erika's parents, grandparents, and brother were in attendance, along with Iliana's parents and four of her seven siblings. Ina, Fonsi, Traudl, Marga, Vreni, and Stefan all witnessed as Üwe's voice shattered our culture's antiquated customs, proclaiming that two

Teutonae—the female word for Teuton—would bind themselves by blood, oath, and love.

Tension slinked along the breeze as a result of my friends' wedding, and I caught the first whiff of it at the New Year's festival just a week later. I heard both women and men muttering amongst themselves about the audacity of two females perverting a primeval rite to appease their unnatural yearnings. At one point, I saw two middle-aged women eyeing me as one of them said to the other, "At the rate things are going, with the *Leitalra* urging the youth to find partners of low blood and teaching children to give offerings to *Eihalbae*, we'll end up extinct within two generations. The fairies will steal away our young and never give them back. Mark my words."

These rumors, coupled with Trudi's poor condition— she was in the hospital on bed rest in an attempt to help her reach her due date of February 5th—put me in a sour mood. I bickered with Hans more and more, complaining that our people would rather pass the blame onto other creatures entirely before they would accept and correct their own ludicrous biases. Seven children had been pulled from our classes, and one little girl had given me a note that her absent friend had written: *I want to be there, Lady Municha. But Mutti says I can't make rocks for Eyhalba or they take me to Wootan.*

"Are these people living in the Dark Ages or something?" I demanded after showing my husband the note. The girl had written it in crayon and drawn a picture of herself with a tree and a fairy that looked more like a butterfly, tears streaming down her sketched face. "I've talked to *three* different *Eihalbae* in my lifetime, and not one of them invited me into some spooky otherworld. Next they'll start fearing changelings." I shook my head in disgust.

"Fairy lore is not well understood among our people," Hans reminded me, sounding far less upset about the matter than I felt. "But it might be best to focus more upon our history and language during the classes. I've deflected complaints of all sorts since you've taken the children under your wing. Adi Dantzler has a mind to attend a few of your lessons come spring."

"No. Absolutely not," I retorted. "The lessons I teach are for children and people who've just entered our conclave, like Beth and Iliana. I will *not* tolerate an old priest listening in for the sole purpose of contradicting everything that needs to be taught."

"Swanie, remember, you're still new at this position—"

"The Old One is *not* invited and never will be." I cut off Hans' attempt to placate my frustrations and stuck my index finger in his face. "*You* are present at every lesson, and *you* are the Keyholder. The buck stops with you. If Teuton priests think they have some arcane wisdom to impart, maybe they should invite women to study for the priesthood, too."

"Enough, Swanie!" Hans snapped, pushing my finger away from his face as his spiritual hands sent a jolt of reproach to my heart, followed by an irresistible surge of serenity. "You're getting far too flustered about this, and that's not good for you or the baby. Come, let me give you a bath to soothe your muscles."

Thus it went for the majority of the first months of 2004. Whenever I opened valid concerns before my husband, he would use his hold over my heart to pacify me. He claimed that he did not need my emotional angst to exacerbate my blood pressure, but the one time my father's doctor visited to check me over, it showed no signs of unhealthiness. The doctor gently tried to convince me to sign up for an ultrasound and the standard tests for fetal disease, but I saw no need. My child was a boy; I could tell by where he had chosen to take residence in my womb. And none of my past children were born with any genetic maladies. My CFTR protein was in good shape, so I would not pass on cystic fibrosis.

Trudi's labor started two weeks early, and she delivered a son by C-section after struggling and failing to birth him vaginally. Although part of me wanted to be there for moral support, I hesitated to step into the labyrinthine corridors of a hospital for fear of reawakening my latent

PTSD from my younger brother's death. The child was healthy, and Mane and Trudi named him Lukas. According to Traudl, who texted me to keep me abreast of the situation, Lukas had Mane's curly hair and Trudi's blue-gray eyes.

At my request, Gregor prepared a collection of one-pot meals for Trudi and Mane to ease some of the stressors of first-time parenthood. When I dropped them off at their apartment, Mane thanked me profusely, stating with a grim smile that he had never expected to learn so much about cooking during the past months. "I've gotten good at spaghetti and scrambled eggs, but I know Trudi will want more variety when she gets home," he said.

"Pretty sure there's stroganoff, goulash, beef stew, vegetable gratins, lobster bisque, mushroom casserole, Sauerbraten, cheese Spätzle, and a whole bunch of other soups and stews in the mix," I noted, nodding at the containers as he stuffed them one by one into a mostly-empty freezer. "No lie, the Thaden house has smelled like heaven for the past few days. If you end up needing more, just let me know."

When the early spring blooms began blossoming in the window boxes, the Old One from the council appeared at the front door one Sunday afternoon, wearing a sport coat and tie as if he had come straight from church. Lise, the housekeeper, let him in, for he apparently said that he needed to speak with Hans. A group of twelve children from the ages of nine through eleven sat in the sunroom with me, Beth and my Keyholder at my side, as I tested their knowledge of Teutonic names for vegetables and herbs.

Lise slipped into the room to murmur something to Hans, just as I opened the subject of dusky spurge and its potentially deadly properties. Hans' hands sent a pointed tap to the heart of my soul, and I halted my discourse to meet his gaze. Very quietly he said in Teutonica, "Adi Dantzler is in the front parlor."

Anger coiled into a knot in my chest, but I had to keep a calm veneer before the children. So I cleared my throat and addressed Beth, asking her to tell them all that she knew about dusky spurge—which at that point was not much. Then I rose from the settee to follow my husband into the family room, where I cut loose in a low, scathing voice. "Get. Rid. Of. Him. I told you he's *not* permitted to intrude on our lessons."

Hans sighed and gestured for me to lower my voice further. "Swanie, it's not wise to put forth the appearance of uncivility to someone—"

"*No,*" I repeated, jamming my fists against my hips as I glared up at my husband. "Use your authority as the Keyholder to send him on his way, and call my Pappi if you want help. This is his house; he can order him to leave. If the two of you won't get it done, I'll threaten him in spirit form."

"You most certainly will *not!*" Hans exploded, black flames leaping into his eyes, though he kept his voice down. "Freezing your mortal body would kill our child. Did your precious Black Priest never mention that to you? How long do you think an infant can last in a frozen womb?"

Augustin had not mentioned that to me, but I had never before sought to enter the spiritual realm when pregnant. The dream world was far different, since a Teuton's element did not need to protect the physical body while the spirit traveled there.

I folded my hands over my abdomen, which had rounded out just a bit over the last month. "Fine then. Do your job as the Keyholder of this city and bring your priests into line. I have children to teach." I spun away from him on my heel and reentered the sunroom, where Beth had engaged her quarry in a folk song about the spirit of the River Isar.

Hans did, in fact, evict the Old One from the house, but his reluctance to do so festered in my heart that entire week. By Friday night, work-related crises had pushed my tolerance past the tipping point, and I railed on Hans once we retreated to our private chambers. I accused him of cowing before his peers when they were dead set on keeping our people unaware of their full potential. The earlier rumors about *Eihalbae* kidnapping children had intensified, and the number of students attending my classes continued to dwindle.

I told Hans that I might give a speech at the upcoming May dances, and tell our people that fairies only punished those who wronged them first. "Since you're too afraid to speak the truth, I might just let everybody know that priests prefer to keep their constituents ignorant of the sorcery they can wield. They took all the spells out of *Der Weg* except for the filial curse; and if that doesn't say something about their true intentions, nothing will. You walk the dark path willingly."

My husband glared at me and said that I ought to go lie down for a while, for my stress had clouded my judgment. But I shot back with a jagged threat. "'Oh, keep her calm and peaceful so she doesn't rock the boat.' I'm sick of you shrugging off the things that mean something, that could actually make a difference.

"Maybe what I need to do is take a quick trip to a pipe organ and play Prince Otto's song. Then I can experience what it's like to have a priest who listens to me and takes me seriously! Augustin, a far better man than any of your ilk, the one who taught me things you'd never think to show me."

Hans sneered at me and gave a scornful laugh. "It'd be wiser for you to air your grievances to someone who truly loves you. That Cursed One chose Wuotan over you when he left you here, remember."

"You sound like you have a suggestion," I charged, narrowing my eyes. I expected him to reference himself, for I knew without a doubt that he loved me. My pregnancy hormones had ravaged my patience of late.

"How about your Mutti, the one who christened you as 'ice princess' before you manifested your element? I'm surprised you haven't thought to speak with her yet, to ask for her guidance on your destiny as *Leitalra*."

I gawked at Hans, his response taking me completely by surprise. *What is he saying?* "But . . . I can't go to my own past. That one book said . . . the temptation to change something . . . ."

"Now you're a rule follower?"

My eyes widened, and I thought I detected mockery in Hans' expression. Hazy images of my mother arose in my brain—her smile, her laugh, the scent of her perfume, her gentle touch when she brushed my hair. And I remembered how happy she had looked when she married my father.

Would she really have advice to offer for my situation? Did my Mutti ever try to influence her friends to push back against our patriarchal system? Would it be a good idea to tell her that her daughter's fated to travel time and become Muniche's Lady? Would she be proud of me?

I excused myself and retreated to our bathroom for a long shower. While I relaxed beneath the warm spray, my irritation tapered off, and I recognized that I had not been fair to Hans throughout the past few months. Experiencing pregnancy again had ignited memories best left dead and buried. The satisfied glint in my ex-husband's eyes whenever I found myself with child in the eleventh century, how he used to say, "Good, that'll keep you from running off with your Cursed One for another year." The swelling, the stressed throbbing of my heart, the weight that clung to my short frame.

I'm only doing this twice. Just two times. After that, Hans will agree to get the snip. I know he will. He's been trying to handle people's complaints to protect me from excess trauma, and all I've been doing is yelling at him in return. Gosh, I'm such a mess.

Maybe he has a point about asking Mutti for advice. She might have some hints about how to handle stupid pregnancy emotions, if nothing else. In the eleventh century I just spewed at Ulka, and she'd bring me tea. I could use some of that right now.

I apologized to Hans after finishing in the shower, and he held me against his chest as I cried out my unhappiness. Sometimes I longed to go public about my time travels, to our people at least, so the older ones would stop judging me as some naïve young fool. But I remembered my Key-holder's warnings, my father's fears: *Wuotan didn't say whether he wants you dead . . . or something worse.*

What was worse than death?

On Palm Sunday, I attended mass at the Frauenkirche and caught up with the head organist after the service. I had not played any concerts there since Hans and I had formalized our marriage, but the two of us were on friendly terms. We chatted about his repertoire for a while, how he had begun to study Messiaen, how his fingers struggled with some of that composer's rhythms. And eventually I asked him where I might find a pipe organ to play in a small town or village, somewhere to practice without fear of being overheard.

Chapter Nine:
Camilla

Hans pulled a few strings once I returned home that afternoon with a short list of chapels and their caretakers. He made arrangements for the two of us to meet with three Catholic priests in three different villages the following Saturday, in order to take notes on each organ and on the security measures. My Keyholder averred that it would be well-nigh impossible to play the Song of Time without witnesses unless we broke into the chapel of our choice. "And of course it wouldn't be hard to do so, if I enter in spirit form and unlock the door."

My husband appeared far too unruffled by such a prospect, as he pored over maps of southern Bavaria in his office, plotting out our route for the weekend. I thought back to the first time I had opened the arcane gateway—when I attended my parents' wedding. Hans had given me an old master key for the locks in the Frauenkirche, a key that worked back in the 1970s. "Did you break into places a lot when you were a teenager or something?" I asked.

Looking up at me from beneath his dark brows, Hans smirked, his eyes glinting with mischief. "Don't a lot of teens dabble with petty crimes?"

I scoffed and ran a hand through my hair, its black tresses thicker than usual thanks to my pregnancy. "I never did that here, but Beth and I broke into the junky community center in her neighborhood once. It was being used as a church. One of the windows was unlocked, so we crawled in and nabbed some saltines. Then the alarm went off. Good thing we had gloves on." I chortled.

"Saltines." My husband sounded scornful. "My buddies and I used to swipe Schnapps from a couple different places years ago."

That figured. I leaned forward and placed my hands on his desk, noting that our course would take us around München in a counterclockwise loop. "So the plan is for us to scout things out, pick one chapel, and then come back late at night. Park some distance away, and then you sneak in as a fiery spirit and unlock the door for me. We'll need dark clothes. And if we happen to get noticed?" I tilted my head at my husband.

"I'll use my fire's speed and obscurity to sweep us away. It's no problem. I'll keep my spirit stretched forth the whole time to check for people nearby."

I nodded, a naughty excitement brewing deep within. "I'm going to have to figure out what to wear. I can't just use Mutti's clothes this time. How did people dress in 1985?" I tried to sift my vague memories of that era and came up empty, although I knew that men's shorts were much shorter back then. Did I need to get a perm first, or use a blow dryer to frizz my hair?

"I'd suggest you go in the winter. Then you can conceal your outfit beneath a long coat. You wouldn't want to go too close to May, because your Pappi has said she was sick for several months prior to Dane's birth." Hans cleared his throat, his forehead wrinkling as he glanced at his computer screen.

I shivered all over at the enormity of what I was about to do—have an actual, adult conversation with the woman whose influence had set me on this path of Teutonic magic, a woman I had hardly known. How much should I tell her about my destiny? Would she believe me when I told her who I was?

"Can you pull up the calendar for 1985?" I asked, moving around Hans' desk to view his computer screen. He brought up the calendar and scrolled back to 1985, and I pointed to Wednesday, January 16th, the middle of the month. "I'll go in the early afternoon on that day. Pappi should be at work, and Mutti should be at home, at Opa Hobart's house, especially if she isn't feeling her best. It'll be interesting trying to evade everyone else just to talk to her." I frowned a bit.

Hans looked from the computer screen to my face. "You can use your ice to do a quick sweep of the area and avoid anyone who isn't the same element as you. None of the Thadens claim ice."

"Hopefully none of their employees did, either," I muttered, trying to plan for any potential mishaps. I felt my son stretching inside of me as I pondered, and my right palm drifted automatically to my abdomen, acknowledging his presence. *You ready to take a journey through time? You're likely the first unborn child to ever do that.*

Surprisingly enough, my husband and I encountered no road bumps as we carried out our plan. Choosing a chapel on the outskirts of an industrial village, we crept inside in the early morning hours. The place had no security, but also next to nothing of value except for an intricately sculpted altar. Hans led me down a pitch black aisle toward the organ, which stood against the wall to the left of the altar. Along the way, he snagged a candlestick and invoked natural flames upon it.

"Getting major eleventh century vibes doing this," I remarked as I switched on the organ, looking over its stops and considering which ones to use. "We should have brought flashlights."

Hans snickered as he set the candelabra onto the organ. "You're the one who can't see in the dark."

I prepared the registration like Prince Otto had written it long ago, noticing when I glanced at my Keyholder that his eyes were a flat black. "Quit bragging. I've got to concentrate."

My husband held his peace as I flexed my fingers and began playing the Song of Time, the inherent power of its melody weaving into my soul. I focused my thoughts on January 16th, 1985, at 3 p.m., envisioning my grandparents' gardens—tall hedgerows dusted with snow, a marble fountain in the shape of a rising phoenix, its frozen waters shimmering. I imagined no people around, willing my arrival to be undetected by any of my family or my grandfather's staff.

When I reached that chord at the end of those lines that had long been lost to history, a resounding *crack* split the air between the organ and the altar, as two labradorite gates appeared from nothing, slowly opening to reveal a tumultuous abyss, streaks of colors warring with darkness, vanishing into infinity. I lifted my hands and feet from the instrument and turned to stare at time's gateway, part of me bemused at the fact that I was doing this *again*. After I had first become Lady Muniche, I had envisioned myself bound to the present day ... but now I would step into the year 1985, when Bertha Lohr held my position ... and Hans held the keys.

"That was magnificent," Hans said at length. I met his gaze, and he gave me an approving nod, his black eyes drifting from the organ's keyboards to me.

"Guess you can step into the past yourself now." A nervous laugh escaped my lips, for Hans was a far better organist than I could ever be. Now he knew the ending to the Song of Time, and he might be skilled enough to play it aurally.

My Keyholder shook his head and smiled, then offered me my floor-length wool jacket. "You might want to get going after making a racket like that. Not sure how long our presence here will remain unnoticed."

"Right." I grabbed the jacket and worked my way into it, concealing both my pregnancy and my outfit. I wore a pair of stylish winter boots, the legs of my jeans stuffed into them, and I had my hair braided and pinned to the back of my head. I was as ready as I would ever be, so I turned for the gateway, running through the subjects I wished to cover with my mother one more time. *A fairy led me to the Torstein. I'm Muniche's Lady. I'm trying to make a difference in the community, working with Pappi, having my Keyholder's child. I wish I'd had the chance to know you better.*

"Swanie." Hans' voice cut through my ruminations just before I stepped into time's currents. I looked back at him, where he stood before the organ. His visage was piercing as he tossed something toward me. I reached out to catch it, the ice churning in my blood improving my reaction time; it was a sheathed knife, maybe ten centimeters long. *What?*

I frowned at my husband, and he nodded grimly. "Just in case."

It took me a second to translate that, as I turned the knife over in my hand. *Oh. A backup plan if I can't get to an organ to reopen the gates of time. Not sure if I'm brave enough to cut the Torstein out of my hip, though.*

But I tucked the knife into a pocket of my coat anyway and nodded at Hans. "Be back in a sec," I promised with a wink. Then I plunged into time's obscurity.

As usual, I felt as though my physical body had left me entirely amid those tornadic currents. I could see nothing solid while I flew into the past, nor could I touch any of the swirls that encircled me, carrying an interloper in a direction contrary to nature. Stifled groans arose from beneath me, wordless pleas for acknowledgement, for freedom, for something I could not give . . . . And I winced as feminine voices clawed at my ears, ridiculing me in Ælte Teutonica.

The brash witch has returned, discarding all warnings, all admonitions. Is our master your master now? No one can serve two masters. Your God will not protect you . . . as you distort Wuotan's sorcery for your own selfish gain. To speak with the dead is necromancy . . . forbidden . . . and you have brought a child with you. Our master should take him for himself . . . eternal damnation . . . .

Though I tried to ignore the sirens' censure, terror gripped me in a vise at the thought of Wuotan seizing my unborn son while I writhed in time's currents. Was that *possible?* It could not be, no, just an empty threat. But when the demon's coarse laughter rang out around me, tearing at every thread of my spirit, I started screaming, questioning what had driven me to face this wretched portal anew. Why did I need to talk to my mother, anyway? I hardly knew her. She had married the love of her life; she would have no counsel to offer me.

Thankfully, when I burst through the labradorite gates onto a hidden path sprinkled with snow, my mortal self was not screaming. I fell to my knees as my left ankle twisted, and I panted, shivers racing through my entire body. My gloved hands pressed upon my abdomen, and I felt my son kick me in response. *Oh, thank goodness. He's still there. We both made it. We're here . . . and I need to shut those damned gates.*

I raised my left hand in a commanding gesture, and they disappeared within seconds, revealing the frozen marble fountain I had imagined not long before. The sky above was gray, the clouds appearing as though they harbored the potential for snowfall. I heard a sparrow chirp from some distance away, and I closed my eyes, stretching my icy spirit forth to take stock of the yard and the stone manor beyond. I sensed no spirits outside, Teuton or not, but inside I picked out fire, dark energy, air, and ice. *Opa Hobart, Oma Toni, Tante Rilla . . . and Mutti.*

"Okay," I whispered, more to my son than myself, "we have to figure out how to get your Oma by herself. Maybe we can get her to come out here, to where your Onkel Dane and I used to hide from our nanny. That'd be perfect."

Stealthily, I made my way to a thicket of holly, wedged between a chimney and a windowless gable, a sundial overgrown with moss the sole ornamentation. Vague memories suggested that my mother had shown me this place when I was very young, that she had taught me how to read the sundial before I understood the hands of a clock. I shuffled my way through the bushes and saw that the snow here was untouched. There was no more appropriate place to meet her now. I sent a silent call to the icy Teuton inside the house, brushing her spirit with mine. *Meet me here. I long to commune with you.*

I sensed an answering curiosity, so I prepared myself to wait for her. Nerves churned inside of me, excitement mingling with dread . . . just how honest should I be with her? I stuffed my gloves in my coat pockets and summoned the icy flakes on the sundial to dance along the tips of my fingers. *Try to keep the subject steered away from Dane. She doesn't need to know that he'll be born sick.*

While I waited, a strange tingling grew more and more evident within my heart, agitation stemming from my connection with Muniche's collective spirit. I frowned a little as I concentrated on the snowflakes swirling around my fingers. In the nearly four years that I had housed Muniche's ethereal presence, she had never unsettled my heart quite like this. It was an inherent inquisitiveness with a hefty dose of tension: *Who are you?*

It occurred to me that Hans, my Keyholder, doubtless sensed our bond, for it was complete in marriage. Even though he had not yet met me. Even though he was bound to an elderly woman, my predecessor. Hans detected my presence, and it disturbed him. I chewed on my cheek and tried to distance myself from the city bond, to filter its questions into a back corner of my brain.

I took several deep breaths of the winter air and spiraled the snowflakes into a glistening cyclone above my right palm. *That man had better not interfere with what I'm doing here. He's probably at work right now, and hopefully that'll keep him from seeking me out. He'd better not trail me to the chapel after I've finished talking with Mutti . . . I'm going to have to jump on the S-Bahn quick.*

There was a soft crunch of footsteps upon the snow, and I turned to face the holly bushes as a woman who could have been my twin emerged from their dark green leaves and crimson berries. A knit hat concealed most of her black hair, and a fur-lined designer parka swathed her form in stylish warmth. Her hands were bare, like mine, and her blue eyes shifted from my face to the snowflakes with which I played. Tears welled in my eyes as I blinked at her, where she had stopped just beyond the bushes. The greetings I had practiced evaporated.

Camilla Fischer von Thaden looked striking. Muted eyeshadow and mascara enhanced the cobalt glory of her irises as they stared at the snowflakes that had transformed into ice to coat my fingers. She looked back at my face, and her full lips parted to speak my name. "Swanie?"

How does she know? Hastily, I tried to fabricate some kind of response, and all I managed was, "Hi." My brain had turned to mush.

My mother raised an eyebrow at me and placed her hands on her hips, as though she had caught me stealing from the cookie jar. "Shouldn't you be in New Jersey?"

"I am," I blurted, my voice trembling over the Bayerisch words. "I mean . . . the five-year-old version of me . . . is with your brother's family." I blinked fiercely against my tears; they were more ice than water. "I . . . I came . . . ."

My mother took a step forward, shortening the distance between us to less than half a meter. My right hand hung frozen in the atmosphere, the sundial beside me cleared of snow. She looked me over from head to toe, and I saw her forehead crease as she met my gaze. "You've traveled time . . . to visit me."

My father had once complained that my mother had immersed herself in Teutonic rubbish before her death. I did not speak to one unversed in the strictures of our magic. "I did. I wanted to tell you . . . about my life . . . about . . . ." *Everything you've missed.* I could not force the words around a lump in my throat.

Her face crumpled in pain, and she stepped forward to fold me in her arms. "Swanie, my dearest child," she murmured, one of her hands gently stroking my hair. "I always knew you had an infinite future before you, my ice princess."

One sob broke free, and I buried my face against her neck, the exotic aroma of Magie Noire perfume tickling my nose along with the fur lining her hood. She had always loved that scent. Childhood memories long ignored splashed my mind with colors: skipping with her through the gardens here, marching my stuffed animals up and down the grand staircase with my mother playing the role of zookeeper, singing songs before bed after reading the fairytales of *Little Red Riding Hood*, *Snow White*, and *Cinderella* over and over again.

I had not realized how desperately I needed this reunion.

Eventually my mother pulled back to hold me at arms' length, her blue eyes damp with tears while I wiped my own away on the sleeves of my jacket. "I won't survive the birth of my son," my mother said, having perceived the wretched truth already.

"I wish . . . I wish I'd spent more than a week here. At Christmas." I remembered fleeting images of a whirlwind trip, my mother too sick to attend the services at church, a brand new Crystal Barbie doll. So stupid. I should have spent more time with my mother instead of running off to play with my cousins.

My mother's fingers reached out to brush a lingering tear from my cheek. "There's no need to worry about that now. You're here, and I want to hear all about your life. You've found a way to travel time, like Prince Otto von Bayern. What sort of enchantments have you wrought?"

She smiled at me, but I saw the pain in her eyes, sorrow that I had faced life's trials without her. I moved back to the sundial and sat in the snow, endeavoring to stifle what remained of my grief. "Well . . . it's been a life . . . that's for sure," I said, my Keyholder's disenchantment twinging my heart again. *Shut up, Hans. I'm not here for you.*

My mother chuckled and came to sit at my side, our coats overlapping as she took my left hand in her right. "Don't worry about hurting me with any of your news," she said, giving me a sly smile that reminded me, oddly, of Beth. "I've had a feeling that my days were numbered for a while now. Wuotan's been stalking my dreams, threatening to bleed me dry when your brother comes."

"What?" I gasped, my thoughts flying back to my cousin Trudi's experience. *Those nightmares mean something. I knew it.*

"Don't worry about me," my mother repeated, squeezing my hand in silent camaraderie. "Pappi bound my heart just before Christmas, so I don't have to face that anymore." My eyes widened.

"He's been studying for the Teuton priesthood," my mother went on, her expression wavering between pride and something I could not pinpoint. "The magic has come readily to him. He had no trouble forming the heart-bond with me."

I kept silent for a moment as my emotions vacillated. Yes, my father stood on the cusp of Teutonic glory right before my mother's death . . . and then he shunned the uniqueness of his blood for seventeen years. "Pappi's a good man," I whispered, a quality his new wife, Beth, had readily embraced.

"He'll struggle after I'm gone," my mother predicted, her tone subdued.

I forced myself to meet her gaze and worked to speak around the fresh lump in my throat. "He never showed me his magic until after I graduated from college. I only just learned that he's energy. If it'd been up to him, I'd have never discovered my ice . . . it was all because of Hans— München's Keyholder. You asked him to train me . . . before you passed away."

My mother's face wore an unreadable expression. "I see." Ice had veiled her irises and seeped from the skin of her fingers to caress my own. She glanced at the sky and sighed. "You didn't come here to bemoan all of our family's faults with me. Tell me about your life. How did you step into the past?"

I cleared my throat as she brought her gaze back down to mine, her frosty irises radiating interest. "The summer before I went to college, an *Eihalbe* led me to the Torstein. And . . . and I studied business . . . and organ," I appended.

"That's wonderful. You've always been both sharp and resourceful."

"I guess so."

My mother touched a finger to my chin, prompting me to look up from my lap, where my gaze had blankly fallen. Had she noticed my pregnancy? My wool coat almost blended me in with the snow's whiteness.

"Don't you downplay your strengths, Swanie," my mother urged me when our eyes met. Hers seemed infused with resolve as she added, "That's something our people do too much of. I've lost count of how many women I've known of high Teuton blood who hadn't learned to conjure their element. We have to do better. If *you're* wielding the Torstein, rather than some withered old priest, that's a *major* accomplishment."

My mother's pride emanated from her spirit, knitting its way into my ice. I clasped her hand more tightly and said, "I've been trying . . . trying so hard . . . to bring our people into the modern age. I've been Lady Muniche since 2000, and I'm working with some of my girlfriends and the council members to launch a shelter for battered women. Going to make it safer for women to come forward if their husbands are perverting the heart-bond. And I'm teaching the children, like Bertha Lohr used to do . . . telling them the things our history overlooks."

For some reason, my mother's face seemed to have glazed over the longer I spoke about my efforts in the local community. She looked away from me before I finished talking, her right hand no longer responding to any touch from mine. But after a few seconds of quiet between us, she nodded once and sniffed, running her free hand along the furry neckline of her parka.

"So you were destined to represent our city," she said, still not meeting my gaze. "That's the biggest responsibility any Teuton woman can inherit, and you'll need a lot of support to change anything for good. Keep your friends close, Swanie." She turned her face back toward me, strange sentiments shining in her eyes.

"I'm doing my best. I think you'd like a lot of my friends." I grinned at my mother as I thought about the coterie of Teuton women with whom I shared my deepest dreams. "A couple of them are helping out with the shelter. One had a bad experience with a Teuton priest a while back, but she's free now and outspoken for equality. Another married her girlfriend in a Teutonic wedding last year."

"Which priest allowed that?" My mother looked shocked.

"Üwe Widermann, the artist."

"Ha! Of course. They always protect their own." She chuckled. I cocked my head at her, the message escaping me; and when she noticed my mystification, she explained in a low voice, "Üwe's gay."

I blinked at my mother. "I . . . didn't know that." I felt like an idiot; it made perfect sense. *I . . . wonder if that's who Hans meant when he said that he'd had sex with yellow fire . . . .*

My mother said something else, but I did not hear her. An intense spasm had seized the heart of my soul, and reality blurred around me as I envisioned my Keyholder's spirit glaring down at me from the cloudy atmosphere, black flames of deprecation enshrouding him. *Who are you? You don't belong here. You're not Muniche's Lady. Why have you falsified a perfect bond?*

I clutched my chest with my right hand and spat a curse. Tugging my left hand free from my mother's, I hefted myself to my feet. "I've got to get out of here," I apologized to her, as she looked up at me in dismay. "My Keyholder feels me here. And I think he's going to come look for me."

Horror crossed my mother's visage. "Shit." She made to extract herself from the snow, and I offered her a hand. Once she was on her feet, her face burned with tenacity. "You know where the garage is?"

Chapter Ten:
The Worst Possible Solution

It seemed like hours later when my mother's silver Porsche 928 pulled out of my grandparents' garage. She drove to the street and made a right turn, guiding the car into a position hidden from the house. I watched her approach from the hedges, my boots having cut a noticeable groove in the snow.

The entire time, I had tried to shut myself off from Muniche's bonds, something that I apparently could not do. Although I had gotten used to funneling away her frustration about my lack of proximity while I was in the U.S.—and her chastening when my heart yearned for Augustin—it was impossible to wholly separate myself from her.

A thirty-eight-year-old Hans was tracking me, silently demanding an explanation for the cords that pulsed between us. I did not know how late his hours had been when he worked for Süddeutsche Getriebe rather than for my father. How long would I have until he appeared before me as a spirit . . . or in the flesh?

My mother opened the passenger door for me, and I slipped in quickly, the luxurious seat cradling my back. I saw that the clock read 16:08, and my heartbeat spiked. "Okay, Swanie. Where do we need to go to get the Keyholder off your trail?"

I breathed the name of the town where I had played the Song of Time in the chapel not long before . . . nineteen years from now. Hopefully it was undisturbed in the nighttime hours now, just like its future version . . . and hopefully I could convince my mother to leave me there to play the organ alone. I did not want to tell her that I had Prince Otto's song *and* the Torstein in my possession, nor did I want to reveal why I could not use the blood red rock to reopen time's gateway. *It's stuck in my hip to hide it from demon-possessed thieves.*

"So how do we get there?" my mother asked at length, working the gearshift as her blue eyes focused on the road before us. "Which Autobahn do we need?"

I told her, then took several deep breaths in an attempt to soothe my frantic heart. "You're not going to ask me why we need to go there?" I blurted stupidly.

My mother chuckled and rolled to a stop at a traffic light. "I was taught that Teutons who travel time are supposed to keep the future under wraps. But you've already said that I'm fated to die, that you're fated to be *Leitalra.* I'm not sure how much more you should tell me."

I gave a weak laugh and laid my head back, shutting my eyes to the scenery around me. The outskirts of my hometown looked different in the 1980s—and the cars all looked ridiculous, coughing up smoke. "This is the fourth time I've gone to the past, and from my experience thus far, what you tell people doesn't change the future. On my first trip, I went to your wedding, and I left a note for Hans to play Buxtehude's Praeludium in C. That's my favorite organ piece."

When I opened my eyes to look at my mother, I saw that her lips were pursed, her polished fingernails tapping the steering wheel. "I wondered why he played that song. I nearly came down the aisle early because I was trying to figure out what it was. That was you?"

My mother caught my eye, and we both started giggling. A blush heated my cheeks as she turned the car onto the on-ramp for the Autobahn I had mentioned. "I love to play that song. It's like dancing up and down the pedalboard. But wait a minute . . . ." My thoughts shifted in another direction, likely due to my Keyholder's persistent pressure upon our connection.

Hans is the one who suggested I come here. I wouldn't have thought to visit Mutti otherwise. That means he remembers how he felt . . . with me here . . . .

"Swanie?" My mother sounded concerned.

"Hans said I ought to come here," I muttered in a dead tone as I tried to work out his motives. "I've been struggling . . . since he got me pregnant. I think the hormones are getting to me or something. He said you might have advice to offer. But he didn't tell me that he sensed me here." *What was he thinking?!*

"I noticed that you're pregnant. That coat doesn't completely hide it, if you thought it did." My mother nodded toward my abdomen and merged into the left lane. An instant later, she floored it, and the Porsche shot forward. "Let's not worry about what your Keyholder might do. What kind of music do you like?"

She reached for the radio dial as I watched the speedometer climb past 170. "Uh . . . I listen to all kinds of music except country. You trying to show me how fast this car can go?"

"I don't get out enough anymore. Your Pappi tells me I ought to drive safely when you're in the car. Since you're just a kiddo." She shot me a toothy smile and finished, "But not anymore." The speedometer passed 200 kilometers per hour, and she turned the radio on. "99 Luftballons" burst from the speakers.

My mother started singing along with Nena, and hilarity swept over me. I had never imagined experiencing *this* with my mother: tearing up the Autobahn while she sang along to an 80s anti-war song, both of us pregnant with sons, both of us careless about what the future may hold. "Just remember you're not supposed to die until my brother's birth. So don't let us crash," I said. Then I sang with her.

We sang through a slew of popular songs before we reached the village, my mother's accent hardly noticeable on the English tunes. She pulled her car into the parking lot of a restaurant on the edges of town and offered to buy me dinner. "I know you're just as hungry as I am after traveling time with your son." She nodded at my abdomen and smiled.

She was not wrong, for my son had grown antsy during the past hour. I had eaten only a small snack before Hans and I struck out for the chapel; and while on a normal night, my son would still be asleep, my shuffling had doubtless grated on his patience. *I promise we'll sleep late once we get back home.*

"I actually brought a wallet with some Marks," I told my mother as we exited the car. "I brought enough for the train ride and some food, so that means I could pay for both of us. Whatever I spend will come to the future with me when I go back."

My mother snickered. "Then their cash box will be really short tonight," she noted, and we entered the restaurant and chose a private booth in a corner nook. I browsed the entire menu, bemused at the low prices, and ordered Leberkäse with potato salad, topping it off with hot chocolate to drink. My mother got Jägerschnitzel with cucumber salad and ordered the same drink.

"So where else have you gone when you've used the Torstein?" my mother asked after our drinks had come. She spoke Teutonica in a low voice, ice veiling her irises as she scanned the patrons and waitresses around us.

I gave her a basic rundown of my eleventh century journey, keeping most of the details to myself. I did not broach the topic of Prince Otto's song, nor did I tell her that I got there in 1044 instead of 1064—and spent fifteen years founding the Thaden family line with Joel, the American Teuton. Instead, I shared the emotional aspects with her—how heartbroken I had been by Beth's death, my deep friendship with Freia, my abiding love for Augustin.

"Don't mention that part to Pappi or anyone else," I begged her after relating how devastated I had been when Muniche's spirit tore me away from my beloved. "Neither he nor Hans has taken well to that whole thing. They think Augustin used the heart-bond to sway my feelings, to create love where it didn't exist."

My mother sighed heavily and rolled her eyes. "Teuton men, especially priests, rarely believe you can find your one true love. I think you found him, Swanie, but your Keyholder will always push against that. Once you've made your choice, no mystic bonds can change it."

She sounded certain, and I longed to believe her. "But Mutti . . . I just don't see how I can ever be with Augustin, now that Muniche claims my heart. Sometimes I want to just flee to the past and never come back, die there by ritual suicide and forsake the duties I have here. But if I do, Muniche will pull me toward Prince Otto. And his dark sorcery has messed up my life enough already."

"Sometimes people find their one true love here in this life, but they can't be together until the next," my mother responded. She took a sip of her hot chocolate with a thoughtful look, her eyes seeming to stare off into eternity. "Barriers of all sorts rise up, circumstances, deaths, sickness, other people. But as long as the man you love puts his faith in God, you'll be together in heaven."

Our food came before I decided how to answer. The empty place in my heart that belonged to Augustin ached at our conversation, for I had not told my mother that he was a demon's servant bound for hell. *It's better for her to imagine him as the noble lord he once was,* I decided as I cut the meat and egg on my plate. *And I need to focus on the future, on improving things for Teuton women and Teutons as a whole. That's what I'm supposed to do. Protect the Torstein, keep my friends close. Pray every day that somehow Augustin will turn from Wuotan, even if I never see it happen.*

I asked my mother about her own experiences, how she met and fell for my father, how close she was with her friends, where she had learned how to invoke her ice. She had studied under Bertha Lohr, as I had, and had a handful of friends whom she loved dearly. She knew Marga's mother and Erika's, and she mentioned that one of their girlfriends had passed away during the blood-transfer back when they were all in high school.

"Doro was so angry when she found out her brother and Rory did it on the sly," my mother said, referencing Erika's mother and father. "After Liesl died at Wuotan's hands, we all agreed we'd never touch blood magic of any kind. There's too much darkness wrapped up in all of that. Rory's still paying for it today."

I watched my mother's body shudder as she turned her attention to her food, leaving out the rest of the story. Erika had told me how her Irish father gained Teuton blood. The Black Priest Günter had conducted their blood-transfer. *Good thing I didn't mention Augustin's curse,* I thought as I chewed on some potato salad. *Mutti prefers the path of light. Good for her; it's safer there.*

Pity her devotion to goodness had not spared her life.

The prickling sensation around my heart continued throughout our meal. By the time we finished eating, it had sharpened into a siren's call, as though Hans had focused all of his intent upon our bond in order to pinpoint my location. All at once, I realized that he must have gotten off work and struck out immediately for this cozy village where my mother and I sat chatting like old friends. It was only a forty-minute drive from München . . . and it was already dark outside. January.

I have to get to the chapel and play that song before Hans gets here and forces me into who knows what. He'll likely try to bleed me, find out everything.

"What time is it?" I cut off my mother's current tale, which involved several of her friends and a wintry romp along the Isar.

Her eyebrows wrinkled, and she looked down at her golden watch. "Just after six. What's wrong?"

"I have to get out of here right now," I gasped, anxiety pulsing through my spirit in tandem with Hans' fingers probing my heart. "He's coming. He might be here already. I have to go back home."

Before my mother could react, I fairly leapt from the booth and charged for the exit, plunging my arms through my wool coat as I made a quick escape. I forgot to leave any of the Marks I had tucked into an inner pocket; my mother would have to buy my meal after all. Out in the parking lot, I summoned my ice to the fore and scanned my surroundings.

"How far are we from the chapel?" I asked my son, who had curled into a ball atop my bladder—his standard sleeping position. I looked down the road toward the industrial part of town, then toward the snug collection of houses. "It's on the other side. Can we get there before Hans gets to us? Or will . . . we . . . have to use . . . ."

An image of the knife my husband had tossed to me before I stepped into time's currents arose before my eyes, and my fear spiked to a new level. *No. That can't be why he gave that to me. Did he know I have to dig the Torstein out of my hip in order to get home? I can't do that! Knowing my luck, it'd be in my hand when we get there, and it's not safe out in the open!*

In a cloud of Magie Noire perfume, my mother appeared beside me, her coat and hat shielding her from the cold. Flurries had begun to fall from the layered clouds above. "I just paid for both of us. Is the Keyholder here already?"

The village where we stood was positioned in a valley, and I caught sight of a pair of headlights cresting the hill opposite the restaurant. I knew they belonged to Hans' car; I felt as though his fiery spirit stared straight at me. My mother's car could doubtless outrun whatever piece of junk he owned, so I hurried toward where she had parked, sweat beading on my forehead. "He's coming from the Autobahn, just like we did. And I'm not sure how to get back to it from this side of town."

I halted at the passenger door, and to my surprise, my mother tossed her keys over the car. "You go. Find your way through the maze. I'll distract him."

The keys landed on the pavement, and I scooped them up and chucked them back toward her. "I can't do that! I don't know anything about this area!" I yelled, terror shooting my heartbeat skyward. "Oh, if only I wasn't pregnant, I'd go punch him in the face in spirit form. Knock him out. Curiosity killed the cat." I growled under my breath, furious at my future husband's meddling.

My mother got in the car while I grumbled to myself, and the passenger door slapped me in the hip that held the Torstein. "Come on. Get in. We'll lose him." She sounded as resolute as she had earlier when she went to get her car.

But my eyes had zeroed in on the tree line, the forest of conifers bordering the village. I could invoke the snow to shield me, to get me far enough away so I could cut the damned rock from my hip. *Freaking gross. How am I supposed to manage that half-twisted around? Hans put it a couple centimeters down; I can't feel it even when I rub my back. Why did I let him talk me into this? This is the last time I'll ever travel time at someone else's suggestion.*

I bent down to meet my mother's gaze through the passenger doorway. "I'm going to go in the woods, open the gateway there. It should only take me about five minutes. Can you distract Hans when he gets here, keep him out of the woods?"

"You got it." My mother stepped out of her car again and slammed the door.

I shut the passenger door and struck out for the tree line, invoking my ice to summon the snow around us into a contained blizzard as the night enveloped us. I touched my left hand to my womb and said, "You stay warm in there." Then I met my mother's gaze one last time, our icy irises gazing deep into each other's souls.

"I'm so glad I came to see you, in spite of this." I gestured vaguely toward the parking lot, where I heard a fresh set of car tires skidding to a stop. "I'm going to do all

I can to guide our people forward. I promise I'll make you proud."

"You already have, and you should be proud of yourself. I love you *so* much, Swanie." She squeezed my frigid hand in hers.

"I love you too, Mutti," I said, choking back a well of tears.

She let go of my hand and made a shooing motion. "Get going. And Swanie. May you reunite with the man you love most someday." She nodded at me with a fierce expression, then turned to face the parking lot. The tree branches swayed as she intensified my blizzard, effectively masking my presence.

I plunged further into the trees, using my element's power to keep my feet from breaking through the snow. There was a lot more of it here than in München. Several branches smacked me in the face as I worked to put as much space between myself and my mother—and my Keyholder—as possible. But I felt my adrenaline ebbing at long last, for I had been here nearly three hours. It had been almost two a.m. when Hans and I broke into the chapel back home; and although I had taken a nap in the early evening, I should be asleep now, like my son.

He had not moved from his ball since my mother had told me the stories of her friends. Why did that seem like ages ago now?

The sounds of voices pierced the air, muffled thanks to the ice and snow that whirled around my body. *How long can Mutti distract Hans? She's no one to him, and I'm his Lady. This isn't going to work.*

I thrust my right hand into the outer pocket of my wool coat, quickly finding the sheathed knife. My hand shook when I pulled it into the winter cold, as my feet doggedly pressed forward, as the whiteness around me seemed to glow in the dark of night. *Can I really* do *this? Where the heck is the Torstein?* I cast the coat to the ground, my focus shifting from my snow squall to my waist.

Unexpectedly, my right foot dipped into a thick patch of snow, sinking down to the top of my boot. The winds surrounding me tapered off, as the fingers of my left hand worked blindly at my jeans, trying to loosen the elastic, to bare the skin of my back. I could not see what I was trying to do with my pregnant belly in the way; my son was due in only two and a half months. I heard voices behind me again, as I grabbed the knife's sheath in my teeth and pulled its blade free. And then I heard a scream, one that pierced my heart like the knife itself: *"Swanie! Go!"*

Hans must not be distracted any longer.

And I could not get my jeans pulled down with one leg trapped in a gully. I could not get the Torstein out before that damn Keyholder came upon me to initiate the worst interrogation I had yet experienced. I could sense his anger, his nosiness, his disgust. He would not be kind to the one who had "falsified" his city's bond. I should not exist here. He would find out about the Torstein, about the song. He would find out about my Black Priest Augustin. He would find out everything.

As my bleary eyes locked on the blade of the knife, shining silver against the snow, I saw that my hand still shook . . . and I saw the dull line of blue that arched downward from the base of my thumb to hide beneath the sleeve of my blouse. The worst possible solution became clear. If I killed myself, my body would vanish into the future. And the labradorite gates would appear in the ethereal realm between life and death . . . not here in earth's forest, where my Keyholder and my mother would see something they were not meant to see.

I would have to kill myself.

It's not ritual suicide if it's not by the Rhine River on the night of the new moon.

What was the moon phase? The cloud cover hid it from me.

But I was in Bavaria, nowhere near that fatal river. And I did not have to slit my wrists and then my throat. I knew blood control. I could just do the filial curse upon myself.

I nearly laughed at the madness of that thought as I moved the handle of the knife to my left hand, securing my wobbling fingers around it. I raised my right arm and wiggled it, bringing the sleeve of my blouse down to my elbow. *Thank goodness I wore a loose shirt.*

There was a commotion behind me, heavy footsteps crunching through the snow, piles of white descending from the trees as a strong force shook them. *Do it now, Swanie, and spray your blood in a fountain.*

I turned my right palm upward and fixed my gaze on the forest before me. "Due to the unpardonable sins you commit in excess," I muttered in Teutonica, touching the point of the blade below my thumb as a lingering hesitation seized me. Could I really do this with my son sleeping so peacefully in my womb?

I had no choice unless I wanted Hans to bare my heart nineteen years too early. Gritting my teeth, I spoke the final phrase of the spell: "Cursed for all of time." Then I sank the blade into my flesh and ripped it with a vengeance, swiftly so there could be no going back. I felt the blood blooming upon my skin, hot and pungent, and I directed all of my power as a Teuton toward that wound, summoning every trace of blood I sensed in my body to rush into the abyss.

It was quick. Within seconds, darkness encroached around the edges of my vision, luring me to a place I had been thrice before . . . the first time Augustin bled me . . . the time I offered my Teuton blood to Freia . . . and the time Wuotan had incited his cursed slave to sacrifice me. A realm of shadowy mist with no sky above or ground below, a place where a blue-fired demon would block my path to the future. *But no. Not this time. This time I go of my own volition.*

Before the labradorite gates of time arose from the mist to welcome a weary traveler home, I imagined that I saw my Keyholder's spirit, robes swept in elegant sable fire, obsidian eyes looking at me, looking through me. I thought I saw his lips part as he spoke a name . . . but I was too far gone to hear it with my mortal ears . . . or to understand his mental voice . . . for time's gateway had taken me . . . bundled me away on a course for April of 2004.

The sirens must have had a field day insulting me as I returned from my fourth trip to the past. But for the first time since I had learned Ælte Teutonica—the dialect of my heathen ancestors—my brain could not decode their phrases. I could not hear anything, actually, nor comprehend the meaning of the oblivion in which I tumbled. It was as though my conscious mind had fallen into slumber, perhaps by nature of the death I had chosen for myself. Cursed for all of time. What sort of madness was this? I could not curse myself.

Somehow, before my body found its way through the other side of the portal, back into the plain chapel where my husband awaited me, I sensed a presence with me, a Teuton spirit not wholly unlike myself. This new spirit seemed to wind itself with mine, offering gifts long lost to my jaded heart: happiness . . . trust . . . hope.

It was my son. He was here with me.

And then I found myself stumbling from the portal, my ankles striking the stone floor with a bit too much force. I staggered forward to grip the altar, my shoulders quivering, my lungs expelling panted breaths, the wool coat seeming to cook my body. It was sweltering, and dark. My right hand touched my abdomen, and a squeaking moan pealed from my lips. *Had I* really *just committed suicide to get back here . . . to this home with a man who would cast me into hell . . . without warning me first.*

Someone took hold of me, and warm fingers touched my neck, tracing my pulse, tilting my head against a sturdy chest. My Keyholder's hands began stroking the heart of my soul, granting me a portion of peace, of acceptance. "Swanie . . . my darling ice princess . . . you need to close the gateway."

To this day, I am not sure how I managed it, but I believe Hans may have held my left arm up himself and pointed it toward the labradorite gates. My entire body quaked—confusion, helplessness, and betrayal mingling in my spirit, in my blood. At least my husband had not lost his grip on reason, for he took me in his arms and called forth the potency of his black fire to conceal us, to shield us, to sweep us away to the far side of the village, where he had left his BMW parked alone in the restaurant's parking lot. The same one from 1985.

It was at some point on the drive back to the Thaden house that I found my voice. I sat motionless in the passenger seat of Hans' car, the wool coat discarded on the backseat, a few scooching movements within assuring me that my son had safely returned. Even though I had killed us both.

"What . . . exactly . . . were you thinking . . . just tossing me that knife before I left . . . when you knew what I'd be *forced* to do with it? What the *hell* was wrong with you back there? What made you think you needed to hunt me down? If you had just gone to bed, I'd have been gone when you woke up!"

And to my irritation, Hans replied simply, "You can't know your own future."

Chapter Eleven:

Fumbling in the Dark

By the time we reached home, my fury at Hans had dulled to a slow boil. Although he responded to each issue I raised, his rationale carefully appeasing my emotions, one stark betrayal remained in the back of my mind even after I lay beside him in bed. *He could have offered a hint about what I'd really do with that knife before I dove into time's currents. He saw me die when he was thirty-eight years old . . . and never thought to give me fair warning.*

According to him, my mother had told him only the basics about the strange woman who bled to death and vanished, taking the duplicated bonds of Muniche with her. She had told him I was destined to be his Lady one day, so he needed to ensure I was properly trained in Teutonic magic and history. She had told him nothing of my journeys through time, of my longings for a man bound for hell. But the fact that my fated master had seen fit to keep me in the dark about my discovery of the Torstein—and my horrific death in the forest—did not sit well with me.

I took Friday off work and spent the afternoon sprawled on a couch in the family room, mindlessly watching old movies. I picked at a vegetable tray Gregor prepared for me, my gaze often drifting toward the minibar. Alcohol's haze lured me, though I had tried to avoid it since I found myself pregnant. My son was active in my womb that afternoon, having gotten what rest he required in the morning. I poked back at him every time he kicked, grateful that my fatal choice in 1985 had not taken him from me.

At one point, I called Trudi at her apartment, for she was still on maternity leave. My mother's offhand comment about her demonic dreams gnawed at my peace, and I wanted to make sure my cousin was okay.

"I feel stronger every day, even though Lukas won't let me sleep through the night yet," she told me. "Mane helps as much as he can, but they're running him ragged at work. He got a promotion just before Easter, and his new position has a *lot* more responsibilities." She sighed.

"I'll have Gregor make you some more meals," I said.

"You don't have to—"

"It's no problem at all," I cut her off, glancing at the hallway that led to the kitchen. "He loves cooking larger meals. He jokes all the time about how awful it was when I was in college. 'Only four people at dinner, if that.'" In those days, Hans and Sebastian normally ate Gregor's offerings before retreating to their cottages, but Lise preferred to cook her own dinners for her and Siggi.

I asked Trudi how her incision was healing, whether she had a sufficient supply of milk, how long it would be before she could start taking massage clients again. She and Traudl had not yet opened their combined business; Trudi worked at another massage parlor in the city.

"It's been tough, to be honest, Swanie," she admitted, sounding weary. "For a while I was having trouble keeping food down. Sometimes I worry Lukas isn't getting enough to eat, because he hasn't liked any of the formulas we've tried. He only wants Mutti's milk. Mutti's been trying to eat more, but that's not going to get this stupid weight off. My entire stomach is sagging; I look like an old woman."

Trudi sniffed, and I did my best to console her, remembering how my weight gain had bothered me in the past. Seeing Freia's perfect figure had not helped my outlook, even though my other noble peers like Lady Adeline and Lady Hildegard had kept some of their pregnancy weight. "Just remember, anything extra proves you're a warrior who carried a child. Not everyone can do that," I pointed out.

"I guess so. Ina told me a few things she did to get her weight off, but she said the stretch marks don't go away. She and Fonsi have been a real help, though. They take Lukas every other Saturday so Mane and I can have some time together. And my Mutti's been really helpful, too, but she thinks I'd better not have another baby. She's worried I might end up with twins if I try again."

Trudi gave a tired laugh, and I chewed on my bottom lip. "Tante Lena may be right about that," I noted. "And I've . . . heard some things about women who have nightmares like the ones you had. The ones with Wuotan. You and Mane might be better off keeping it at one."

"I don't know. We both really want at least two. A boy and a girl."

Nervousness churned in my gut on Trudi's behalf. But she had always wanted to be the mother whenever we played house as children. I knew that she would gladly give up her career if Mane and Traudl earned enough to let her stay at home. "Well, just take all the precautions you can," I advised her before hanging up the phone and hefting myself off of the couch en route to the bathroom. My son was treating my bladder like a soccer ball.

That evening after dinner, Beth and I ambled out to the gazebo beside the trickling stream in the backyard. I wanted to tell her of my latest trip through time without my Keyholder snooping around. During the winter, Beth had made great strides in her elemental aptitude; she could conjure snow from her spirit, invoke it into her eyes to improve her vision, and project its traces in a sphere to watch for other Teuton spirits. The real test would come in summer, when the atmosphere's warmth would strive against inherently chilly elements. But for now, I trusted her to keep our tête-à-tête off Hans' radar.

Beth sat at my side and listened as I spilled my guts, a character trait of hers that I highly respected. At the end, when I related my violent return to the present day, her irises turned from brown to white. I sensed an enhancement to the snowy aura that encompassed us as she cried out, "You tried to *curse* yourself?!"

"I mean, not really. You can't curse yourself. Nobody has the authority to curse me anymore, anyway. Marriage bonds negate filial bonds."

"But you figured it'd be better to cut yourself *that* way instead of slitting your throat or something." Beth looked revolted.

"Slitting my throat would have been too close to ritual suicide for comfort," I explained, though I had not considered cutting any other artery. The radial one had caught my eye and held it, a whispering voice across the threads of time.

"Hans should have left you alone," Beth said, sounding disgusted by what his inquisitiveness had incited me to do. "Or he could have told you what time he got to the restaurant, so you would have known to get out of there sooner."

I winced a bit and shrugged, leaning my back against the railing. "I agree with you, but . . . you're not supposed to tamper with the past. And he knew what was set to happen. I've been seriously questioning my entire life since this morning. It's like I'm fumbling in a dark tunnel with traps everyone else can see, and no one wants to share their light with me."

"That's why he led you on romantically since that first dance. Because your Mutti told him you were fated to be his. And that's why he didn't force you to hand the Torstein over to the council or Bertha Lohr after you found it. Because he saw your body vanish, so he knew that you would travel time."

My best friend had just put all of my uncertainties into words. She slipped an arm around me as I exhaled in frustration and rubbed my forehead with my right hand. "One of these days I'm just going to have to get over the taste of blood. I wish people would be honest with me when they know things about my future. Who cares if I'm 'not supposed to know'? People should *tell* me if a past version of myself is going to commit suicide!"

"I hear you," Beth murmured, tilting her head against mine. We sat that way for a while, my tears unshed, her wintry spirit reaching out to support mine in the realm beyond mortal sight. And my muddled reflections alighted on an entity long gone, one that possessed the insight of nature.

The price of Wuotan's sorcery is death.

"I died to get back here. I wonder if that means my price is paid." I pulled away from my cousin's embrace and met her gaze, seeing confusion. "The *Eihalbe* from the eleventh century, the one who spoke to me five times. It told me that the price of Wuotan's sorcery is death. You and Joel paid the price, but I didn't . . . until now."

Beth's face darkened, and her forehead crimped in thought. "I don't know. If Wuotan's anything like his servants, then he'd probably consider that just one payment. And you've done the blood-transfer and traveled time four times."

"Crap. Good point." I frowned and looked toward the stream to the right of where I sat upon the gazebo's bench, silently asking its waters to reassure me. "If he's keeping score, I owe him a darn lot. You're still working on Günter's project, right?" I gave my cousin a meaningful look.

She turned her face toward the trees but gave a single nod. "I've been fitting it into what Max has me doing for Süddeutsche Getriebe."

My father had given her a part-time position in copyrighting, primarily for the English market. That was not exactly Beth's dream job, but she was polishing several manuscripts to submit to agents and publishers on the side.

"You know, if you're going down the Teutonic research rabbit hole on Günter's behalf, I might need you to check a few things for me," I said, my thoughts lingering on the *Eihalbe* I once considered a friend. She raised her eyebrows at me, so I clarified, "Find out if there's any actual history of tree fairies stealing Teuton children, or any children. I want to know the background of that claim the mothers are tossing around."

"I can definitely check on that. I'm going to the archives in a couple weeks."

"It's so utterly ridiculous," I went on, irritation roiling within me at those damaging rumors. "Nobody in eleventh century Muniche ever hinted that *Eihalbae* might steal children. Nobody. People warned about witches and wolves, but never about the fairies. They were considered sacred, as were their trees. Silver oak leaves really come in handy if you don't know blood control. Gretchen even used them to stave off infection."

"I wonder if that idea came after the Saxon invasion. You said that Teuton traitors cut down every silver oak they came across. That might be what started the bad blood between Teutons and *Eihalbae*."

"But there's not really bad blood," I argued, my eyes following the stream as it snaked toward the trees . . . and the single silver oak on Thaden grounds. "Unless . . . maybe that's when it became a faux pas to question the fairies. They'd certainly have reason to distrust Teutons after that whole ordeal. It was like the traitors were trying to commit genocide."

"Like their Saxon handlers," Beth supplied.

I harrumphed and shook my head, my icy spirit reaching out toward that aged oak beneath which I had danced many times as a young maiden. "I need to talk to the *Eihalbe* that claims our property again. But I'll have to wait until I can go in spirit form. I need to find out where I should plant the sapling; it'll outgrow its planter by next year. It's already a lot taller than me."

The *Eihalbe* on Thaden grounds had spoken to me only once, on the night when it offered me an acorn to establish its legacy. Lise and I had cared for it ever since, and its shimmering branches granted welcome shade to my balcony. But its roots needed to spread, and we had already swapped out its planter for a larger one. *That night when the fairy spoke to me, I was reading Augustin's pages on the Torstein . . . unaware that within two years, I'd be inextricably devoted to him.*

"I might see if I can find a book on how to make healing potions from silver oak leaves," Beth mused, a faraway look on her face. "That would be an awesome thing for you to start teaching the kids."

My thoughts were a thousand years in the past again. "The *Eihalbe* I knew best called me by name on the day Muniche burned, on the day the traitors cut its tree down. It came to where I sat with Augustin at the turret of the town hall . . . and it said it wanted to see me with him. It was about to die, and it wanted to see me with Augustin. *Why?*"

Beth wound her fingers through those of my left hand and drew me close. "Maybe the two of you aren't quite finished yet," she whispered.

My nigh-dormant hope warmed my heart, beating against Muniche's chains anew. "If that's the case, then the *Eihalbe* here knows it all. But I doubt it'll be any more forthright with me than any of the fairies have ever been. They enjoy speaking in riddles. I just want to know that Augustin will eventually turn from evil. That's all I really care about." Icy tears welled in my eyes.

Beth squeezed my hand and said, "I didn't learn anything along those lines when I was at the Black Castle . . . but I did see one thing."

"What?" I prompted, nearly choking on the word.

"There's a hallway somewhere on the main floor," she said, her expression wavering between mystery and dread. "You can get to the lower levels from there, and those are dark places, so it wasn't a place I preferred to spend my time. But it has stone effigies of every known Black Priest, from Günter all the way back to the earliest ones."

"Augustin's was there," I guessed, my heart skipping a beat as I wondered how it looked. *Striking, magnificent, perfect.*

"Wolfgang Wolfrik Wolfe, it said," Beth confirmed. "And beneath the name, the years 1045-1493 in Roman numerals."

My jaw dropped in slow motion, and I *stared* at my cousin. "Fourteen . . . ninety-*three?*"

"Yep." A few unintelligible phrases spilled from my lips as I shivered all over. My devoted lover was to be trapped on earth until Christopher Columbus returned from the Americas. Beth embraced me and brought her head close to mine as she asserted, "*I* think if that man doesn't turn from Wuotan in four hundred years, he's not as smart as you've told me. He'll do it, Swanie. For you."

The week before I finally met my son, Erika called me to give the news that Iliana was pregnant with their first child. She was due in January of 2005, and they were already making preparations, lists of potential names, potential elements. "This kid is going to have the biggest family ever," Erika exulted. "My parents and brother have already started buying stuff, and Iliana's family is over the moon about it. Our kid's going to attend *all* of your classes, just so you know."

I shared in my good friend's joy and promised to help out as much as I could, even though my own son would take up most of my time quite soon. A small cactus nudged my happiness as I inquired after their baby's father. Had they made a deal with Günter, made use of his sperm bank? Erika giggled at my query and answered that the father wanted to remain anonymous for now, but that they were safe from Günter's sinister machinations. "There are more open-minded Teuton men around here than I thought, to be honest," she said, and I breathed a sigh of relief.

On Wednesday, June 30th, my son entered the world, to the delight of the entire Thaden household. I birthed him on the floor of our private parlor, a thick blanket absorbing all of the assorted liquids. My water had broken early, like it had during my first childbirth experience in the eleventh century; but once the majority of it had made its way out, I kept moving. I dusted and cleaned his room on the third floor and did several loads of laundry downstairs, pausing to brace myself against doorjambs and counters whenever a contraction struck.

Hans trailed me like a puppy, concern radiating from his black-fired eyes, for he feared that I might need to be rushed to the hospital at some point. But I trampled his expectations with stalwart defiance, cradling our newborn son at my breast, his silvery gray eyes gazing into mine. The doula I had hired praised my fortitude and remarked that I had a high pain tolerance for a first time mother. I chuckled tolerantly while my brain filed this experience away as its ninth.

After a bit of consideration, we decided to name our son after his father and grandfather: Maximilian Johannes Meissner von Thaden.

Chapter Twelve

Times Are Changing

During my four months of maternity leave, I passed countless hours with my son, relearning the triumph of parenthood—a glory I had experienced long ago in a far different setting. Now I did not need to sew clothing for my child; instead, I found myself purchasing what seemed like a boat-load of diapers, then sorting through ever-multiplying baby outfits thanks to generous friends and family. Beth and Lise helped me take care of Max whenever their duties did not hold them back, and each evening, he napped with Hans on the couch in the upstairs parlor.

I introduced my son to music in his earliest weeks, for I sang a wide variety of melodies to him whenever I held him to my breast. Along with religious and children's songs in both English and German, I crooned my favorite metal tunes to my son. Sometimes I sang the old Teutonic and Rhenisch ballads I had learned in medieval Muniche and from Freia. I envisioned little Max becoming quite talented in the language arts, for I intended to teach him German, Bayerisch, Teutonica, and English as soon as he learned to talk. Then he could speak each dialect without the impediment of a foreign accent.

Throughout my vacation from the office, I also adopted a stringent diet and exercise program with the intent to drop the four kilograms that had clung to me after childbirth. Every evening, I walked briskly along the nearby streets, usually accompanied by my husband. Once my body had sufficiently recovered from the birthing experience, I began doing sit-ups and spending time daily in the exercise room.

My father poked fun at my strict agenda, but I brushed off his comments. He had no concept of how unhealthy I had been in the past, nor did he know how uncomfortable excess weight could be, for he was still in decent shape for his age. Hans smiled tolerantly at my efforts and joked that I had better not get too thin, or the Torstein may stick out of my hip like a cancerous lump.

In September of that year, a group of contractors broke ground on what was to become München's newest shelter and rehab site for domestic violence survivors. It was on an undeveloped stretch of land several kilometers south of the city itself, and the property included a tributary to the River Isar. Hans and I worked hard to obtain all of the necessary approvals, and I laid down what was left in my personal bank account from my college days to purchase the land. Hans managed to get our nascent enterprise non-profit status, and my father used his influence in the local business community to drum up donations. I remarked to my husband that I may have to step back from Süddeutsche Getriebe once the resource center had opened, since I wanted to protect it from corruption.

"I'm not sure what my boss would think of that," he pointed out as he studied an accounting document for our venture.

"I'm not sure whether his business is for me," I said, cradling a somnolent Max in my left arm while reflecting on what I had experienced since joining my father full-time two years prior. "Everybody's just so greedy and arrogant. I want our shelter to reach beyond that, to the brighter side of humanity. *Selakerza*, just what our people and society in general need—a light for the soul."

Hans chuckled at the name I had chosen for our enterprise. It was a Teutonic word that meant *soul candle*, different enough from the German terms to stand out to anyone who knew Teutonica. The word came from a folktale about *Eihalbae* summoning moonlight to help travelers find their way. Although I wanted to help the community as a whole, I planned to promote the shelter's resources before my people first, so that those bound in silence would know they had options.

On a brisk afternoon in early October, I passed Max off to Lise and retreated to my bathroom with the intention of entering the spiritual realm for the first time in several years. While Hans and I spent nearly every night together in the spiritual dream world, I rarely entered the actual *Gæstelort* anymore. There were too many outsiders in the Thaden house, and I did not wish any of them to come upon my frozen body lying in some hidden alcove. So I locked the bathroom door behind me and stretched out in the empty hot tub, closing my eyes as I called my ice forth in all of its power.

My element encased my body from the toes up, slowly at first, then more swiftly as my Teuton blood recognized the magic I invoked. Living frost swathed my physical body in a protective coating that no outsider could breech, and I felt its wintry chill slaking my hair, sinking into my pores, my tissues, my organs. Ice hardened my lungs, stifling my breath for one terrifying moment—and then my spirit leaped free, into the air above where my body rested.

I flashed my frozen body a grin before propelling my spirit toward the sky, through the ceiling, the empty suite above, the attic, and the roof. No clouds broke the deep blue of autumn, but a slight breeze tickled my spirit, swirling my cerulean robes around me. I felt invigorated and powerful as I took in the overhead view of the Thaden house and grounds, of the wealthy neighborhood in which I lived, of the crystalline waters of the Isar slinking northward, of München's russet roofs in the distance. This was my city, my home . . . my domain, my destiny.

It's fantastic, I murmured to myself, the cords of Muniche's spirit humming joyfully around my heart. *This is truly my soul's calling . . . guiding my people to the path of light and truth . . . building a strong foundation for my son and those who follow after me.*

But I turned my attention toward the tiny forest on my family's property—and the aged silver oak that stood tall amid its lesser relatives. I hoped that its fairy would deign to acknowledge me, for I had no wish to disrespect it as I had once done to its ancestor. Did this silver oak tree, planted not terribly far from where another had grown a thousand years ago, trace its lineage to that very tree? Did it know that *Eihalbe's* name?

Did any *Eihalbae* have names?

I descended gracefully toward the tree, rolling my eyes at my muses. I ought not to pry into this fairy's personal business. My purpose was to learn the best place to plant its successor, and to get the fairy's opinion on the caustic rumors. When I reached the silver oak's crown, I positioned my spirit comfortably in a notch between one of the branches and the trunk, looking here and there in a vain attempt to catch sight of the *Eihalbe* who lived there. Birds of all sorts chattered to each other, and the breeze ruffled the leaves around me, but I saw no fluttering sprite of silver.

Noble Eihalbe, I began, projecting my mental voice in a fairly wide radius, *I would like to speak with you, if you would grant me the honor.*

I spoke formally in Teutonica, as was proper, then laced my fingers together and waited. A gray squirrel scampered along a branch of the neighboring elm, its nose sensing hidden messages in the wind. It occurred to me to wonder whether animals could detect the presence of a Teuton spirit. Though I had danced in spirit form as a teenager countless times, I had never pretended to be a fairytale princess who could talk to animals. Part of me suspected that they knew, for the squirrel looked my way at one point, its nostrils noticeably twitching.

Just before I sent a thought to the squirrel's mind, a delicate voice threaded its way into my spirit's ears. "*Zoubaraera Teutona,* welcome to my home."

The *Eihalbe* appeared seemingly from nowhere and settled its squirrel-sized body upon a thin branch at eye level. Its beating wings held it in place as it crossed its silver legs and directed its mesmerizing eyes to mine. It ran the fingers of one hand through its argentine hair, while the other took hold of a yellowed leaf nearly as large as its own body.

Thank you, I said, still clinging to propriety; a Teuton must thank a fairy for any advice, and I figured an actual welcome deserved gratitude, too. *I should have visited you when I first came back from the past. I apologize for snubbing you all this time.* Regret dulled the blues of my robes a few shades. I highly suspected that the *Eihalbe* had watched me open time's gateway by the gazebo, though I had not thought to look for it that night.

"The *Leitalra* has innumerable responsibilities." The *Eihalbe* wrapped its yellow leaf around its body like a cloak, its eyes shifting from mine to the distant roofs.

So it knew that I was Muniche's Lady. Had it sensed that when I returned from the past, or had it gleaned the truth from seeing my wedding take place here beside the stream? *You're right. I've been neglecting your offspring. It needs to find its place in the earth's vast network, but I'm not sure where the perfect spot would be. I haven't really dabbled much with earth magic.*

"A wearied linden succumbed to a recent squall and offered its corpse to the stream," the fairy stated without emotion, as though such events were a mere part of life. I knew of which tree it spoke; Siggi had just recently finished cutting it into firewood. "Four paces upstream from its grave, the earth yearns to nurture my kin."

I met the fairy's kaleidoscope gaze and nodded. *Thank you so much.*

"Plant it by the full moon before the longest night, so its roots may ground themselves in winter's steel," the *Eihalbe* added.

Very well. I really appreciate your guidance, I said, tracing my icy fingers through the ethereal robes that arrayed my spirit. The fairy was both resourceful and sagacious.

"You have come here for far more guidance than this," the fairy gathered, its eyes intent upon my face. It had removed the stem from the leaf that blended it in with the others, its fingers nimbly peeling shreds from it one by one.

I have, I confirmed, narrowing my eyes a bit as I considered how to phrase my most pressing concern. *There has been . . . unrest . . . among some of the local mothers, ever since I started teaching their children what happened to your kind . . . during Prince Otto's defeat.*

The *Eihalbe* looked at the activity of its fingers, its silvery visage appearing contentious. "Your cousin's judgment was not wrong," it said.

Shame washed over my spirit on behalf of the Teuton people. *I'm so sorry for what my people did to your kin. I felt so helpless when your ancestor told me how the Teutons of low blood uprooted your trees. I wish I could have helped . . . done something to stop them . . . but I was so sick and weak then . . . .*

The fairy's slim lips curled on the edges, and it looked up from its stem to gaze beyond where my spirit balanced on a crook of its tree. "You helped. But your people turned to their own devices during their scattering. Irrational blame spread like a parasitic growth, though individuals yet proved themselves worthy."

I sighed, my spirit's robes dulling further toward gray. *People are so quick to follow the easiest path, the one where they're not at fault. Human history is loaded with situations like that. And it's hard to see what a single person can do against the big picture. I hate it so much.*

I dropped my head into my hands and shut my eyes, the translucent quality of my skin impeding but not canceling my vision. What the *Eihalbe* said proved that it had overheard my conversation with Beth at the gazebo, after Hans had betrayed my trust all over again.

Go to the past to give Mutti a message that would set me on this path of time travel . . . this path where I have no control over my destiny whatsoever. Would Muniche have chosen me if I'd remained ignorant of my ice, of the magic inherent in Teuton blood? Could I have led a quiet life, or would I have submitted to a transactional marriage with one of Pappi's colleagues?

"The truth you have shared with your young has not gone unnoticed among my kin," the fairy said at length. I exhaled again and worked to get my discontent under control, placing my hands back in my lap when I raised my chin to look my companion in the eye. The *Eihalbe* appeared to smile again as it added, "Thank you for that, *Leitalra.* There is hope yet, even in the depths of darkness."

My thoughts traveled back to the first time this fairy had spoken to me, on the night that it entrusted me with its offspring—a silver acorn. *The first time we talked . . . I was reading Augustin's papers about the Torstein,* I mentioned, my mental voice nearly breaking over my medieval lover's cursed name. Whether tree fairies had any knowledge of romantic love or soulmates, I could only guess; but the empty space in my heart festered with grief at the thought of Augustin walking the earth alone for four hundred years, forsaken, distrusted, hated by all. Wuotan would keep wearing him down, tempting him to renounce the glories of love.

"The Cursed One of Muniche," the *Eihalbe* responded, the colors in its eyes seeming to swirl as it studied my expression.

That title brought me up short. My eyebrows came together as I gawked at my wispy companion. *The Cursed One of Muniche,* I repeated, trying to figure out what the fairy meant by that. Lady Maria, Prince Otto's partner, had dumped his condemned blood into the Isar after the Price pronounced the filial curse upon him. Maybe that was what the *Eihalbe* referenced?

Right after I became Leitalra, *I attacked him for not defending me from the Saxons,* I recalled, ashamed. *I love him, and I just perpetuated the cycle. Maybe I should start telling the kids about Black Priests and why they shouldn't curse a sibling or a child. It's unfair. Murder.*

"He spurned his fate for many years," the *Eihalbe* said, its fingers flicking the final strip of stem into the atmosphere. "But . . . ."

But? I blinked at the fairy, blades of hope and anxiety jabbing at my heart.

The *Eihalbe* blinked back at me and rose from its branch, the yellowed leaf tumbling toward the ground in a gust of wind. "But his course is murky, treacherous . . . and infinite."

Of course the fairy would not be forthright with me. It was quite obvious that our conversation had reached its end. I gnawed on my cheek as well as I could with spiritual teeth and lifted myself into the air, nodding at the *Eihalbe* on its descent into the autumn colors. *Thank you for your counsel. I'll make sure the youth know to never disrespect your kin. Your healing magic is a great gift.*

In subsequent months, I returned to work with my father, ultimately finding a fairly stable balance. Corporate racket from eight to five, Monday through Friday. Family time in the evenings and on Saturdays. Church and teaching children on Sundays. Preparations for *Selakerza's* official opening sprinkled throughout.

My good friend Vreni had offered her services as office manager, and thus she would be our first real employee. Hans began holding interviews for licensed therapists, security guards, and social workers as 2005 progressed. Iliana's daughter Sophia entered the world in January and quickly became her mothers' pride and joy. And my son Max began speaking words and phrases in Bayerisch, German, Teutonica, and English by year's end, his silvergray eyes radiant whenever we listened to music together.

I became pregnant again in early 2006, shortly after I had weaned my son. Hans and I both agreed that this child would be our last, so we intended to follow my fertility cycle when it came to sex in the years to come. He had no desire to get a vasectomy, while I had no wish to mess my hormones up with pills or undergo the knife myself. Since my Keyholder was mature enough to actually control his urges—unlike the hapless Joel—I felt certain that we would meet no surprises.

To my chagrin, my body seemed to have a vendetta against me as I met my second modern pregnancy, and my eleventh overall. Nausea struck me hard at the start; and after that tapered off, my baby—definitely a girl this time around—spent half of the day kicking at my ribs and spine. I began bleeding prematurely in the middle of August. At first I shrugged this off, for I had experienced it with baby Erika in the eleventh century and pushed through with the help of bed rest.

But my hopes of another peaceful home delivery dissolved as my husband put his foot down and demanded that I get an ultrasound, which revealed major placenta praevia. It covered my cervix entirely, and my daughter was breech, which meant that I must face the hospital's menace to undergo a C-section.

Chapter Thirteen:
I Do Not Cast Him Out

The next few months are ones I prefer not to remember in detail, but I suppose I ought to relate some of the facts here for my son's edification. Doctors attempted to bully me into checking myself in at the hospital to be monitored until my due date; but to Hans' consternation, I stood my ground. I would rest at home and confine myself to my bed if necessary, but I refused to be treated like a medical experiment until my daughter's birth. Flashbacks to Dane's final sickness fueled my tenacity. I lacked faith in modern medicine.

Hans reprimanded me when we went home, arguing that I may very well end up like my mother if I refused to accept my situation. He believed that Wuotan had caused my condition, that this was his latest effort to eliminate me. I responded tartly that if I lost too much blood due to my placenta's abnormal position, Hans could grant me a portion of his own in medieval fashion. I had exchanged blood with Augustin from palm-to-palm on three occasions, and each time it served its purpose—even when his blood was dead.

"You need to *stop* pretending you're in the Middle Ages," Hans snapped at me, as I worked to organize my things in a way that could keep me occupied while bedridden. "Even with your precious Cursed One's expertise, you would *not* survive a breech birth. You're in the present day, Swanie, and you can't dance with death here. Your children need you, and I need you. I don't want to raise Max and our daughter alone."

I plugged my laptop into the outlet nearest to our bed, then turned to sneer at my Keyholder. "I'd better stick around to make sure you don't curse Max once he comes of age. I haven't forgotten your stupid promise to Günter. I agreed to the C-section against my better judgment, and you'd *better* keep your magic focused on my blood the entire time they're tearing my body apart. Especially if I'm too drugged to concentrate." My daughter jabbed at my spine, and I winced.

"You won't die on the operating table," Hans pledged in a husky voice, his fiery hands stroking the heart of my soul. "I'll keep your heart beating. And even if you lose a lot of blood, Wuotan's river holds an unbounded supply. I know how to channel it into your mortal heart, though I've never had to do it."

I hefted myself onto the bed and gave a weary snicker. "Teuton priests all sneaking around with dark sorcery despite their pious façade. I hope you're as good at it as Augustin was. Pretty much all the blood left in my veins on that last morning in Muniche belonged to Wuotan's river." He had bled me so much the night before, but in the throes of eroticism, I had hardly noticed. I looked toward the burn marks on the wall from where Augustin clawed at it on the day he had broken our heart-bond forever. *Oh, if only I hadn't let him leave me . . . .*

"Keep your focus on the present, on your family, your friends, your duties here." Hans sounded like he was pleading with me, and when I looked back at him, I saw heartache in his dark blue eyes. "I can't lose you, Swanie. Please take care of yourself. Don't let our enemy win." He clasped my hands in his and bent his head over them in prayer. So I promised that I would push through, just like I had always done; yet a niggling anxiety took root in my spirit at the prospect of facing the doctors, the surgeons, the anesthetists. Loss of control.

Though I could recount the events of October 12th in detail, I shall simply say that Freya Swanhilde Meissner von Thaden entered the mortal world late that afternoon. The procedure went smoothly overall, but I believe that Hans may have controlled my heartbeat himself from the second we walked into the hospital. Old traumas sent my anxiety through the roof, and I struggled to relax and control my breathing as the anesthetist gave me the epidural to numb my lower half. Once the medicine kicked in, I felt utterly helpless, and I cried so hard that the doctors talked about sedating me.

Thankfully, my husband refused on my behalf, cradling my head with his physical hands as his spiritual ones infused my heart with peace. When I heard our daughter cry for the first time, most of my terror slipped away, replaced with a welcome relief and devotion. We chose the name Freya Swanhilde to represent my best friend in the past and Hans' "best friend in the present." The altered spelling came as a result of popular naming conventions in Germany; neither of us wanted our daughter to face mockery on account of her name.

While our daughter looked nothing like her Rhenisch namesake—her hair was black like her brother's, and her eyes dark blue like her father's—I felt a strong sense of maternal pride as I held her to my breast later that evening in a private room. I used a pillow to protect my stitches and grant me a bit of stability, for my arms felt feeble after such a harrowing day. Despite everything, my daughter and I had survived the treacherous experience of childbirth. So I sent a silent thought in Wuotan's direction as she suckled my breast: *Your move.*

When Freya and I came home from the hospital several days later, she slept in my arms as I introduced her to the friends and family who populated the Thaden house: her grandfather and grandmother, her older brother—who excitedly asked me whether she could talk yet—Lise and Siggi, Sebastian, Gregor, and the other cleaning and landscaping staff. They all pronounced her gorgeous, though small; she had been just under three kilograms at birth. Her father shadowed me while I made my rounds, his face alight with pride. I could sense Muniche's spirit drawing us closer together in the shared victory of parenthood.

I handed Freya off to Hans so I could make my way upstairs to our bedroom. Although I had summoned a bit of blood magic to heal my incision more quickly, I got the impression that my guts might spill out whenever I took larger steps. My plan was to remain on the second floor for the next week or two, taking my meals in our private parlor and relishing the summer sun on the balcony.

Beth and Sebastian aided me as I climbed the stairs one at a time, cringing more often than not. Beth remarked that modern medicine was a godsend, since I would not have survived a breech birth otherwise. "I'm so glad both of you are safe at home," she said.

I managed only a fake smile in return. Although I had endeavored to face my fate with poise, images of my little brother choking on his breath while doctors worked to save him had haunted me every second I spent in the hospital. A dark part of my brain predicted that I would have to return to the past before I became elderly, if only to avoid a pile of medications and doctor visits. If Augustin ever discovered a way to loosen Muniche's hold on my heart, I would have to return to him long before my physical body failed me.

I waved Beth and Sebastian away when we reached the private parlor, urging them to go marvel at the Thaden family's latest addition. Upon entering my bedroom, I breathed a sigh of satisfaction, truly happy to be at home again. But as I headed for my closet to unpack the bag I had taken to the hospital, my eyes fell upon the balcony doors. Their glass was tinted now, darkening the sunbeams that arched into the bedroom. The scratches from Augustin's anguish were gone.

I froze in place, ice veiling my vision as my eyes moved to the right, to the wall his skeletal hands had charred. It had been repaneled, the singe marks gone.

Betrayal scratched at my heart when I realized that Hans had taken it upon himself to remove some of my cherished memories of Augustin during my three-day absence. *That jerk,* I thought to myself, glancing back at the doorway through which I had come. Hans had not followed me upstairs. He likely entertained the toddling Max, who had seemed thoroughly invested in his newborn sister.

I dropped my bag onto the floor and hurried to my desk, checking the wire bin where I stored Augustin's pages on the Torstein. They were still there, looking no worse for wear, so at least my Keyholder had not returned those to Günter in some desperate bid to square his debt. *I'll have to make sure I keep Augustin's last letter with me all the time, stuff it into my purse so Hans doesn't think to throw it in the trash. Not sure why he's so bothered about my cursed lover now, when we have two children and we're running a nonprofit together.*

As before, I took four months of maternity leave and did not return to my father's corporation until February of 2007. During my time off, I spent many wonderful moments with my children, lavishing tenderness upon them in my fleeting opportunity to completely share their world. I remember sitting on the black couch in our private parlor with my daughter wiggling in my arms, singing along with the stereo while Max played with his toy trucks on the floor. Sometimes his childish voice joined me on the simpler choruses of the metal songs I loved most. Along with old favorites like Nightwish, Haggard, and Therion, many newer bands had entered the scene since I came home to München for good in 2002. Evanescence's Gothic anthems conquered the U.S. airwaves; and Vreni and Erika kept me abreast of fresh sounds by Draconian, Epica, Leaves' Eyes, and Sirenia. Sebastian kept me up to date on NDH as always, his favorites including Rammstein, Eisbrecher, and Oomph!

On a crisp morning in January, I took the U-Bahn downtown with my sights set on Üwe Widermann's art studio. I had browsed his shared gallery several times since Marga and I first visited in 2001—back when I believed my Keyholder to be any Teuton priest except for Hans. Üwe was a priest of yellow fire who had recently turned sixty. He had a talent with oils and watercolors, his skills ranging from landscapes to human portraits.

While I had grudgingly forgiven my husband for renovating our bedroom without telling me first, his decision to do so bothered me deep inside. It was as if he wanted to replace Augustin in my life and erase my precious memories of him, despite his vows not to attempt such nonsense. Thus, I had concluded that I ought to commission a portrait of my cursed lover, one that could ornament the wall beside our balcony doors as a memento to the priest who accepted all of my faults.

I did not tell Hans my intentions, but I knew that he would not dispose of a painting created by his comrade Üwe. They were good friends because they had become Teuton priests around the same time, and Üwe visited the Thaden house for dinner once every few months. I had not yet told the artist that my mother outed him to me back in 1985, but if I could catch him in private today, I might do that very thing. Hans mentioned more than once that Üwe could be trusted to keep a secret, and I rarely got the chance to discuss my time travels with anyone outside the Thaden household anymore. Real life had cut down on my free time.

I slipped through the door into the Fantasia Galerie just after nine a.m., and to my surprise, I found it bustling with people. It appeared that Üwe and his partner Herr Ellinghausen were holding a sale, which had lured a batch of tourists in from the cold. Üwe, in fact, was running the register, and I caught his eye as he rang up a young man with studs in his ears and a wrapped painting bundled under his left arm.

Turning my attention to Herr Ellinghausen's glass sculpture of the Norse goddess Sigyn, I waited for Üwe to finish helping his customers. The lighting inside the gallery was warm and radiant, a welcome transition from the wintry chill. My Teutonic spirit sensed the aura of Üwe's yellow fire present in a variety of jarred candles positioned around the studio. *Not sure if I'll be able to talk to him privately with so many customers here today,* I realized, somewhat disappointed. *But I can browse the sale anyway, see what new paintings he's offering.*

I had reached the sculpture of Odin—fashioned as a bearded warrior rather than as his sinister Teutonic counterpart—when Üwe came to my side. He greeted me in dialect and said that it was nice to see me out and about.

I turned to smile at him. "It's good to see you too, Üwe. It takes longer to heal from a C-section than from a normal birth, that's for sure. But Freya and Max are keeping my spirits up."

After we had spoken the usual pleasantries, I lowered my voice and switched to Teutonica, asking whether I could speak with him alone. Üwe answered that we could talk in the hidden gallery that contained his dark Teutonic art, which he had closed off to the public during the sale. The artist offered me a brass key to its door and gestured for me to go, saying he would corral his partner and have him handle the customers while we conversed.

I had spent several minutes staring at Üwe's rendering of a Black Priest clad in ragged robes and chained to an evil representation of Wuotan, when the artist slipped into the chamber and shut the door behind him. "Forgive me, Swanie, but I shouldn't spend too much time away from the guests today," he apologized, his yellow fire brightening the sconces that shed light on each painting.

"It's fine. I'm . . . just wanting to talk to you about something." The gloomy nature of the painting I studied prompted my voice to tremble a little. I turned away from it with a sigh, my eyes catching the more vibrant colors of a happier image: *Formation of the Heart-Bond of Love.*

"What's troubling you?" Üwe inquired. He approached me at a respectful pace, his silvery gray hair reflecting the golden light of his candles. Concern etched itself across his features. "Are the priests on the council giving you grief?"

"Thankfully, no." A wavering smile curved upon my lips, for along with Hans, we had laughed about Herr Dantzler's insistent prying into the subjects I taught the local Teuton children. Üwe had recently proclaimed that the Old One ought to take himself into the background and allow the younger generation to step forward and lead. I had a notion to nominate the artist as Herr Dantzler's replacement after the elderly man passed away.

I found myself standing before the wondrous painting of the red-fired priest forming the heart-bond with the woman of light. Moisture welled behind my eyes as I recalled the devotion on Augustin's face when he had first held my heart in his hands. "You're someone with experience in forbidden love," I observed, stuffing my hands into the pockets of my winter coat.

Üwe smiled and removed his glasses to wipe the lenses on the hem of his flannel shirt. "Has Hans been telling stories about me?"

I realized abruptly that I had been far too blunt with my statement. *But you came here to talk about forbidden relationships, so there's no point in treading lightly,* I reminded myself. When the artist put his glasses back on, his blue-gray eyes met mine, and I responded, "No, Hans isn't that sort of man. But I found out some things about you recently from someone . . . very close to me."

"Erika Kenney?"

A squeak of laughter escaped my lips as I remembered what my mother had said on that snowy winter day—a day much like today. "No, not her. A few years ago, I took a journey to see someone I lost when I was a child. Someone whose portrait you've painted . . . and she told me about your preferences."

Üwe's eyes grew round, golden flames glinting in their irises. He held his peace for a few moments before murmuring in Teutonica, "You took a journey into the past . . . to speak with Camilla." I nodded, a lump forming in my throat at the subject, and realization dawned upon the artist's countenance. "That's why Hans knew that you'd be his Lady."

"He told you that?" I cocked my head at Üwe as my trust in my Keyholder took a fresh nosedive. *He thought it'd be awesome to just jabber to his friends about the child who was his fated mate.*

"He implied that he'd learned it from a reliable source," Üwe said, clearing his throat delicately and turning his attention to the cheerful scene in the painting before us. "I didn't believe it myself, since our people don't have much of a history where prophecies are concerned. The future is always wreathed in shadow. But if you told Camilla about your destiny, then that makes perfect sense."

I told him a little about what it was like to travel time, how the Torstein had been an encumbrance ever since Wuotan sent his brutes after me while I was in college. Üwe listened attentively, and when I mentioned that my Keyholder and I disagreed occasionally on whether I should travel time or not, he said something that brought me up short. "It could have been me, you know."

I blinked at him from behind my own glasses. "What?"

"Hermann Lohr offered the keys to me before he offered them to Hans." The artist grinned apologetically and placed his hands on his hips, awaiting my reaction.

My brain solved the puzzle in seconds. "You didn't want to be bound to a woman through the city bond."

"Correct," Üwe said.

"Well . . . I mean . . . I wouldn't either, if I was in your shoes." My cheeks flushed at the subject, and I wondered if Üwe had faced censure for his refusal. *Like Augustin.*

"You're very kind, Swanie. Not everyone has agreed with my choices over the years." A subtle grimace crossed Üwe's face.

Then he had been criticized just like the man I chose to love in a different age. "Muniche tore me away from the man who held my heart, like in that painting . . . one thousand years ago," I whispered, suddenly unsure whether I could tell this talented priest the truth about Augustin.

Would he think worse of me once he learned that I had explored the dark path myself?

But his kindness drew the story from me at length, his fiery spirit radiating understanding the entire time I talked. He readily agreed to take a commission of any painting I wished, exiting the studio to retrieve a notebook and pencil. In his absence, I turned my attention back to *The Black Priest of Death, Wuotan's Slave*, defiance rising inside my heart. *He's not Wuotan's slave as long as he holds the memory of our love*, I told myself. *He still has a chance to turn from evil, to step into the light. I just hope our love was enough to guide him there.*

When Üwe returned, I said, "I'd like you to paint me a new rendering of a Black Priest wandering alone in a snowy forest, a wintry river before him under the midnight sky. He should be clad in black robes, his hair like silken ebony, falling to his shoulders, his eyes the blue of fire . . . and a trail of sparse cobalt flames should follow his path in the snow. His visage should be turned toward the river and the stars, his face melancholy, desirous of a way to find that one woman he loved, the one whom fate took away from him." Tears trembled on my eyelashes as I finished speaking, the hole in my heart aching anew.

It seemed a long while before Üwe addressed me again, his tone sounding quite distressed. "Does the Cursed One ever find his long lost love?"

"He will. I'm sure of it," I answered, willing myself to keep the flames of hope alive in my heart, though they dwindled with each passing day.

"And how should I title the painting?" he asked, his blue-gray eyes appraising my face.

"Call it *Augustin*," I replied, lifting my chin as certainty swelled within me. I nodded firmly at the artist and said, "My arrogant predecessor may have dumped his blood into the Isar, but he's not lost to me. *I* am Lady Muniche now, the embodiment of our city's grace, and I do not cast him out."

Chapter Fourteen

An Unexpected Side Plot

Now seems to be the time to jump ahead several years, but first I must give a brief overview of what happened in the meantime. The year 2007 brought its share of grief along with joy, for my cousin Trudi did not survive the birth of her second child, the daughter for whom she had yearned. Her beloved Mane did not handle the tragedy well and ultimately had to quit his job in the corporate world while he mourned.

Traudl and her parents took over for him, though the light left her eyes after her twin sister's death. She cast herself into her work at the repair shop and went out only rarely, spending her free time caring for Lukas and his sister Selina. As time went by, she grew closer with Mane in a platonic manner. The two of them eventually started a new repair shop, Mane handling the books and the front desk while Traudl used her skills to mend ailing vehicles.

My Opa Hobart von Thaden also passed that year, which brought on a new round of shuffling in Süddeutsche Getriebe's upper management. I admitted to my father that I might not be the right one to succeed him after all, since I got more joy from my work behind the scenes at

Selakerza. Our team there had helped our first Teuton client that spring—a young woman from a small village whose parents planned to force her into an arranged marriage. We gave her the resources to gain employment in München, and she moved in with Marga after she started to find her way.

Vreni grasped her fire at last in early 2008, and she came to my front door bubbling over with elation as she created a crimson fireball above her left palm. She invited me to her Teutonic wedding with Stefan, set to take place the Saturday after the May dances. I agreed without hesitation. With a grin that seemed to stretch all the way to the North Sea, Vreni told me that Stefan had already formed the heart-bond with her, and that she could reach the spiritual realm on her own.

"After all these years of learning about Teutonic magic from the outside, it's just coming naturally to me, like I had it all along," she said. I hugged her with gusto, her fiery spirit communing with my icy one beyond the mortal sphere. Vreni had hovered on the sidelines for too many years, ever since she and I first became friends. Now, she finally claimed Teutonic magic for herself.

She and Stefan got to work making babies immediately after they married, for Vreni declared that eleven years of waiting was long enough. By the summer of 2011, they had two boys, Fabian and Manuel; and Vreni planned to try for one more before she called it quits. Of all of my Teuton girlfriends, she had the least trouble with childbirth, or with losing the excess weight afterward.

Both Iliana and Erika—who had a son named Sean back in 2007—remained pleasantly plump, while I worked doggedly to maintain my pre-pregnancy weight. I discovered that the scar from my C-section would never fully heal, for its flesh remained numb to the touch. Occasionally, I would get fleeting abdominal pains, which brought back memories of how broken my body had been after Augustin's abuse.

Herr Dantzler succumbed to a heart attack in late 2010, and his elderly wife Ada struggled in the wake of their severed heart-bond. The two had been married for over five decades, and Ada ultimately had to enter a nursing home after her master's death. That situation disturbed me deep inside, for I remembered how shattered my heart had been after Augustin severed our bond. My Keyholder had completed the city bond with me through marriage less than a day later, but Ada Dantzler had no one to heal her devastated heart.

Hans and I also had to find another Teuton priest to fill the empty space on München's council, and after some deliberation, we nominated Üwe. The moment when he and the other priests—Rudi, Oskar, Warren, and Jürgen—joined hands and united their elements in a rite much older than the city itself, a strong sense of pride warmed my heart. The man who once refused the keys for a valid reason now stood together with Muniche's guardians, to support and defend her until the day of his death. When I offered him my frosty hand, our elements contrasting gloriously beneath the starry sky, I smiled as I repeated the ritual words: "Serve me well, as I serve you. May Muniche's gates welcome the Teuton people forever."

Like Augustin once predicted, my relationship with Hans deepened as the years passed, gradually superseding the painful recollections of a time long gone. For a while I locked away the memories, aside from those recurring moments when I found myself alone in our bedroom, watching photos of my cursed lover scrolling across my computer screen. My eyes would shift from them to Üwe's artwork of the Black Priest seeking the one he had lost, and from there to the painting he had made for Bertha Lohr, of the Keyholder and Lady separated by whirling obscurity. And what little remained of my free will would ruminate on what would be left of me once Hans had gained his eternal reward. Would I be obliged to offer my heart to a naïve young child? Or could I find the courage to dive into the past in one final quest for the Cursed One whose devotion spanned infinity's abyss?

Though it seemed somewhat ironic at the time, now I simply look back and chuckle at the new and unexpected camaraderie that took root in my soul. It found its place between my son and me, the seed planted early with tales of Teutonic lore and careful lessons on that exquisite language of old. We shared a lot of the same hobbies, for Max began guitar lessons at age six in hopes of mimicking the chords and riffs we admired in metal. He loved to listen to me play the organ in the music room, and he often mused about the Teutonic sorcery inherent in all of creation. His childish insight impressed me, his pure heart inspiring me to tackle each new challenge as it came.

To Hans' credit, he became more open with me as the years passed. That brought me to the forefront of a gross reality in the Teuton community. Fulfillment boosted my optimism whenever *Selakerza's* resources brought someone out of darkness, and I became closer with many of my girlfriends in the shared glories of motherhood. I started to see familiar faces in my children's classes—Lea and Alison, Sophia, Lukas, and my very own Max—and fewer parents complained about the topics that I chose to address. Some of my earliest pupils matched themselves with Teutonic partners, and Erika gave a lesson to the older teens each year on how to survive the blood-transfer. It seemed as though my small steps were leading my people in a positive direction.

But Hans informed me on the first Saturday in June 2011 that there was to be a priestly conference on the subsequent Friday. "Every Keyholder has been asked to attend, along with two priests from each city council," he informed me as we prepared for bed.

I worked my way into an oversized FC Bayern T-shirt and tugged my black hair free. It still fell to the middle of my back, though I normally wore it up at work. "Is this conference like the one from 1904 when they decided to take all the spells out of *Der Weg?*" I asked, suspicions brewing within me.

My husband's expression was inscrutable as he laid himself upon our bed, clad in nothing but a pair of gym shorts. "I don't think this one's going to involve any changes to tradition. But I'm pretty sure this is the first time a conference has been called since just before World War II."

"Okay." I raised an eyebrow at Hans and climbed onto the bed, lying down on my left side and propping my head up on one elbow to look at him directly. "So are you going to keep beating around the bush or tell me what it's about?"

Hans sighed and leaned back against the headboard, his eyes on the closed door to our private parlor. "Three suspicious fires happened in separate cities on the Wednesday before the May dances. The Teuton priests— members of the council of each city—who resided in the affected structures have not been seen since."

My jaw dropped further the longer Hans spoke. "So . . . what . . . is someone hunting Teuton priests or something? Is that what you're trying to find out?"

My husband closed his eyes, his age evident in his profile; he had turned sixty-five just two months prior. "I'm not sure. The known facts will be presented at the conference, and afterward comes the speculation. There's likely something wicked involved, something that could affect our community as a whole."

Shivers ran up my spine, and traces of ice entered my veins, an instinctive reaction. "Which priest called the conference? Was it a Keyholder?"

"Yes. Miche Hoffmann from Innsbruck."

"Innsbruck? That's out in the sticks," I commented, wishing my husband would look at me. I could tell by his expression that this was serious.

"He's having us meet out in the sticks, too," Hans noted, turning his head to the right to meet my gaze. "Some castle ruin on a hilltop in the forest. They'll likely rent it out for the evening, maybe the entire night."

"Hope there's not an altar there for sacrifices," I joked, trying to shake the nervous twinge in my stomach.

"I don't think he invited Günter," Hans said with an answering smirk. "But I wanted to ask your opinion on which of München's priests I should take along."

"Me," I responded instantly, sitting up straight.

Hans gave me a dark look. "Swanie—"

"I know, I know." I waved a hand at him dismissively, but my curiosity converged with my unease. *Maybe I could sneak in as a spirit so I can make sure all these patriarchs behave themselves.* "Invite Rudi and Üwe to tag along with you. I trust their judgment."

"Not so much for Oskar, Warren, and Jürgen?"

I scrunched my nose and shook my head. "Oskar will probably be out of town, Warren's too wishy-washy, and Jürgen gives me the creeps. I don't know how Eva puts up with him, to be honest. He gives off an unsettling vibe."

"You just don't like smoke."

I laughed and tossed a spare pillow at Hans. "Be serious. Would you be mad if I attend in the shadows, as long as I keep my thoughts to myself?"

My Keyholder chucked the pillow back at me, and it hit me in the gut. "That might not be the wisest thing to do. If enough priests show up, they'll probably use supernatural security to keep the conference private. You can't pass through an energy shield undetected, not even as a spirit."

He had a point, but after thinking about it for a second I said, "You can if you imagine yourself inside the shield and change reality around you."

Hans breathed a heavy sigh and sank down upon his pillow. "Swanie, you could get us both in trouble if you're caught."

I lay down myself and grinned at him while switching off the lamp atop my nightstand. "Good thing I'm skilled enough *not* to get caught." He muttered a few phrases about witches and spells, and then we kissed goodnight, his tongue seeming desperate to claim every portion of my mouth. Despite Hans' dignity, I knew that he was turned on by the thought of my forbidden knowledge. If we had not already made love earlier that evening, I would have gotten far more than just a kiss for my brazenness.

Once all of the six-to-eight-year-olds had been retrieved by their parents the following afternoon—the lesson that day had been on *Eihalbae* and the importance of respecting a silver oak's gifts—Beth and my father took my children out to dinner while Hans and I traveled in spirit form to the castle ruin where the conference was to be held. He had scouted out the location earlier that week, and we entered the *Gæstelort* with our physical bodies joined, so he could carry us both to the hilltop. We worked our magic beside a ripple in the stone wall around the Thaden property, his black fire and my ice concealed behind a thick hedgerow.

When we met in the ether, the youthful perfection of my Keyholder's spirit stunned me anew, his thin lips forming a beatific smile as he reached out to caress my face. My longing for him erupted along every nerve, and my robes transformed into a frosty wonderland. *You'd better not keep this up, or we'll spend our whole time here sticking our tongues down each other's throats,* I warned him, though my cheek leaned into his hand in unspoken bliss.

Hans' laughter tickled my brain, and he backed away from me just a little. *True. I wish we had more time to enjoy each other like this outside of our dream world. This is one of the only places where our powers are equivalent.*

I gave my husband a chiding look and turned my gaze to the east. *You'll be my master no matter how old you get. Fire's a destructive element that conquers all. Now carry us to the castle,* Leitaeri, *so we can scope things out.*

Hans chuckled again and caught me in a blazing storm, and I closed my eyes to focus on his darkness as the ground below changed from München's skyline to a tangled forest. A thin trail led uphill from a grassy parking area shaded by a patch of pines. A gravel road curled away toward a distant village, and the first thought that popped into my head was, *You might want to take the M-Class.*

I had traded my Maserati for an SUV shortly after Freya's birth, and it had more clearance underneath than my husband's BMW. *You're probably right,* Hans replied, his spirit descending toward the ruins themselves. *I don't sense anyone else around, aside from a couple tourists. Let's see what we're up against.*

There was not much left of the castle, which was of gray stone. It was more like a manor than a castle, its weed-coated walls reaching to my shoulders when I set my ethereal feet upon the ground. The fortifications were weathered and broken, several slabs lying here and there, the remnants of a spiral staircase winding part-way up a turret. My Keyholder and I traversed the entire edifice, keeping our distance from a pair of hikers toting maps and backpacks; their American English stood out to me. They sounded like New Yorkers.

Hans figured that the conference would convene in the largest remaining chamber. Several glassless windows offered views to the north and south, with two modern benches standing out against the aged stone. Three steps rose to a landing at one side of the chamber, and a ring of stones marked its center—a place for a fire. *That's where you'll summon Wuotan,* I said to Hans, gesturing at the ring.

My husband rolled his eyes at me and noted, *I'm going to bring my own chair. I'm too old to perch on some windowsill for who knows how long, and those benches will get claimed by whoever arrives first. I'll tell Rudi and Üwe to do the same.*

I nodded thoughtfully, looking from a shadowy corner, to the windows, to a turret that reached several meters above my head. *So I'm going to sneak in, but some of the priests might be on the lookout for Teuton spirits. It might be helpful for you to invoke the darkness in your aura, so I could slip beneath your robes to watch. If you stake out territory in that corner there, I could probably pull it off without drawing attention.*

Hans looked toward the corner I indicated and pursed his lips. *It might be better for you to just watch from above. The stones are wide enough for you to hide along the wall and peer over it. If Rudi, Üwe, and I can get that corner, you can lurk above it, and I'll send extra darkness up to conceal you.*

Afraid you'll get too cold with my spirit all cozied up beneath your robe? I raised my eyebrows at Hans before rising into the air to observe the corner he had mentioned. The stones of the wall were about as wide as my arms were long; more than enough room for me to prowl. *What if some of the priests with security duty do a sweep of the walls every now and then?*

Then you'd better prove yourself quick as a hare, my husband answered, his spirit hovering in the atmosphere before me. He blew me a kiss with a sly look.

Are any of the priests coming as spirits? I asked, that possibility shooting a dart through my plans. If so, I would have to hope for clouds.

My Keyholder shook his head. *No, Miche expects us to come in person. He has some suspicions about the fires, that they may be a result of Teuton arsonists. He and the other two Keyholders are planning a degree of interrogation.*

I shuddered at that idea. *You mean you might get bled?*

Hans shrugged one shoulder and looked toward the west. *It's possible, but that'll happen only if some priest or other seems guilty. Teuton priests don't bleed every neck when a crime takes place; there has to be solid evidence for it. I think Miche's trying to cover his tracks, so if the perpetrators* are *there, they won't be able to flee the country.*

They'll get chucked in the dungeon instead, I finished for him with a grin.

He invited me into the ether for an elemental dance, before we left the forest behind to return to our physical bodies. The darkness of his fire, coupled with his seductive heat, infused my heart with rabid desire. When we found ourselves back in our mortal prisons, I practically dragged Hans to the cottage he once called his home for an intimate tryst. Afterward, he complained good-naturedly that he knew not how long his body could keep up with my verve. "Your cousin might not appreciate how we've used her couch," he said, as he put his shorts back on.

I heard his knees creaking in the process and frowned a little, for I did not particularly like thinking about my Keyholder's age. "Ah, it can give her inspiration for a steamy scene," I rejoined, glancing around what had once been Hans' front parlor. Now the room held a writing desk and chair, computer, filing cabinet, loaded bookshelf, the flowered couch, and several wintry paintings that spoke to Beth's snow. The two of us struck out for the main house hand-in-hand, leaving my cousin's home office behind.

On Friday June 10th, Hans left the Thaden house with Üwe and Rudi en route to the castle ruins, just before five p.m. The conference was set to begin at exactly eight-thirty, before twilight would descend, which meant that I would have to be extra sneaky when I arrived in spirit form. Hans and his two comrades planned to get dinner at a local beer garden; and he promised to text me when they arrived, and when the gathering adjourned. Rudi and Üwe assured me that they would create a diversion if anyone caught wind of my spirit. It pleased me that Muniche's representatives were in full agreement about their Lady's attendance.

Gregor prepared pizza for dinner, a favorite of both Max and Freya, neither of whom was happy about their Pappi's absence. We usually held a family night on Fridays, with my father and Beth as well as Sebastian, Lise, and Siggi. My children adored all of my father's employees, and Sebastian had even allowed Max to tag along to his family's Seder that year. My son had gushed about that for the rest of the month, for at age six he had become fascinated with cultural traditions, Teutonic and otherwise.

In my husband's absence, we sat together to watch *Beauty and the Beast* on the giant TV in the family room. Max and Freya acted out the movie with their stuffed animals as it played, and I was thoroughly engrossed in their interpretation of the story when my phone vibrated on the side table. I glanced at the clock first—it was seven-twenty. When I brought up Hans' text, I nearly burst out laughing. *All the priests from Linz and Rosenheim are wasted. Might have to cart some of them up the hill myself.*

Are you guys at the beer garden? I texted back, grinning.

This place is loaded with Teuton priests. It's freaking obvious.

I imagined a small beer garden stuffed full of men in black robes. *The more who get drunk, the fewer I'll have to worry about. You can't invoke your element if you're drunk,* I responded.

True. Still set to start at eight-thirty, came Hans' reply.

Great. Gaston's headed for the Beast's castle, I updated him.

Hans texted again shortly after eight p.m. *We've got the corner.* I sent a brief acknowledgement and kissed Max and Freya goodnight. "I've got something to do to help Pappi. You two obey Omi and Opa when they say it's bedtime," I told them.

I exchanged a look with my father before heading upstairs; he knew what I planned to do. He nodded at me rather grimly, and part of me wondered whether he might appear at the gathering himself after putting my children to bed. He had better be ready to hide if so. I made my way upstairs to the bedroom I shared with Hans, discarding my phone on the bedside table before heading for the bathroom. I would enter the spiritual realm in the empty hot tub to contain my ice's dampness.

In spirit form, I rose into the sky above the Thaden house, casting my eyes toward the setting sun. Night would not come for another four hours, and I sensed very little moisture in the atmosphere. My ice would have no help from nature; I had to do this on the power of my Teuton blood alone. *But Hans is going to toss me a bit of darkness,* I remembered, summoning all of my courage as I envisioned myself among the trees that cloaked the hill and its ruins.

Reality transformed around me, and I sensed a moment of swift travel as my spirit appeared between a thick white oak and a younger birch. I stood in a batch of brambles, and I felt them scratching at my ethereal form. No matter; they could not injure me. Raising my eyes to the gray ruins upon the hilltop, I caught sight of several black-clad figures congregating in the yard, between the outer wall and the manor itself. Their hoods raised, they appeared deep in conversation.

Cautiously, I extended my ice in a tight sphere, trying to detect any security measures. I drifted forward a few paces, sensing naught but the trees and shrubs, the fresh breeze of a summer evening. The group of priests disappeared into the ruins, and my ears might have heard a few more walking the trail from the parking lot—I had sent my spirit to the opposite side of the hill. I kept my icy aura contained to the area around me, not wanting any priests, drunk or sober, to detect my presence.

So did they raise an energy shield or not? I wondered, creeping gradually through the underbrush as through a labyrinth, my spiritual heart hammering all the way. *What if they planted booby traps instead? Should I just float into the air and hope nobody's looking up? What did that corner wall look like again?*

Although Hans had claimed that all of the attendees should be in their mortal bodies, edginess had transformed my robes into a stark white, hardly helpful in the forest's gloom. What if I ran into some Teuton priest probing the area as a spirit before the conference started?

I had reached the tree line without coming across any trace of a shield; my icy essence nearly touched the ivied fortifications now. I hung back to eyeball the corner wall. *I just have to go for it.*

But before I created a clear picture of my hideout in my mind, an unknown voice slinked into my brain, prompting me to freeze in place. *You might want to be a bit subtler with that ice if you're trying not to be noticed.*

My eyes practically leapt from their sockets, and my element snapped back around my spirit. Another ghostly Teuton emerged from the forest, passing straight through a thick oak in the process. The interloper raised leaden eyebrows at me, rippling robes the exact color of the stones seeming to cascade in tandem with charcoal locks of hair. The spirit offered me a coy smile.

She was *female.*

Chapter Fifteen:
An Atrocious Scandal

Silence stretched between us, as I kicked myself for not returning to my body the instant that her voice entered my mind. If she had been a priest, my cover would be blown. But now I grappled with innumerable questions. Another Teuton woman, a Lady perhaps, who wanted to infiltrate the conference? Did her master know that she was here? How long had she been here, creeping up on me? Was I really *that* unobservant, oblivious to the spirits around me? I had heard a number of priests approaching the hill from the far side!

My companion, meanwhile, continued to smile at me, and at length she jerked her chin toward the overgrown fortifications. *They do have a shield raised, if that's why you were sweeping around like an ice witch. Where are you planning to perch yourself? You're hardly invisible.* Her slate gray eyes took in my spirit from head to toe; my robes were still a wintry white.

On top of that corner. The thought left my brain before I could stop it. Here I was, telling an unknown entity far too much about myself. Something about her countenance gave me pause. Although her skin radiated the standard shimmer of a Teuton spirit, her complexion looked darker, and not the gray of her element. She was obviously stone—that was why her robes matched the ruin's walls—but why did her insubstantial arms look . . . foreign?

Her lips opened into a real smile, and she held out her right hand. *Come on. I've got you. I know every wall on this hill like the back of my hand.*

I looked from her luminous fingers to her countenance, hesitation seizing me in its grip. Amity pulsed outward from her essence, but could I really trust someone who had surprised me in the middle of an irreverent act? The spirit before me caught wind of my misgivings and lowered her arm a tad as she said, *Right. Where are my manners? I'm Zehra of Erlangen. And you?*

Her name was hardly Teutonic, but I could not mistake the authority that surged from her spirit. This was the *Leitalra* of Erlangen, a smaller city north of Nürnberg . . . and she was a foreigner.

I'm Swanie of München, I managed to answer, trying to work out how to ask respectfully about her background. Long ago, I had read that it was indeed possible for a foreigner to be chosen by the spirit of a Teuton city if she met three criteria: the city in question was her birthplace, she was unmarried, and she had gained Teuton blood by one of the two standard means. To my knowledge, that had happened only once in Teuton history, when a Jewish-born woman became the Lady of Wels in the 1700s.

You did the blood-transfer? I finally asked, wondering wildly *how* I had not heard of this astonishing twist of fate. I did not mingle among my people enough; I hardly had the time to keep up with the Teutons in my own city.

Zehra grinned, and I heard her chuckle in my mind. *I did, and my parents were Turkish. But if you want that story, we'll both miss out on whatever the patriarchs have to say. I, for one, think they need some supervision.* She winked.

You're not wrong. Does your Keyholder know you're here?

Of course. Miche Hoffmann didn't want to invite us, actually, which tells me there's something really bad going on with all this arson stuff. And I bet it's not what you might think. Zehra turned her face toward the inner walls, her eyes narrowing in suspicion.

Well, if we don't keep our thoughts to ourselves, they may not be upfront about any of it, I predicted, looking up at the corner again.

I scouted this place out last week. Spent a whole day passing through every wall. I can drop you off on that corner and then get in the turret.

I looked back at the spirit before me. *Which turret, the one by the landing?*

You got it. Zehra smirked and held out her right hand again. *I promise I won't leave you inside the stone, even though it's way easier to spy that way.*

A shudder raced through me at the idea of that. *I kind of like the air around me, thanks,* I said, reaching for her hand. Our spirits passed through each other, but I felt her stone clutching my essence . . . and the next thing I knew, we stood upon the corner of the wall, more black-clad men gathered in the chamber below than I had ever seen in one place.

Get down! Zehra hissed, having sunk into the stones of the wall all the way up to her neck. I had to stifle a laugh at that, but I crouched down onto my stomach and peered over the edge of the wall. I saw what had to be Hans sitting beneath me in his bright red camp chair, with Üwe on his left in a blue chair and Rudi on his right in a green one. I recognized his companions by their size and build, since I had to keep my ice contained around my spirit; I felt as blind as my mortal eyes were without glasses or contacts.

Give me a heads up if you're going to make a scene, Zehra requested, and when I turned to acknowledge her, her head sank into the stone wall where I lay. I heard her chortling again as I shook my head in bemusement. This was the first time I had ever thought that it might be useful to be a solid element, and have no compunctions about a lack of oxygen.

In her absence, I sent a thought in my husband's direction. *I'm here, and I'm not alone. The Lady of Erlangen had the same idea I did.*

Hans stroked the heart of my soul in response, and I sensed relief emanating from his spiritual fingers. He was glad that I was here. I saw him murmur to his companions, likely informing them of my presence; and I averted my focus to the scene below as a whole.

It was debilitating to look down upon a multitude of Teuton priests without the privilege of detecting their elements. I dared not extend my ice outward to any extent, not even behind where I lurked in an attempt to sense the energy shield Zehra mentioned. The priests had lit a fire in the stone circle, and its flames leapt skyward in all the hues of Teutonic pyromancy: red, yellow, blue, and black, along with muted natural tones. That meant that there were priests of each shade of fire here at this conference . . . and the sight of those blue flames brought pain to my heart. *Oh Augustin, if only one of them was you.*

Nine priests gathered upon the landing opposite of where I skulked, and of the nine, three seemed thoroughly invested in a raucous discussion about a local soccer team. The scent of alcohol hovered around another group of priests who had claimed the windowsill facing south. I wondered which batch was from Linz and which was from Rosenheim. At least six of the men below did not take this meeting seriously.

Other priests approached Hans from time to time to converse, which did not surprise me, since München was the largest Teuton city. His word, if asked to give it, would likely hold more weight than any of the others. It occurred to me, as my eyes scanned the final few priests wandering in, that I had not asked Hans which cities other than Innsbruck had experienced the fires. And of course I could not ask now, since he could not reply without giving away my presence.

Zehra? I sent a tentative thought toward the spirit of stone, shifting my gaze to the turret at the far corner. Its top was shaved off, but it stood at least two meters higher than the rest of the walls.

I'm here. I just blinked at you.

I tried to make my ice sharpen my vision even further; I could already trace each crack in the turret's stone, even in the low light. Suddenly, a bronze nose came into focus, and a pair of slate gray irises blinked at me again. She had literally melded her spirit with the wall.

That's just . . . insane, I thought to her. She laughed, her teeth flashing pearly against the turret for an instant. *I mean, I guess it's not, since I've done that with ice and snow before. But still.*

It took me a few months to get used to it, Zehra admitted, her eyes trained on the activities below us now. *But the stone welcomes me. Pretty sure my Teutonic magic is healing some of this castle's ailments.*

That was an interesting concept. *You don't happen to know which cities had the fires aside from Innsbruck, do you?* I asked, trying to keep my attention on the events below. There had to be nearly a hundred Teuton priests down there now, so the conference must be about to begin.

Regensburg and Linz, Zehra said, adding in a tone filled with censure, *and it's obvious that nobody from Linz gives a damn what happens here tonight, even though they lost their Old One. He must have been a charlatan.*

It was the Old Ones of each council who disappeared? I asked.

You got it. A bunch of fossils who might have fought with Hitler for all we know. Zehra did not seem concerned about that coincidence, but a fresh quiver ran through my spirit. Hans was the eldest member of München's council after Adi Dantzler's death last year, although as Keyholder he would not take the lesser title of Old One. Would we have to fear arsonists at the Thaden house?

One of the priests upon the landing descended to the bottom step, a ring of ancient gate keys hanging from a golden chain around his neck, the firelight casting him in an uncanny glimmer. He introduced himself as Miche Hoffmann, *Leitaeri* of Innsbruck, and beckoned his two companions forward before relating their names. He called the meeting to order and asked each Keyholder to introduce himself and his city's representatives.

I watched and listened as each Keyholder did so, most of the names floating out of my memory as soon as they entered. I recognized a few surnames shared by business contacts, and I realized that I actually knew one priest from Freising and another from Ingolstadt. White teeth flashed another smile upon the turret when the Keyholder of Erlangen rose to address the crowd; he looked about my age if not younger, and I caught the cerulean glow of fire in his eyes. His poise was straight and commanding, a young man confident in his position.

At least Zehra claimed a master close to her own age. Her way of speaking matched that of my girlfriends, though her dialect was a bit different. A brief coil of envy squeezed me deep inside, as my gaze dropped back to my own master, a man whose joints cracked, whose hair had long since relinquished its ebony shine. But I forced the jealousy aside, for such sentiments brought no gain. And when Hans stood from his camp chair and declared himself *Leitaeri* of München in a tone of stoic assurance, Muniche's spirit filled my heart with elation.

Impressive, Zehra thought, as Hans sat back down alongside Üwe and Rudi.

Thanks, I answered, not sure how to respond to that remark. But that single word from my own peer transformed Muniche's elation into something much more primal. I could sense the deference my Keyholder's words inspired in the others gathered below, and I sent a rebuke to his mind. *Thanks a lot,* Leitaeri. *Muniche wants to screw you now.*

A snort reached my ears from Hans' chair, and his spiritual hands clasped my heart, exuding both seduction and power. I tolerated that for exactly five seconds. *Jeez, Hans, quit it or I might try to take you in spirit form. Not sure if that's possible, but either way, it'll mark the end of this serious conference.*

Hans muttered something to Üwe and gave my heart one last caress. Üwe tilted his head toward where I peered over the wall, and his yellow-fired eyes met mine as he smirked at me. He rolled his eyes at Hans' expense, and I giggled, my humor and desire having altered my icy robes to a crystal blue that melded better with the evening sky. *These stupid priests are going to get me caught.*

After everyone introduced themselves, Innsbruck's Keyholder stepped further into the firelight and broached the topic of the blazes. As he recounted what was known about each one, I listened intently, trying to work out connections, motivations. Each of the three priests lived alone, so no family or other persons had succumbed to the fires. No remains had been found at any of the burnt houses, so all three priests were currently listed as missing and not dead. The three were not equally wealthy. The one from Innsbruck was a financier whose name I recognized from my high school years, when I had mingled with Morgen and Ava; the other two were middle-class. It was unknown whether the three men knew each other, or if they shared business or personal contacts.

One memory lingered on the edges of my mind as Regensburg's Keyholder stepped forward to describe what little had been found at the affected site in his jurisdiction. He noted that the Old One's retirement accounts had been plundered, with no electronic traces of where the money had landed. The older man continued speaking as what I was trying to remember became clear. *Pappi told me once that Florian von Hollen of Innsbruck is a scoundrel,* I said to Hans. *His family made a killing during the Second World War.*

Hans brushed my heart in acknowledgement, and I pondered it further. What did a financier have in common with two Teuton priests in different cities? They were all the eldest priests on their city councils, they were all retired, they all lived alone, they were each involved with training young men who studied for the priesthood—Innsbruck's Keyholder had mentioned that.

I had not paid attention to the discussion for over a minute, and I when I looked toward the landing, I saw that Miche Hoffmann spoke again. His visage haunted, he said, "One aspect of my city's case stands apart from the others, and that is the story that ran on the TV stations and in the newspapers. Somehow, the media got hold of some evidence they claim was found in Herr von Hollen's house, and from the evidence they concluded that he was involved in"—the man gave a discreet cough—"trafficking. That, of course, is utterly false."

Trafficking? The word revolved in my brain, echoed by Zehra's mental voice. I met her gaze from across the vast chamber, and her irises altered from slate to a gray that was nearly black. *The bastard held slaves,* Zehra translated.

What? I had not yet caught the implications. But one of the priests below—it might have been Salzburg's Keyholder—raised a pertinent question. What exactly *was* this evidence that had surfaced in the media?

Miche Hoffmann's face hardened into a stern mask. "Passports of females. Papers written in Teutonica, and photos of a . . . graphic nature."

An uproar exploded below at the same time the word *Shit!* leaped from my mind. In my horror, I did not keep my thoughts to myself.

An instant later, I heard Zehra growl, *Twenty Euros says they all rented out young women so the priests in training could practice bleeding them. And screwing them. And hurting them with their elements.*

I cursed again and unleashed my vitriol at Hans. *Is this some tradition for Teuton priests when they're training new recruits? The Lady of Erlangen says they were probably using these girls as practice. What. The. Hell?!*

Hans' hands closed around my heart, sending a harsh order for me to control myself. But Zehra was talking again, letting me in on a dark secret my Keyholder had never told me. *It's an old custom nobody likes to talk about. Whenever young men train for the priesthood, they have to practice their sorcery on someone. And a woman can be used and discarded like trash for that. If her heart is bound to the priestly tutor, he can wipe her memories afterward.*

How . . . how do you know all this? I asked her, pressing my hands against my temples as the colors of my icy robes churned in agitation.

I've been around the block a few times, Zehra replied grimly, and I directed more venom in my husband's direction. His hands clutched my heart even more firmly; but to his credit, he pushed himself out of his camp chair and spoke over the multitude of voices, demanding both silence and attention. As I watched in anguish from above, the chatter died down at the thunder in Hans' tone. He spoke with Muniche's authority. I gripped the stones of the wall and stared.

"Were the passports found at Florian von Hollen's house of outsiders or of Teutons?" Hans questioned, slowly approaching the fire.

My elemental eyes watched Miche Hoffmann's face grow pale. Hans' tone demanded truth, and an aura of dark heat rippled in his wake. The five brass keys of München stood out starkly against the black background of his robe, and while I could not see his expression, I could imagine how withering it must look. At first I thought Innsbruck's Keyholder would either back down or run, as all eyes below looked from my husband to the man whose Old One had committed an atrocious iniquity. Only the sound of the flickering flames pierced the stillness.

Miche glanced around at his peers, his jaw shifting as though he knew not what to say. But at length he straightened his posture and met my husband's gaze. "They were Teutons."

A gasp rose from the gathered priests, and Hans halted two steps from the fire, more of its flames darkening to black. "The evidence suggests that Florian, in his infinite wisdom, chose to reinstate a primeval practice that should have never existed in the first place. Need I remind you, Miche, that my predecessor, God rest his soul, and the *Leitalra* I served for over three decades set out to end that practice eternally? And need I remind you that the penalty for permitting such perversions is akin to the penalty for staging blood sacrifices to our demon lord? Has your city and those of your compatriots lured your people back into the days of darkness?"

Power crackled along Hans' hands, and the fire blackened further. But for some reason, Miche's face appeared even whiter, his eyes as round as the full moon as my husband's indictments sliced his dignity.

A rumble spread through the black-robed figures, their unease and disgust reaching upward to where my icy spirit skulked. I sensed Muniche's power infusing me with otherworldly vitality as her Keyholder's words seized light over darkness, justice over mercy. *Make him pay. Make* all *of them pay,* I hissed at Hans.

Miche rose to his own defense at last, his voice sounding kicked more than confident. "Herr von Hollen trained young priests on his own. I had no knowledge of his—"

"Then you admit to allowing your priests free rein among the community to its detriment?" Hans cut him off, sounding wholly incensed. "And yet you hold the keys to your Lady's heart. What a travesty, to permit the torment of her daughters while claiming the station of master guardian, of *Leitaeri.*"

The anger seething below rose to a fevered pitch. Miche repeated that he had no knowledge of his missing Old One's machinations, and Hans directed the Keyholder of Salzburg to bleed him and verify his claims. The gathered men seemed to have unified behind my husband's declarations, for they stood in each doorway and window, blocking the exits. At long last I sensed the humming of a thick energy shield just a few handbreadths from where I lay upon the wall.

Salzburg's *Leitaeri* bled Miche for a mere ten seconds before confirming that he indeed knew everything that his Old One had done. The man had gone through five Teuton women over a period of twenty-two years; he had used each one in his priestly instruction and bred them with the young trainees. That tidbit prompted my thoughts to race back to Günter Setzer, the undead breeder of Teuton children. *Is that why all three men had their ghastly empires overthrown? Did Günter view them as a threat to his business?*

I wanted to share my ruminations with Hans, but he still stood by the fire, overseeing the conference that had become something of a trial. Separate priests bled the Keyholders of Regensburg and Linz in turn—I wondered briefly if Linz's *Leitaeri's* blood tasted like alcohol—and corroborated that the Old Ones of those cities also had enslaved Teuton women.

And someone found out and decided to burn their houses down and do who-knows-what to the priests and the women, I recognized, uncertainty agitating my ice. *These Keyholders need to be punished, along with the entire councils, probably . . . but who was responsible for all this? Pretty sure we'd have some common ground.*

While the priests below debated on how to handle this horrific scandal, I sent my thoughts to Hans, wanting to ensure he was on the same page. He needed to direct the discussion back to its initial purpose—to reveal the perpetrators behind the three fires. One of his hands squeezed the heart of my soul in agreement, and he raised his voice once more to address the crowd.

Every single priest on the councils of these cities needs to be questioned, Zehra stated while my husband and his peers speculated on the arsonists. *Names of the enslaved women should be unearthed and their families questioned, as well. They probably got paid by the Old Ones to give up their daughters.*

If I had not been in spirit form, I might have vomited. *Are Teuton parents really that vile? That Hollen bastard used five women. How many did the others violate? How has it come to this?*

I placed my hands on either side of my head and shook it, feeling as though my efforts to improve Teuton society had fallen flat. The community in München was more open and charitable than it had been just a decade ago . . . while trafficking was still in force in Innsbruck, Regensburg, and Linz. The Teuton populations of those cities were not especially large.

While Zehra and I bemoaned the intolerance of our people, the priests below had concluded that there were only two plausible options in regards to the fires. Either they had been planned by a group to take place on the same night, or they had been lit by a Cursed One. The sloshed Keyholder from Linz pushed back against the second idea, for he argued that there had been no trace of lightning among the ashes. "Found some . . . uh . . . black sparks in the rubble, though," he said.

Dark energy? I looked toward the tower to meet Zehra's gaze. Her stone-colored irises appeared as leery as the men below at the subject of Cursed Ones, and she made a mental noise that seemed the equivalent of a shrug.

"Has anyone actually *asked* Günter if he's responsible?" Zehra's Keyholder posited the question, his hands on his hips as he gazed around at his comrades. He stood behind the Keyholder of Regensburg, having read the truth in his blood. "He might have viewed these slaveholders' business as competition to his own."

Miche flinched at the term *slaveholder*, and the drunk piped up, "It wasn't a business . . . not a *business* . . . ."

No one had spoken to Günter, and if they had, they were unwilling to admit it publicly. A few men tossed around some theories about the black sparks, whether it was difficult for the dead to change light to darkness, whether they were planted to obfuscate the facts. And a memory from years ago rose to the forefront of my mind: that night in the Leutasch Gorge, after the *Eihalbe* led me to the Torstein and I lost my grip on the cliff. A hooded figure cloaked in midnight's obscurity stood above me in silence, watching me scramble for footing, watching me look death in the eye.

Time and tide wait for none but the dead.

Had that mysterious priest claimed dark energy as his element? Was that what had fashioned that potent storm that carried me to safety, along with water from the stream and the sleek summer breeze? Dark energy?

Certainty took hold of my heart as my spiritual robes shifted into a snowy translucence. *That* Black Priest—an unknown, not the one who inhabited the infamous castle—had saved my life in 1998. Maybe he had saved the lives of the three enslaved women before incinerating their cages and . . . .

The conversation below had shifted to the fate of the three guilty Old Ones, all of whom had vanished without a trace, just like their financial assets. *I bet that Black Priest of dark energy is a computer geek. He pocketed all of their money.* A chuckle escaped my brain, and I saw Zehra's eyes dart in my direction. I was the only person here who had spoken to that enigmatic priest, the only one—aside from Hans, perhaps—who knew he existed.

"There's one way to find out whether those three met their appointed end." The declaration cut the air like a knife as the Keyholder of Salzburg stepped into the firelight, baring his arms. "Or are all of you too frightened to summon our demon lord into his preferred medium?"

You could have heard a pin drop; I think none of the men dared to breathe. And the flames flared red to match the priest's irises as he produced a knife from beneath his robe, nicking his right palm and casting the blood into the fire with the incantation, "By the power of this fire and the strength of my blood, I call you to earth from your . . . ."

Hans whirled away from his peers to face me directly, black fire igniting around him in thick obsidian. "Swanie, get OUT of here!" he ordered, his voice jabbing at my heart. "I can't hide you from him! GO!"

Our eyes locked, and I read terror and resolve in his. *Make sure they don't get away, that they pay for what they've done,* I begged him. *And get Zehra's number. And text me when—*

"*GO!!*"

I condensed my spirit without further delay, gasping as I found myself lying in the empty hot tub. My heart raced and sweat beaded upon my brow, though my body had spent over an hour coated in ice. I pulled myself to my feet, climbed out of the tub, and staggered to the bathroom mirror to stare at my reflection, the events on that secluded hilltop replaying in my brain.

The Lady of Erlangen knew about Teuton priests enslaving women for use in priestly training. Florian von Hollen had gone through five in two decades. And this atrocity was permitted to continue by three Keyholders, three men who held the same position as my husband. Three men meant to honor and serve their Ladies.

"Why are Black Priests the only Teuton men who call it like it is?" I asked myself, shaking my head as I reached for my glasses lying upon the sink. "The only ones who believe in a fair trade, who believe all Teutons are worthy."

In a haze, I made my way out of the bathroom and practically fell into my desk chair, my eyes locking upon Augustin's three pages about the Torstein as I retrieved a pad of notebook paper and a pen. I needed to know if that dark priest who had saved my life was responsible for punishing the slaveholders. And I had a notion that the *Eihalbe* on Thaden property might be able to find out.

Chapter Sixteen:
Steps So Small

While I worked out what to say in my note to the mystery Cursed One, I heard a light knock on the bedroom door. My ice sensed my father's energy in the private parlor—I had cast it in a wide net after having to stifle it so cruelly during my hour as a mole—so I called out, "Come in, I'm back."

My father entered and shut the door behind him. "Max and Freya are both in bed. We spent a good half hour imagining how different *Beauty and the Beast* would have gone if they were Teutons."

I laughed at that and laid my pen down, turning my office chair around. My father wore a Süddeutsche Getriebe T-shirt and baggy shorts, his dark hair peppered with gray now at the age of fifty-six. "The Beast must have been a Cursed One, alone in a castle and shunned by the living. He could have hidden in the shadows and invoked his element's illusion to appear like a monster."

My father grinned and sat down upon the bed, his gray eyes sparking with energy as he said, "Max doesn't know about Cursed Ones yet, but he envisioned the Beast as a Teuton Prince of darkness who creates shadow figures. He

160

tried to make some himself before I sent him off to his room. Pretty sure Freya's scared of what's under her bed now thanks to her brother." He winked.

I sighed and rolled my eyes on my son's behalf, though my maternal heart swelled with pride at how adept he had already become with his element, darkness, at the age of six. "I'll go kiss her goodnight again after I get this note written. All sorts of craziness going on at that conference, by the way." I turned back to my desk and retrieved the pen.

"Did they notice you there?" my father asked, sounding tense.

"Of course not. But I had to leave because they summoned Wuotan."

My father made a strangled sound, and I heard him leap to his feet. Keeping my back turned, I gave him a brief rundown of what had already happened; and I mentioned that I may need to go back to make sure the Keyholders from Innsbruck, Regensburg, and Linz got taken in for formal questioning.

"I'll go," my father declared after I finished speaking, as I wrote a sentence onto the notepad before me. "I'll make sure those bastards don't get away with it. And if they paid the families for their daughters, I'll see to it that the parents donate the exact same amount to *Selakerza*, even if it puts them in dire straits. Ach, every time I think our people can't get any worse, they prove me wrong again."

My father sounded as disgusted as I felt, and I gestured for him to make use of my balcony. "Why don't you enter the spiritual realm out there, so when you're done, you can just jump to your own balcony from the outside? Hans and I need to have a serious conversation when he gets home, anyway." I cringed.

Chuckling, my father headed for the tinted doors. "Might freak Beth out if I do that. She'll expect me to come to bed from the hallway, not from outside."

After he left, I sat looking at the note I had written, considering my words carefully. I crossed out a few things and changed them, then rewrote it on a fresh sheet of paper. *You saved my life in the Leutasch Gorge thirteen years ago. Did you save the enslaved women, too? The living priests are in an uproar.*

I did not sign my name, and I sealed the note with a piece of Scotch tape—hardly arcane in any way. I wrote it in Bayerisch since the inscrutable priest had spoken his apothem in dialect. *Time and tide wait for none but the dead.* It sounded like something Augustin would say, but I knew that Cursed One could not be my long lost love. Augustin's body had looked like a goblin from hell when he came to the present day to break our heart-bond, and the priest who had saved my life stood tall and self-assured, his voice that of a man, not a growling specter.

The *Eihalbe* on Thaden grounds deigned to appear after I had waited a good fifteen minutes, pacing around the aged silver oak and recalling the days when I had practiced using my element beneath its branches. Those were the days when having Teuton blood was simple and straightforward; though I must not display my magic before the unversed, I could use it in subtle ways to cool me down on a hot day, to chill a beverage, to rescue Vreni from high school bullies. I had wanted to use my gifts for good since I first learned about them at age thirteen, but my life had taken such startling twists that I hardly knew right from wrong anymore.

Selakerza had helped a good many people since its founding, though only two had been Teutons. Both were building their own lives now, and I had spread the word of my nonprofit's services far and wide, to any Teutons silenced in abuse. But how many of them walked among us behind masks so meticulously placed by one who could torture their hearts at will? How many would never dare to come forward for fear of losing their children, their income, their very lives?

Had I hoped for a quick reply to my message, I was to be disappointed. The *Eihalbe* said that it passed my note along the respective channels, but only silence trailed in its wake. Hans spent weeks working with Teuton authorities to enact punishment upon the offending priests. The Keyholders of Innsbruck, Regensburg, and Linz donated hefty chunks of change to their local shelters as well as to *Selakerza,* and Hans decreed that they publicly apologize for permitting slavery in an era when humanity had progressed beyond such things. The families of four of the victimized women were chastised and required to donate on behalf of their discarded daughters.

According to Hans, when Wuotan had appeared in the fire at the Keyholder of Salzburg's behest, the demon behaved quite coarsely. He scoffed at the priests' cries for justice and proclaimed that the blood of Teuton females restored his fiery river to a far greater extent than any outsider's blood could accomplish. After a bit of back and forth, Wuotan admitted that the three slaveholding Old Ones had indeed passed into eternity, but he refused to expound on the arsonist's identity. *Leave the tumult to those who follow me,* he had advised in parting.

From that I gleaned that the Old One of Innsbruck must have sacrificed his four prior slaves on the heathen altar, which prompted me to shudder in repulsion. I told Hans that Wuotan must have lied about what Teuton blood offered to his infernal river, because our people had never been in the habit of slaying our own, even two millennia ago.

My husband agreed with me and said that I should not pry too far into the secretive Black Priest's affairs. He may have played a part in shining a light onto one of our people's worst deeds, but if he preferred to remain incognito, we should respect his wishes. "Remember that it's unwise to anger a Cursed One," Hans said.

I pondered it off and on as the years went by, recalling that assertion I had seen repeated in various tomes. *Black Priests eventually lose control over the fatal gift that comes with their curse, and they shall find themselves unable to mingle with the living for fear of stopping hearts with their anger. Death consumes them from the inside out, destroying everything good inside of them, leaving them as eternal slaves of Wuotan, shackled in anger and hatred.*

Prince Otto had leveled the filial curse upon Augustin in June of 1045, nearly a year after I arrived in the past with Beth and Joel. Subsequently, a Cursed One guarded the heart of my soul for twenty-one years, and another year and a half once I returned to the present day. In all that time, Augustin's anger had never reached out to kill me, or anyone else that he did not intend to kill. He had called the death that lurked in his blood his secret weapon, useful in a fight and in hunting game. Not once had he mentioned it lashing out indiscriminately.

I recalled the epiphany that had struck me the evening when Augustin and I watched his ex-brother leading his soldiers into the besieged Muniche. Wuotan had tempted Augustin to kill Prince Otto then, to allow his deadly anger to punish the one who murdered him with the curse. And I had begged Augustin to stay his hand for fear of changing history—and turning his gift of death into a curse.

Had my assumption been correct on that lurid night so long ago? If a Black Priest killed the one who cursed them, was that the act that cut them off from the living?

Hans' take on it did nothing to appease my concern. "I don't know all the workings of Wuotan's deadly curse, but I do know that some Teutons have gone to the Black Castle and never been seen again." A non-answer, and neither Rudi nor Üwe had any further insight. I would never know the truth unless I asked Günter himself . . . or unless the elusive Cursed One stepped out of the shadows.

One autumn night in 2016, my son came to me in the dark, long after my husband had retired to bed. I had stayed up late, for it was a Friday night; and I lay upon the couch in our parlor, listening to my old Gothic favorites on my iPod and browsing *Der Weg Teutonisch* for the first time in a while. I sensed Max's presence the moment he slipped through the door, clad in a pair of gym shorts and a black tank top, his disheveled appearance suggesting that he had just crawled out of bed.

Max closed the private parlor's door behind him and stood in silence at the threshold, looking at me. I shot a glance at the nearby digital clock and saw that it was long past midnight. I removed the ear buds from my ears and rose from the couch, casting *Der Weg* aside. "What are you doing up so late, Max? Is something wrong?" I asked. I moved to his side, brushing a hand across his bangs, smoothing his mussed black hair.

"No, not really. I just couldn't sleep," Max replied, blinking at me with an expression that suggested some sort of inner turmoil. Before I could question him further, he looked toward the candles lighting the window and said, "This night has been calling to my blood, to the darkness inside me." A sigh escaped his childish lips. In his silvery eyes I saw that unique yearning for Teutonic glory, the hunger I often felt in winter, when the frost called to my ice.

I glanced toward the window myself, noting the blackness of the sky at the new moon. Then I smiled at my son and nodded my head toward the couch with the words, "I know how you feel."

Max drifted slowly in the direction I had indicated, moving as if in a dream, his darkening eyes focusing on the encyclopedia of Teuton history that lay upon the middle cushion of the couch. He murmured something softly in Teutonica—the only words I caught were *"Der Weg"*—and then he looked significantly at the door to my bedroom with the query, "Is Pappi asleep?"

I eyed him coyly, wondering how Hans' unconsciousness factored into our meeting in the night. "I'd expect so," I answered, closing my eyes for a moment to sense his quietude through our bond, peaceful repose. "He probably wonders why I haven't joined him in his dreams yet." I cocked my head at Max.

"Well, I was wondering," Max began in an uncertain voice, shifting his gaze to the floor while his toes dallied with the fibers of the carpet, "if maybe you'd tell me . . . some Teutonic tales, now . . . since this seems to be such a

Teutonic night." He looked out the window again, his eyes flashing black for an instant.

A wave of pleasure washed through me, and I gestured for my son to join me upon the couch. "Your Mutti is always up for Teutonic tales, my darling boy, no matter how late the hour. Which story would you like to hear?" I plopped onto the couch after setting the iPod and *Der Weg* onto a side table, patting the cushion beside me.

But my son did not approach the couch. Instead, he cast his eyes toward the bedroom door again, pausing for one last moment of hesitation before asking in a tentative tone, "I'd like to hear the story . . . of that painting that hangs above your computer . . . the one called *Augustin*."

My eyes bugged and my ice veiled my vision, so I laid my glasses down on the side table. "You waited to ask when Pappi can't influence my answer," I guessed.

"Pappi always looks frustrated when he sees you gazing at that painting, and you always look sad," Max noted, pointing his feet toward the couch at last, meeting my eyes with a searching expression.

I shook my head at my son's perceptiveness, and I placed my left arm around his shoulders when he sat beside me. "Oh Max, your curiosity will get you into trouble," I scolded.

He shrugged away from my embrace in a moment of pre-teen awkwardness, then muttered, "I still want to know."

I sighed and leaned back against the couch, shutting my eyes as I allowed my muses to travel deep into the past, to a time before Muniche guided my destiny. "Augustin is the man your Mutti loved long ago, before God saw fit to hand me the responsibility for this city," I related, the vagueness of those memories tugging at my contentment. Max was but twelve years old, and I had never opened the subject of my past to him before. Was he mature enough to handle the worst of it, to learn that his Mutti harbored the power to bend time?

"You mean . . . Muniche pulled you away . . . from the man you really loved?" Max whispered, tragedy lacing his tone.

I opened my eyes and turned my face toward my son's, my icy spirit sensing his distress. "We don't always get what we want in life, no matter how hard we work for it. Sometimes our callings don't match what our hearts long for, and in the end we have to claim the path before us. Muniche gave me your Pappi, and you know he's the best. She also gave me you and your sister." I smiled at Max, though deep inside my individuality wept anew, clawing at the thick bars of its cage.

"Did you . . . have the heart-bond with . . . Augustin?" he inquired, his black eyebrows crimped in contemplation. He and the other young Teutons his age had just learned of that deep commitment in their recent class. Iliana and Erika always spoke on that subject, since the two had exchanged hearts after doing the blood-transfer. The youth needed to understand that the heart-bond was a serious step, something meant for adults in loving, respectful relationships.

Icy tears began to form in my eyes, and I brushed at them and said, "I did. He cared for my heart as though it was his own, gentle, protective. It was one of the best experiences of my life." I sniffed and silently ordered myself to get a handle on my emotions. My son did not need to see me mourn a Cursed One.

"He was a priest," Max observed.

I laughed quietly through my nose. "He was. That's why he wears the robes in Üwe's painting."

"And Muniche broke you up from him." Max's hands fidgeted with his shorts, his brow furrowed on my behalf. Before I could repeat my earlier statement about destiny, his shining eyes gazed into mine as he asked, "Is he still alive?"

I felt as though a knife had pierced my heart. My right hand rubbed my chest instinctively, old anguish groaning from the grave. I could not tell my son that my one true love was a Black Priest. All he knew of Günter was that he was an undead ghoul whose blood had been cut off from the Teuton people—the basics. "No. He's not . . . still alive," I murmured, shaking my head slowly.

Max leaned against my left side, and I gathered him into an embrace. "I'm sorry, Mutti," he said in a muffled voice, "I'm sorry you can't be . . . with Augustin."

"It's fine, my darling boy, it's fine," I assured him, my ice stretching forth to comfort his desolate darkness. "I'm glad Muniche chose me, actually. Augustin was a very broken man, not a Christian."

"Was he atheist?" Max looked up at my face again, his eyes damp with tears.

"He was more agnostic, I'd say. He knew God exists but chose to reject Him. I'm much better off with your Pappi, with you and Freya. I don't regret turning away . . . when Muniche's spirit made her home within my heart."

I had never told a more ridiculous lie, though I tried day by day to believe it. With each passing year it became easier, my devotion to Hans growing ever deeper, though his aging body and dwindling stamina often sent my thoughts deep into melancholy. But his spirit remained resilient as we continued to work together to improve the lives of those in our community.

That same year on Christmas Eve, I slipped outside after reading the story of Christ's birth in front of the large tree in the family room, its branches concealing a slew of presents waiting for morning. Clad in naught but pajamas and a bathrobe, I strolled through the freshly fallen snow into the trees, my course set for the trickling stream.

Unexpectedly, the *Eihalbe* waylaid me on the trail to hand me a slip of paper, an answer to my note from five years ago: *The living had best hold the dead at a distance. But if they perpetuate crimes of a ghastly nature, it is my prerogative to effect lasting change.*

Chapter Seventeen

The First Tragedy

Late that night, as Hans and I prepared for bed, I passed him the note the fairy had given me. Then I headed for the bathroom to brush my teeth and hair, noticing a few new strands of gray while I did so. The past few years had been difficult for my career. My father had stepped back from Süddeutsche Getriebe in early 2014, and despite his hopes that I would eagerly take his place, I chose to focus my efforts on *Selakerza*. But I retained my part-time position in administration as my cousins Leon and Lothar took over the drive business, both of whom required too much oversight. It was a constant struggle to balance my two jobs with my children's classes and family life.

Something had occurred to me when I read the mysterious Cursed One's note. It had certainly come from him, for he had written it on the back of the letter I sent five years earlier. He did not sign it, but he wrote his cursive in the old style—someone who had learned to write long ago. That Black Priest was out there in the ether, apart from the Teuton community . . . and he stood against the enslavement of women . . . and he was *not* Günter Setzer.

"So apparently that Cursed One has some morals left in his black heart," I remarked when I reentered the bedroom, nodding at my husband.

Hans had stretched himself upon our bed, his face weary from our children's exuberance, his eyes shut. He sat up against the headboard when I spoke and looked toward me. "I certainly hope you won't allow your heart to pine for another dead ghoul."

I frowned at my husband as I crawled into bed beside him. "I haven't pined for Günter yet, have I? You're the one who holds my heart. I just think it's interesting to know there's a Cursed One skulking in the shadows who takes a stand for morality."

"I wouldn't assume such things if I were you," Hans said, eyeing me in the dull light from my glitter lamp. We still used it as our nightlight; it sat upon my bedside table, where it had been for nearly twenty years now.

"Well, apparently this mystery Cursed One *isn't* Günter Setzer," I pointed out, glancing toward my desk, where Hans had left the note. "And technically that means you're off the hook for finding him a successor. He already has one. And an old one, judging by his handwriting."

My Keyholder made a scoffing sound. "If the man has kept his existence under wraps all this time, I highly doubt he'd be willing to offer himself up for Günter's purposes. He's likely been on earth longer than the *Unmensch*. Wuotan has kept the two apart, and I don't think that'll change anytime soon."

"The *Unmensch?*" I raised my eyebrows at my husband. The word meant *monster* or *cruel person,* and it prompted me to envision torture chambers. "Didn't know Günter had a nickname."

"An appropriate one for a torture artist."

"Right. But the point is, Günter isn't the only Cursed One on the earth, and that means he can enter eternity if he and the other one come to an agreement." I gave Hans a pointed look. "And that means you totally *don't* have to curse our son or persuade anyone else to curse their son."

Hans sighed and leaned his head back, closing his eyes once more. "Swanie, please don't entertain notions about bringing two Black Priests together. The one who saved your life in the gorge isn't as noble as you think. When my peers and I sought out the person who offered Regensburg's Old One his final slave, we found her. But he'd gotten to her first, and he cut her eyes out."

Horror rushed through me, and an icy sheen crept over my vision as I put a hand to my mouth. "He *cut* her *eyes* out?!"

"Black Priests operate under Wuotan's laws, not ours," Hans reminded me. "Therefore, it's best to hold them at a distance, just like the note said."

That tidbit brought a fresh wave of specters to haunt me. I began to wonder whether all Cursed Ones ultimately went mad at Wuotan's hands. Demons crafted torments that human beings could not fathom, and I feared again for Augustin's soul, as he faced over four centuries of devilish chastisements. Without someone to remind him of love and goodness, would he fall into hell's bowels like his modern counterparts?

In the subsequent spring, the day came for me to give my lesson on the filial curse to the Teuton children ages twelve through fourteen. That was the first time I ever discussed the subject formally with my son Max, as well as two of my friends' children, Sophia and Lukas. Obviously I presented the topic as someone who had learned of its horrors from the writings of history, leaving out the deep connection I once had with the greatest Cursed One of all, Augustin von Bayern.

Beginning with the creation of the curse in the early days of Christianity, I related the tale of the four priests of Wuotan who refused to convert, whose clans chose to force them into the deadly level of the Teutonic priesthood. I emphasized the results of that wretched curse—the death and forced slavery, the loss of control over what gifts Wuotan could offer, and the constant longing for something forever gone—life. I argued that it was murder to level the filial curse on anyone, since a Cursed One must die, either from the spell itself or afterward, through sacrifice.

I hoped that through my discourse I could convince my pupils to never attempt to curse a relative, no matter how much the situation seemed to demand it. That spell should never have been written, the worst treason any Teuton could commit against their own blood. I even mentioned that the current Black Priest was a mad villain who bred Teutonic women for gain.

After the other children had gone, my son came to me in the music room, where I sat listening to Freya practice the piano. Her teacher was trying to develop her skills at memorization; she currently worked on Bach's Prelude in C. Max slipped into the room unseen and crouched beside my chair, invoking the shadows to conceal him from his sister, who hated having him "listen in" on her practicing.

"Mutti," he whispered to me in a voice so low I had to summon my ice to sharpen my hearing. "Are priests the only ones who can survive the filial curse?"

I looked down at him as I sat with a tumbler of wine in one hand, seeing what appeared to be curiosity mingled with trepidation in his silvery eyes. "History implies that very thing," I murmured to him, "and that means anyone who curses a son or daughter who hasn't studied for the priesthood commits blatant murder."

Max shuddered and wrapped his arms around himself. "Why is the spell for that curse still in *Der Weg?* Shouldn't it be taken out since it kills people?"

"That's a question you'll want to ask your Pappi," I responded, for I tended to agree with my son's opinion. "Maybe priests think it needs to be left on the table, to make sure no Black Priest ends up trapped on earth forever. Someone like that could initiate an apocalypse, or genocide."

"But still, I don't think—"

Freya's abrupt screech cut off whatever Max was about to say. She had spun upon the piano bench to face me and caught sight of her brother—dark energy flashed in her irises. "*MUTTI! He can't be in here! Make him leave!!*"

"Keep practicing," I ordered my daughter, gesturing for Max to depart. "He just had a question about the class I taught today. And you've got twelve minutes left before you're done." Freya eyeballed Max with a nasty look as he muttered an apology and headed for the kitchen. And I relaxed back into the chair and took a sip of wine, grateful for my son's sensible view of the filial curse.

Time passed, and my children grew older. Max's interests ranged from soccer—he played goalie for a local team—to guitar, a pastime that kept me caught up on newer sounds, though he was a fan of rock and metal, too. Freya spent her free time playing video games and creating odd electronic contraptions from spare parts, trying to run them using her element alone.

She faced an unfortunate rash of bullying in school once her brother had moved ahead, for she was not skilled at sports or at classes in general. Nearly every morning, Freya begged Hans and me for permission to use her dark energy against the jerks who harassed her. We forbade her from invoking magic before outsiders, and my Keyholder warned her that if she disobeyed, she would be required to take a dose of dusky spurge each morning to suppress her element.

Beth gained traction as an indie author of contemporary romance, her sweet tales launching her into bestseller charts. After my father semi-retired, they had moved their family—which included two sons now, Connor and Logan—south to Mittenwald, forsaking city life for the country. Whenever we visited them, I would see signs for the Leutasch Gorge on the road into Austria . . . and my muses would range from the Torstein, safe within my right hip, to the mysterious priest who had saved my life, rescued three subjugated women, and cut out the eyes of one who discarded her relative like trash.

I grew closer with Zehra and several other Teuton Ladies as the years went by. We occasionally met to discuss the progress made in our local communities, for the Ladies belonging to younger generations agreed with many of my assessments. While we continued to stress the importance of preserving Teutonic magic for the future, we backed off from the traditional emphasis on blood purity. Teutons who chose to be mothers were still exalted, and those who could not conceive were welcomed to contribute in other ways. Zehra started a class on how to survive the blood-transfer, since she had done it herself, offering her wisdom to any outsiders interested in joining our people.

Life had settled into a semi-pleasant routine despite everyone's separate personal trials. Sometimes I even lulled myself into the belief that I truly belonged here in the twenty-first century, *Leitalra* of München, wife to my aging but faithful Keyholder. It seemed that Wuotan had forgotten his vendetta against me, or maybe he considered my suicide in 1985 sufficient payment for dabbling with time travel. No dark consequences had arisen yet from Hans' pledge to Günter or from Beth's. The priests had eliminated the three rogue conclaves that perpetuated slavery, and *Selakerza* provided resources for domestic violence survivors daily.

But I shall never forget that night in August 2018 when peace forsook my family permanently. It was a Friday night, and Hans had already gone to bed while I sat in our private parlor, reading Beth's most recent novel on my e-reader. Then my smart phone rang, extracting me from a fantasy land of seashells and young love. I laid the e-reader aside and reached for my phone, my forehead wrinkling at the sight of Marga's number. I had not heard from her in years now, not since she had moved out of the city to live with her boyfriend.

"Swanie?" Marga's voice scratched at my ear when I answered the phone, her tone sounding harried. "Something's happened . . . and . . . I . . . it's not . . . what it looks like . . . ."

"You're breaking up," I said, checking my reception, which was fine. "What's going on?" I stood up anyway and paced toward the window, its panes open to invite the evening breeze into the room.

I heard more static, and then her voice came through. "Sorry. There's not a lot of service here at the Plansee."

"The Plansee?" I repeated, looking out at the back gardens. That was a lake in Austria, one frequented by the wealthy—something Marga was not. My father and Beth were on a yacht there now, vacationing with one of his friends.

"I have to tell you . . . something awful happened a few hours ago," Marga said, her voice still sounding strange. "Your Pappi and your cousin . . . were found unresponsive in . . . police have been called. People are saying—"

"*What?*" I cut her off as my ice erupted in my veins, hardening my fingers.

"Suicide. But I don't . . . ."

"*What?!*" I yelled, my heart dropping into my gut.

"Sorry, I . . . ." More static on the phone, and then the connection was cut. In a daze, I brought the phone down from my ear, staring at its screen in shock. *Beth and my Pappi . . . are dead? But why? It can't be. No, it can't be.*

Somehow, I managed to wake my husband, who took the initiative to call the police department nearest to the Plansee. While I sat in shock on our bed with my arms wrapped around my body, my ice shedding traces onto the blanket, Hans told me a tale that completely shattered me. My father and his wife were found dead in their cabin on the yacht, having detached themselves from the partygoers on deck shortly after lunchtime. A paramedic on the yacht had tried in vain to resuscitate them. By the time the boat came into port, it was far too late to save either of them. Hans had ordered a private autopsy, since he could not fathom that my father and Beth would have any motivation to kill themselves.

They were parents, with successful businesses and a happy home life. Their sons were so young—only six and four years old. In fact, they were with Beth's parents right now, enjoying a beach holiday in New Jersey. Their world was about to crash and burn, as mine had done when I learned of my mother's death while crafting a lifelong friendship with my cousin.

"This just can't be real," I whispered when Hans came to sit beside me, his fiery arms binding me to him. "How could this happen? What does anyone have against my Pappi, against his wife?" I began to sob, tears of solid ice falling from my eyes. I remembered my father's promise to me after I faced Wuotan's wrath at college. *I'm always here for you, and I always will be.*

Hans comforted me gently until exhaustion cast me into slumber, and in our dream world we discussed the implications. If evidence came forth to prove that my father and Beth had not committed suicide but had been murdered, then we would need to open an investigation. We would also have to scrutinize my father's business dealings and financial status in an effort to determine what might have prompted such a thing. I asked Hans to hire a P.I. firm to probe everything from top to bottom, starting with each person aboard the yacht.

Why had Marga been there? Was it pure chance?

We also mourned on behalf of Connor and Logan, who would return from their U.S. holiday to attend their parents' funeral. Beth and my father had named Onkel Jens and Aunt Linda as their guardians, so the two young boys were about to be uprooted from their homeland. I knew that Beth's author business would pass to me, though I had no experience with that field. I told Hans that this might be the final blow for Süddeutsche Getriebe and me; I could not run three corporations at once. "We'll be picking up the pieces for a while," my Keyholder noted, "and I'll do all that I can to help you. Üwe and Rudi would be glad to offer their services, too."

Subsequent months chugged by in a hazy shroud. I tried to speak eulogies for my father and Beth at their joint funeral, but I collapsed in tears and could not finish reading my notes. My son stepped up to do so on my behalf, his own voice breaking as he added memories of camping trips with his Opa, baking cupcakes with his Oma. Freya cried in the pew throughout the ceremony. She had loved her Opa dearly, for he taught her most of what she knew about her element.

The investigations showed that my father and cousin had died due to an excessive amount of dusky spurge in their bloodstreams. The business and financial probes revealed nothing amiss—the investigator said that my father's records were the cleanest he had seen in his entire career. And dusky spurge was a poison unknown to outsiders, who saw the plant as a worthless weed, not knowing of its ancient uses—to temporarily suppress elemental magic . . . or to still the heart when used in excess.

Had one of my own people—or perhaps someone with a hatred of magic—caused my loved ones' deaths?

Chapter Eighteen

An Insidious Threat

On a Thursday toward the end of November 2018, I spent the afternoon in my private office at Süddeutsche Getriebe, packing up the last of my things so I could vacate my position in the company that very Friday. Although I would retain my place on the board, it was high time for me to relinquish the corporate world and focus my efforts on *Selakerza* and Beth's books instead.

The past few months had shown me the complexity of the indie author racket. I spent several hours each evening with eyeballs on her slew of ads, trying to keep them profitable. I needed to write an official announcement to her newsletter subscribers, too, to let them know that their goddess of romance had graduated to the heavenly realm. Thankfully, she had scheduled three months' worth of emails before her passing—Beth had always been organized—but those were about to run out.

I sighed a little as I unplugged my decorative fountain, as its trickle that whispered so tenderly to my ice tapered off into silence. I would have to call one of the delivery boys to get it cleaned up and boxed; it was too heavy for me to carry down to my car. Several weeks ago, Leon, Lothar, and I had cleaned out my father's office, with all the awards his company had achieved and the prototypes he had introduced into the drive market. Now, no one who held the Thaden name remained in this business that had been my Opa Hobart's pride and joy.

Leon and Lothar will keep it running. They have to, I told myself, standing in the center of my office with my hands on my hips, my eyes passing over what items I had deemed meaningful. *Connor or Logan may want to get into this business one day, or even my son Max. The Thaden line hasn't gone extinct.*

The intercom on my desk buzzed abruptly, indicating a message from my personal secretary, who would work under Lothar starting Monday morning. She informed me that three envoys from a northern German corporation wished to confer with me about some pressing business matter, something that may grant Süddeutsche Getriebe an economic boost.

My eyeballs rolled toward the ceiling as I headed for my desk and pressed the button. "Shouldn't they extend their offer to Leon?" I said. He was the acting CEO, as he had been since my father's retirement. I had spent the last six years on the outskirts of management.

"He's out with a client, and they claim their offer is time sensitive," came the reply. I sighed again and put my hands on my hips, trying to bring my thoughts to the present. Süddeutsche Getriebe had struggled a bit since my father's death, and as his representative, I ought to at least consider the offer. So I told my secretary to send them to me, for I had closed multiple deals before. What was one more?

Within a few minutes, I rose from behind my desk to receive my callers—three men clad in business attire, two tall, one of medium height, all appearing between the ages of thirty and forty-five. I nodded at them and introduced myself, speaking a few words of welcome on behalf of my business and München, since my secretary had mentioned that these men were visitors from the north. I apologized for the state of my office—boxes stacked everywhere and naught but a single extra chair stuffed in the corner beside the door—and admitted that they had caught me at a transition point.

The medium-sized man standing in the midst of his larger companions took several steps forward to bow with a courteous smile, pearly yet crooked teeth evident beneath a bushy auburn mustache. "Thank you very much, Frau von Thaden. I am ashamed to say that I didn't expect such a gracious reception, after interrupting your duties so suddenly." His blue-green eyes seemed to appraise me with a strange combination of interest and mockery. He spoke in a gravelly voice, his German otherwise perfect.

The intensity of the brown-haired spokesman's regard disturbed me, but I determined not to show it, to conduct myself with proper decorum—though I had noticed that my caller had not introduced himself or his companions. "I'm always prepared to hear the proposals of colleagues, especially from those who wish to accomplish business in the drive industry. Your presence has not inconvenienced me in the slightest, I assure you." I smiled brilliantly at my three callers, catching sight of the tiniest smirk tainting the thick lips of the blond hulk standing to my right.

I had not yet retaken my seat, and now I silently pondered whether I ought to suggest that the spokesman make use of the single chair that remained in my office. Boxes—some already upon dollies—lined the wall to my left, while my silent fountain stood to my right, before the large window with the view of downtown München. I had plastered the façade of gentility upon my face and deportment at this point, for while I felt somewhat annoyed by my guests' ambiguous behavior, I saw no cause for serious concern. Conversely, I wanted to draw this tête-à-tête out to its very end, if only to discern a means to mock my visitors, vocally or just in my mind.

As I opened my mouth to invite one them to sit, the spokesman finally introduced himself as Markus Oster-mann, head of a group known as NVH. He also mentioned the names of his comrades—Emil and Arne—but I hardly heard him, for I was too busy trying to identify the term

'NVH.' I had never heard those letters in succession before, in business or anywhere else.

Herr Ostermann had finished speaking and handed me a business card. I gave it a cursory glance, noticing a P.O. box in Dresden listed as the group's address, along with a website. The card did not reveal the identity of 'NVH,' but I casually urged the spokesman to sit, so we may turn our attention to their proposal. That should give me a better view of what this group represented.

As I settled myself upon my own chair, I thumbed a button underneath my desk, activating the hidden sound recorder in my office, so I could study the proceedings more thoroughly later. My guests were already on camera as it was, but I had a hunch that I had better keep tabs on the conversation. Herr Ostermann had dragged the single seat forward to the center of the office, situating himself there to have a better view of me; I judged that immediately. The others planted themselves behind him, the bald one near the boxes, the blond near the window.

Opening the topic of commerce, I inquired whether their interests lay in the domestic or foreign markets, assuring them that I could assist them with either. Herr Ostermann's lips curled into a wry smile, and he cleared his throat, pressing his fingertips together in his lap and addressing me in an apologetic tone. "I fear, Frau von Thaden, that our offer has little to do with the drive industry."

This did not entirely surprise me, but I pulled my eyebrows together and said, "If that's the case, Herr Ostermann, I must admit that your decision to speak with me here puzzles me. If your interest is in my nonprofit—"

"Our offer does involve Süddeutsche Getriebe," my charge interrupted, his propriety escaping him, "just not in the production sector, *per se.*"

Now we were getting somewhere. "Do continue," I requested, leaning back in my chair and folding my hands.

"My colleagues and I are considering making an investment in your company," Herr Ostermann said, looking as though he had no suspicion of Süddeutsche Getriebe's sagging earnings. "A considerable amount of capital lies at our disposal, and we'd like to put it to use in the Bavarian market." His blue-green eyes appraised me.

I began to wonder whether these three men were involved with illegal smuggling; I had dealt with enough tainted offers over the years. Herr Ostermann's casual reference to the Bavarian market was unusual. Why would businessmen from some northern metropolis wish to plant their currency into the southern German market? "May I inquire after the source of your interest in Süddeutsche Getriebe?" I eyed my visitors in speculation.

The bald man coughed into his elbow at my query, and Herr Ostermann's friendly but intense eyes darkened a tad. I waited, lifting a pen from my desk and fiddling with it, trying to give the impression of vague interest. The spokesman cleared his throat again, then completely changed the subject. "We've heard that you hold considerable influence in this Bavarian capital, and not merely as a representative of a lucrative company." He squinted at me, and his bushy mustache twitched.

My mind raced now, trying to come up with a logical end to this . . . a reason . . . a rationale. The man did not seem interested in *Selakerza,* and the only other "influence" I had in the local community had no connections to either of my careers. *What could my position as Lady of Muniche mean to these businessmen?*

I said nothing in response to Herr Ostermann's assessment save a simple "Oh?" Best to pretend that I did not follow his implications.

But the spokesman was not fooled, and neither were his colleagues. Both of them straightened their posture, as if in preparation for some sort of conflict. My eyes darted unconsciously toward the silent fountain, my spirit seeking relief in the camaraderie of water. In the same instant, I deduced that none of the three men here before me were Teutons. Their spirits all felt incredibly empty.

Herr Ostermann responded to my interjection with brutal frankness. "Yes, Frau von Thaden, for you are the

Lady of Muniche, a highly respected woman in the esoteric circle known as the Teutonic brotherhood."

A choked squeak escaped my throat at that label. The fool made it sound like some freaky Masonic order, or maybe the Illuminati. I spent a few moments regaining my composure, scratching the tip of my pen on one of the papers lying at the edge of my desk. *Outsiders who know about Teutonic customs . . . .*

A new realization struck me, and I raised my eyes to my questioner's, inquiring blandly in Sächsisch dialect, "May I ask how such private matters relate to my business, or why they might interest patrons from the north?"

This caught all of them off guard. Both of the bulky men fidgeted on their feet, glancing at their leader, who looked quite displeased. Thus far he had spoken his German with no trace of a Saxon accent, and still I had blown his cover. "I did not know . . . that you are fluent in Sächsisch," he said in the same dialect, rubbing at his mustache.

I smiled beguilingly, basking in my momentary victory. "I speak a number of German dialects. It's a hobby of mine." And it was also useful for business.

"Indeed." Herr Ostermann appeared even more disturbed. He thrust his hands into the pockets of his pin-striped pants before glancing once toward Emil, the blond.

"You have not yet answered my question," I reminded my charge, flipping the pen between my fingers as though it were a knife. My guard was up, and my element lurked in traces throughout my veins.

"That is true, and I suppose there's no point in further delay." The Saxon huffed, the disgruntlement on his face transforming into irritation. He leveled his blue-green eyes upon me and stated, "My colleagues and I are highly interested in preserving the heritage of all German peoples, and thereupon keeping all records correct. We've encountered some irregularities regarding your group in particular, and we believe you may be able to assist us." He gave me a withering look, and the bald man cracked his knuckles.

I frowned, working to shove aside the nervousness his words invoked. "If I understand you correctly," I began, maintaining my show of ignorance for the moment, "your group—NVH, you named it—wishes to offer Süddeutsche Getriebe a monetary sum for information you believe I could grant you on Teuton history? Or perhaps it's in the 'esoteric' matters that your interest lies?" I smirked in spite of myself, wondering what these three Saxons would think if I froze the still waters of the fountain right before their eyes.

"That is essentially correct. As Lady of Muniche, you undoubtedly have greater insight into the traditions of your people than most . . . or rather, than the uninitiated." Herr Ostermann's eyes narrowed.

I almost laughed again. "I fear that you ought to have brought your questions before the Teuton Council of München."

"This discussion has no place for scorn on your part, Frau von Thaden, for I speak of a very serious matter." A sneer appeared beneath the Saxon's auburn mustache as he explained, "No *priest* could satisfy our interests, for no priest living today has dabbled with the mysteries of time travel."

It took all of my control to keep my ice at bay as I stared at these three Saxons before me—menacing enemies, it appeared, adversaries who wanted to harness that deadly power that I kept so carefully under wraps. But I managed to chuckle, laying the pen down and looking gravely into the eyes of the spokesman. "Perhaps you've misinterpreted my children's classes on Teutonic history, or the subjects discussed on my internet forum. There are countless tales in the lore of my people that are nothing more than imaginary stories for children, fables to teach them life lessons."

"On the contrary, I aver that this matter of time travel is not a legend. It is a potential that far outweighs any twenty-first century technology, and you are the first human being to have controlled that power in over five centuries." Herr Ostermann's eyes glittered, and the blond gave a satisfied sigh.

I blinked at them, trying to figure out *how* this random group of Saxons had gotten wind of the Teutonic rites of time travel. And more, *how* had they connected this sorcery with me? As though guessing my thoughts, Herr Ostermann went on, "Our sources are quite sound, I assure you. And may I remind you that we came here to offer you substantial payment for your secret means of time travel. Such an incomparable power should not be held by a mere—"

"If your sources all stem from the internet, a den rife with untruth—" I cut my opponent off before he could finish his sentence. Under no circumstances did I wish to be slapped with modern-day chauvinism, from an outsider to boot.

"Oh, we have far more trustworthy sources than that online rubbish," Herr Ostermann interrupted me in turn, scowling.

"This conversation goes no further until you reveal your sources," I shot back, wracking my brain to recall every person in the twenty-first century who knew about my journeys. Who had betrayed me? *Hans . . . Erika . . . Üwe . . . Joel . . . Marga . . . .*

"You know our source, Frau von Thaden, and he knows you." Herr Ostermann laughed a throaty laugh. "He has scorned you more than once, each time you've summoned the arcane gateway."

I gasped, and this time I could not stop my eyes from turning an icy blue. Herr Ostermann continued speaking in a tone loaded with ridicule, but I hardly heard his words. I caught just a few snippets *. . . has a vendetta . . . forsook him long ago . . . disapproves of your success . . . .*

Images from a millennium ago appeared before my eyes: *the Saxons getting hold of Prince Otto's song, using it to pull half-demon warriors from ages past—an immortal force to destroy the Teuton kingdom forever.* Was *this* the price I must pay for using Wuotan's sorcery? Did that wretched demon want to eliminate the Teuton people for good? A tenacious resolve began to coalesce in my heart, a sacred pledge on the honor of my city. *I will not bow to Wuotan's minions.*

When I focused again on Herr Ostermann, I saw that he had pulled a small leather booklet from somewhere within his suit coat. "As I stated earlier," he was saying, "we're prepared to pay you any sum you require, in any sort of currency, even in land or industrial investments. Our resources are at your disposal the very moment you relinquish possession of the Torstein to us."

That struck me for another blow, though I suppose it should not have. If these thugs had consulted with Wuotan about my adventures, they would know of the Torstein . . . *but what of the song?*

I kept quiet for a lengthy interval, attempting to sort my thoughts, to solidify my resolution. I would never give some group of Saxon purists the Torstein, even if they paid me several trillions. If Süddeutsche Getriebe fell prey to the ill will of investors and all of my assets perished in flames, still I would refuse. If *Selakerza* could no longer extend resources to those in need, I still must protect that stone at any cost. It could be used to eliminate Teuton blood from the earth.

I rose from my chair, placing both hands upon my desk as I addressed my opponent in a firm tone. "Let me make this clear to you, Herr Ostermann, and you may pass it on to the rest of your cronies in NVH and elsewhere. No circumstance, and no sum of money, will convince me to reveal the mysteries of time travel to the brutes who ravaged my city under Wuotan's direction one thousand years ago, and afterward chose to write that vile chapter out of history. Muniche shall not bow to your machinations a second time. You speak now to her Lady, not to some pious coward whose loyalties were too celestial for earthly good." I glowered at the three men, watching incredulity creep across their faces one by one.

The spokesman stood with a cursory nod, leaving his chair aptly displaced. Herr Ostermann placed his leather booklet back inside his coat and straightened his lapels with the remark, "I had hoped you would prove more cooperative, Frau von Thaden. I fear that we may have to resort to more persuasive methods to obtain our objective." He bowed once toward me and turned for the door, ushering his cronies to precede him.

I narrowed my eyes as they headed for the hallway. When Herr Ostermann reached the door I called after him, "Should I construe that final sentence of yours as a threat?"

"Interpret it however you wish," he replied smoothly, pausing at the doorway to regard me with an inscrutable expression. "My colleagues and I will venture to refine our offer and contact you later. In the meantime," he concluded, raising one thick eyebrow at me, "I suggest that you tread carefully . . . *Leitalra*." A moment later he vanished into the hallway.

It took me some fifteen minutes to sit down again after they had gone. When I did, I glanced at my right hip, thinking of that numinous rock that rested beneath my flesh.

How seriously should I take this new development? For too long I had banished the memories, preferring to relish what glories the twenty-first century offered—that sense of belonging as a Keyholder's wife, pride in my children, contentment in what I offered to those in need.

Now, visions of the past troubled me, dropping a fresh batch of darkness while my family reeled from my father's and cousin's deaths. *What if . . . what if the NVH had a hand in that? What if some Saxon thug crept into their cabin to interrogate them about time travel, and poisoned them afterward? Neither of them knew where I've hidden the Torstein.*

After switching off the sound recorder in my office, I retrieved my smartphone from a drawer and dialed the Thaden house. My husband answered on the second ring, about his business as usual, and I greeted him with the words, "Hans? I think we have a problem."

Chapter Nineteen

Persuasive Methods

During the winter, Hans and Üwe dove into extensive research about the NVH group, though their efforts uncovered much less than we hoped. Their website told us that the letters 'NVH' stood for *Norddeutscher Verein Historikers*—the North German Historical Society. Apparently, this was a cover for a cabal of Saxon men obsessed with the horrid truths of the past, particularly the poor relations between Saxons and Teutons in the Middle Ages. This group had not forgotten those tales that had long been officially suppressed, and it seemed that they had also not forgotten how to invoke a certain demon.

As for Herr Ostermann, we found little about him aside from reports on his extensive wealth and investments. Both Hans and Üwe advised vigilance on my part. They applauded my refusal to give the NVH concrete information, suggesting in addition that I must continue to keep my adventures with the Torstein a secret, even from the other members of München's council. Hans reminded me privately that at least no one knew the current location of the rock aside from him and me. We swore to each other that we would not disclose that information to anyone.

Whether the NVH had any connection to my relatives' deaths was anyone's guess. Although Üwe uncovered a list of the group's members, none of them had been on the yacht when my father and Beth met their doom. I noted that since Herr Ostermann had presented his financial offer as their first effort to collect the stone, the NVH may be more likely to toss money around for forbidden knowledge rather than murder those who might harbor it. Hans and Üwe did not seem so sure. Üwe remarked that they had enough capital to hire professionals to commit such crimes and cover the traces.

The one thing that simmered in the back of my mind that winter, as I shifted my focus from the drive industry to *Selakerza* and Beth's legacy, was that Marga had disappeared into the ether after calling me on that awful night. I thought I saw her at the funeral, sitting alone toward the back of the church; but once the service ended, she had gone. Her number was disconnected, and both of her emails came up as invalid. She had not signed onto the Teuton forum in nearly a decade, though few users did these days thanks to social media.

I asked my friends whether they knew Marga's address or had any contact with her recently, and all of them replied negatively. Ina—once her best friend—said the last time they had gotten together was the previous winter. "She seemed to be drifting away from Teutonic life," Ina told me over the phone. "I think she was starting to feel left out, with the rest of us pairing off and having kids, and you being Muniche's Lady and teaching those classes. She got with some guy who works in a warehouse, and not to judge, but she can do better."

This news would not have bothered me had I not wondered what brought her to the Plansee the same day that my father and Beth died. As far as I knew, she still worked in medical billing. If her current partner was a warehouse worker, the two of them together would not earn enough to warrant an invitation onto a yacht. Unless Marga's boyfriend had connections with its owner?

I asked Hans to visit Marga's father in early January, to find out whether he had any knowledge of the NVH or of his daughter's whereabouts. The man had retired to Freising, Marga's birthplace, and his wife had passed away not long after Hans and I married. My Keyholder returned that evening with a look of pity. He said that Marga's father had not heard from his daughter since she hooked up with her latest boyfriend. He thought the man might have run afoul of the law at some point, but his daughter believed him to be faultless.

As the days went by without evidence connecting the NVH with my relatives' deaths, I began to relinquish my suspicions there. Part of me suspected that Hans and Üwe wished to link the NVH with those losses to simplify things. A cabal of power-hungry Saxons wanted the Torstein and had offered a vague threat—reason enough to tread cautiously, to question every connection.

Truth to be told, it was a relief to work primarily from home and leave my father's business to others. At *Selakerza* I need not fear some odd businessman probing my knowledge of time travel. Vreni always greeted me with a smile when I spent the morning there, the red fire in her spirit assuring me that I was not alone. Rudi and Üwe stopped by regularly to do maintenance and grounds keeping, their presence quelling my anxiety.

After four months without further word from the NVH—right when I had begun to relax once more—Hans and I received news that tore me to pieces all over again. Traudl and Mane had taken Lukas and Selina to Italy for the Easter holidays, visiting a wide range of attractions along with Traudl's parents, my Tante Lena and Onkel Beni. Traudl had messaged me a picture of the children with the Leaning Tower of Pisa in the background, both of them posed as if they held the entire edifice on their backs. Just two days later, we learned that all six had fallen victim to a drive-by shooting at an outdoor restaurant.

The word came from Mane's father, his voice grim and dejected. Lukas was the only survivor, but he was currently in a coma at an Italian hospital, one bullet lodged in his spine. If he woke, he would probably never walk again. My son broke down in tears when I told him, for Lukas was one of his best friends; they both played on the same soccer team. I held him against my chest as he choked out a few phrases of sorrow, his grief gradually transitioning into something more like resentment.

"Do you think . . . do you think it was the mafia?" Max wiped black tears onto his sleeve and blinked at me, pain evident in his eyes.

"We don't know yet," I answered gently, reaching out to capture some of his tears. They were a lovely liquid darkness, leaving no stain on my skin. "I don't think the mafia would have anything against Traudl and Mane, anyway. It may have just been random, senseless violence."

"As soon as Lukas can come back to München, I need to see him," Max said, sniffing and backing away from me. "Even if he's not awake. I need to see him."

"We'll all go see him as soon as he's home," I promised my son, my shoulders drooping under what felt like never-ending burdens. If Wuotan wished to saddle me with grief, he had certainly succeeded. I spent hours crying out to God in prayer as I prepared to face yet another tragic funeral. Had I experienced too many years of plenty, of peace and progress? Must I sit back and watch as a helpless observer while my dearest relatives left orphans behind, while innocent children had their lives upended?

To my dismay, another horrific event took the lives of two of my friends on the night before Mane's and Selina's joint funeral. Fonsi pulled me aside before the ceremony began, his eyes shadowed with a combination of exhaustion and heartache. "I'm so sorry," I murmured to him automatically as I directed Max and Freya to follow their father toward a pew. "Mane was a good man. He didn't deserve this."

I assumed that Fonsi's distressed appearance was on Mane's behalf, since the two had been close friends throughout their lives. But he gestured for me to follow him to a corner beside a confession booth at the back of the church, his dark gray eyes passing over the people drifting in as though they were mere drops in the ocean. It suddenly occurred to me that Ina was not with him. He was here alone, dressed in black from chin to the ground, the aura of his light agitating the air around us.

"Fonsi . . . where are Ina and the kids?" I lowered my voice and leaned on the wooden edge of the confession booth, my instincts screaming that something sinister waited on the horizon.

Fonsi shut his eyes for a moment, and I saw moisture welling around them as he took a measured breath. "Last night we went to a concert. All four of us. At a local venue . . . it was Lea's choice. She loves synthpop." Anguish broke across his face, and he opened his eyes to stare into mine, light sizzling deep within.

I blinked at Fonsi, trying to figure out how a family outing could inspire such agony. "Something happened to her . . . at the concert?" I guessed, bracing myself for the worst. Had an abuser drugged her drink?

"I stayed at the bar the whole time since I'm not into that stuff," Fonsi said, running one hand restlessly through his graying brown hair. "Lea and Alison were dancing with the crowd in front of the stage. Ina—" He choked, his visage twisting in a way that reminded me of my son.

"Ina had gone to the bathroom. And while she was in there, someone . . . I didn't see it happen and neither did Alison . . . it was too dark in the crowd . . . but somehow, someone slit Lea's throat. She collapsed to the floor and died *right in front of her sister.*"

I felt as though we were surrounded by ghosts. My lips parted in shock, and I put my right hand to my throat, an instinctive reaction. "Someone *slit* Lea's *throat?*" Nausea churned in my stomach. Violent crime was rare in Germany.

"She died in a pool of her own blood. I didn't know anything happened until Alison pushed her way out of the crowd, screaming. They stopped the show, called the police, did a bunch of interviews. Not even the people on stage saw who did it. I just . . . ach, Swanie, I just feel so helpless. I don't know who killed my girl."

Fonsi shrank back against the wall, crossing his arms and shaking his head. I sensed that a hug or gentle words would not soothe him; he seemed to have the need to bare his heart before a supportive listener. So I waited with my right hand resting against the confession booth, trying to work out how to tell my children that another one of their acquaintances had entered eternity.

The silence stretched long between us. Fonsi fidgeted, a dark look creasing his brow. "I think it's really brave of you to come here and support Mane's family after all of that," I said at length, impressed that he had managed to get out of bed after such a terrible tragedy. "I guess Alison's at home with Ina?"

His face broke, and he let his hands fall listlessly to his sides. "She's with my Mutti. I wish she could be with Ina. But . . . in all the confusion after the concert stopped, I forgot she was in the bathroom. Someone found . . . her body in there . . . when the police were escorting everyone out." Fury blazed in his eyes.

"Her . . . *body?*" I repeated, horrified.

Fonsi shook his head again, his anger prickling against my element, which had cooled my veins since he told me about Lea. "She had no marks on her body, no evidence of a struggle. Of course the police assume she overdosed, but Ina's never been an addict. Never. Someone's after my family, and when I find out who it is, I'm doing the *Virstohran*. I don't care if people think it's too archaic. Nobody hurts my girls and gets away with it."

I stared at Fonsi, at a loss for words. "Uh . . . you . . . you realize . . . you just told the *Leitalra* of Muniche that you're going to invoke ritual vengeance."

His answering regard leveled a challenge. "Are you going to stop me?"

Should I? I placed my left hand against my temple and closed my eyes to think. "You don't want to do anything rash until we find out who's responsible," I noted, my voice sounding shakier than I liked. "Are you going to hire investigators, or do you need some funds to do it?" I raised my eyebrows at him.

"I've already ordered an autopsy for my wife," he muttered, looking sick. "And I'm going to look around on the dark web to see if there's any talk about why. Why my wife and daughter? Were the same people responsible for both? I can't really imagine two unconnected crimes like that happening in the same place on the same night at almost the same time."

I could not disagree, and I urged him to sit with my family as Mane's and Selina's funeral commenced. He ended up sitting at the opposite end of the pew, his fingers scrolling his smartphone while friends and family spoke their tributes to a beloved father and daughter. And I told Hans later that Teuton authorities needed to contribute their resources to solve these wicked felonies.

On the first Thursday in May, an email from an anonymous sender landed in my inbox with the disquieting title, "Have You Reconsidered?" When I opened the message, I read the following:

"What a pity that innocent lives mean little to the selfish Leitalra. Children dead and maimed, orphans grieving, Teuton blood forever lost. And you cling to that amulet like a celestial talisman. Heartless bitch."

Chapter Twenty:
Drowning

An onslaught of guilt washed over my spirit, and I pushed my chair back from my desk, breathing shallowly as the truth became clear. The NVH was indeed behind my family's recent losses. Sadistic cowards who murdered the innocent and pushed the blame onto me. *Is the Torstein more important to you than your friends' and family's lives?*

Hans was at a doctor's appointment, so I had no supportive master standing beside me to talk me down from my emotional storm. My hands shook, my element trapped inside like a solid knot in my chest. Was this what Herr Ostermann meant, when he hinted that his group would turn to "more persuasive methods" in their quest for the Torstein? Did he intend to slay everyone close to me, even those who had no knowledge of my journeys through time?

But why the *children?* Selina was not yet twelve, and Lea had just turned twenty back in December. She had been in college studying social work and planned to join *Selakerza* to help others after graduation. She had been such a vibrant soul with a strong desire for justice. Had her connection to me been her only crime?

At some point I managed to retrieve my smartphone and dial Erika's number. I desperately needed to hear her voice, to know I had at least one friend still living. When she answered, I begged her to have lunch with me tomorrow at the Thaden house. "There's something evil going on, and we need to talk in private. It's serious," I said.

After a pause, Erika answered, "Okay then. What time?"

"One o'clock, in the sunroom?"

"I'll be there," she promised. We hung up shortly thereafter since she needed to pick up Sean from school and take Sophia to her ballet lesson. The dark corners of my mind showed me images of those two beautiful children with lifeless eyes. *I can't let the NVH get to Erika's family, too.*

I tried my best to put forth the appearance of peace before Max and Freya at dinner that evening. But the mood was somber, my husband's expression drawn. He had not yet told me how his doctor's appointment had gone, and I feared that he may have received bad news. Hans had recently turned seventy-three, and some of the medical issues common to aging had caught up with him. During the past few months, he had begun to forget things, and frequent headaches hampered his ability to concentrate on his work. Though we no longer held parties at the Thaden house, Hans still handled the investments that were in my name, and he continued to do administrative tasks for *Selakerza*.

When we shut ourselves in our bedroom for the night, I trailed him into the bathroom as he prepared to shower. Although I desperately needed his advice on how to handle the NVH's latest threat, angst about his condition clutched my heart in a skeletal grip. "So how did the tests go?" I asked him, seating myself upon the toilet lid, my eyes tracing his body while he adjusted the faucet.

Hans grunted and glanced at me before stepping beneath the showerhead and closing the glass door. "The doctor doesn't think it's Alzheimer's, so that's the good part," he said.

I breathed a sigh of relief, for I had not wanted our children to have to face their father's gradual deterioration. "And the not-so-good part?" I prompted.

The crisp scent of Hans' body wash wafted out of the shower. "He's going to do a few more blood tests and send me in for an MRI. To rule out cancer."

Shuddering, I hunched forward and dropped my hands between my legs. My knowledge of brain cancers was slim, but I had a strong suspicion that such afflictions tended to be incurable. "I'll go with you when you get the MRI. You don't need to have Thomas take you." My father's chauffeur had returned to München after his employer's death, and we used his services on an occasional basis.

"You sure you can handle that sort of thing?" my husband queried after at least a minute of silence. My distaste for doctors and hospitals had not ebbed much over the years.

I sighed and straightened my back, wrapping my fingers around the toilet seat to steady myself. "There are worse things I'll have to handle," I admitted. Then I opened the subject of the anonymous email that had brought an unnatural chill to my spirit. Hans remained silent while I repeated its contents and unloaded the terrors that lured me to the edge of reason.

If this Saxon cabal has the means and desire to murder the people I love, can I really refuse to give them the Torstein? Would they use it to eliminate the Teuton people from the earth, or try to alter historical events? How was I to balance my friends' lives against the very essence of history? If I just give the NVH what they want, they'll leave us alone, and no one else will die.

After Hans finished his shower, he toweled himself dry and gradually talked me down from my hysteria. He would pass the information on to the investigator Fonsi had hired—a Teuton of air with a decade of experience as a detective. Under no circumstances could we offer the Torstein to a group that proved itself willing to kill to obtain its objective. Such felons would attempt to upend our world if they grasped the power to bend time.

"I just can't understand *why* they killed Traudl's family, and Ina and Lea," I said to Hans as we sat together on our bed. "I mean, none of them knew anything about the Torstein. If that's what they really want, why don't they just confront me directly? Kidnap *me*, torture *me* . . . not these . . . ." A sob contracted my chest.

"They are likely trying to attack your conscience," Hans mused, massaging my shoulders gently while I wept. "Since they already offered you money and you turned it down, these terrorists may believe that they can crush your opposition through guilt—by spilling the blood of those close to you."

I shivered all over and crumpled against him. When I finally choked back my tears enough to speak, I murmured, "But if that . . . if that's what they're going to do . . . then they might go after you and the kids." I lifted my face to meet Hans' eyes, noting the pallor of his visage and the lines of worry creasing his mouth. My Keyholder had once been a powerful man, but now he looked far too frail to withstand Saxon torment.

"Don't fear for me," he responded, the hands of his spirit enshrouding my heart in solace. "My time is short already, and there'd be no point for the NVH to detain the Keyholder of the largest Teuton city in Bavaria. That would raise all sorts of alarm, and I think these fanatics wish to keep their schemes under wraps."

I nodded, trying to force my frightened brain to accept Hans' logic. "I guess you're right, or else they would have gone public and posted about the Torstein all over the internet." Blotting my tears on my sleeve, I leaned against my Keyholder's chest, his arms still my faithful shield, despite his advanced age.

"The problem is, *we* can't go public either without bringing every power-hungry human to our doorstep," I realized. "The police and the government would think we're crazy if we claimed that a secret society has been pressuring us to surrender a rock that opens the gates of time. But our people would know . . . and the priests might band together and force me to give the Torstein to them, if not to the NVH."

"Sadly, I have to agree with you," Hans sighed, stroking the locks of my hair. "For now, it'd be best to allow the detective to do his work, while Üwe and I probe into things on the side. Tomorrow I'll look into hiring security for our house. That way if these Saxons dare to attack us directly, we'll be prepared."

"Erika's coming over for lunch tomorrow," I said, "and I'm going to try to convince her to go into hiding with Iliana and their kids. She and Vreni are the only girlfriends I have left, and I'll have to talk to Vreni about it in the morning. Her family may be okay since Stefan's a priest. They haven't attacked any priests yet." I leaned into Hans' embrace, and he assured me again that we would figure out a way to combat this insidious menace.

When I arrived at *Selakerza* in the morning, I called Vreni into my office and informed her of the connection between the recent deaths of our friends and my family. She did not know about the Torstein, so I left that out, telling her that a group of Saxon purists were on a crusade to wipe Teuton blood from the earth. "It seems like they've targeted me as Muniche's Lady first," I said, "and I don't know if they might go after you since we're good friends."

With a pensive expression, Vreni pledged to inform Stefan but said that she did not want to go into hiding. "Our clients here need our services. I don't intend to bow before some fringe batch of Saxons. I'll talk to Stefan about hiring a tutor for our kids if things get dicey."

That was something that had not occurred to me, but I filed it away for later. Freya would be overjoyed to withdraw from school, but I knew Max would be devastated if I ordered him to quit the soccer team. Hopefully Hans' security plans would allow us to live as normally as possible with the NVH's threat hanging over our heads.

When Erika came for lunch, Gregor set up a dish of goulash with seeded breadsticks for us to consume while we discussed the dangers drawing near. I asked him not to bother us for at least an hour, since thus far Hans and I had not informed any of our staff about the NVH. None of our employees were Teutons, and at that point the Saxon cabal had attacked Teutons only. Sebastian, Gregor, Lise, Siggi, Thomas, and the other cleaners and groundskeepers should have nothing to fear.

To my relief, Erika seemed to sense the tension emanating from my spirit, for when we sat upon the settee with bowls in hand, she listened in silence as I narrated the tale. A lump formed in my throat at the subject of Lea, Selina, and Lukas—three young people lost or disabled thanks to mad brutes who wanted the Torstein. "Hans says we can't give them what they want under any circumstances, but I don't know, I'm just not sure whether the detective will be able to trace them and bring them to justice before more children die. Connor and Logan had to leave their homeland to be raised among outsiders. How can I just do nothing when I have the means to end this?"

Erika's face appeared grim, her hazel eyes darkened with grief. "I don't know what to tell you," she sighed, taking a small bite of breadstick. "I get where Hans is coming from, especially with what you saw in the past. The last time the Saxons got hold of time travel, they brought half-demons to the future and nearly pulled off a genocide. Fanatics who can't stand others wielding power they don't."

I shivered at her words, and my friend gazed at the blooming peonies across from where we sat. "It just seems so impossible," she added, shaking her head. "Our people's magic has been concealed or disbelieved for centuries. Centuries. And this NVH shows up out of nowhere to steal the Torstein? Where were they when it was in the Leutasch Gorge? Why now?"

All of the nebulous warnings the fairies had offered repeated themselves in my mind. *Sorcery always exacts a price. Respect the price. The price of Wuotan's sorcery is death.* My father told me years ago that Wuotan wanted something from me, that my use of his powers to open time's gateway must come with a cost. I shut my eyes for a second as the truth tried to drive me to the ground.

"It's my fault this is happening now," I said to Erika, my voice barely more than a whisper. "Not long after I found the Torstein, I learned that Prince Otto made a deal with Wuotan to create the stone. That means anyone who uses it uses a demon's power, and demons—like their cursed servants—require a fair trade. Hans warned me to tread carefully after we found out about that, but . . . I used the Torstein anyway when I went to the eleventh century. And I traveled time twice after that. Wuotan had a hand in the Teutons' fall, and I think he has a hand in this, too." I shuddered and took a bite of goulash, its flavor not soothing me at all.

"Then Wuotan's punishing you by killing the people you love? That's not very fair," Erika observed, scowling.

"It's not, but it seems typical for a demon. Wuotan killed Augustin's child in the past, so I guess that's his favorite way to 'punish' a Teuton who pisses him off. Drown them in guilt. It's working." I tore into a breadstick, trying to disperse the lump of tears in my throat.

"You're afraid the NVH might come after my family next," Erika gathered. When I met her gaze, I saw fear lurking therein.

"I am. That's why I asked you to have lunch today," I replied. I used a fork to blindly push a chunk of beef around in my bowl as I spoke swiftly. "Please, Erika, you need to take Iliana and your children and get out of here, go far away where the NVH can't find you. Or somewhere out in the middle of nowhere so if they *do* find you, you'll be prepared to take them out. Please, I don't want to watch more innocent people die on my account. You're one of the only friends I have left."

Erika looked at me, her countenance thoughtful as she nodded. "I'll talk to Iliana about it as soon as she gets home tonight. She's nearly done with her new designer collection. Once that's sold, we should have enough to disappear for a while."

"*Any* of my funds are at your disposal," I told her, grateful that she took my concerns seriously. "You'll need to go into *hiding*, as in, not getting a job or sending Sophia or Sean to school."

Her red eyebrows crimped. "Just how long do you think it'll be before Hans and the priests take care of this? Even after my wife sells her collection, we won't have enough to stay afloat for long if we can't make new art."

"I'll give you enough to last for a year," I said, "and please don't ask me not to. I have to do something to protect my friends."

Erika pressed her lips together, appearing unhappy but resigned. She ate a few bites of goulash before murmuring, "Maybe we should let Rudi know, so he can help Sophia set up an energy shield around wherever we set up camp."

"Rudi?" I repeated, surprised at her reference to one of the Teuton priests on München's council. Iliana's daughter Sophia claimed the element of energy, though. A shield would be a perfect defense mechanism.

Erika winked at me and said, "Rudi's Sophia's father. And before you ask, no, he and Iliana did *not* fuck. He donated a nice little sandwich bag of sperm."

I blinked at my friend, nonplussed. Never had I *ever* suspected that Rudi was open-minded enough to do such a thing. "Is he . . . is he Sean's father, too?"

Erika cackled. "Nah, he's Fonsi's kid. Since Ina didn't want any more after what happened with Wally, she agreed to let me make use of her husband." Erika looked down and cleared her throat, a blush blooming on her cheeks.

For some reason, this news thrilled me. "Then you screwed a man?"

"Once," Erika emphasized, shooting me a pointed look. "And that doesn't mean I'm bi. Not a fan of having a sausage thrust into me. It's gross."

I found myself chuckling for the first time since I had read the email, a tiny portion of the weight lifting from my shoulders. We spent the next half hour trading ideas on where her family could settle while Hans and the others tracked the NVH. At least one of my close friends would be safe.

On the second Monday in May, we received the results of Hans' MRI, which cindered what little hope remained in my heart. His doctor solemnly informed us that Hans had a brain tumor, one that stretched across much of his frontal right lobe. He would need to have surgery to remove it, and then a biopsy could identify the type of cancer. Once my husband and his doctor started discussing median survival rates and such morbidity, I left the room to wait in the hallway, the sterile scents of the medical office combining with the terrible report to drive me to my knees.

Chapter Twenty-one

A Burden So Great

How I managed to rise from that floor and follow my husband to our car, I know not. A thousand anxieties battled within my spirit, rendering me mute, though my Keyholder surely heard the screams pealing from my heart. Somehow he drove us home. My eyes were blinded to reality as images of the most destructive ends mired me in depression. Last week I had done a quick internet search on brain cancers; my faithful husband was destined to leave this earth, and soon.

He'll have the surgery and then go through chemo and radiation. That'll make him sick and weak, unable to help me combat the NVH. Max and Freya will have to witness their father's decline . . . and then . . . he'll have to find a new priest to take the keys of München. A new master who will learn all of my dark secrets. One of the kids who used to attend my classes, perhaps . . . but will he have the heart to pardon my steadfast loyalty to a Cursed One?

And how could I allow the city bonds to ignite a craving I did not want?

Once at home, I retreated to our bedroom and shut the door, seeking relief through tears and prayers. I was in no state to inform our children of what would come. At one point I retrieved Augustin's letter from its hidden pocket in my purse, my ice-tinted eyes reading its lines again and again. His last promise burned into me like the cobalt flames of his fire: *I shall devote all of my resources and intellect to solve the conundrum of that cord that shackles you apart from me. And if by some twist of fate I discern a solution, I shall come back for you.*

Augustin was fated to remain trapped on earth for over four hundred years. And he had not yet appeared to free me from this wretched bond. Had he never found a way to pry the soul of a Teuton city from her Lady's heart? He should have come for me already if he had figured it out. I would turn forty in August, and he was a Black Priest, immortal in death. Though my middle-aged body was in much better shape now than when medieval Muniche fell, why had he waited this long?

But . . . it's not possible to travel to the future, only to the past. Augustin's connection to the modern era broke when he severed our heart-bond.

Maybe that was what I should do once Hans chose some young priest to take his place as Keyholder. Maybe I should play Prince Otto's song again, asking time's currents to carry me to my cursed lover. There I could enjoy true devotion whether Muniche's soul rebuked me or not. Once I grew old and frail, the option of Teutonic ritual suicide offered a direct path to eternity. I could leave the twenty-first century forever, and the young Keyholder could have a Lady closer to his age, one with no lingering wisps of memory to taint her loyalty.

Hans came to my dreams that night, as he had done almost every night during our marriage. He approached me softly, like a ghost in the fog, pulling my attention away from the chattering stream in our backyard, where I huddled with my bare feet beneath its waters. When I raised my head to look at him, denial sliced my heart. In the *Gæstelort Troumerae*, Hans looked eternally young, forever healthy, his black fire casting his robes, hair, and eyes in magnificent sable. His spirit glowed with an inner light as he held one hand out to me, his expression so anguished I nearly started to sob.

"Swanie, please talk to me," he pleaded, his right hand slipping beneath his robes to stroke my heart. "It's not healthy to bottle up your grief, my love."

"Oh, Hans," I groaned in a plaintive voice, "my master . . . my Keyholder . . . I can't see . . . how I can possibly go on . . . without you." My spirit quaked, and my eyes closed in silent torment. Behind my translucent lids, my aged husband's youthful perfection twisted my emotions. The thick black fires of his hair looked so resplendent . . . it was impossible that this man faced death.

"My ice princess . . . ." My husband's love surrounded me in a protective shroud, a safeguard against life's trials. "Don't let the doctor's report discourage you like this. We don't know everything yet. It may be a benign tumor, and I might have ten years left, or even twenty." He stroked my heart tenderly, bringing it out into the cool night air.

"That may be true," I allowed, opening my eyes to look upon my beating heart, resting in the hands of my faithful Keyholder, this priest who had been my loyal guardian for over sixteen years. For a few moments, I gazed at my heart in a reverie, concentrating on the touch of Hans' fingers, feeling the love we shared that outweighed anything mortally possible—the destiny of Muniche.

But at length I sighed and beckoned for Hans to sit beside me at the banks of the stream. While he did so, I said, "Whether your tumor turns out to be cancer or not, the truth of the matter is what's been bothering me all day. You're seventy-three, and I'm almost forty. Unless the NVH gets to me first, you'll probably enter heaven before I do. And when that happens . . . you'll have to pass the keys on to someone else."

"You're not wrong," Hans admitted as I kept my gaze fixed upon the waters of the stream, their currents whispering to my ice. "Are there any Teuton priests in this city who attract you?"

Ice floes appeared in the stream, and I turned to stare at my husband. "Did you really just ask me to give you advice on my future Keyholder? To pick one that *attracts* me when I haven't felt a thing for any priest in this era but you?"

I sensed Hans' embarrassment as he placed my heart back within his robes. "Fair point. But I'd like to get your input on München's next master guardian. I don't want to choose someone who would mistreat you or undo all of the progress we've made these past sixteen years. You have more insight on the younger priests than I do, since they've all taken your classes."

I shook my head a little, flexing my toes in the shallows. "I'm pretty sure all of them have gotten married. I don't know which priests in this city are single other than Üwe, Rudi, and Oskar. It wouldn't be smart to pass the keys to another man in his seventies."

"I'll look into that before my surgery. Then after I've healed, we can invite each of them to dinner separately so we can get to know them."

Grimacing, I pondered whether it would be wise to let Hans know about my earlier ruminations. It might be better to let him assume I planned to stay here and let Muniche's bonds awaken a new attraction in my heart. "Did you tell Max and Freya about the tumor?"

"I did, and I told them both to give you space while you come to grips with the news. Max spent most of the evening in our private parlor, hoping you'd open the bedroom door. Freya shut herself in her room playing Mario Kart."

I sighed, feeling like a failure as a mother. My selfish heart latched onto the prospect of gaining a fated mate I did not want, plotting insurrections around that instead of granting solace to our children. "Hans, can you let me wake so I can comfort them? I'll catch up on sleep later."

Not long afterward, I found Max curled up on the sofa in our private parlor, still in his Powerwolf T-shirt and jeans, his eyes shut in sleep. But he jolted upright when I opened the door, and we spent a half hour talking through our grief and fear. When we went upstairs to check on Freya, we found her passed out on her bed with her controller in hand, the trash can beside her bed chock full of crumpled tissues. She woke when I reached down to stroke her hair and kiss her cheeks, and the two of us clung to each other while we gave voice to our sorrow.

Hans had his surgery on the 20th of May, and the following week we learned of the biopsy's results while he recovered at home. His tumor was stage IV glioblastoma, an aggressive cancer treatable by surgery, radiation, and chemo pills. Unfortunately, such treatments were considered palliatives only, methods to postpone death by a few short months. My Keyholder would likely have only one year left, it seemed. Thus we began to prepare for the trials to come, consoling our children, scheduling family dinners with each unmarried Teuton priest in München.

While Hans coached Sebastian on how to handle Thaden finances, strange news reached us through the Lady of Amberg, one of the women who aided my quest to guide the Teuton people along the path of light. Lady Zehra of Erlangen and her husband had been victims of an awful accident in the mountains. Their car had plunged off a high cliff onto jagged rocks, and neither survived. She rattled off the name of the new Keyholder of Erlangen—the priests on the council had to vote on someone, since Zehra's husband had no time to properly pass on his legacy.

I did not know what to think after I hung up the phone, shaking my head as I looked at the date on the bottom right of my computer screen. Thursday, the 4th of July. Connor and Logan should be celebrating today with my aunt and uncle. Maybe they would go to Ocean City to watch fireworks from the boardwalk. Here I sat a continent away, my gut churning as I shouldered yet another loss.

Hans sauntered into the bedroom, his right hand gripping the cane he had used ever since his surgery. "What happened?" he asked when our eyes locked. He had doubtless felt my distress through our bond.

"Zehra and Henning are dead. Car wreck in the Alps." My voice came out flat, and I exhaled as I tried to sort my feelings. Zehra had been a good friend, one who sought to give back to the community even though so many authority figures in her life had failed her. I remembered the last time we got together, several years before my world had crumbled before my eyes. With a conspiratorial smirk, she had told me that her husband had completed six blood-transfers with twelve survivors—a record for our people.

My Keyholder approached me and placed his free hand on my shoulder. His face looked frail, his hair still buzzed short from his surgery. He murmured a few words of comfort before heading for our bed. This was his first week of radiation and chemo, and the daily journeys to the hospital and back tended to tire him. I was trying hard not to think about the inevitable side effects of cancer treatment, as the distrustful side of me imagined that his final months would be better without such poisons. He chose to undergo the treatments for our children's sakes alone.

With a sigh, I averted my focus to Beth's books. After modifying a few of her lower-performing ads, I asked Hans whether he wanted dinner in our parlor or if he could handle it in the dining room. We had recently gotten a chair lift installed at the back staircase so he would not have to negotiate them.

Hans requested that I wake him for dinner, and a moment later I opened my personal email account, my eyes zeroing in on another disturbing title: "A Tragic Symphony." I saw that it was from an anonymous sender.

Nervously, I opened the message and read, "Did you believe Keyholders and Ladies were safe from us? The blood of the Turk cries out from the stones that tore her to pieces. Guess elements aren't all-powerful, are they? Her husband led us on quite a chase!"

Now I had a strong suspicion that the Saxon cabal was racist among other things. The message implied that they had gone after Henning and Zehra due solely to her ancestry. And, of course, her connection with me. Just how far could I let this go? I heard a quiet snore escape Hans' lips, and I was not cruel enough to wake him. We could discuss this in our dreams tonight.

Hans drew me into our dream world shortly after I fell asleep, having thus far suppressed the truth about my acquaintances' fate. Both Max and Freya had grown more withdrawn since their friends' deaths and their father's diagnosis. At some point I knew that I ought to tell my son the truth—that his mother had messed with demonic time travel and the bill was coming due. He had just turned fifteen and was quite mature for his age. As for Freya, I wished to shield her as long as possible, since she tackled enough trials at school each week.

Once my master met me at the stream, I beckoned him to follow me to our bedroom. I had kept my desktop on, so I could pull up the latest email as a spirit. I sensed Hans' anger as he read it, the heat of his robes licking harshly against the still air. "I'll call Frau Diesen tomorrow afternoon for an update on the progress," he said.

He referenced the detective Fonsi had hired; she currently worked on our family's case as well, since the two were intertwined. "Has she found any proof of their crimes yet?" I asked. I had not kept up with the investigations.

Hans shook his head. "The NVH appears to have extensive experience with covering their tracks. Hired mercenaries with mafia connections were responsible for the shooting in Italy. I've passed the information on to Mane's parents in case they want to pursue it, but that may not get anywhere with it being mafia-related. Frau Diesen has yet to trace whoever poisoned your Pappi and cousin, and all she's discovered about Ina's situation was that fentanyl killed her. If anyone at the venue happened to notice the perpetrators slipping away, no one's talking."

Frustrated, I left our bedroom behind to drift outside onto the balcony. "So the only proof we have are those two emails. Frau Diesen isn't a tech person, is she?"

My Keyholder trailed me onto the balcony and set his spirit upon one of my lounge chairs, his flames appearing dangerous against its plastic. "She's not, but she has a few others looking into it. I'll be interviewing a young man on Monday for the position of head of security here at the Thaden house. He has experience in the electronics sector along with security itself. If he appears to be the right fit, we can have him set up protective surveillance around the house."

"Good," I said, a hint of relief lightening my icy robes a few hues. "Is he an outsider like the rest of our staff?" I sat down on the other lounge chair.

"He claims to be a Teuton of ninety-one percent. His name is Sango Litke, raised in Straubing."

"Sango? That's an odd name for a Teuton," I remarked, thinking back to the moment when I first met Zehra. Maybe Sango was a Teuton by blood alone.

"Not the strangest name I've run across," Hans noted.

He was right, and I leaned back on the chair to gaze at the stars. "We have to think of something to do about the Torstein," I commented after a short silence. "I mean, we can't just let this go on and on with people dying on my account." Part of me had begun to reconsider giving the NVH what they wanted.

"We have few options when it comes to fully solving this problem, unless we decide to eliminate the NVH entirely. To do that, we'd need the help of others, which would require speaking of the Torstein, quite likely. But I'd rather not have my wife and children embark on the path of crime because of some Saxon sect."

Hans sighed, slipping his right hand beneath his robes to caress my heart. "I only wish I could be of more help, but my strength is failing, Swanie. I doubt I could fight anyone with my element today. I'm so old and weak."

I endeavored to offer him some reassurance, though my spirit had nearly lost its grip on hope. I sighed as my eyes traced the points of energy glowing across the sky. "If only . . . if only . . . Augustin were here . . . he could kill them all," I whispered, my worst desire put into words.

A coolness entered my heart through Hans' fingers. He chuckled, a strained sound, and said in a wry tone, "Be careful what you wish for, darling ice princess . . . for your desires have often led you into darkness."

On Monday, Hans dispatched me to meet the young computer whiz. He had managed to plant himself in his office that afternoon, giving Sebastian a bit more guidance about our family's investments. As yet, he had not faced any side effects from the chemo pills aside from tiredness, but we both knew the honeymoon phase would be temporary. His doctor had already prescribed steroids and anti-nausea medications in preparation for the inevitable.

I cannot begin to describe my astonishment when I opened the front door myself after hearing the bell. Despite my recollection of the man's unique name, my imagination had already conjured pictures of a Teuton geek in his twenties, nerdy-looking, dressed sloppily, and carrying a laptop. Instead, I blinked my eyes at a man of African descent, attired in a navy blue suit and matching tie, his tight curls shaved nearly to the scalp, his dark brown eyes seeming to smile as brightly as his mouth. He greeted me enthusiastically and ducked his head as he introduced himself as Sango Litke, here for his interview with Herr Johannes Meissner.

At first, I could not form any reply. I could not even shake his hand, though he offered it with a luminous smile. I detected no trace of a foreign accent in the young man's voice; he spoke perfect German, and with a Bavarian inflection. My ice sensed the energy inherent in his spirit, an aura that struck me with memories of my father. *This man may be the head of security our family needs, especially if he's good with electronics. He could raise an energy shield around the property.*

I mirrored Herr Litke's smile and introduced myself as Swanhilde Meissner von Thaden, Johannes' wife. I added that due to his poor health I had been sent to guide him upstairs for the interview. The young man nodded politely, voicing a few considerate phrases on behalf of Hans' health, and I led him into the vestibule, my curiosity piqued. "Forgive me, Herr Litke, but I can sense the energy in your spirit," I said as we ascended the front stairs. "Did you do the blood-transfer?"

Herr Litke grinned at me and answered, "Yes I did. It's been six years now since I changed my blood, and my element aids me greatly with my work."

I thought I noticed a trace of sorrow in his eyes, and I wondered who had granted him his Teuton blood. Had his donor not survived? Maybe the priests in Straubing were not particularly adept at the blood-transfer.

"That's really awesome that you gained an element that matches your skills," I said, thinking back to the other Teutons by blood alone that I had known throughout my life. Iliana claimed blue fire, not useful for clothing design, but an appropriate manifestation of her personality. Zehra had been stone, a powerful element to uphold her against repressive patriarchs. Joel claimed wind, and over time had come to appreciate its magic. And Freia had been light.

Herr Litke mentioned areas of security where his energy had already proven useful, and I nodded along, my thoughts a millennium away. When we paused at the closed door to Hans' office, I said, "I did the blood-transfer once, long ago."

Herr Litke's brown eyes searched my face with a look of abrupt awareness. "And . . . your friend?"

"She's in heaven today, but not because of the ritual." I lowered my gaze in memory of Freia Denlinger, my sunny sister from the past.

"Please accept my deepest apologies for your loss," Herr Litke said gravely, and I thanked him before opening the door to Hans' office.

Chapter Twenty-two:
Prelude to Disaster

Our new head of security soon settled himself into the routine of the Thaden house. Freya was overjoyed when she learned that his element was energy, and she started asking him for help with her electronic creations. He and Max shared similar tastes in music. On weekends, he, Max, and Sebastian would set up camp in the game room after dinner, with albums by Powerwolf, Sabaton, Rammstein, and Oomph! booming from the stereo as they played pool and darts.

Within a month, Sango proved to be a priceless comrade in our struggle against the NVH. At my request, he raised an energy shield that spanned the entire Thaden property, one that would alert him of any comings and goings. He also set up hidden cameras and motion sensors connected to a veritable electronic heaven he fashioned in what had once been Hans' cottage. The hut had stood empty since my father and Beth moved out, and it was nice to see its lights glimmering at night once more.

I asked Sango about his past one evening in early August, for I wanted to talk with him about the blood-transfer—the ghastly ritual the two of us had in common.

His childhood had been much more difficult than mine. He had never known his real father, and his mother died when he was eight years old. Afterward he had been passed here and there to various foster families and ended up joining a gang in an attempt to find acceptance.

Although tolerance had been taught for years throughout Germany, Sango still faced prejudice from both peers and his foster families until he went to live with the Litkes right after he turned thirteen. They were a middle-aged Teuton couple who had remained childless but wished to adopt an orphan. With the Litkes, Sango learned the true extent of family love, welcomed with open arms into a culture the likes of which he had never known.

"It was my adopted father who gave his blood for me," Sango told me that evening, his eyes moist with sorrow. I bowed my head in deference to this noble Teuton man who had given his life for his adopted son.

"To this day I can't understand how he could do such a thing," the young man continued, blotting his eyes rather self-consciously upon a handkerchief. "For an outsider I can see the necessity for the blood-transfer . . . the longing to be a part of such a special group and grasp the wonders of elemental magic. But how . . . *how* can a Teuton sacrifice himself or herself so willingly, facing a demon for the sake of a stranger?"

I sighed, thinking back to that Friday afternoon a thousand years before, when I had bravely lain my body upon the bench of torment, trusting Augustin to triumph over the most dangerous Teuton ritual. Sango did not yet know about my journeys through time, for Hans and I agreed to keep that under wraps until we were absolutely sure we could trust him. The time would soon come to let him in on the secret, but right now I needed to reassure him about his father's sacrifice.

"When I did the ritual, I didn't know what I was doing," I said, shivering at the memory. *Augustin's horror, his fury, his violence . . . tearing the veil from my hair, baring my neck, bleeding me . . . his resignation: "I see now. You love her, and you want her to be your equal. You have no choice."*

Lifting my eyes to Sango's, I murmured, "I loved my friend, and my blood was the best gift I had to offer. Every day I'm glad when I see the scars, knowing that I gave a good woman the gift of Teutonic magic."

Sango's lips parted into a mournful smile, and he glanced down at his own shirt as he said, "The magic is the greatest gift, along with the community. I believe my father is pleased with me, serving our people by helping you and your family."

The remainder of the summer passed without further incident from the NVH. In early September, Sango pinned down their official headquarters at an office building in Leipzig. When he scouted it out in spirit form, he reported that it was a simple suite with a lobby, bathroom, meeting room, and a few offices. All of their paper files were locked up tight, but Sango mapped the hard drive of the sole computer there to sift for evidence.

Max and Freya returned to school that same month, for Hans insisted that they not neglect their education, even though my maternal instincts shouted at me to keep them on the Thaden grounds. I decided to drive them to school myself each morning and pick them up after lunch, since it seemed that our enemies preferred to harm others instead of me. They should not be able to hurt my children while I hovered over them like an ice witch. I ordered my son to quit the soccer team that season, something he resented, though Hans and I had told both of our children about the looming "threat" to the Teuton people—our excuse for the heightened security.

Hans struggled with the side effects of the chemo pills as the months passed. Nausea, headaches, and fatigue became his constant companions, and his already slim form began to drop kilograms. Now that his radiation treatments had ended, he tried to ride the stationary bike in the exercise room in the mornings, his attempt to maintain a degree of strength. The treatments seemed to be doing their jobs for now, since his most recent scan showed no further tumor growth.

A horrific incident occurred on the first of October, while Sebastian was on his way back to the Thaden house after celebrating Rosh Hashanah with his family. They lived in Freising, and on his drive back to München that night, he stopped to fill up his gas tank. As he stood at the pump, a vehicle drove by, and its passenger lobbed a Molotov cocktail at Sebastian's car. The resultant explosion lit up the entire gas station, leaving six patrons and two employees dead.

Hans read the news in the morning paper, and for a moment I felt as if I could not breathe. I had noticed that Sebastian had not come home, but since the holiday was not yet over, I figured he had simply crashed at his parents' house. An investigation was already underway, according to the article, but I knew without question that the NVH was behind this latest massacre. I had lost too many people close to me in the past year to brush it off as pure chance.

The following day, the expected email arrived, its message prompting me to choke with sickness. "Now we have touched your household. Expect no mercy until you grant us what we seek. Pity the swine felt the need to celebrate a so-called 'New Year.' Good riddance."

The NVH was comprised of filthy racists. I abruptly began to wonder if they were actually neo-Nazis, if they wanted to wipe Teutons out since my people had naturally dark hair and magical blood.

Our staff did not react well to the news of Sebastian's death. He had been a mainstay in the Thaden household since before my college years. I sat down with Lise and Siggi and told them that if they wanted to retire somewhere off the grid to escape this nonsense, I would give them the means to do so. The couple, who were in their sixties now, thought it over for a few days but decided to stay. "Someone needs to stick around and keep things organized," Lise declared, for the other cleaners had quit, along with the groundskeepers.

Her loyalty touched my heart, but I begged her and Siggi to never leave the property unless I went with them. "We can do the grocery shopping together," I asserted, and my former nanny hugged me hard in response.

On the first Monday in October, I had scheduled a lunch date with Vreni at an outdoor beer garden. I had not spent much time at *Selakerza* since before Hans started his radiation therapy, and she wanted to catch me up on some recent offers. One of the largest industries in the city recently held a food drive for the shelter, and Vreni was finalizing a partnership with a local trade school to grant survivors opportunities for professional study.

I arrived at the beer garden about a half hour early, grateful for the chance to sit alone at a table for two, watching the patrons and relishing the cool weather. The owner's little Bichon made her way from one table to another, likely hoping for a handout. I smiled and scrolled social media on my phone, feeling content for the first time in a while.

That was when a disturbing voice suddenly spoke in my ear, and I almost dropped my phone. "Good afternoon, Frau von Thaden. It's been a long time."

I started and spun to the left to face the interloper. A thousand bolts of electricity seemed to shoot through my veins at the sight of Markus Ostermann standing two paces away from my table. He wore a tan suit and greatcoat, his hands resting casually in his pockets, his crooked teeth displayed in an enigmatic smirk. The Bichon ambled over to him and sniffed at his brown dress shoes.

I recovered myself as quickly as possible, sitting up straight and addressing him harshly but tactfully. "Your presence here surprises me, Herr Ostermann. I'd believed you could not find the nerve to meet me directly ever again, considering all the unsigned emails your historical society has sent to me."

The brown-haired Saxon grunted and booted the inquisitive Bichon away before plopping himself onto the chair across from me. The tiny dog yelped and retreated beneath a table with friendlier occupants. I frowned at my unwanted companion as he laid his hands atop the table.

"It seemed about time to officially inquire whether your resolve has faltered yet," he stated with a caustic snort, his blue-green eyes viewing me so fixedly that I fidgeted. "We're still prepared to pay you enormously for the item we require," he said with a wink, his smirk widening.

"Your presence here may interrupt an important appointment," I said in an acerbic tone, ignoring his declaration.

"Your dear Teuton friend isn't scheduled to arrive for fifteen minutes," Herr Ostermann rejoined, his eyes glittering ominously. He chuckled when he saw my vexation at his careless remark and added with a shrug, "Oh, we know all about your comings and goings, my dear Lady of Muniche. And we've also been keeping tabs on your company's earnings . . . still tenuous, are they not?"

Süddeutsche Getriebe had not fared well at all since I had stepped away last November, but I had attributed that to my male cousins' poor business sense. "So *you're* behind all of this financial mess! What do you plan to do, drive my family into poverty?" Best to let him imagine that Süddeutsche Getriebe was the Thaden family's sole source of income.

Herr Ostermann leaned forward, close enough that I could have poked his crooked teeth. "We plan to do whatever is necessary to get that rock from you," he murmured in an odious voice.

My body had frozen, for I could clearly see the outright loathing in his stare. My stomach sank to the ground as I considered the possible results of his threat. *They'll go after my whole family and all of my friends . . . maybe even force me to watch them suffer . . . ruin my father's company until I have no funds left.*

"Of course, we would like to bring all of this unpleasantness to an agreeable conclusion," Herr Ostermann was saying, his blue-green eyes searching my face. "Surely, as a respectable businesswoman, a faithful wife, and a caring *mother—*" he paused rather forebodingly on the word *mother* "—you hold the fates of your loved ones and corporation in their proper perspective."

I scooted my chair several centimeters back, taking deep breaths, focusing my gaze on the road beyond the shrubs that lined the beer garden. *The fate of the Teuton people as a whole is still most important. I can't imagine otherwise, not with Muniche's soul residing inside of me, and not after what I experienced in the eleventh century. Their threats are a modern form of torture, like what they did to Paulus. And I am no coward.*

"I ought to warn you, Frau von Thaden," Herr Ostermann added, appearing irritated by my prolonged silence, "that if our current methods of negotiation fail, we are prepared to touch you directly. And we will, if you prove so pitiless as to watch your people die without granting us what we seek." He narrowed his eyes at me and rubbed his mustache.

"If you resort to such techniques, I'm afraid you'll be rewarded with a corpse." I leered at the Saxon, part of me glad that he had finally threatened *me*, personally. I did not fear death, and I had no plans to stay here long after Hans passed. "Then your gracious society of historians would lose all that they seek, for I'll be sure to take the secrets of time travel to my grave."

"There are ways of keeping you alive despite physical discomfort, *Leitalra*." The Saxon cracked his knuckles, a clatter almost as galling as hearing him speak my title with such deprecation.

"There are also ways to die of which you know not," I shot back, thinking of blood control, and the option of bleeding to death from a paper cut.

"Something tells me that your resolve may falter once your dear Keyholder has succumbed to his cancer," Herr Ostermann said, seeming to backpedal.

"If you seriously believe that my tenacity stems from my husband, you are greatly misled," I informed him, drumming my fingers on the table. "You seem convinced that I am the great and mysterious time traveler extraordinaire. If that were the case, shouldn't you attribute just a portion of my resolve to those events I witnessed in history?" I raised an eyebrow at my charge.

"Oh, we know what you saw in the eleventh century," Herr Ostermann assured me with a smirk. "He told us."

"Then why hasn't *he* told you where to find the item you seek?" I wondered about that myself. If Wuotan had informed the NVH of my adventures, why had he not told them that the Torstein was hidden in my hip?

My opponent gave a faux cough, then changed the subject again. "You still underestimate our resources, dear *Leitalra*, for our influence far outweighs that of your pitiful Teutonic brotherhood. The day will come when you'll regret that you so arrogantly refused our initial offer of capital."

Something more occurred to me, and I leaped at the chance to finally defeat this Saxon thug, at least for now. I needed to scare him off, for Vreni would be here very soon. "Herr Ostermann, you're gravely mistaken if you believe that you're the only one at this table capable of threats. If your source truly told you all about my escapades in the past, then he should have enlightened you about my immortal ally, the one to whom death holds no meaning."

I watched with satisfaction as the first spark of worry appeared in my opponent's eyes. "Has it ever occurred to you to wonder what exactly became of that 'unconquerable army' your people used to vanquish the Teuton kingdom? I am sure you know of them, for you seem well informed on everything else. What happened to those unbeatable warriors after the Teutons fell? Why didn't they aid the Saxon armies for ages to come?"

My charge remained silent, though I gave him ample opportunity to comment. I took a sip from my glass of Apfelschorle, glancing at my smartphone. I should have thought to record this conversation, but it was too late now. My phone lay upon the table, in plain view. I rolled my eyes internally at my short-sightedness, then looked back at Herr Ostermann. A shadow had fallen upon his countenance, and he looked agitatedly from me to his hands in his lap.

"Muniche's greatest avenger was a Cursed One," I informed him, using the traditional phrase, which Herr Ostermann recognized, for his whole body jerked. "And if I asked him to come here and take vengeance on your group, he would do so gladly." I narrowed my eyes at the now very disturbed Saxon.

"You may ask why, what cause for loyalty from an outcast? I'll tell you plainly. He would protect me because he held my heart first. He was my husband."

Herr Ostermann stared at me like I had turned into a witch, his complexion hued a dead white. But at length he collected himself and gave a single nod, rising from his chair without further ado and stating in a rather shrill tone, "I see." Then he spun on his heels to stride away from me.

Before I could breathe a sigh of relief and prepare myself to meet Vreni, the Saxon laid one hand on my left shoulder and whispered in my ear, "I don't think even a Cursed One could protect *everyone* you love."

Sango tightened our security further following my tête-à-tête with the NVH leader. He spoke with Max and Freya, asking that they eat lunch together at school and check in with each other when possible between classes. Max took this advice very seriously, seizing the role of the protective big brother. He had begun to study some of Hans' priestly tomes, his inquisitiveness about Teutonic magic as insatiable as mine had been in my younger years.

Actually, Sango advised Hans and me to pull our children out of school and let them learn at home with a private tutor. My Keyholder disagreed, insisting that they be educated with their peers. Besides, I drove them to and from school each day, and Herr Ostermann had admitted that his group did not plan to murder me. I was getting used to traveling here and there with anyone who left our house.

The Friday before Freya's thirteenth birthday dawned with heavy clouds and cool winds, omens of a coming storm. I drove my two children to school as usual, their excitement palpable as my daughter chattered about the party we would hold for her tomorrow. We had invited her friends from school and from my classes, which I had not held since the murders came to a head in the spring. Sango, Hans, Lise, and I had been preparing for the party for weeks, ensuring that everyone who attended would be safe.

I spent the morning scheduling emails for Beth's newsletter and checking with the parents whose children would attend tomorrow's party, ensuring that they had no change of plans. Hans was on the recovery days from his chemo regimen, so he spent a few hours in his office showing Sango some of the financial pointers he had given Sebastian. Now someone else would have to manage our investments after he had gone.

When I went to retrieve my children from school, I waited for longer than usual, singing along with Nightwish's "Ghost Love Score" as familiar exclusive cars pulled away one by one. My children attended the same school I had, and all of their classmates were from wealthy families. Heavy raindrops splashed upon the windshield, their dampness calling out to my ice.

Suddenly, Max flung himself at the car, yanking open the passenger door, his irises a solid black that matched his soaked hair. "Mutti, I can't find Freya. She wasn't with her classmates or at the fountain where we usually meet. Her class had an assembly today, and I don't know. I don't know what happened to her. I think . . . I fear . . . I've failed her."

Chapter Twenty-three:
Cruel Reality

With trembling hands, I retrieved my phone and called Sango, asking him to come to my children's school right away and bring Lise. My son's desperation rubbed off on me, and I feared that I would be unable to drive us safely home. Max did not want to come home, in fact. He declared that when Sango arrived, they could probe the school together, speak to the administrators and Freya's teachers. How had they lost track of her? Had she merely slipped out with one of her friends?

Once Lise brought me home, I called all of Freya's friends' mothers a second time, stumbling over my words as I asked whether my daughter had come home with any of them. If she had, she would be in serious trouble, for my children knew they were not allowed to hang out with friends without express permission from Hans and me. That rule had been another point of contention when we established it after the rash of crimes around the Easter holidays. Being the "bad guy" was one aspect of parent-hood I did not enjoy.

Freya was not at any of her girlfriends' houses. Eventually Sango called and informed my husband that he had found our daughter's flip phone in a restroom trash can. Her teacher insisted that she had gone to the assembly, but she might have stepped out to use the restroom at some point. Her backpack and schoolbooks were still in the building, undisturbed. The administrators would check through the security cameras and report any findings on Monday.

Hans took the call in his office, while I sat crumpled into a ball on his extra chair, my ice shedding traces onto its fabric. He put Sango on speakerphone so we could both hear the report. By the time I heard him say, "Thank you, Sango. You can do no more there. Come home," I could no longer see, frozen tears having caked my corneas. A cry like that of a wounded animal burst from my lips as Hans hung up the phone. I buried my face in my hands and collapsed in sobs, guilt washing over me in a tidal wave.

The NVH had my daughter, and she knew nothing, nothing of this. Why hadn't I taken Herr Ostermann's latest warning more seriously? I knew he would go after my kids, and I let them stay in school, convincing myself that Max could protect his sister. They don't share any of the same classes. What have I done?

Late that night, Hans and I had a wicked argument. My despair boiled over, falling upon my weakened master, this dying priest whom I had trusted to be my perpetual tower of strength, though his cancer treatments had drained him to a shell. I railed on him for insisting that our children remain in school while these Saxons breathed down our necks. If he had listened to Sango and me earlier, Freya would still be safe. I would take Max out of school immediately, whether Hans approved or not. He could study at home under a private tutor like Vreni suggested. And we would have to think of something, some way to crush this extremist group, to kill them all and rescue my daughter, my poor, innocent child.

Hans tried to calm me, but his efforts were in vain. I could clearly sense his frailty through our bond, and it infuriated me. At some point I began throwing the past in my husband's face, though he hardly deserved such unfair treatment. I pushed him away when he touched me, shouting that there seemed no purpose in this mess, if we must fall prey to Saxon fanatics. And what help could my Keyholder be? He was dying, and I would have to seek assistance elsewhere, perhaps from a Cursed One, one who held some sway with Wuotan. What more could I do, aside from giving up the Torstein? Was this really worth my daughter's life, my father's life, my cousins' lives, and all the others?

My husband grew angry with me then, snapping with a hint of his old tenacity that under *no* circumstances should I even *think* about giving up the rock, not even if the NVH murdered everyone I loved, himself included. He argued that the NVH depended on a subservient demon for their information and thus could never truly vanquish us. Why else had they not taken hold of me and ripped the Torstein from my hip? Why else had they not demanded that I tell them the Song of Time? The NVH knew only the facts that Wuotan was permitted to divulge. Hans felt certain that God had silenced the demon on some of the particulars, that this was all part of His plan.

"It's God's plan that a bunch of innocent people died? Really?" I glared at my husband from where I sat on the opposite side of the bed. "That sort of thinking is what turns people against God. It's Wuotan's plan to drive me insane, to force me to kneel before a heartless demon."

Hans sighed and eased his body beneath the covers. "I see your point. But either way, we need to trust God to bring this to His appointed end. Sango is still working with Frau Diesen to nail the NVH for their crimes. And Swanie, trusting God does *not* include requesting help from a Black Priest," Hans said, his spiritual hands tightening upon my heart to reinforce his words. "All Cursed Ones—even your beloved Wolfgang—serve Wuotan first and may be incited against us."

I could not sleep that night, for each time I drifted off, images of Freya's torment inundated me before my husband could transfer my consciousness into our dream world. Then I would wake in terror, gasping for breath, the chill of my element doing nothing to soothe me. I finally gave up and froze my body in bed, seizing the palliatives I had once held dear as my spirit leaped into the ether. Parking myself atop the gable that once held my father's chambers, I sat beneath the rainfall and reflected.

Despite my grief telling me to blame Hans for Freya's disappearance, I knew most of the fault lay upon me. If I had controlled my shock when Herr Ostermann confronted me at the beer garden, I could have swept my smartphone into my lap instead of leaving it on the table. Then I could have called the police, or Sango, or at least recorded part of the conversation. Though the man had not openly admitted to any of the murders, the implications of his words might have been enough to condemn him. He had certainly threatened me along with my family. If I had not sat at that table like a stunned fool, he might be in custody now.

But my reason had forsaken me, and now my daughter was gone. Although no anonymous email had arrived yet to confirm the NVH's involvement, nothing else made sense. Freya would have no reason to just leave her school without her phone or coat. She was not really a people person, anyway. After the party she was supposed to celebrate later on today, she would doubtless have spent the rest of the week shut away with her electronic contraptions and video games.

What did the NVH plan to do with her? Would they murder her outright or hold her hostage and demand the Torstein as the ransom? Would they torture her? Starve her? Would they . . . .

God, I really need Your help, my mind cried out to the stormy sky, sorrow churning around me, turning all of the raindrops into ice crystals. *I know this isn't just part of 'Your plan,' but does the Torstein really mean more than Freya's life? How can I defeat this wretched demon who wants to destroy me? Where is Your infinite grace? Why must my daughter suffer because I traveled time? Show me how to survive this . . . I've got nothing left . . . .*

Words failed me, and I wrapped my ethereal arms around my robes as I gazed blindly out at the back gardens. The lights in Sango's cottage still glimmered in the trees. Sebastian's cottage was empty and dark. Most of our staff had left us this week. Gregor had found a place at an upscale restaurant, and Thomas finally retired at Hans' insistence. Now the Thaden property held only six people by day and by night—me, Hans, Max, Sango, Lise, and Siggi. While Sango's energy shield would give us fair warning of any intruders, were we strong enough to stand?

Memories of Augustin arose before me, the despair in his tone when he told me the story of his mother's death. And afterward, when he spent a year before her tomb, begging God to send her back to him. But his mother had never returned, and Augustin turned his back on goodness, following Wuotan down the dark path of power, sadism, and hatred.

I felt like God ignored me now, as my loved ones fell victim to the Saxons one by one. But there must be some way to conquer this, to triumph despite what my enemies wished. My faith had not failed me yet, and I determined that I could not become what Augustin had become. Eventually the NVH would make a mistake and we would bring them to justice. I clung to that belief like a lifeline.

On Sunday I received the expected message, an anonymous email that read, "Do not fear for your daughter's safety. We'll take good care of her until we run out of resources to finance her welfare. We trust that by then, you'll have found some compassion and sent us the item we require. Once it is in our possession, tested and secure, your daughter will return home."

Sango went to work tracing the email, hoping to find some clues about our enemies' hideout. Thus far, none of the emails had any connections with the single computer at the official NVH office, so he opined that the group must have a secret lair. Max, meanwhile, shut himself in his bedroom with his tomes on Teuton traditions, promising that he would not leave the house without permission from Hans or me.

I told Hans that afternoon that I could no longer keep the full truth from our son. He had matured noticeably over the past few years, and I wanted his thoughts on our situation. Hans agreed and said that he would inform Sango about the Torstein while I spoke with Max. He believed our head of security might gain fresh insight on how to defeat the NVH once he knew their intentions. Neither of us would reveal the stone's current location, but it was time to pull the veil from the other Teutons in our household.

Since Gregor had gone, Lise took it upon herself to cook a hearty lunch and prepare sandwiches for dinner each day. After she and Siggi departed the main house Sunday evening, I invited Max to join me in the upstairs parlor, while Hans spoke with Sango in the family room.

I shut the parlor's door behind us and turned on the overhead lamp before moving to sit at one end of the couch. Max wore black jeans and a plain turquoise long-sleeved shirt, locks of his black hair falling below his jawline. He stood with his shoulders hunched and his hands in his pockets, his eyes following me to the couch.

"There's more going on than you're telling us," he discerned, his tone more weary than reproachful.

My son was always perceptive. "You're right, and Pappi and I think it's time for you to understand why the NVH has been hurting our loved ones."

Max's silver eyes darkened a shade, but he shuffled forward and sat on the opposite side of the couch, leaving one cushion between us. "I thought they were killing Teutons at random because they're afraid of our magic. You mean they're actually after *us?*"

I swallowed, then rose to head for the mini fridge. "Do you want a soda or something? I'm getting some sparkling water." I snagged a small bottle.

"I'll take the same," Max said. When I handed him a bottle, I saw that his irises had returned to their natural silver. He kept his element contained, in control. A young man who studied for the Teuton priesthood.

I sat back down, running through all the possible ways I could broach the subject. I sighed and shifted my legs, thinking about that blood red stone buried deep within my hip. "You know the stories of the Torstein," I said.

My son's eyes widened, and his lips parted. "You have it?" he gasped.

Well, that was easy. "Yes. And that means you're looking at the sole person responsible for all of this tragedy. Your Opa and Oma, Traudl, Mane, Lena and Beni, Selina, Ina, Lea, Zehra and Henning, Sebastian. Plus the others at the gas station. All of them died because I refuse to give a Saxon cabal the power to open time's gateway." Nineteen people gone on my account. How many more would die before we resolved this?

"And Lukas . . . and Freya," my son whispered, a crease forming above his nose. He flexed his fingers on his bottle of water, then blurted, "Mutti, how are you handling that?"

The anguish in his tone pierced my heart, and I chewed on my bottom lip. "Not well," I confessed, grief clawing a fresh wound in my soul. "I know I can't give the Torstein to our enemies, and I know Sango and Frau Diesen will pin it on them eventually, bring them to justice. But they just keep killing people, and they're very, very good at covering their traces. They hired mercenaries to kill Traudl's family, and for all we know they did the same with the others."

My son was breathing hard. My ice sensed his darkness seeping into the room, seeking an outlet for his emotions. The overhead light did not flicker, and I knew that he struggled hard to keep his element contained. "Mutti . . . don't you think . . . maybe . . . you should get more priests involved? People who can hunt for these . . . these fiends in the spiritual realm?"

He met my gaze and I considered my response for a moment. Max grasped at strands of hope, at resources thus far untapped. "I know you've been reading a lot of your Pappi's books and talking with some of your older friends about it," I began, wincing at the knowledge that I was about to trample my son's beliefs about Teuton priests.

"You don't want me to become a priest?"

"No. No, you certainly have the aptitude for it, and you're respectful. There needs to be more Teuton priests like that, actually. In my experience, too many of them tend to hold to outdated views of women, treating them as lesser, unable to wield the priestly levels of magic. I've done my best to take apart those perceptions, but if your Pappi and I tell the council that I have the Torstein . . . well, they'd likely get an inferiority complex. Üwe knows, but as much as I'd like to build an army of Teuton priests to destroy this Saxon sect, I just . . . don't think that would work."

Max appeared thoughtful, and he took a swig of water before saying, "They would probably want you to give them the Torstein. And they might use it to screw everything up."

"Right," I said. "I'm always careful when I travel time and make sure I don't tamper with recorded events. But the Torstein is a result of Wuotan's sorcery, and he incited the NVH to punish me."

Max looked frustrated. He cast his eyes around the room, a sneer forming upon his upper lip. "I know you don't want me to leave the house, but could I talk to Matthias as a spirit and find out whether he'll start officially training me for the priesthood now? He and Jan have shown me a few things, but . . . you need a real priest to shield you, to force Wuotan to yield."

I chuckled softly. "You can ask them to come here to train you. But I wouldn't advise you to summon Wuotan the second you earn the priestly robe. I don't need him getting a vendetta against my entire family."

My son was quiet for a moment, and I took a sip from my own bottle. This conversation had gone much better than I expected. He seemed to agree that the Torstein should be protected no matter the cost, and he had not even asked where it was hidden. I hoped that his friends Jan and Matthias would be willing to train him even though he could not officially earn his robe until he turned sixteen.

"You met Augustin when you used the Torstein, didn't you?"

The new topic caught me off guard, and I sensed my ice cooling my blood. I looked at my son and saw that he watched me closely, his silvery eyes fathomless.

"I did. I met him when I took my longest journey into the past, when I went to the eleventh century to watch our people fall." Max gasped, and I nodded once at him and said, "The history books don't tell you this, but the Teuton kingdom fell because the Holy Roman Empire—controlled by the Saxons—stole Prince Otto's Song of Time and used it to build a half-demon army."

Max had put a hand to his mouth. "They want to do it again."

"That's why I can't give up the Torstein, no matter what."

My son dragged his hand down his chin and groaned, "Shit." He chugged water from his bottle, his free hand now clenched into a fist. "There's got to be some way to take them out. If they realize you're not going to give up the Torstein, they might just start killing everyone until our people go extinct."

"I've thought of that, too. And as much as Pappi doesn't like the idea . . . I'm starting to think I might have to get some . . . immortal help once he's gone." I told Max that Augustin was a Black Priest, emphasizing that Prince Otto had cursed him out of spite and jealousy. My son stared at me with an unreadable expression as I admitted that I had considered asking Augustin to come to the modern era to eliminate the NVH. It was a dark desire, one I probably would not fulfil.

The next time Max spoke, he brought up something I had not considered. "If you bring Augustin here before Pappi dies, maybe he could give him the keys."

I blinked at my son with my mouth hanging open for a good long while. He looked back at me with his eyebrows raised, taking a casual swig of water. "I . . . don't think . . . that would work," I hedged, though my individuality had burst into cerulean flames at the idea. *Claim your chosen lover as your Keyholder.*

"Why not? You said you had the heart-bond with him before, so you know he won't misjudge you for what you've done. And . . . I don't like any of the priests who've come to dinner." He sounded hesitant, looking down at the bottle in his hands.

"I don't want one of them to be my 'new' Pappi. I know he's leaning toward that one guy, Herr Brennemann I think? He's been to dinner three times now. I just . . . don't like the idea of you being stuck with somebody you haven't had time to love."

I winced at how my son phrased it, for the bonds of a Teuton city did indeed awaken love and devotion whether the Lady wanted it or not. "That's just a part of my destiny I have to accept," I said.

"But you love Augustin already. So if he comes here to take the NVH down before Pappi dies, he can offer him the keys."

I shook my head and looked toward the door to the hallway, my element sensing Hans' and Sango's presence nearby. "I'm probably not actually going to ask him to come here. It's just something to think about, an idea to toss around. I trust Sango and Frau Diesen to get this solved and find where they're keeping Freya."

"I'm going to help, too," Max declared as I stood up and stretched, ready to open the parlor to my husband. He came to my side and promised, "I'm going to be a good Teuton priest like Pappi. I'll make sure whoever takes the keys doesn't use Muniche's bonds against you."

I wrapped an arm around Max's waist and laid my head upon his shoulder, for he stood twelve centimeters taller than me now. "Thank you Max."

Chapter Twenty-four:
New Confidantes

Exactly one week after we received the email from the NVH, the five Teuton priests on München's council graced the Thaden house at my Keyholder's invitation. Hans had decided that we must tell the council about the Torstein, both to silence gossip about our family's misfortunes and to grant me further protection against Wuotan and his human minions.

I did not particularly agree with my husband's decision, and part of me wondered whether Max had given him the idea. Üwe was aware already, and Rudi would not cause any trouble. Erika and her family had gone off the grid in Finland, establishing their hideout during the summer's eternal day. Rudi was the only person who knew their address, and he had helped Sophia raise a strong shield around their property. He would doubtless be glad to learn the reasons his "family" had gone into hiding.

But the other priests were a question mark in my mind. Jürgen Peninger bothered me the most, since he tended to drop chauvinistic remarks at the festivals. His children were all out of his house now, and his wife Eva appeared content with their marriage. As one with experience on

Teutonic heart-bonds, I knew that outward poise often concealed turmoil behind closed doors.

Would Jürgen, Warren, or Oskar demand that I relinquish the Torstein to the council? Would they assert that they could protect it better than I could? Hans reassured me when I unloaded my apprehensions that Sunday morning, pledging that he would speak for both of us. "You need not fear their judgments," he said, "for none of them can take action against you without my consent."

The council members arrived in the afternoon and met Hans and me in the sunroom as requested. I sat on the cushioned settee beside my husband as the men trickled into the room. With grave expressions, each of them greeted us and peered closely at Hans' countenance, likely trying to discern the state of his health. He had recently finished another regimen of chemo pills, and his face resembled that of a wizened wraith, hollow cheeks and eyes that had long lost their spark.

Hans received our callers with what etiquette he could muster, nodding at each in turn though he did not stand. He wore the imposing priestly robe I knew so well, the black hood covering his bald head and protecting his eyes from the glare of the sun, which exacerbated his headaches. The withered fingers of his right hand were laced with those of my left.

I sat as close to my Keyholder as I could get, clad in the dress of a Teuton matron, eyeing the five council members with a look that I hoped appeared calm and unashamed. Hans and I had agreed to present a united front before my guardians in an attempt to mitigate their initial reactions. I felt a tiny flame of courage when my gaze locked briefly with Üwe's. At least he knew about my adventures already, and I trusted that he would defend me, even if the others did not.

"I do apologize for calling such an unorthodox gathering," Hans began once the five priests had positioned themselves relatively comfortably around the sunroom. Üwe sat closest to us on a stool to my right, while Rudi took a seat to Hans' left. Warren and Oskar sat upon lawn chairs

Sango had brought in from the deck, while Jürgen Peninger stood rather stiffly near the door to the family room, maybe on the lookout for snoops.

I sat quietly while Hans directed our companions' attention to the recent events surrounding our family, asserting that he and his Lady had decided that it was time to bring our situation before München's council, for the sake of advice and support. He then opened the subject of the NVH, solemnly informing my guardians that a group of Saxon terrorists were behind the calamities that had fallen upon our household. He intimated that the NVH may prove a threat to the Teuton community in general, if their schemes continued unchecked.

The atmosphere in the sunroom seethed with elemental activity, a strangely damp breeze springing up from the direction of Warren and Oskar. But my eyes were on Üwe, for I had heard him curse. Now he lifted his yellow-fired gaze to me, a look akin to grudging resignation upon his face.

My husband paused when he finished relating all we knew about the NVH, allowing his fellow priests to mutter amongst themselves. They appeared rather disgruntled at the fact that Üwe had known about this menace from the beginning without saying a word. I saw Oskar glowering at him after Hans mentioned the artist's role in our research. Part of me wished my husband had kept mum about Üwe's involvement, but I also understood the need for openness after a prolonged silence. We had brought the council members into this mess to gain their help, so we must be honest despite the cost.

And just as that thought crossed my mind, Jürgen voiced the question I had hoped to avoid, though that would have been unfeasible. "May I inquire as to the cause of this sudden onslaught, *Leitaeri?*"

I heard Üwe sigh once, and I could sense the interest in each of the other four priests in the sunroom. There was no getting around the issue, but I sidled closer to my husband, my façade of composure wavering as he told my guardians the truth, at long last.

By the grace of God, my Lady found the Teutonic Torstein some two years before earning her current position. She has used it on several occasions, gaining vast knowledge and wisdom from the past, as is proper according to the writings. But there is a darkness surrounding Prince Otto's grand invention. My Lady has learned that its power stems from Wuotan himself. Thus she has resolved never to use it again, and he has chosen to persecute us because we harbor his gifts.

My body trembled when Hans finished speaking. I closed my eyes, feeling the coolness of ice creeping up my fingers, suffusing my blood. He had lied primly to cover my butt; I fully intended to travel time again, though probably not by way of the Torstein. I felt thankful that he had not mentioned Prince Otto's song, the musical sorcery with notes that played daily through my brain.

I heard the priests murmuring again, more loudly this time, and I smelled smoke in the air. A strange moisture fogged the glass that fashioned the sunroom, a buzz of disrupted currents pealing forth from the outlet beside the doorway to the family room. I hid my face against Hans' shoulder, afraid to face the questions, the accusations, the incredulity. Then a warm hand squeezed my right arm as both of my husband's hands covered my fingers, and I heard Üwe's voice whispering in my ear, "Be strong, Swanie. You don't face this alone."

I tried to take his advice, to pull myself together and lift my eyes to those priests that likely glared at me with expressions more terrifying than the stare of Augustin in his devilish madness. But I remained an icicle frozen to my fiery Keyholder, not daring to stir while he responded sternly to each heated query. His defense of me never wavered, though I knew it taxed his strength.

No, there was no necessity to disclose this information earlier, since the Torstein itself had no bearing on my position as München's female representative. The rock was a personal matter, useful only for edification on history. Yes, the NVH likely wished to use it for wickedness, but there were limits to the Torstein's power, and not even foreigners could tamper with Wuotan's devices without consequence. True, the Torstein did hold a measureless amount of possibility, and therefore it must be protected from outside threats at all costs, preserved forever by Teutons alone, who alone respected its immense capabilities. That, in fact, was why we had chosen to bring this problem before our city's council at long last—in hopes of gaining allies in our struggle.

Throughout my husband's discourse, I kept my face bowed upon his sleeve, gradually regaining my composure. Üwe's fiery touch gently persuaded my ice to thaw as he stroked my right sleeve, whispering constant solace: "It'll be fine, Swanie. Trust me. Your master won't fail you . . . they cannot hurt you . . . your Keyholder wouldn't allow it . . . and neither would I."

At last I raised my head from Hans' shoulder, tugging my left hand free from his grasp. Üwe lifted his hand from my arm and I turned my head to look at him. To my surprise, he sat upon the arm of the settee, his priestly robe making him appear more formidable than usual. He caught my glance and my shaky smile, returning both and patting my shoulder. Three of the priests were on their feet now, but Rudi remained upon the chair to Hans' left, his countenance alight with comprehension as he looked from my husband to me.

About the same time, Oskar asked a question that pulled me from my silence. He stood nearest to the three of us perched on the settee, his gray eyes fixed severely upon Hans' face. "Where is the Torstein now?" His wind wafted through his robe as he spoke, and two others crept closer to him—Warren Haas, his eyes glittering a watery blue . . . and Jürgen Peninger, the youngest of them, his bearded jaw working in frustration, his eyes the swirling gray of smoke.

"It is best to keep that information classified," I answered before my husband had a chance to gather his thoughts. "The more people who know, the more likely it is that the information may leak." I narrowed my eyes at the priests, my courage having returned rather violently and unexpectedly.

Oskar looked taken aback. His wind calmed a bit, leaving his robes draped more naturally around his feet. "That is true," he stated, sounding rather subdued; but Jürgen huffed audibly, stepping forward to address me directly.

"Forgive me, *Leitalra*," he began in a clipped tone, "but we may consider the information to be endangered already, held in the heart of a woman."

I rose from the settee immediately and glared at the smoky narcissist with the rebuke, "Do *not* address me in such an insolent manner, Jürgen. Perhaps you have forgotten that you speak to Muniche's Lady, and that she, in fact, watched and *felt* her city burn one thousand years in the past."

Gasps of shock resounded in the sunroom; Hans had said nothing about the eras I had chosen to observe. I continued to stare into Jürgen's eyes as I declared, "I assure you that I have no intention of letting München fall again. I am *not* Paulus von Bayern. I am Swanhilde Meissner von Thaden."

I felt my Keyholder's hands upon my heart a moment later, more firmly than usual, an unspoken order to back down. I had rendered all of them speechless, so I figured there was no harm in retaking my seat. When I did so, Hans wrapped his right arm around my waist and muttered, "Be cautious," in my ear. As for Üwe, he nodded once at me, his lips twisted in a grim smile.

Once the council members regained their composure, Oskar suggested that we part ways for now, so each of them could have some time to think things over, to put the situation in its proper perspective in their own minds. Perhaps they could meet again in a week or so, leaving Hans and me out of it, to discuss solutions in private before presenting any plots to their Keyholder and Lady. My husband agreed to this, and shortly afterward we vacated the sunroom, our black-robed guests gravitating toward the front door, conferring quietly with one another from time to time.

Üwe and I shared a brief conversation in the vestibule after most of the other priests had gone. "I don't know, Swanie. I think you may need greater help than what we can offer, especially with Freya in Saxon hands." He eyed Oskar's back with a dissatisfied grimace.

I cocked my head at Üwe, not following his implications. "It wasn't Prince Otto and his council members who eliminated the Saxon plague from Bavaria," he reminded me.

My thoughts raced to Augustin and my darkest desires. "But Üwe . . . I can't bring *him* here, not when I'm bound to Muniche."

"Augustin isn't the only Cursed One on this earth," Üwe said in a whisper so low I could hardly hear him. Then he passed swiftly through the door.

Before I had the chance to process his hint, I found myself meeting the critical gaze of Jürgen Peninger, his eyes still a smoky gray. "I find it troubling that Muniche's Keyholder has allowed his Lady to develop such an audacious character, especially in regards to a matter as serious as the Torstein. If I were in his place, *you* would not have used it at all." He scowled at me.

"Then I am grateful that *you* are not my master," I replied.

Chapter Twenty-five:
An Audacious Attack

Sango approached me after the council members had gone, beckoning me to the music room, away from where Max hovered near the front door, his silvery eyes lifted to the autumn sky. "Do you think they'll be able to help us?" Sango inquired once we were alone.

I sighed and shook my head, leaning against the organ bench as I said, "I really don't know. But we certainly need *some* sort of help with this mess. I can't expect you and Max to fix everything yourselves."

"It's getting harder to keep the situation under wraps," Sango murmured, drifting toward the karaoke equipment, his countenance fraught with frustration. "This morning I disconnected the land line to the house, because every call we've gotten in the past week has been from inspectors or the media, seeking a statement on Freya's kidnapping. And the spam in your husband's email." He rolled his eyes with a caustic grimace.

I gave a weak snicker, tracing the fingers of my left hand along the patterns on the organ bench. "Tell me about it. I might just trash my smartphone since I don't plan on hiring extra detectives or officials to pry into our business. The idiots don't realize that their 'concern' does nothing but aggravate my anxiety. Poor Vreni has been fielding a lot of questions at *Selakerza,* too." I groaned and rubbed my forehead, longing for the return of serenity.

"If you want to get rid of your phone, I'll take it apart myself," Sango said with a half-smile. "We're going to have to send a statement out to the media," he went on, his mien growing more solemn, "if only to silence the rumors. This misfortune has been wreaking havoc on Süddeutsche Getriebe's profits, and we can't let it go on unless you want to lose your family's legacy."

"I know it. There's also the honor of München to consider, for we both know that if the Saxons do get the Torstein, they'll try to annihilate our people." I sighed again, leaving the organ bench behind as I crossed the floor to the window that revealed the gardens, tears dampening my eyes at the sight of the deciduous trees bare of leaves already. It had been a cold October.

"If only there was a way to *destroy* the Torstein. That would keep it out of Saxon hands forever," I mused, my gaze on the sky, the dark blue of Hans' eyes.

After a short pause, Sango spoke softly into my ear, having come to join me at the window. "If you believe those ancient writings Max has unearthed from the archives, the Torstein can't be destroyed. Its royal creator put it under some sort of mystical protection to make it an eternal gateway to the past."

"So I can't be the noble Frodo and cast it into the fires of Mount Doom," I translated with a humor I did not feel. "Prince Otto may have been a respectable Keyholder, but he certainly made a lot of stupid decisions."

"He was the same as all of us," Sango reflected, leaning his elbows onto the windowsill. "If we knew the consequences of our choices, we'd spend our entire lives in isolation."

"That rock has been a burden since I first found it," I said, remembering the burdens I had shouldered as a direct result of the Torstein. The rape I had faced in college at the hands of a brute possessed by Wuotan . . . the secrets

I could tell to so few . . . the disillusionment about Teuton history and my people in general . . . two marriages that would have been far more fulfilling had I not hoped that one day Augustin would keep his promise.

"And now my daughter suffers because of my failures. I just hope . . . I just hope they don't . . . keep her captive for too long. I know Freya's a Christian, bound for heaven . . . and she won't be the first child I've lost due to my sins." My grief overpowered me, and I collapsed onto the windowsill, shaking with sobs. During the past week, I had come to terms with the fact that we likely would be unable to rescue Freya before the NVH ran out of patience.

Eventually I found myself on the music room's plush couch, placed there by the kindhearted Sango, who sat beside me, urging me not to give up hope. "There is still a chance to save Freya as long as she's alive," he assured me.

"I hope you're right," I whispered, dabbing at my tears and trying to regain my composure. It was so hard to be dignified and confident when my daughter's cries haunted my every waking moment.

"In the meantime," Sango stated after a thoughtful pause, "we ought to consider your own safety, Swanie. You said that Ostermann threatened to harm you personally, if his current methods prove ineffective. I figure that the NVH may hold Freya for several months while sending nasty hints. We should be able to track down their lair before long, and we can get her out. If we aren't able to bring all of the members to justice at once, I fear that they may attempt to attack us here, with a large group of thugs. This household is weak in comparison."

Sango had a point. My mind raced through the elements my family boasted, and I listed them aloud. "Ice . . . darkness . . . energy. I know Hans would be too weak to use his fire. My element could probably protect me from their bullets, but if the NVH raided the house I might not be able to escape."

"And if they captured you, would they gain what they seek?" Sango asked the question gravely, his serious eyes searching my face.

I looked away, for I knew that they would indeed get the Torstein if they managed to abduct me. Though I would never willingly give it up, I also knew that once they had killed me, they could take my body apart—and find the rock buried deep in the flesh of my hip. So at length I responded, not meeting my comrade's gaze, "Please don't ask that question, Sango. We'll have to find a solution before it comes to that."

The next week passed without any new developments. Sango sent a brief message to the local media at my request, stating that the youngest member of the Thaden household disappeared from school two weeks prior and that our family requested privacy. This stilled the rash of inquests for the moment, although Sango continued to receive messages from private investigators looking to gain revenue from our misfortune. He refused all of them with utmost decorum and broke my primary smartphone down to its tiniest components, depositing them in various dumpsters around the city.

As for me, I remained at home taking care of Hans, who had grown ill after speaking with the council members on Sunday. My husband insisted that I was such a compassionate nurse as I sought to encourage him. I maintained a smile when I took his temperature and checked his vitals, offering him a variety of foods to tempt his failing palate. But my heart broke while I watched him struggle with his illness, remembering the days of old when Hans boasted a vigor that could shake off any infection. Now, his appearance hardly reminded me of the Keyholder to whom I had pledged my heart until death. He had lost all of his hair thanks to the chemo, and his withered skin looked so pale and *old*, clinging to his thinning frame like papery ivy stuck upon a crumbling wall, waiting for the slightest touch to peel it away forever.

On the evening of Saturday, October 26th, Hans rested on the couch in our private parlor while I sat at his feet reading a book on my e-reader. An album of organ pieces by Buxtehude played on the stereo, prompting Hans' legs to twitch occasionally, his feet longing to tackle the pedalboard as they once had. At one point he remarked that the composer's Praeludium in G minor was his favorite, though he knew that I preferred Praeludium in C.

Things were getting spicy in the paranormal romance novel I read when an unexpected voice entered our minds. *Hans, Swanie. Sorry for bothering you.*

I jerked into an upright position and summoned my ice into my eyes, casting them in the direction of the curio cabinet. Üwe hovered before it in spirit form, his yellow flames licking around him in a frantic manner. My heart plunged into my gut as I sensed the horror radiating from his essence.

"What happened?" Hans asked in a sharp tone, trying to lift himself from his recumbent position. I leaped to my feet and supported him, easing him against the back of the couch.

We were meeting at Oskar's cabin this weekend, all five of us, Üwe replied, his ethereal hands combing the fires of his robes. *Planning to talk about what's going on with the NVH, come up with some ways to stop them. Turned out the maid hadn't stocked the fridge with anything other than beer, so Oskar sent me out to grab some groceries. When I was on my way back up the drive, a gigantic fireball lit up the heavens.*

Hans and I both cursed, speaking separate Bayerisch terms. "Are the woods on fire?" Images of tree fairies arose in my mind, for a silver oak grew between the cabin and the lake. Had our enemies decided to start uprooting the sacred trees along with those who harbored Teuton blood?

I don't think so. The blaze was brief and contained, Üwe answered. *I'm not sure if any of my peers survived, but if they did, they're in bad shape. Emergency services have already cordoned off the area around the cabin.*

I exchanged a glance with Hans. "Is your body somewhere safe?" he asked, his expression alert.

Üwe nodded. *When it happened, I hit the brakes and turned my car around. I knew I couldn't do any good with something like that. Called 112 to report it, then left my car at the far side of the nearby town. My body's in the church right now; its clergyman is a Teuton, so he let me make use of a confession booth.*

Shock had snapped something in my brain, and I had to stifle a coarse groan at the mental image of Üwe's fiery body lurking in a confession booth. Good thing Teutonic elements stayed contained when the spirit traveled unseen. My husband questioned Üwe further, asking if he had done a sweep of the affected area before coming to us. He nodded and said that the entire cabin was in shambles. He had sensed no trace of Teutonic life—or any life—among the ruins.

I don't know how the NVH pulled this one off, but it was certainly them, Üwe said, his thoughts prickling my brain like a growl. *They've just eliminated a significant number of priests, so it's clear that they're done playing fair. None of us are off their radar.*

"Sophia . . . ." Her name whispered its way through my lips as pain seized me, icy tears welling in my eyes. The girl had just lost her father. I knew not how important a part Rudi had played in her life, but he had helped her fashion a shield to protect her mothers and brother. I leaned into my husband's embrace and wept.

While I cried, I vaguely heard Hans and Üwe exchange a few more phrases. Yes, all four council members were either inside or near the cabin when it erupted in flames. Rudi, Oskar, Warren, and Jürgen were presumed dead. Üwe had not noticed anyone creeping away from the site afterward, although the perpetrators could have bolted before he arrived in spirit form. The fire department had gotten there first, about fifteen minutes after the blaze began.

Eventually their conversation turned to the two women whose hearts faced a devastating loss—Claudia Haas and Eva Peninger. Both were alone and would require support; Hans murmured that he would send Claudia's son a message to have him check on his mother. But my thoughts had drifted a thousand years into the past, to when the Holy Roman Empire colluded with a semi-demonic legion

—and with Teutons of lower blood status—to conquer my people.

"What if Teutons are helping the NVH?" My query prompted Hans and Üwe to lapse into silence. Slipping away from my husband's embrace, I looked from his face to that of our yellow-fired friend. "What if they didn't find out about the Torstein from Wuotan at all? What if our own people are betraying us again?"

Üwe's translucent face appeared blank, as if he had not thought treachery was possible. I had not thought of it before, either, but . . . .

"Maybe that's why you couldn't find any traces of the culprits when you went to the cabin. Maybe the fire was set by Teuton spirits who returned to their bodies after the deed was done. And that may be why the cameras didn't record Freya leaving the school grounds. What if the NVH is paying a Teuton of energy to betray us all?"

Swanie . . . . Üwe's mental voice sounded pained, and he laid a hand upon his forehead. An instant later, Hans voiced the possibility that had evaded me.

"We haven't seen or heard from your friend Marga since the incident on the yacht. She's the one who told you it happened."

My lips parted in horror as I stared at my Keyholder. Black flames flickered in his irises, the situation grim enough to animate his failing strength. "But . . . she's earth. Marga couldn't be behind all this," I squeaked, not wanting to envision the alternative. "Maybe it's her boyfriend who has connections with them. And if he's the type to bleed his woman . . . that means he knows all about the Torstein, and what I used it for." Why had I not realized this earlier? It made perfect sense.

I never should have told *any* of my girlfriends about my adventures with the Torstein, not when Teutons could read blood memories.

We don't have any evidence for Marga's involvement, Üwe noted, *but I can do some extra digging.*

"Please," I said, angst gripping me as I met his fiery eyes. "And Üwe . . . when it's safe to drive home from the village, don't go back to your apartment. Come here to the Thaden house. Please. I've lost too many friends in this mess, and I don't need them to get you, too. They've probably already noticed that they missed one."

I've thought of that, too. Üwe shifted his gaze from me to my Keyholder. *Do you agree with your wife? Should I take refuge on your property until we get this under control? We probably ought to send out a notice to all Teuton priests, letting them know their lives may be in danger.*

Hans nodded once, weariness becoming more noticeable on his face. "Come here as soon as you can get away. I'll have Sango wait up for you. In the morning we can craft a message to our people."

The hues of Üwe's fire brightened a tad, and he looked away from both of us as he admitted, *There's somewhere else I have to go first.*

I figured he wanted to stop by his apartment and pack a bag or two. I opened my mouth to assure him that Max and I could go in spirit form this very night and retrieve whatever he deemed most precious; my son had been practicing his skills at concealing things with his darkness in recent weeks. But before I could broach the subject, my husband said one word that derailed my train of thought. "Eva?"

Dead silence in the parlor. Blinking, I looked from Hans' face to Üwe's. His visage had grown taut and determined, and my element sensed a hint of longing weaving through his fires. "Eva . . . Peninger?" I asked, bewildered.

Üwe trained his eyes on the floor, and Hans laid a hand upon my shoulder. "Eva's parents forced her into marriage with Jürgen years ago, because they didn't want her to be . . . spoiled by a sodomite. That was the exact phrase they used."

My jaw dropped, and my vision went completely blue. *"What?!"*

I'll go to her first, make sure she's okay. She might be willing to come here, too, once I tell her what the NVH is doing.

I hardly comprehended Üwe's thoughts, for my ice had cast its sheen upon my skin from head to toe. Rising to my feet, I glared daggers at my feeble husband. "You mean to tell me . . . *all this time* . . . one of the priests on München's council . . . has been mistreating his wife . . . and *you knew* . . . all this time . . . and never did anything to help her?" Wrath churned in my soul as I stared at my Keyholder.

"We don't know whether Jürgen mistreated her or not," Hans responded, shutting his eyes and leaning his bald head against the back of the couch. "Swanie, we can't break every marriage apart just because we *think* there might be—"

"Stop." I cut him off and thrust my right palm in his direction, shifting my stance to face Üwe instead. "Just stop. Üwe, when you talk to her, please let her know that any of *Selakerza's* resources are available to her. If she needs therapy or counseling or funds or even a listening ear. But please invite her to come here as soon as she can. Lise and I will start preparing all the extra rooms in the morning, including Sebastian's old cottage. We're going to need to bring as many of our loved ones as possible under Sango's protection."

Will do, and I agree. Üwe nodded at me with a fierce expression and jerked his head toward the door to the hallway. *Would you mind stepping out with me for a minute? There's something else you need to think about privately.*

I raised my eyebrows at the fiery priest, half expecting Hans to interject a complaint. But he likely sensed my anger at him through the pulses of my heart and discerned that it would be best to give me space. Their revelation about Eva Peninger had floored me, and not in a good way. After over a decade of going along believing that my efforts were making a difference in the Teuton community, a destructive marriage had unfolded right before my eyes.

Hans had known the entire time.

And he had kept his mouth shut.

I sincerely hoped that Eva's children had not ended up in similar marriages. As I recalled, she had a son and a daughter, both of whom attended some of my first classes on Teutonic history and traditions. I prayed silently that my lessons had taught them to respect others, since they would not have learned such things from their maternal grandparents or from their father.

Üwe drifted all the way to the back staircase before halting and turning to regard me. "I'm so, *so* sorry about what happened with you and Eva," I whispered, keeping my voice low in case Hans had an urge to snoop. "I wish I could have done something to help."

Thank you, Swanie. I appreciate that. What I had with her was beautiful, but it couldn't have lasted. I'm going to do all that's within my power to help her heal from whatever that bastard may have done.

The resolve pouring from his spirit joined with a pure desire to invigorate my waning hopes. We would work together to get this figured out, to find the NVH's lair and rescue my daughter, to bring these murderers to justice. A smile curved upon my lips as my fury at Hans gradually dissipated. A mistake had been made, and now it was time to fix it.

The thing I wanted to say to you alone is that I stand by what I said a week ago, Üwe informed me, his expression grave. *It's becoming quite obvious that living Teutons don't have the wherewithal to bring these fiends to justice.*

My eyes widened as I remembered his words from the previous Sunday. *Augustin isn't the only Cursed One on this earth.* "I can't make a deal with Günter Setzer. He breeds and traffics his own people," I protested softly.

Üwe cocked his head at me and answered, *There have been intriguing developments on that front in recent years. Günter has been trying to keep it on the down low, but he supports himself through his investments now. He hasn't adopted out a baby since 2016.*

Chapter Twenty-six

Castle of the Dead

Early Thursday afternoon, I left Thaden property in Hans' black BMW, giving the excuse that I needed to help Vreni and Stefan pack their things. They were about to move into the Thaden house temporarily at my insistence, along with their three young sons. When I visited *Selakerza* briefly on Monday that week, Vreni told me that Stefan had noticed several unsavory characters trailing him on his way to and from work the previous week. So I put my foot down and demanded that they stay with my family, and that Stefan and Vreni work from home until we eliminated the NVH's threat. Both of them wavered at first, but Hans added his voice to mine, and they would move in on Saturday.

In truth, my plan that day was to drive to the Black Castle to confront its immortal occupant and convince him to help us destroy the Saxon conclave. Üwe had not expounded further on the alleged "intriguing developments," but he would not suggest that I bargain with Günter if he thought I could not make it out of the castle alive. I knew how Cursed Ones operated: gain something in return for a fair trade. While I had no clue what the man would require for his help, I suspected that he might have a few things in common with Augustin.

He'll want sex or blood, and I can give him either.

I clothed myself warmly for the journey to the Black Priests' domain. I knew from both gossip and what Beth had found in the archives years ago that the winding mountain road to the castle ended a little less than a kilometer below the actual stronghold. Thus, any intrepid visitors must climb the rest of the way using a rock-strewn trail. I wore hiking shoes and thick black jeans, a bulky wool coat wrapped around my silver-flecked sweater. I had also applied a suitable amount of makeup and wound my hair into an elegant braid so I would appear attractive if nothing else. Hopefully my efforts would appease and interest Günter.

I glanced in the rearview mirror occasionally as I left the highways behind, progressing into the mountains at the southern tip of Bavaria. I felt just a little on edge at the possibility of pursuit. I knew that NVH lackeys watched my family's house, so they might follow me. Maybe they would try to force me off a cliff, like they did to Zehra and Henning.

"They won't do that," I told myself quietly, working to still the uncertainty that flecked my bloodstream with ice. "If they killed me that way, they'd never get the Torstein."

Whether I made it out of the Black Castle alive depended primarily on one thing. I knew not whether Günter retained control over his death gift, or if a wrong phrase might stop my heart for good. A few pangs of regret struck me as the car ascended the final narrow road. I should have written last letters to Hans and Max in case I did not return from "helping Vreni." They deserved better, but my desires had led me into darkness, as Hans said before.

"I'll have to survive this, one way or another," I told myself, looking at the patches of sky between the trees. The car's clock read 4:15, and dusk would soon come, along with colder temperatures. "I can promise Günter anything, blood, sex, riches, whatever. Even to be his mistress. It's all for Freya and for Max. I can't let them live in fear of the

NVH forever, no matter the cost. And he had a wife . . . and Üwe says he's no longer selling babies . . . so he must have *some* humanity left."

There were no vehicles behind me by the time I stopped the BMW not far from the overgrown foliage that practically hid the "Dead End" sign from view. I smiled a bit dubiously at the sign, thinking that it seemed pointless to set up such a marker when it was quite obvious that the road went no further. It had been a long and tedious climb to reach this place, the mountain boulevard having twisted here and there, passing through a tunnel and over several stone bridges. Ever since I had turned onto this road from one of the main thoroughfares at the base of the mountain, I had not encountered cars, ski resorts, or cabins.

I paused for a while after shutting the car door firmly behind me, stuffing my gloved hands into the pockets of my coat as I looked at the dark forest beyond the sign, then back the way I had come. My ears picked up no sounds of civilization, naught but the chirping of birds and rustling of squirrels preparing for slumber. Twilight had already fallen amongst the trees, and the air possessed that thin quality of a high mountain peak, cold and bare.

"What a lonely place," I murmured, wondering if I should abandon my mission and drive back home. If the Black Priest decided to kill me despite my good intentions, no living soul would know it. But I pushed my fears aside, allowing my ice to gain prominence over my body, so I could better navigate the dense path just barely discernable beyond the sign. I had come this far, and there was no point in giving up now. So I struck out for the woods . . . and the unknown.

It took me longer than I anticipated to reach the far end of the trail, for it wound through tight thickets and across two streams, offering no bridge. I felt thankful that my element was ice when I encountered the first brook. The frigid waters cheered me, their voices seeming to whisper that hope still remained, although I trod a dangerous path.

Eventually I broke out of the forest. The trail snaked along a rocky ridge with an impressive view of the nearby peaks, many of which were coated with snow. A few centimeters of the white flakes crunched under my boots the further I climbed, and by the time I scaled one final heap of boulders, my hands sank entirely into the crusty snow that cloaked the stones beneath me. When I attained the summit of the crag, I halted, my mouth falling open as I viewed the scene before me in the fading daylight—the Black Castle of the Cursed Ones.

It was an imposing fortress built of solid stones of the same gray hue as the jagged rocks I stood upon. The castle had been erected into the cliffs which faced north, its interior seeming to extend into the mountain itself, as though the main portion—semicircular in shape—had not been deemed large enough. But its central tower rose above the cloud bank, soaring to the sky, a spire with a deadly point. Four smaller turrets framed the castle walls, square in shape, topped with rather stately cupolas. I saw a myriad of rectangular windows dotting the towers and the walls, a handful of which glowed with a reddish light.

*Some*one must be inside the castle, though it would take the entire night to find anyone if I had to rely on feeble human senses apart from my ice. As I stared at the fortress standing about the distance of two soccer fields away from where I stood, my thoughts rehashed the very few facts I knew about Günter. His element was lightning like Rudi. Short black hair slicked back from his forehead. Dark blue eyes similar to Hans'. Tall, broad shoulders, strong fingers, a six pack.

And he had awakened Beth's Teutonic magic through repeated anal sex.

Would I be willing to grant him that, if that was the allotted cost? My anus clenched as memories of the assault I faced in college blurred the castle from before me. I shut my eyes for a second and shook my head, knowing that this mission of mine was bound to grow more complicated the longer I procrastinated. I forced my lungs to breathe deeply of the frigid air and squared my shoulders, ordering myself to be strong. *You can do this. It's for Freya and Max.*

So I scrambled down from the rocky crag, sliding a bit through the snow, and set my course for the stone bridge that led to a sort of veranda and an ornately framed doorway between two of the smaller towers. I observed the castle's architecture again as I crossed the bridge—this time noting the artistic balustrades that encircled the veranda, the intricately carved marble of the entryway, the two pillars bearing rather impressive sculptures that stood on either side of the bridge nearest to the castle.

I recognized the statues as angelic beings, both winged and prepared for battle, neither of their faces looking particularly joyful. I eyed each of them in turn when I stepped onto the veranda, not sure which angels—or demons—they were meant to portray. Then I saw that two hideous gargoyles stood at the corners of the railing that surrounded the porch, their tongues and claws outstretched toward those who approached their domain from the bridge. I smiled in spite of the chill that crawled up my spine; this Black Castle was certainly no welcoming place.

Turning my attention to the main door, which was made of iron and bolted shut, I observed a verse from the Bible etched into the stone above the entryway. Written in Latin, I read the words of Pharaoh to Moses after Egypt faced the ninth plague: "Take heed to thyself, and see my face no more; for in that day thou see my face thou shalt die."

The second thoughts that had needled my resolve since I left my car flooded my spirit like the Red Sea covering Pharaoh's army. I froze, my ice-tinted eyes blinking at that statement, obviously meant as a last warning to intruders.

Do I really want to do this? That's not Augustin in there. It's some other wretch, one who might see me as a fool fit for his heathen altar. Hans left this place long ago without fulfilling his pledge. How can I imagine that this Cursed One will show me mercy, when we've never met before?

I actually looked back toward the bridge with the angels, seriously believing that I should leave now, before the Black Priest himself appeared on the veranda to demand my rationale for infringing upon his solitude. I may have heard sounds within the walls—scrapes and clatters, growling voices and sinister laughter. I turned completely away from the door, clutching my coat more tightly around my body, the darkness of nightfall having obscured my intentions. *I can't do this. I have to get out of here and forget this nonsense.*

Just as I took my first step toward the pathway framed by the grim angels, a rattle upon the iron door behind me prompted me to freeze, my braided hair crystalizing into streaks of ice, my trembling lips expelling a frosty breath of shock. I heard the door swing open with an ominous creak, and then a spectral growl reached my ears—a voice similar to Augustin's when he came to the future as a wraith. "I thought I smelled something alive out here."

Menacing laughter followed that statement—which had been spoken, to my surprise, in Teutonica. Then another voice pierced the air, deeper than the first. "Be vigilant, Kasimir. This one appears to be a Teuton, unless she fought with an ice storm further down the mountain." More laughter, and the second voice proposed, "Perhaps she did not come here to die."

"Of course she came here to die. She stands under Azrael's wings, and she graced this fortress on All Hallows' Eve. There is no other logical explanation."

I smelled death in the air, a putrefaction that reminded me starkly of Augustin's rancid odor on his final visit to me. A mental image of the calendar surfaced in my brain for the briefest of instants, and I swore silently. I had forgotten that today was, indeed, the 31st of October. It figured that there would be some sort of demonic orgy at the Black Castle on Halloween, and it also figured that I had not seen it coming. Why was I always so clueless?

My whole body shivered now in spite of my element, but I knew that escape would be impossible with two of the undead standing behind me, bantering about my fate. So I gathered all of my courage and circled around to face my adversaries, ordering myself not to appear afraid or surprised.

"Ah, so she is not frozen to the ground after all."

"No, and thus we ought to greet her as proper hosts." The shorter phantom stepped toward me, his disintegrating toes sinking into the feathery snow on the threshold. His features were ugly as an ogre, but he wore a decent-looking gray wig on his misshapen head—akin to those old portraits of George Washington—and his robe was of a faded gray. His eyes glinted metallically as he addressed me with a grotesque smile.

"Welcome to the lair of the Cursed Ones, dear child of ice. Curiosity compels me to inquire as to your purpose in visiting this anteroom to hell . . . for I must say that you chose an extraordinary night to come . . . assuming you wish to leave this place alive."

Before I could comment on this, the taller wraith bounded forward rather excitedly, mist dampening his robe as he halted just a few centimeters from me, his straggly white hair shimmering. "You *certainly* must not intend to leave this castle alive," he declared in a growl that was almost a purr, his watery eyes appraising me with apparent satisfaction, one skeletal hand lifting slowly to touch my frozen hair.

"You cannot," he whispered, his eyes widening when his mist melted the ice on my hair, "for your blood smells very . . . succulent . . . and it has been too long, yes . . . too long since we have drunk pure Teuton blood at one of our celebrations."

The vampirical specter leaned his head close to mine, his sharp teeth spread in an awful smile. His expression suggested that he wished to sink them into my neck here and now, draining my blood before any of his cursed comrades could get their share. I had a notion to scream or flee, though neither would have done me any good against the dead; but in the next instant, the wigged wraith clapped a hand down on his companion's shoulder, dragging him a few steps back.

"For pity's sake, Kasimir, have you been taking lessons from Ubel during our last stint in hell? I doubt she came here to offer us her blood. I think she is here to speak with

Günter." His metal-tinted eyes locked with mine, silently demanding an answer.

At last I found my voice, though it sounded high and fearful, destroying my hopes of portraying a confident demeanor. "Yes, I'm here to speak with Günter, if the two of you would be so kind as to tell me where to find him?"

The wigged priest chuckled darkly and gestured toward the shaded doorway from whence he and his comrade had come. "We will take you to him ourselves, if you would be so kind as to precede us." He grinned.

To obey seemed my only option, unless I wanted Kasimir to bleed me dry. So I ducked my head at my skeletal hosts and advanced into the vestibule of the castle, which was dimly lit by several electric bulbs set into the walls. I heard the door creak shut behind me while I looked around at the tapestries adorning the walls. Most of them depicted macabre battle scenes.

I heard Kasimir grumble to his companion, "Günter is still with the others, quite likely, and if we take her to the dungeons, Ubel will unquestionably sink his claws into her veins before we can chain her to the altar."

The other snorted gruffly. "It is high time we had some real fun at one of these gatherings. Günter's style of sacrifice is not particularly amusing, since he always drugs the victims senseless—"

"And I especially hate the taste of contaminated blood. Damn doctor he is."

Both wraiths laughed raucously, and I chose to ignore their repartee as we passed through a gloomy hallway beyond the vestibule. Hans had said that Günter had gone insane back in the 1960s; now I was beginning to believe that *all* Black Priests ultimately went mad. Why else would my hosts chat incessantly about past sacrifices and their distaste for victims who were too stoned to struggle?

But a faint trace of hope arose in my heart, though I walked in the castle of the dead. If Günter 'always drugs the victims senseless,' he must indeed retain some vestiges of mercy. Maybe I could manage to escape this place alive, assuming Ubel—whoever he was—did not sink his claws into my veins first.

Towering columns rose high above me as the wigged wraith directed me into a lengthy corridor. I could hardly predict just where the ceiling lay, since even with my elemental vision the darkness debilitated my sight. The only light that pierced the gloom stemmed from occasional niches cut into the stone walls.

Natural candle flames illuminated marble busts of men whose carved expressions appeared as mirthless as the angels guarding the bridge. Despite their dour faces, each statue boasted very attractive features, the perfection of death—Wuotan's gift. I glanced at the first two as I continued onward, seeing the name *Konstantin* inscribed above the bust to my left, and a *Nemo* to my right. That last Black Priest must have had a morbid sense of humor, to choose such an appellation as a result of the filial curse—Latin for *nobody*.

When my gaze moved to the light flickering within the niches further down the passageway, it occurred to me that Beth had told me about this place. This was where she had come upon the eternal memorial to Augustin, with the years 1045-1493 inscribed beneath his likeness. Yearning burned in my heart, and I quickened my pace.

Both of my ghoulish hosts overtook me before I got very far. Kasimir wound his emaciated hand around the arm of my coat, tugging me to the left with the assertion, "You must look at *mine* first, child of ice."

The other wraith grumbled something about the misty specter's vanity. A moment later I studied a handsome-looking sculpture of jade-flecked marble, its hairstyle and beard clearly evoking the era stenciled on the wall beneath the ever-burning candle glowing upon its visage: 1798-1896. Underneath the dates I saw a short phrase in Teutonica: ... *and in the end, death is ever victorious.*

I frowned slightly, then looked at the name written above the bust. My frown turned into a smirk of disbelief, as I read aloud, "Kasimir Ulbrecht Markus Moritz Eduard Ralf Viktor Oswald Ludwig Laudenslager?" I shot a glance at the mist-coated phantom, who had drawn himself up into a regal pose, pride written all over his rotting face. "You must have a proclivity for names, Herr Laudenslager."

He gestured at the ten epithets inscribed above his image and explained, "None of *those* names can be taken from me, dear child. And perhaps you did not perceive that my ten names are, in fact, an acronym. Their initial letters spell the German word *Kummervoll*, which seemed too terribly apt when I first fell under the dreaded curse." He heaved a wistful sigh.

I cocked my head at my charge, then looked again at his bust, wondering what had happened to him during his years of death on earth to alter his attitude so remarkably. He had been cursed as a 'sorrowful' man, yet his epitaph lauded the triumph of death. Before I could voice any inquiries on the subject, fingers of steel latched upon my right arm as the wigged wraith pulled me toward the bust directly across from Kasimir's.

"Come, come, leave this misty wretch behind and view *my* statue. It was fashioned, at my command, out of solid metal. You may be pleased to discover that *I* have only four names, ones which are easily pronounced."

Kasimir scoffed, and I heard him mumble, "Yes, *Archibald.*"

He articulated the name in the English manner, but I hardly noticed. I was too busy studying the sculpture before me—an imperious-looking man sporting a wig exactly like that of the wraith who had at last freed my arm to round on Kasimir in a fury.

"You rascal, *stop* calling me *Archi*bald! I'm not some jackass from England, and I outrank you by blood, elemental power, *and* seniority. How would you like it if I started calling you Käse?" Kasimir hissed, and he likely would have leapt upon his companion for a good-natured scuffle had the latter not added, "Remember your manners, friend, for there is a lady present."

I was attempting to stifle a snicker at the nickname of 'cheese' for the misty specter. The phrase written beneath the bust before me did little to help me regain my dignity, for it read in Latin, *I came, I saw, I cursed.* Such a ridiculous modification of that ancient idiom did not seem to fit with the haughty statue before me. I seriously began to fear that I had fallen into a den of lunatics.

Suddenly, a ghostly voice spoke in my ear, the scent of its breath a bizarre combination of metallurgy and the grave. "You may call me Konrad, lovely Teuton of ice."

"Konrad Archibald Griswald Reichel." I read his full name, pronouncing it in proper German fashion as I turned away from the bust to cock an eyebrow at the wigged phantom.

"See, this one is educated," Konrad praised me, favoring his comrade with an arrogant sneer. Kasimir waved one damp hand dismissively, and I looked once more at the statue depicting the Black Priest of metal, this time noting the dates of his stay on earth: 1682-1824. A long time, but not nearly as long as . . . .

My mind flew back to Augustin, and I started off down the corridor again, my feet moving automatically, my gaze fixed upon the next two niches. Maybe I would find my medieval lover's memorial there. My hosts fell in behind me, Konrad commenting to his pal, "Yes, we must go if we wish to confront Günter before the sacrifices begin."

The next two sculptures were from further back in history—a *Jakob* from the sixteenth century and the illustrious Ubel, who held the position of Cursed One directly prior to Konrad. I did not pause long at either bust, though I did see that Ubel's epitaph lauded the 'glorious savor of lifeblood.' I shivered as I continued on, images of vampires filling my mind. My predecessor Bertha Lohr had once hinted that the European tales of vampires began with the Teuton people. Maybe Ubel had something to do with that.

To my left I read the name *Ritter* inscribed over a Cursed One whose purgatory spanned the late 1400s and early 1500s. Finally, as I turned to my right, my eyes fell upon an image I would recognize anywhere, in any form. Locks of hair falling around the shoulders, bangs pulled back from the face . . . *that gorgeous face* . . . the eyes so unfathomable even carved in stone.

A small squeak escaped my lips, though I endeavored to control my reaction for the sake of my ghoulish company. But how could I not race forward, just to put forth my hand and touch that frozen face, the eternal candle beneath it barely warming the stone? Tears clouded my vision as my fingers dropped to the base of the statue, then to the wall, tracing the years etched thereon: 1045-1493, exactly as Beth had told me.

"Almost five . . . *hundred* . . . years . . . oh . . . my love." My jaw quivered, and I closed my eyes, ordering myself to be calm, not to fear, not to hope.

But my eyes sprang open as the impossible desire grabbed hold of my heart. I spun to face Kasimir and Konrad, who stood not far away, muttering quietly to each other, probably labeling me a fool for weeping over a statue.

"Is . . . is . . . this one . . . ." My voice cracked, and I cleared my throat, gathering all of my gall to ask, "Will . . . Wolfgang . . . be at the . . . the gathering . . . tonight?" It took all of my control to not say *Augustin*.

Kasimir guffawed. "*Him?* Of course not. He never comes. We're not good enough for the almighty Herr Wolfe." The misty wraith scowled at the bust, and Konrad made an obscene gesture with his wasted hand.

My hopes shot down with poison darts, I sagged, lifting my eyes to the name written above my cursed lover's form: *Wolfgang Wolfrik Wolfe.* I shook my head at my own folly, then addressed Kasimir again. "Why wouldn't he come? What do you mean, you're not good enough for him?" I frowned at Augustin's sculpture as I spoke, wishing those eyes were alive, that they could see me and remember.

"That fiend never partakes in our celebrations because he committed the unpardonable sin," Kasimir responded with a leer.

"And Günter himself may be headed for that same misfortune," Konrad put in with a grimace, beckoning me forward before I could ask any more questions. "There is no use lingering here, child of ice. The night is not growing any younger, and once the blood of the first sacrifice is spilled, you can hardly expect to *talk* with Günter before one of us bleeds you dry."

"That would be Ubel," Kasimir supplied, earning a hoot from his comrade.

I sighed, my eyes remaining upon Augustin's bust as long as they could while my feet returned to the main walkway, urged forward by my spectral hosts. A thousand new issues had surfaced in my mind thanks to what I had seen in that niche, and my thoughts preoccupied me so entirely that I completely missed the other four sculptures that represented Anubis, Osiris, Tartarus, and Erebus.

So he remained on earth until the late 1400s, until Ritter came to relieve him at long last. Augustin was probably the one who oversaw the building of this castle. That would explain all the records that are stored here . . . the pages Hans found on the Torstein . . . and so much more.

But what could he have meant by that phrase beneath his statue, his last thoughts for posterity. "This Eternal Slavery—Not So Lamentable A Fate." That'll bug me for the rest of my life. Augustin could have been less enigmatic in his epitaph . . . but it's typical of him to confound me even in death. What did *Kasimir mean, that Augustin committed the unpardonable sin?*

I said nothing more as we threaded our way down tortuous stairwells, my thoughts completely consumed with memories and questions that would never be answered—unless I took one final journey into the past. Before I knew it, I stepped through an archway into a round stone chamber lit by four flaming cauldrons at each point of the compass. Each one held a separate color of Teutonic fire—yellow, red, blue, and black—and they framed an altar at the center of the room, upon which lay an unconscious naked woman.

Nine apparitions cavorted around the altar, some cackling devilishly, some haggling over whose right it was to make the first cut with the knife. I froze in the doorway, wrinkling my nose against the stench of death and uninhibited elements. Then one of the wraiths swung around to face me with the cry, "They've brought us a live one, untainted with drugs!" It bounded forward with outstretched claws, its eyes brighter than the sun.

But Konrad arrested his advance with the calm assertion, "Her blood is not your gift, Ubel. She has come to speak with Günter."

Chapter Twenty-seven

My Deliverer

At those words, a tall form in a robe much darker than the shabby clothing of the wraiths stepped out from behind the cauldron to my right. Striding forward to meet me with confident steps, his face appeared much livelier than those of the ghouls surrounding the altar. He carried a stone dagger in his right hand, its blade glowing with heat from the fire and perhaps with something more. A vibrant electric current coursed along his fingers, and his eyes flashed a striking whitish-gold, alternating between that and their natural shade of deep cobalt.

He stopped several paces away from me, lifting his free hand in a backward gesture to the specters, who swarmed around him, ogling me with a wide range of elemental colors. "If she has come merely to *speak* with me," he began in a dark voice, his midnight blue eyes raking over my face and garments, "she has chosen an inopportune moment, for she interrupts our sacrifice." He peered at me forebodingly from beneath the hood of his robe.

"We told her that, but she's incorrigible," Kasimir chimed in, sidling away from me with Konrad at his heels. They retreated to stand amid the other damned priests, many of whom hurled insults at me, primarily wishes for my death. But I heard one of them—a large one who wore a pair of stone horns upon his misshapen head—whisper a name I could not catch. When I looked more closely at him, he blinked his stone-gray eyes at me with a look of despair.

Günter snickered, flipping the dagger around his hand in a movement too fast for my eyes to follow, drawing their attention back toward him. "Speak then, unfortunate woman, and do so with celerity, for I know not how long my authority as master of this castle may keep these devils in check."

He threw one glance at the grimacing ghouls, all of whom had apparently forgotten about the woman upon the altar. "They think your Teuton blood smells much tastier than the blood of the working women in my dungeons." Günter smiled, his teeth glistening a pristine white—demonic perfection.

"Forgive me, Herr Setzer," I whispered, though I barely heard my own voice. Terror had gripped me in a vise, and I stood stock still several steps from the archway, not far enough away from Günter's ghastly companions.

I pulled a deep breath into my lungs, sending a silent prayer heavenward for God's protection to spare me from these blood-drinking wraiths. I looked Günter square in the eyes and said, "I didn't realize this was such a bad time . . . but I came because I need your help."

"Ah, and at what cost, I wonder?" The smirk had not left Günter's face. The specter with the luminous eyes—Ubel, I guessed—suggested that he listen to my demands and then spill my blood as payment for his aid.

"I may consider it," Günter mused, prompting Ubel to chortle and rub his skeletal hands together. "However, the cost depends on the nature of the assistance you seek. It's a rare occurrence to have a middle-aged Teuton woman grace the doors of this castle. Most of my supplicants are elderly, seeking medical miracles. And the younger women, of course, who beg for demonic help in childbirth."

My thoughts flew again to Augustin, the eleventh century Cursed One who assisted Teuton women in childbirth.

I wondered if that was a duty all Black Priests performed, or just the ones with a medical background. "My situation has nothing to do with those things," I informed my host, watching the curiosity glittering in his eyes, which still occasionally sparked with whitish electricity. "I came to get help for my family. We're under attack from Saxon extremists."

Several of the ghouls snarled at this revelation. Günter himself took a step forward, the blade of his dagger glowing under the touch of his fingers. "May I ask why a Saxon group singled out your family for persecution?"

Of course he would have to ask *that* question. But there seemed little point in beating around the bush, especially considering how excited Ubel's eyes looked, his gaze fixed hungrily upon my neck. Hans had come to this place years ago in a quest for information on the Torstein, so Günter probably assumed that it had been found.

"We have something . . . in our possession . . . that they want to take from us. From me in particular." I fidgeted, scuffing my boots on the stones of the floor, hesitant to reveal the truth in company like this. But the specters and their master waited in silence, studying me with evident interest, so I pressed on.

"They've been killing my family and friends . . . and they kidnapped my little daughter just three weeks ago." I paused to blink against the tears threatening to well in my eyes; I did not need to break down sobbing in front of a collection of dead men. "They're trying to provoke my emotions and my remorse . . . to force me to give up the item they want."

I exhaled, trembling, and thrust my hands into the pockets of my coat, touching the leather gloves I had deposited there when I first entered the castle. Konrad and Kasimir muttered to each other, while Günter remained silent. His expression seemed to grow darker the longer I spoke, the fingers of his left hand tracing the blade of his dagger.

"What the Saxons don't realize," I went on, passion beginning to layer my words, "is that they could kill all of my friends, all of my family, and it would do them no good. I would *never* give them what they seek, for I can't betray my München . . . my city . . . I *cannot* watch her fall again."

A spectral growl pierced the air, and Günter pointed his dagger at me with the indictment, "So *that's* it! You're harboring the power over time travel, and they want to get it from you, to crush the Teutons as they did once before."

"Yes," I whispered, cringing away from his blade, but he flew in a wave of electricity to plant himself between me and the exit, his eyes sparking a warning. My heart practically leaped into my throat, for now I stood between the fearsome master of the Black Castle and his swarm of animated corpses. I heard them snarling eagerly amongst themselves, probably taking bets on how long it would be before Günter's dagger slashed one of my veins.

Suddenly, I sensed a misty presence behind me, accompanied by one of metal. Konrad's familiar voice growled a quiet encouragement in my ear, pledging that he and Kasimir would keep Ubel away from me until I had concluded my deal with Günter.

I hardly had a chance to acknowledge their support, for the blade-wielding priest advanced a step toward me, his hood falling back to reveal a thick mass of black hair, cut in the old style of James Bond like Beth had said. "So you've come to ask *me* to kill them all, to spare your family and your precious city from a catastrophic fate."

The lightning in his eyes cindered me, and I began to gasp, wanting to kick myself for coming to this cursed place when its landlord had no desire to offer aid. Ubel chuckled somewhere behind me, a sinister sound, and I heard one of the others murmur a few words in Ælte Teutonica to one of his comrades, a mockery of my impending doom. Had I not been so seized with fear, I might have whirled around to see who had spoken, to ask if his name was Anubis, or Osiris, or one of the others . . . for only the ancient ones spoke Ælte Teutonica.

Then Günter threw a new accusation at me that made me quake. "*You* are Swanhilde *Meissner* von Thaden, the Lady of Muniche and the *wife* of Johannes Reinhard

Meissner—the wretch who came here twenty years ago and *drank* of my knowledge without repaying his debt!"

I could say nothing to counter him. Günter obviously guessed my identity thanks to my stupid comment about 'my München.' He stepped toward me again, his face livid, the fingers of his right hand flexing on the handle of his dagger.

"*How* could you dare to come to me for help, when your precious Keyholder has thus far defaulted on his payment? Has he sent *you* here to pay? Are you prepared to give your life to take my place, *Leitalra?* Or should I keep you here, chained as my prisoner, until your Keyholder finally fulfills his pledge?" Günter's voice rose to a shout as he spoke. I saw the lightning dancing on the black hairs of his head, turning his irises into a blistering electric fire.

I sank to my knees on the stones, icy tears dampening my cheeks, my hands clasped in a gesture of desperate entreaty. "Please Herr Setzer . . . have mercy."

"Mercy from a Cursed One to whom you owe your very life? I think not." The ghastly crowd behind me murmured more loudly. A misty hand fell upon the nape of my neck, its grip strong, its elemental power thawing my ice, eliminating my defense.

Günter stood just centimeters from where I cowered, bending over me like a heartless judge as he growled, "You and your beloved Keyholder have a son, one who studies for the priesthood, I believe. Are you willing to curse him to fulfill your husband's pledge, handing his life over to me? Or should I simply kill you here and now, to give my cohorts a pure-blooded sacrifice?"

The grip on my neck grew tighter, and I choked on my tears, squeezing my eyes shut as I felt those invisible knives stabbing the air around me, the hands of death reaching for my heart. A shock of electricity raced through my veins when Günter took hold of my chin, prompting me to cry out in pain. He touched the point of his dagger to my throat with the command, "Beg me . . . *beg* me not to kill Muniche's Lady."

My eyes sprang open as my shoulders shook with sobs. I saw a thousand things in that endless moment—Günter's eyes, his fury. My son Max bending over a priest's tome. My daughter Freya practicing piano. Hans in the days of happiness, tracing his fingers tenderly down my thigh. The children I had taught. Üwe's artwork. My father's smile. Beth's happiness when she summoned snow in summer's heat. Cammie dancing underneath a silver moon. Freia pledging her eternal love to Heinrich at the Teutonic altar. Prince Otto, beaten and worn, leading his troops into Muniche for one final stand. And Augustin.

Augustin . . . my *husband* . . . a darkened cathedral . . . a green-draped bed . . . a sapphire ring . . . a promise that had been all but forgotten beneath Muniche's influence. But it would return, for death would free me at last. My lips parted, and though I did not beg for mercy again, I may have put my heart's defiant cries into words: "Augustin . . . forgive me . . . I love you."

And an ear-splitting crack resounded off of the stone walls of the chamber, a bright light exploding upon the periphery of my blurry vision. Gasps and shrieks filled the air. Günter's dagger clattered to the floor, my chin and neck loosed from his grip and Kasimir's. My mind was in a daze, and I could make no sense of what was happening.

I had been about to die—prepared, even—but now I heard the scratching sounds of the specters' claws upon the floor, scrambling away to the walls of the chamber. Then a voice spoke calmly, but with an underlying tone of disparagement . . . a resonant voice, a *perfect* voice . . . one I had not expected to hear again in this modern era. "The life of *this* Lady of Muniche is not yours to take, Günter Emilian Setzer."

A wretched croak split my throat asunder, and my eyes opened wide, the last traces of tears evaporating in the heat of the brilliant priest who stood now to my right, clad in cerulean robes that swirled with fire, his obsidian hair plunging to his shoulder blades. This new apparition glowed with an inner light, and the potency of his element had altered the flames of each cauldron to a radiant blue.

In his right hand he held a blazing sword of pure cerulean fire.

My mouth dropped open, but I could not speak, nor could I blink for fear of erasing this impossible vision before me: *Augustin*, looking as though he had stepped out of the spiritual realm. He glared away from me, toward Günter himself, whom I saw shrinking backwards out of the corner of my eye.

"I . . . I . . . didn't . . . her husband . . . he . . . he owes me." Günter stammered, his face blanched white, his lightning extinguished.

"It is not proper justice to hold the crimes of a family member against one who held no part in the matter," Augustin rejoined, pointing his sword at the groveling Black Priest. "How would you like it if I ascribed the sins of these dead wretches onto your account?"

"No! Please, Herr Wolfe! Have some pity on us . . . we didn't mean—"

"You meant to kill her, you beast, and as I stated earlier, *her* life does not belong to you." Augustin looked away from Günter for an instant so transitory I could not be sure it actually happened, but I think his eyes locked with mine. A choked sound escaped my lips, but he had already turned back to Günter with a solemn command. "You shall allow Muniche's *Leitalra* to return to her home unscathed, and afterward never torment her again, unless you wish me to burn all of you to ash and rend this fortress apart stone by stone. Do you understand me?"

"Yes, Herr Wolfe, we will keep her safe. I swear it!"

"See that you do not forget," Augustin warned him. He glanced toward the cluster of ghostly specters who clung to the walls, gaping at him around the flaming cauldrons of blue fire. Then, at long last, he finally looked directly at me, a chiding expression on his face, his light blue eyes smoldering.

I was still crouched upon the floor, too shocked by this unforeseen turn of events to have considered climbing to my feet. But now, as I stared into the eyes of my cursed husband for the first time in seventeen years, I managed to drag myself toward him just a little, reaching out one quivering hand. "*Augustin . . . .*"

But he shook his head and lifted his left hand in a sign of farewell. "Swanhilde," he murmured, his voice prompting my heartbeat to race, though Muniche's spirit rebuked my treason. "I advised you not to tamper with death in your era, for I cannot continually cross this border to save you."

Before I could respond, Augustin vanished as quickly as he had come, with the accompanying din and flash of light. My eyes blinked fitfully, and I crawled toward the spot where he had stood, cursing myself for *not* saying the most important thing, like he had done at our last farewell. Why could I never find something more profound to say than *Augustin*? I was such an idiot.

I had no idea how he had come, or from whence, but he *had* been here. So I whispered one phrase in Teutonica, hoping it may follow his spirit: "*I love you.*"

I felt a hand upon my shoulder, a pair of sturdy arms pulling me to my feet. I lifted my eyes to Günter's face, which showed no trace now of rage, only concern and what might have been respect. "Come, *Leitalra.* Let's go to another chamber to speak of your troubles privately."

He eyed the eleven ghouls who had begun to emerge from the shadows and said, "You may proceed with the sacrifices here, and I'll return once we have finished. Do not attempt to disturb us."

Günter led me from the fiery chamber once I was certain that my feet could support me. Konrad offered me a parting word, "Good luck, my Lady Muniche." He bowed low, almost losing his wig in the process, and I gave him with a wavering smile as I exited the room.

Chapter Twenty-eight

The Modern-Day Wraith

Once we returned to the ground floor, Günter led me to one of the four turrets. We ascended a tight, uneven stairwell without pausing at any of the first few landings. Weariness had begun to catch up with me by then, for I had already hiked up a mountain and then descended and emerged from the Black Castle's dungeons. I started to think I never wanted to see another stair step when Günter turned at last onto a landing I judged to be halfway up the turret.

He guided me into a decently-furnished parlor that sported a stone balcony accessible through double wooden doors draped with deep maroon curtains. The chamber had a chandelier, but Günter switched on a couple electric lights. He asked me to make myself comfortable on one of two scarlet sofas with black tassels sweeping the floor, before apologizing that his castle was not especially suited for receiving guests.

At that point I was grateful for the chance to rest; I would have been happy enough to simply sit on the floor. I assured him with a casual wave of my hand that the room was very welcoming. Removing my coat to lay it upon one of the couches, I settled myself there and glanced at the doors beneath the curtains, wondering if the balcony boasted a view of the mountains.

Günter sat at the opposite end of the sofa from me, looking rather agitatedly at the decorative lamps on tables in the corners of the room, then at the embers in the fireplace and at the portrait of a field of wildflowers that hung above the mantel. He muttered that he should have stopped at the kitchen to retrieve some wine or snacks, that he had never been a courteous host.

My curiosity about my companion piqued, though I suspected that like his living counterparts, he would not prefer to waste time exchanging stories that had nothing to do with the matter at hand. I assured him that I needed no food or drink, though my stomach had already given a few growls—he had doubtless heard them. After clearing my throat and trying to relax my stiff posture, I reopened the subject of the NVH and my family's predicament.

I told Günter more about the situation, mentioning Freya's abduction again with the remark that I would very much like to have her return home. I also cited Hans' illness and the fact that I would soon have a new Keyholder, likely some young fool I could not trust with my secrets.

"You said before, when we first met, that sometimes elderly people come to you seeking medical miracles," I reminded him, eyeing his stoic face.

"I have no cure for cancer, *Leitalra*," my charge said with a sigh, his gaze still fixed upon the fireplace, away from me. "I've been a doctor since before I was cursed, but my studies have yet to uncover an elixir of life. Youth can be regained for a time, but such spells are deadly, and shorten the hours."

Disappointment dimmed my ridiculous hope, but I pushed it aside. Even if Günter had discovered some sort of miraculous panacea, he would have no reason to give it to Hans. So I turned the conversation back to my request for aid, watching the Black Priest's face closely as I spoke, trying to detect a trace of humanity.

"I realize that as a Cursed One, you have little need for loyalty or honor, for a city, a people, or anything else," I said, contemplating how exactly I ought to word my appeal. "But I also know that, as a Cursed One, *you* know the histories that are hidden from our people. You know, as I know, what really happened in 1066, and that it all came about because of Prince Otto's Song of Time."

I paused, and Günter nodded once, glancing briefly at me. "Yes. That is true."

Before I could reiterate his earlier prediction—that the Saxon cabal would use time travel in a fresh attempt to eliminate Teuton blood from the earth—a noise in the corridor caught my attention. When I looked toward the doorway, I found myself staring at a young woman in her early twenties. She wore skinny jeans and a long-sleeved purple shirt with a neckline that revealed her cleavage. Her curly dark brown hair reminded me of Marga's; she had it pulled back in a clip. Her pale lips parted as if to speak, but Günter addressed her first.

"The sacrifices are not yet finished. You know better than to wander around when hell's minions are in the castle." Günter turned his face toward the girl, who had stopped just inside the doorway with her hands clasped in front of her. I saw his black eyebrows plunge downward, his visage hard with reproach.

"Oh," she breathed in a quiet voice, her hazel eyes widening. "I sensed you coming up from the dungeons and thought they had all gone."

"Get back to your chambers and return to spirit form. Now," Günter ordered.

"Yes, master," the young woman whispered, sounding chastened. She left the room in less than a second, and I heard the Black Priest sigh.

I had been too caught by surprise to offer a greeting to the woman, but her eyes had not acknowledged me once. They had remained riveted upon Günter, the man she called "master" . . . and he had told her to return to spirit form. A Teuton, then, though I had not stretched my icy spirit forth to discern her element. Was she here of her own volition, or had my undead companion taken her heart to use her as his blood slave?

With effort, I turned my torso back toward the man who sat at the far end of the sofa, working to dispel the knot of distrust that had formed in my stomach. "Is . . . she . . . your . . . partner?" I asked, unsure whether I wanted to know.

Günter's gaze had returned to the fireplace. "You didn't come here to pry into my affairs, *Leitalra*."

I pursed my lips and stuffed my hands between my thighs and the scarlet fabric of the couch. That response implied that my judgments were likely correct. *So he's not breeding Teuton babies and selling them anymore, but he now he has a Teuton blood slave locked away in this castle. He'd better not punish her heart for coming to look for him. She probably believes he loves her.*

I gazed at the portrait of wildflowers, silently praying for wisdom on how to handle this Cursed One. As much as my family needed his help, did I really want to collaborate with a man who held a blood slave? His expression had revealed no attachment to her when he ordered her away. Almost two decades of guiding my people down the path of morality, and here I sat about to make a deal with a dead slaveholder.

"I . . . I was going to say before . . . that my Keyholder and I fear what will become of the Teuton people if the NVH gets hold of the Torstein," I managed to say, keeping my focus on the portrait. Günter did not speak, so I went on, "I'll never give it to them as long as I live, but if they murder everyone I know . . . and take hold of *me*, to kill me at last . . . ." My voice trailed off.

Günter averted his eyes to me, his expression just as severe as it had been while he regarded the curly-haired young woman. "They will get it from your dead body, I presume?"

I bit my lip and looked down at my hands, shocked that I had actually given *that* away. Until now it had been a secret kept by only Hans and me. My husband would not be pleased with my lapse. Günter continued to analyze my face, and at length I nodded, then met his eyes.

"The man who came tonight to save me . . . Wolfgang, you call him"—my charge squirmed—"it was he who drove the Saxons and their devilish army from Bavaria after the defeats in the 1060s. And he could do it *because* of his gift of death, *because* of his immortality. That is why I came to you, Herr Setzer, because this threat can't be crushed without supernatural help. If there *is* a way to destroy the Torstein, the information would be here among the writings of Wolfgang."

The Black Priest stared at me, and I folded my hands again, a silent plea. "Ach, *Leitalra*, you mustn't demand that I make such a choice without deliberating first," he groaned, his expression aggrieved. "Loyalty has meant little to me for decades, not since the fall of the Nazis, and that allegiance is what brought me to this." He bared his right arm, displaying the black scar of the Cursed Ones.

"Though I comprehend your desire to save your daughter and bring these terrorists to justice, if my master incited this attack against you, my hands are tied. I could not work against my master in so blatant a fashion when my choices have already enraged him in recent years."

"Why then was Wolfgang able to eliminate the Saxons' immortal warriors, when Wuotan himself guided their steps?" I rejoined, not accepting his excuse. If Augustin had slain all of them, Günter could certainly stop the NVH. There were no indications that they claimed any immortal allies.

Günter's upper lip curved into a haughty sneer as he said, "If I did consider taking up your crusade, you realize there would be a hefty cost."

A chill crept up my spine, but I leveled the Cursed One with a determined look. "Name your price."

A hint of amusement twitched his lips into a smirk. "Your son."

I blinked at him, taken aback. "Excuse me?"

"Your Keyholder owes a debt to me, *Leitalra*."

He had mentioned that earlier in the dungeon, and I abruptly recognized that I had no riposte to offer. "I can't let the filial curse happen in my family," I hedged, knowing that such an indignity would hurt Augustin more than any other poor choices I had made. "There must be something—"

"I know what you've taught to the young Teutons of München," he charged with a scowl, crossing his arms. "I find it strange that one of us came to defend you less than an hour ago, while you urge your people never to curse, to leave the dead shut out of eternity forever."

I winced and leaned back against the couch, my thoughts many years in the past. "The one who came to defend me wouldn't forgive me if I allowed one of my children to be cursed. When I walked down the corridor with the busts, I saw that the number of Cursed Ones has multiplied in recent years. There have been four men cursed in the past two hundred years. This sad trend must stop."

Günter shook his head, not altering his stiff posture. "I have no intention of remaining here until kingdom come just to spare your son or anyone else's. This death of mine isn't a fate I prefer to carry. The choice is yours, *Leitalra*. If you want my help against the NVH, bring me a successor first."

My shoulders drooped, and I took hold of my wool coat, bringing it onto my lap. "I appreciate you hearing me out, either way," I said as I rose to my feet. "I'd suggest, though, that if you want a successor that much, maybe you should start exploring the mountains instead of holing up in this castle. You might not be the only Black Priest on the earth today."

I heard the man snort as I thrust my arms through my coat. Another option poked the edges of my brain along with memories of my experience in the Leutasch Gorge ... and the note I had gotten three years earlier.

Maybe that's what I can do while Sango and Üwe search for the NVH's lair. Maybe I can get Vreni or Max to join me in a hunt for the mysterious Cursed One, the one who freed three women, killed three slaveholders, and gouged that one bitch's eyes out. He might be willing to help us, and if not, I can tell Günter where to find his true "successor."

Resolved, I turned to regard Günter, who had risen to his feet himself, his countenance suggesting that he yearned to return to the dungeons and revel in his heathen sacrifices. In an effort to maintain my politeness, I asked to see the view from the balcony before I left. The Black Priest's dark blue eyes went round at my request, but he nodded and drew back the curtains with a flourish.

We stepped onto the balcony, and I found the vista as splendid as I had hoped—an idyllic snowy night, moonlit peaks spreading out into hills beyond. My ice rose within me as I leaned against the stone railing, and I decided that I would not bother to return to the main entrance, with its gargoyles and grim angels.

"I'll just leap into the forest from here," I murmured, "for this frost speaks to my blood."

"Would you deign to share a dance with me first?"

Baffled, I raised my eyebrows and circled to the right to regard Günter. He stood several steps away from me, his robe billowing with the night breeze. "Here?" I queried, nodding at the floor of the balcony.

He shook his head once and replied with a mysterious smile, "There." He cast his right hand toward the starry sky. I started in surprise, but the Black Priest stretched both hands out to me, allowing them to glow bright with lightning. "If you're so intimate with a Cursed One from the past, I have no doubt that you are also able to dance in spirit form."

I gaped at him, looking from his blazing hands to his face. *Does he want to make me his blood slave, too? Is one not enough?* He could not do that, of course, for Muniche's bonds secured my heart in Hans' hands. But hesitation caused me to vacillate, along with the brilliance of his lightning. I had never joined hands with an energy-related element with the intent to leap into the spiritual realm.

Günter favored me with a reassuring look and said, "Do not fear, my dear Lady. I have no wish to dishonor my hometown's elegant matron."

That threw me through another loop; I had not known that Günter had been born in München. Maybe if I heeded his whims, he might one day decide to go after the NVH of his own accord. So I threw caution aside and took his hands, letting my ice explode from my spirit at the same moment, coating my body entirely before I could register pain from the contact with lightning.

My spirit soared into the sky, the snowy landscape sprinkling my ethereal robes with frosty flakes. The peace of the intangible realm soothed the turmoil in my heart, and the icy breaths rising from the snow atop the peak reinvigorated me. Presently, Günter touched my shoulder, and I turned to face him, caution clothing my spirit in layers of ghostly ice.

His brilliance almost blinded my acute vision. His robes were solid waves of radiant electricity, a shimmer somewhere between pure white and the pleasantest topaz. He laughed as I ogled him, his eyes glittering like jewels. Then he offered me his hands once more and coaxed, *Come, icy goddess, manifestation of the Alpine splendor. Let's play amid the stars.*

And we did, likely longer than we should have. Günter led us into the firmament surrounding the mountains, where we whirled around his castle. My element summoned a dusting of snow from the peak to swirl around me, while my partner fashioned moonbeams into swords of powerful lightning. I thought back to the blue-fired blade Augustin wielded when he appeared in the dungeon and compared it privately to the ones Günter created.

I would have much to ponder when I returned to the Thaden house.

At one point we waltzed atop the main fortress' roof, from which München's lights were visible far to the north. My essence had grown enamored by our dance, the chill of snow in autumn, the cloudless night sky, the ancient stone castle with its cupolas and single carillon. Just as I started to acknowledge that we needed to halt our frolic, so I could drive home—it was nearly seven p.m. now, and the drive would take around two hours—my ice sensed another Teuton spirit lurking in the shadows beside the southeastern turret.

The Black Priest noticed our company and sent a thought into both of our minds. *Curiosity can be deadly in a place like this.*

A quiet gasp entered my mind, and I shifted my gaze from the spirit—the same woman who interrupted us earlier, her robes the wild translucence of wind—to Günter. His feet still moved in the proper steps of our waltz, but he had slipped one hand into his yellow-white robes, a position I knew well. He had wrapped his spiritual fingers around the woman's heart, sending a pointed message.

Are you . . . angry with me? Her hesitant words agitated my brain.

I stared at Günter, disgust building within me; but before I could act on my judgments he answered, *You should know better than that. Join us.*

Yes, master. Her mental voice was like a whisper on the breeze, and in the next instant her wind caught our robes in a graceful draft. Her face radiant with what appeared to be delight, she began to waltz along with us, her airy eyes locked upon Günter's luminous energy. I followed along in silence, my jumbled emotions wreaking havoc on my spirit's loveliness. The young woman adored him without question, but how did he see her?

After Günter ordered her back into the shadows, the two of us returned to our bodies. As I unlocked my frozen hands from his sparking ones, I lifted my chin to look the Black Priest in the eyes, needing at least a few answers. "My Keyholder once told me you went insane in the 1960s, and that's why you started a business trafficking Teuton children. But someone else recently told me that you don't do that anymore. Was that truth or a lie?"

I shoved my still-frozen hands into the pockets of my wool coat, watching the sentiments play across Günter's face. He tugged his hood back over his head and said, "I no longer adopt out Teuton children because of her."

"Because of . . . the windy spirit who joined our dance?" I had to be sure.

Günter turned away in response, but my ice sensed his tension mingling with something much purer—devotion. She was not his blood slave. She was one who had begun to unearth him from hell's bowels, a trait I knew well. Relief wiped my disgust away and lit a renewed flame of hope within me. *The filial curse has no meaning where eternity is concerned. Any Cursed One can find redemption.*

Turning for the railing, I summoned my ice magic to the fore again, so I could simply leap into the forest in a straight trajectory to Hans' BMW. But first, I considered my cursed companion and asked one last question. "Herr Setzer, tell me about that gift of death that all Teutons fear."

His shoulders tensed beneath his midnight robe, his back still turned to me. "You were angry with me earlier, and I sensed the gift pricking my heart, but you didn't kill me." Günter nodded once, still looking away. "Is it just a myth then, that Black Priests eventually lose control over that gift?"

He chuckled despondently. "You may call me Günter, *Leitalra*, and it is no myth. I retain control over that atrocious curse only by the grace of my predecessor, Konstantin. He killed the woman who cursed me before I could do it myself. He thought it may give me some advantage before my master." He moved to face me at last, a dark grimace sharpening his jaw.

"So only those who kill the one who cursed them lose control," I translated, suddenly fearful of Augustin's fate, since he was the one who wrote of Prince Otto's suicide. *I hope he didn't lie about it just to cover an act of revenge.*

"Yes, it is so, for my master considers that act the pinnacle of hate, the final nail on the coffin of the accursed."

I nodded, troubled, and prepared to go. "May I ask you something in return?" Günter inquired, prompting me to pause at the railing. "Who *were* you . . . to Wolfgang?" He stared at me in what might have been awe.

I smiled and answered simply, "I am his wife." Then I leapt into the snow.

Chapter Twenty-nine

Novel Perplexities

When I returned home some time later, my son accosted me first. He stood like a sentry beside the front steps, both his outfit and his element concealing him from the untrained eye. He met me in the garage as I parked the BMW, embracing me the moment I stepped out of the car. "Mutti, where *have* you been? Pappi's worried sick about you!" He spoke in a low but urgent tone, pulling back to stare at me with eyes as black as coals.

I smiled at him faintly, knowing that I would tell him the whole story some other time. "It looks like your Pappi isn't the only one who's been worried," I observed, running a hand through his slightly tousled hair.

"You're right," he admitted somewhat reluctantly, trailing behind me in my course for the side door. "When Sango called Vreni and learned you hadn't been there, we all assumed the worst."

I sighed and ruffled my son's hair again. The greater part of me dreaded the confrontation I was about to have with his sick Pappi—the argument I could not avoid, since I had no desire to lie to Hans. "You run up to your room, Max," I urged my son when we entered the laundry room, giving him a light shove on the back. "I'm going to find something to eat down here and get Sango off my back. Then I'll come tell you goodnight."

Max mumbled his assent, sounding as though he much preferred to remain downstairs and witness whatever was about to happen. He dawdled at the bottom of the back staircase as I switched on the kitchen lights, en route to the fridge in search of leftovers. I heard him inquire very softly, "Mutti . . . what *were* you doing . . . being gone so long?"

I shot him a conspiratorial look, yanking a can of Fanta and a container of Lise's *Eintopf* stew from yesterday out of the fridge. "I was at the castle of the Cursed Ones, looking for help in our fight against the NVH."

Max gaped. "Is Günter going to *help* us, Mutti?" he demanded, right when I heard the distinct sound of approaching footsteps—three pairs.

"Get *out* of here, Max!" I ordered in a low hiss, shooing him away and sticking the stew in the microwave. My son vanished in an instant, and I gathered all of my courage as I turned around to face the exasperation of my husband, Üwe, and our head of security.

It soon became apparent that while Sango and Üwe were willing to accept the short explanation for now—it was nearing ten, after all—Hans ordered that I tell him everything right away, while I ate my dinner in fact. If he waited until after I had finished eating, his weariness might get the better of him, and my rashness had irritated him enough to rekindle his tenacity. My husband's recent tests had revealed that traces of his cancer had returned despite his chemo regimen, so his doctors were research-ing other ways to halt its course.

Hans dismissed Sango and Üwe from the kitchen shortly after I told them I had sought assistance from a new source and was detained longer than expected. Once we were alone, my Keyholder pulled up a chair across from where I sat, gazing into my eyes with a concerned expres-sion, his gaunt hands clasped in front of him.

"Speak to me, Swanie," he said, his voice strained, his eyes circled with exhaustion. "I sensed your fear through our bond, some four hours ago . . . and it was a fear unto death. Do you realize how helpless I feel, when you run off on some foolish errand while lying to everyone, and then I hear your heart screaming for deliverance when I can do *nothing?*" His jaw trembled.

Guilt descended upon my shoulders then. I heard the passion in his words and felt the fingers of his spirit wrapping securely around my heart, desiring to comfort, protect, and rebuke all at once. I nearly choked on a bite of potato in my mouth, and I dropped my head into my hands.

"Oh, Hans . . . master . . . please forgive me. I shouldn't have done it, not without telling you first . . . but I was afraid . . . afraid that you wouldn't allow me to go."

"And where did you go?" he prompted.

I lifted my head and met his gaze as I told him, seeing all of the horror, the disappointment, the reproof. "I *had* to do it, Hans, please don't be angry. It was nothing you've done, no fault of yours. I'm just getting so desperate, unable to do anything tangible to save our daughter. Ach, my love, I *had* to do something, if only to get my mind off this mess! Everyone else who has tried to help us has been killed, so why not appeal to the one who can't die?"

Hans held his peace for a few moments, looking down at his hands as he gathered his thoughts. "So you went to the dead man," he said, "and nearly joined the dead yourself, judging by the cries of your heart."

"But he didn't kill me," I pointed out, taking up a forkful of stew once more. "He didn't even hurt me. You'll find no blemishes on my body tonight."

"Was your quest successful, then? Did the Cursed One pledge his inglorious help to Muniche's *Leitalra?*" Hans eyed me distrustfully, rubbing a hand across his pale forehead, likely attempting to ease a headache.

I sighed and looked down at my food, not wanting to reveal this part to my husband. "Well . . . he said he'd help us if . . . if . . . we curse our son." Hans held his peace, but

I sensed his disapproval. "I told him I couldn't do that, and I dropped a hint about the priest who saved me in the Leutasch Gorge."

"You didn't." Hans sounded horrified.

"I talked around it," I clarified, not wanting my husband to fear that I had given away too much. "And I told Günter about Augustin . . . Wolfgang, they call him . . . about his defense of Muniche."

My Keyholder stiffened at the subject, but I quickly explained, "I wanted him to see the parallel—if it was a Black Priest who defeated the Saxons in the past, maybe." I let it hang.

Hans asked little more after that, to my relief, and soon we left the kitchen behind and returned to our private parlor, ready to put my irrational escapade onto the back burner. I did not mention the other eleven wraiths, or the sacrifice, or Augustin's sudden appearance to rescue me from Günter's fury. Nor did I tell Hans about the young woman who inspired Günter's devotion, whose influence had somehow convinced him to stop breeding women and selling babies.

A host of other perplexities troubled me later that night as I lay beside my sleeping husband, contemplating the day's happenings. Most of my questions revolved around Augustin, for I had not yet completely recovered from the shock of seeing him so unexpectedly—and so briefly. I smacked myself mentally over and over, knowing I should have said so much to him, told him I was happy with Hans, like he had wished, and that I had been serving München as her Lady should, thanks to the wisdom I had gained in the past. I should have told him about the bond of the city, how profound and gratifying it was, how nothing could compare with the glory of feeling my Keyholder's love.

Maybe it was better that he had vanished so quickly. If I'd had the time to say those things, my mad defiance would have resurfaced, as it did hours later while I lay wide awake in my bed. *I would have told him that I still loved him so much, always, forever, just like we promised . . . that Muniche's bonds meant nothing . . . though it be heresy . . . that I wanted him to take me with him . . . to leave this duplicity behind . . . .*

And there were countless questions I wished I could have asked him, a myriad of new dilemmas addling my heart. How had he come to the future in the first place? Did he unearth some other portal to time, something that Prince Otto never discovered? From what era did he come, and how had he been getting along without me? Had he actually eliminated the *Toteheri*, and had he ravaged the Saxons as well, scaring them away from Bavaria for a few centuries at least?

Why did he look so brilliant and faultless, when the last time he had come he had looked like those wretches from hell? How had he known to come at *that* moment, right as Günter was about to end my life? Did he still think of me, dream of me, remember our triumphs, our love . . . our promise . . . the sapphire ring? Had he ever put his faith in God and turned his back on Wuotan? And would he take me with him, if I asked . . . even if it would scar my soul forever?

Friday was Jürgen Peninger's funeral. Üwe and I went for the sole purpose of supporting Eva. He had invited her to move onto the Thaden property, but she said she had to settle her husband's affairs first. Lise and I had finished setting up every spare chamber for company, though Üwe had chosen to make use of the pull-out couch in the family room instead. On our way to the chapel, he mentioned that I may want to ask Fonsi and Alison to join our unofficial safe house, since the NVH had targeted their family once already.

Some of Jürgen's business colleagues spoke eulogies on his behalf, along with an older brother whose deep-seated eyes gave me the creeps. I sat with a few women I knew vaguely from the festivals, while Üwe took his place in the same pew as Eva and her two children. Neither she nor the children took part in the memorial at all.

I kept my ice on high alert throughout the ceremony, brushing the spirits of each Teuton present, silently wondering whether any of them had betrayed their own people. Did the arsonist sit among us unseen? As the clergyman droned on about goodness and conscience—two platitudes I knew had no power to save—my muses shifted to Claudia Haas, wife of the deceased Warren. Her son had found her dead in her apartment. She had slit her throat and left a note intimating that she could not live with the ache of her severed heart-bond.

Eva, on the other hand, had reclaimed her agency with impressive celerity. From what Üwe told me, she was well on her way to keeping herself afloat thanks to Jürgen's investments. She had expressed an interest in *Selakerza's* resources and confessed that she had longed to make use of them much earlier. "If I'd tried to escape his sway, he would have hurt our children. He told me that over and over, as soon as our son was born." Üwe had repeated her words to me a few days earlier, and they addled my soul as I sat at a memorial to an abusive man.

Though the selfish part of me longed to forsake the modern era after Hans' death, leaving the responsibilities of the Teuton community to others, I could not do that without readying people to further my causes. As long as Vreni remained safe, she could continue to help abuse survivors through *Selakerza.* Erika and Iliana would surely take up my mantle along with Sophia and Sean, once they could come out of hiding. My son Max had made it clear that when he became a Teuton priest, he would uphold my lessons of respect, acceptance, and honest partnership. He promised not to fall into the lure of dominating a woman, training his future children to view every human being as their peers rather than rivals or subjects.

On the way home from the funeral, I told Üwe about my experience at the Black Castle. I focused mainly on Günter—leaving out the sacrifices and Augustin's role—admitting that the man refused to help us unless we found him a successor.

"I'm actually pretty sure that there's another Cursed One stalking the Alps, one who hides from the Teuton people and his undead fellows. I might go on the hunt during the next few months, see if I can figure out where he hides."

Üwe's jaw clenched as he turned Hans' BMW onto Thaden property. "I haven't heard of any such thing."

"Hans thinks Wuotan's keeping him apart from Günter and from the rest of us. But *I* think if Günter won't help us, maybe he will. He's the one who killed those slaveholding priests back in 2011."

I heard Üwe's intake of breath as he parked the car in its rightful spot in the garage. "You think a Black Priest was responsible for that?"

"I *know* it," I corrected him, retrieving my purse and reaching for the door's handle. "And if that one's willing to break down one of our people's worst practices, he might be willing to stop the NVH, too." Üwe did not seem sanguine about my assessment, and he warned me to conduct my hunts in spirit form only.

Vreni, Stefan, and their three sons moved into the Thaden house over the course of the weekend, transferring their meaningful possessions beneath Sango's energy shield one carload at a time. Vreni informed me that her father insisted she allow his most trusted security guard to accompany them. "He's the type to build a bunker in a cave, with all this suspicious activity going on," she told me Saturday afternoon as I helped her carry a couple bags upstairs. She and her priestly husband would set up camp in the gable that once belonged to my father.

"We may end up needing something like that before this is sorted," I sighed, scooching toward the wall as her sons charged down the front stairs in a rowdy group. They would take up residence in one of the upstairs suites along with Vreni's security guard.

On Sunday afternoon, I sat with Vreni in the gazebo by the stream as her sons explored the gardens under Max's guidance. Although I did not wish to relate the entire story of my time travels to her, I admitted that our people might be under attack by a sect of racists. That was the excuse that drove Fonsi and Frau Diesen in their investigations, reason enough for the ongoing spate of murders.

"Stefan's of the same opinion," Vreni said, sitting on the bench across from me with her fingers scrolling her smartphone. "My Pappi has noticed a dip in his company's profits lately, same as yours. They've gone after priests, regular guys, women, and children, so they clearly have no compunctions about who they kill."

I shuddered and stretched my spirit toward the stream, wordlessly seeking its comfort. "We know their alleged 'headquarters' in Leipzig, but our moles have seen only a few people come and go from there, and not every day. Same with their P.O. box in Dresden. The person who checks it always cloaks their features and vanishes among the U-Bahnen afterward."

"No luck tracing the two blokes who crashed your office with Ostermann?"

"Not yet. He only gave their first names, and there's a lot of Arnes and Emils out there." I frowned, and Vreni slipped her phone into her jacket's pocket, raising her head to meet my gaze in sympathy. "It really pisses me off that it's been next to impossible to pin anything on Ostermann himself. There's no traces of his family or connections anywhere, even in government records. The only things we've found under that name involve stock trades. It must be an assumed name."

"Has Sango or Fonsi ever thought to scout out the office in spirit form? Grab whoever goes in and bleed the truth from them?" Vreni raised her eyebrows at me, crimson fire smoldering in her eyes.

I grinned at that idea. "A Teuton can't bleed someone in spirit form, at least, not with the intention of uncovering information."

"Too bad. It'd be nice to get these Saxons frightened about vampires."

The two of us giggled for a moment, and afterward I told her about my visit to the Black Castle. I explained that we may need help from darker sources in order to defeat the NVH. Vreni listened to the tale with rapt attention, and when I ended it with Günter's awful demand, she curled her upper lip. "How dare he ask you to curse your own son? Max doesn't deserve such treachery."

"I know, but I kind of see his point. It'd be dreadful to be trapped on the earth when you're already dead. But I've been thinking about his requirement, and I might try another way to find him a successor."

So I shared my plans to embark on a hunt for the elusive Cursed One responsible for the fires of 2011. And to my relief, Vreni pledged to accompany me, her fiery eyes glimmering with anticipation.

Chapter Thirty:

Trifling Progress

During the month of November, Hans and I faced the task of choosing four priests to reestablish the Teuton Council of München. This proved more difficult than one might think. There were more than enough Teuton priests in München, both young and old, and many of the younger ones had attended my classes. Hans knew all of them more intimately than I did, and he said that quite a few would play the role of Teutonic guardians very effectively—if we asked it of them under normal circumstances.

Six of the men we spoke to refused the duty, citing excuses from lack of time to a sense of inadequacy. Hans and I privately labeled the whole of them cowards, for we suspected that they were too afraid to take up the duty when the previous four had been brutally murdered. We both agreed not to broach the subject of the Torstein before any of the novices in hopes of protecting them from the NVH as long as possible, though we knew that our efforts would come to naught after Hans' time was up.

To my delight, Vreni's husband Stefan eagerly accepted a position on the council. He had spent a lot of time with Sango and Üwe since moving onto Thaden property and helped with their investigations whenever he had a break from his corporate obligations. Matthias von Uffel—one of the priests in the process of training my son—also agreed to take up the duty, becoming the youngest council member on record at only twenty-four years of age. By the end of the month, we had completed the council at six priests, Helge Brennemann and Josef Fehr the final two.

As autumn progressed into winter, my husband's health slowly declined. He continued taking his chemo pills on schedule, but his doctors advised that if his next scan showed that the tumor continued to grow, it may be time to discuss end-of-life treatments instead. Hans suffered his first seizure in early December, and afterward he chose to confine himself to a handful of second floor chambers—our bedroom, private parlor, and his office—for the most part. Whenever he heeded my entreaties to join everyone else for lunch or dinner, two of us shadowed his every footstep, ready to support him if he stumbled.

By December every spare chamber in the Thaden house was occupied. Along with Vreni's family and Üwe, Fonsi and Alison had moved in, as well as Eva. Alison and Eva shared the other suite on the third floor, while Fonsi planted himself in Sebastian's former cottage. He insisted upon keeping his management position at Lidl, so on days when he needed to appear at an office or storefront, the two of us drove there together. Fonsi usually kept quiet during those trips, his grief from having lost his wife and stepdaughter clinging to his aura in a thick cloud. But once he grumbled that he was about to stop paying for Frau Diesen's services, since she had yet to locate the NVH's lair after a half year of research.

Dinners proved the most festive moment of each day, when my friends and family gathered around the large table in the formal dining room to eat and chat about the day's events. The adults would discuss topics from the NVH situation to everyday tasks like cleaning and business. Sometimes Max or Fonsi mentioned sports, while Üwe kept us abreast of the local news. These gatherings reminded me of meals in the great hall back in the eleventh century, when Freia and I sat with Count von Meldorf and his vassals, discussing the planting, shearing, harvest, and local gossip. And while I sat chewing my food as the conversations droned on, I found myself yearning for simpler times, for an era when no criminals kidnapped my children.

The NVH sent an email just before Christmas. Their latest message mocked me for not sending the Torstein to their P.O. box in Dresden. "Our spokesman left you his business card at your first meeting, so it's your own fault our disagreement drags on. The child cries for her family in her sleep, aware that her circumstances are a product of her Mutti's selfishness."

That final line chilled me, and I seriously considered giving them what they wanted all over again. Hans ended up asking Sango, Üwe, and Stefan to talk me out of it, and they did. But the guilt weighed on me, dragging me into very dark environs. I withdrew from the others in the house while they celebrated the winter holidays, and I did not attend the New Year's festival for the first time since I had become München's Lady. Vreni and Eva passed on well wishes from my people, none of which found their way through the mire enclosing my soul.

I grew frustrated with our lack of progress. Sango had just hit another dead end, and Fonsi had indeed released Frau Diesen, so I felt as though our efforts went backwards rather than forward. Vreni and I had searched the mountains around Mittenwald in spirit form thrice without finding a trace of the elusive Cursed One, not even any hints of errant dark energy. Vreni suggested that we may have better luck checking the area near Innsbruck, since that Keyholder was the one who called the priestly conference in 2011; she even proposed that we question the one who lost her eyes to the enigmatic specter.

But depression shackled me in iron fetters, and I could not maintain my interest in our hunt. Two outsiders on Süddeutsche Getriebe's board were found dead under mysterious circumstances at a New Year's party, and the Keyholder and Lady of Freising died of carbon monoxide poisoning in their home just three days later. Whether those deaths had any connections with the NVH or not, I felt as though I plodded through a sunless land of decay and anguish.

Max departed the house on the evening of January 11th to make his first attempt at the initiation into the Teutonic priesthood. He would not turn sixteen until June of that year, but he managed to persuade Jan, Matthias, and Stefan to facilitate the rite anyway. He and his priestly comrades had been plotting some sort of insurrection against the NVH ever since Freya's kidnapping, and I feared that my son may take his first step into the world of crime after he earned his priestly robe. Hans, Üwe, and I sat together in the private parlor after dinner that evening, solemnly conversing about the young priests' plans. To my irritation, it seemed that neither Hans nor Üwe was opposed to their involvement.

"We need all the help we can get, Swanie," Üwe reminded me while I sat stiffly on the couch with a wineglass in hand. "And you know your son's not going to tell his friends about the Torstein."

"But he's still underage!" I complained, my maternal instincts jabbing at my peace. "I don't need my child running off to the north to do who-knows-what."

"I'll remind him he's not allowed to leave the property without permission when he comes home tonight," Hans said in a weary voice. He sat in the recliner with a blanket draped over his body, his withered neck barely appearing sturdy enough to support his head.

I shuddered and took a sip of Riesling as Üwe said, "If Max and his friends want to stir up trouble with the NVH, it'd be best for them to do it as spirits. That way outsiders couldn't track them."

He and Hans exchanged a few phrases on that subject while I frowned in the direction of the hallway. Would my son actually pass the initiation at the tender age of fifteen? How would Wuotan react when he summoned him into his darkness?

The next thing I knew, Hans gave a ragged cough and leveled his eyes upon me. "Have you felt any camaraderie with Helge Brennemann yet?"

It took all of my control to avoid rolling my eyes at my husband. He asked me that question every day, sometimes more than once, although usually he did so when we were alone. When Herr Brennemann joined the council, Hans saw it as divine confirmation that the man should succeed him as Keyholder—a thirty-three-year-old meteorologist at the local TV station. Üwe turned his face toward me from where he sat at the opposite side of the couch, looking interested.

"Master, please don't ask me to do something I can't, or to be someone I'm not," I responded. "Seriously, you can't expect me to fall head over heels for a damn snowman or any other local priest. You've been my loyal partner all this time, and you know how these heart-bonds work. You can't direct my affections to a stranger while you're still alive."

Üwe made a sound in his throat that could have been agreement, then took a swig from his bottle of dark beer. Hans sighed and shut his eyes, his expression grieved. "Swanie, darling, you need to consider it with an open mind. At least be *willing* to look ahead for the sake of our city, of our people."

"Well, you clearly believe Herr Brennemann is the perfect man for the job, so don't let my utter disinterest stop you from handing him the keys," I said, taking a final sip from my wineglass and rising to my feet. I turned for the hallway with the intent of taking the glass downstairs. I had no desire to put up with two elderly priests begging me to open my soul to some media personality.

"Offer the keys to Günter Setzer."

Üwe's statement froze me in my tracks, and I pivoted to gawk at him. "That wouldn't work. Günter holds someone else's heart," I said.

"I refuse to offer this responsibility to a cursed madman," Hans answered in a peevish tone. Üwe assured him with a casual wave of his hand that he had been joking. But as I made my way down to the kitchen not long after, my sons' words arose in my mind, the true nature of my heart's yearnings.

But you love Augustin already. So if he comes here to take the NVH down before Pappi dies, he can offer him the keys.

Hans would never agree to that. And neither would Augustin. But it was pleasant to imagine him taking vengeance on my behalf, his visage resplendent with light and fire, his curse reaching out to still the hearts of those who murdered without restraint. *I might need you before this is over, Augustin,* I thought while I washed out the wineglass in the sink. *But what could I give you in return when my heart is bound to this city as long as I live?*

By the time my son came home late that night, most of the household had gone to bed, Hans included. I sat in the front parlor rereading one of Beth's books, while Sango and Fonsi sat with their heads bent over a laptop in the corner of the room. When I heard the front door open, I trained my eyes on the vestibule, watching a black-robed figure close the door carefully behind him.

My ice recognized his darkness immediately, and my lips stretched into a proud smile as he stepped into the parlor and let his hood down. Sango and Fonsi rose to their feet, and Max gave us a brief rundown of his experience in a voice that sounded more ethereal than normal. He revealed none of the details but admitted that priestly rites were more complex than he had realized.

"What happened to Stefan?" Fonsi asked as Sango and Max shook hands rather austerely.

My son jerked his head toward the side of the house and answered, "He had to park the car, so he's probably coming in through the garage." Fonsi headed for the side door while Sango packed up his laptop with the remark that he ought to be getting to bed himself. We spoke our farewells, and he exited the parlor, leaving me alone with my son.

Max's black eyebrows came together as he looked at me, his darkness reaching out to brush my ice. "Mutti, are you proud of me? I did this for you and for Freya, to protect you from Wuotan's wiles."

I offered him a small smile and studied his appearance. The robe he wore matched his element exactly, its folds indicating that it could accommodate Max's future growth. His attire made him look far more mature than his fifteen years.

"I hope you're not planning on cutting any deals with a demon," I noted, resting my hands casually against my hips and lifting my chin to meet his gaze. "I don't want my son walking the path that leads to eternal torment."

"I won't," Max assured me, "but my friends and I won't let anyone hurt you or Pappi. And we're going to get Freya out." His irises darkened a shade.

"No crime," I reminded him, holding up the parental finger. "And you need permission from Pappi or me before you leave this property, remember."

"I know, Mutti," he murmured, drawing me into his dark embrace. I closed my eyes and tried to believe him as his youthful voice promised me, "We're going to make the NVH wish they'd never thought to attack our people."

Another anonymous email arrived shortly after my son earned his robe. It stated rather petulantly that if I refused to mail the item they wanted, I should send a message to their P.O. box listing a date and time in which I planned to grace the doors of their headquarters, alone, with the Torstein in my possession. Sango rolled his eyes when he read the email and joked that if they were so intent on my visiting them "alone," maybe I ought to let Max come with me under cover of darkness. "It seems like they're hoping for a battle of threats," Sango observed, "and we can give them that, for my sources are making progress in tracking down these criminals. It'll buy us time."

I asked Sango to send a note to the P.O. box on my behalf, warning the NVH that my P.I. had tracked their emails and would soon bring them before the courts to be tried for kidnapping and murder. That was not entirely true, but I hoped such a threat may give them pause. The tactic seemed to work for a time, as no more messages came for over a month.

Hans' health worsened exponentially during the month of February, which did little to ease my stress. He began having regular seizures and spent much of his time in bed. He had stopped taking the chemo pills in January, after his doctors admitted that they could do little to improve his quality of life. Scans of his tumor showed that it had begun to spread, and by the end of the month we arranged for hospice care, since Hans wished to die at home with his family.

Because of his illness, I hid the worst of my fears any-time I spoke to him. Instead, I preferred to talk of times past, of the triumphs we had shared, our marriage, our community service, our passionate activities in bed. My husband smiled at these subjects, but then he would ask for my thoughts on his successor, something I did not want to confront. I feared that if Hans offered the keys to Herr Brennemann, the man would use Muniche's bonds to enslave me, bleed all of my secrets from me and distort my cherished memories of Augustin.

On the sixteenth of February, a Sunday, Lise and I helped Hans make his way to the chair lift so he could enjoy lunch with our friends. Despite my husband's frailty, he generally tried to amble from room to room at least once each day. While he could not eat much anymore, his face always brightened at the sight of Vreni's sons squabbling over the food, at his son sitting primly beside him, updating him on recent soccer matches.

After we helped Hans into his seat at the dining room table, I stepped into the family room for a quick breather, my eyes zeroing in on the brilliant rays arcing into the chamber from the sunroom. I needed to get outside more. I had started to feel like I lived at a hospital, since Hans' bed was set up with railings and monitors now, while I occupied a single mattress beside my balcony doors. The room I had loved for so long had become a veritable cage, a place of grief and pain.

Sango sat in a chair beside Üwe's pull-out couch, his serious face fixated on the screen of his laptop. "Hey," I greeted him. "Lunch is almost ready, but I need a few minutes to myself. Can I use your laptop to check my email?"

"Sure," Sango answered, tapping a few keys before handing the computer to me and stretching his arms and legs. "What's on the menu today?"

"I think it's a farmer's breakfast, courtesy of Fonsi and Alison," I said. Sango made an approving hum before departing the room. Directing my steps toward the sunlight, I smiled at the scents of peonies and roses mingling with the fountain's trickling stream to welcome me into nature's indoor grandeur.

I made my way to the settee and sat down, relishing the serene atmosphere of the sunroom for a lingering moment. Sometimes I wished I could just lose myself in the realm of nature, among the Edelweiß on the mountains, a place where my Teutonic magic invigorated me, restored me, shielded me from the world's troubles. Stories of a new virus had begun to taint the news reports, my Keyholder's health waned daily, my son spent half the days in spirit form conspiring with his friends, and my daughter suffered somewhere out of reach.

Eventually I pulled myself from my reverie and focused on Sango's laptop, opening the browser and signing into my email. Any sense of peace evaporated in an instant when I saw the message sitting at the top of the screen, its title filling me with trepidation: "So Little Time Left . . . ."

There was a file attached to the email.

I forced myself to take several deep breaths, stretching my ice forth to call for my most trusted supporter—my son Max. He came running into the sunroom, clad in jeans and a tan sweater, his thick locks rumpled, his eyes already black. I gestured at the computer screen before he could ask any questions, and he sat at my side, his eyes catching the title that had thrust a dagger through my heart.

Max cursed and yanked the computer onto his own lap, his fingers tapping the mouse to open the email. What I read prompted me to squeak in terror.

"Frau von Thaden,
We regret having to send you this file, but perhaps once you've listened to its contents you'll come to your senses regarding the item we seek. She is such a feisty whore, satisfying in a macabre way. What a pity we'll soon have to kill her. You have one week."

Max spewed a stream of Bayerisch curses before he looked at me and said, "This may not be something you want to hear, Mutti." The malevolence in his eyes provoked me to edge away from him.

"You know we can't do anything about it. Not from here, at least," I pointed out, blinking at my son's ire.

"I realize that," he answered in a dead voice, glancing once at me with the query, "Are you sure you don't want to leave?"

I grated my teeth and summoned all of my courage. "It was sent to me, not you. Play it."

The audio file proved to be a minute long, but that was more than sufficient.

It began with a quavering voice I knew well that said, "Mutti, they're going to hurt me because you won't give them the Torstein. I don't understand. Why would you let them do this? I thought you loved me!" A girlish cry pierced my eardrums, and then came a few seconds of static.

Followed by sounds that sickened me to the core.

Chapter Thirty-one

So I Must Lose Them Both

Within seconds, it became clear how the NVH intended to "hurt" my daughter. My body crumpled to the floor, my limbs tucked into the fetal position as salty tears poured from my eyes. My heart shattered into pieces, and I knew I had no other option now. I would have to give up the Torstein before they killed her.

One week.

How Max managed to keep his cool long enough to silence the audio file and set Sango's laptop onto the table, I know not. Even though my ice had contracted into a brick in my chest, I sensed his darkness churning around me, infiltrating the entire sunroom with unadulterated hatred. I had not wanted my son to turn to crime just to crush our enemies, but now? Now, after I recognized Ostermann's aroused voice as he took advantage of my daughter?

I heard something crash to the ground, and I found out later that Max had upended one of the putto statues before stomping into the house in a wave of fury. I croaked out a few words as he fled, pleas for him not to tell Hans, not to ruin lunch for everyone else. Forsaken, I wallowed in my anguish, my ever-multiplying afflictions breaking me at last.

I would have to cut the Torstein from my hip and give it to a sect of Saxon purists, of racists, murderers, pedophiles. But how was I to do that when we had yet to find their lair? The P.O. box in Dresden was out. Should I visit their office in Leipzig "alone," as they had wished? Would Freya be there waiting for me, or would they rob me and lock me away somewhere to never see another day? Whether they had Teutons working for them or not, the NVH knew the methods of restraining an element, or my daughter would have used her dark energy to escape.

Vreni came to my side at some point, her vibrant red fire reaching out to console my spirit. She sat with me in silence for a while, and eventually everything spilled from my lips. I told her about the Torstein, how all this time I had protected it to keep our people safe. But this was the final straw. Those foul men had raped my innocent child, their latest threat tearing away the last of my resolve. I could not sacrifice Freya for some imagined "greater good." Her suffering far outweighed the previous murders —swift ends.

Vreni held her peace until I managed to push myself into a sitting position, blinking teary eyes at the childlike angel, face down on the floor with its dainty hands broken off. That statue and its counterpart had come with the property, vestiges of an era long gone. The first casualty of Max's anger. I sniffed and wiped my eyes on my sleeve, fear gnawing at my soul as I wondered what my son would do now. Would he lead his priestly friends in a charge against our foes?

I sighed and leaned my head upon Vreni's shoulder. "Did . . . did my son . . . tell everyone at the table . . . what happened?" I could hardly get the words out.

"He asked me to look after you and then snagged Sango and my husband," Vreni answered, her tone heavy with sorrow. "Fonsi's eating with my kids in the kitchen, or Max likely would have grabbed him, too."

"He's going to want to lead some kind of rescue brigade," I muttered, shivers running their way down my spine. "But the NVH probably beefed up their security before they sent that message. They might have laid traps to catch Teutons."

"I don't know," Vreni murmured, her right arm sturdy around my shoulders. "I just don't know if you should give them what they want. Especially if they want the power to bend time. They could find a way to completely pervert reality if they got that."

"I can't let them keep hurting Freya. I can't," I said, my heart wailing within me.

"I agree, and I think that once we catch them, we should punish them under Teuton law instead of the official courts. These villains need to suffer." I met my friend's gaze and saw scarlet flames sizzling in her eyes, her expression set.

"Well, we know Fonsi's all about the Virstohran," I noted, realizing that I needed to read up on exactly what that rite entailed. "But I still think we could use the help of a Black Priest, someone who doesn't abide by any mortal laws."

Vreni raised her eyebrows at me. "You want to check the mountains around Innsbruck for a couple hours this afternoon?"

Sighing heavily, I allowed my spirit to accept the gift of vitality my girlfriend offered. Maybe we could rescue my daughter without setting our people up for destruction. "I guess that's better than giving the NVH a way to destroy the world. We probably ought to eat something first."

Word of our antagonists' latest crime struck Hans' stamina, and he spent the entire afternoon in bed, drifting in and out of awareness. As much as I longed to join Vreni's search, I ended up staying by my husband's side, uncertainties about my fate after his passing joining the tumult of my thoughts. He admitted at one point that he should have heeded my instincts and taken our children out of school much earlier. I gently admonished him not to blame himself, for our enemies—and Wuotan—were the ones at fault. He merely groaned in response, the skin of his face blanched and paper-thin, his pulse visible in his neck.

The next morning Hans remained in bed when I went downstairs to snag a quick bite for breakfast. I encountered my son in the kitchen; he sipped at a mug of coffee, his countenance appearing much older than his fifteen years.

"We're going to get Freya out on Tuesday, Wednesday at the latest," he told me as I poured myself a glass of orange juice.

I glanced from my son's face to the doorways at each side of the kitchen. We were alone. "Is that so?" I retrieved a croissant from the counter.

"Matthias, Stefan, Fonsi, and I scouted out their headquarters last night," my son said, his eyes drifting toward the ceiling. "We didn't get back here until just before seven. Pretty sure they're going to sleep late."

"Sounds like you might need a nap yourself," I observed, taking a bite of the croissant and beckoning him to the kitchen table. We sat across from each other, taking positions where we could see if any company arrived in the room.

Max shrugged one shoulder. "I'll get one. There were two men in the office all night long, working on the computer and sifting through the files. They left at six and two people replaced them, a man and a woman. We're going back tonight to bleed them, find out where they're keeping Freya."

I eyed him suspiciously. "You're not driving there, are you?"

My son smiled at me over the rim of his mug. "Of course not. We'll collect their blood using syringes. It's not that hard."

I recoiled, abruptly wondering if that was something else priestly trainees learned. "Syringes, huh? Where'd you get your medical training? You'd better be careful when you stick them; they might bleed to death."

Max chuckled, a mocking sound. "Three Teuton priests, and you're afraid they'll bleed to death. It's not *that* hard to slow an outsider's blood flow."

It was my turn to smile now, and I looked down at what remained of my croissant. "I know." Before my son could comment on that, I gave him a sharp look. "Remember, no crime. At all."

Max drained his mug and stood. "Don't worry. We know what we're doing."

Vreni and I scoured the mountains east of Innsbruck that afternoon without finding any signs of stray dark energy. The only interesting thing happened while our spirits passed over a snowy village on our way to the adjacent alp. Another Teuton spirit appeared about fifty meters away from us, her small size identifying her as a prepubescent child. She noticed us right away and gave a shriek before her form vanished into oblivion.

Guess they teach kids how to wield their magic pretty early around here, Vreni thought with a chuckle.

We'd better get out of here before she sends an adult to investigate, I put in. The two of us plunged into the forest at the base of the peak and renewed our search.

That night I had trouble falling asleep, even though my brain was tired from hunting a Black Priest who did not wish to be found. Traces of elemental magic lingered around villages with a high number of Teutons, but we found nothing that implied a dead man resided in some secret nook. Depression clamped my heart in its teeth again, telling me that there was no point in looking for help, that Freya would never come home. Even if Max's group managed to save her, how long would it take her to forgive me? She would need therapy beyond my capabilities.

On Tuesday I had to drive Fonsi to work. His face haunted, he kept his gaze riveted on his phone for the entire drive. I longed to ask him how it had gone last night, whether they had gotten the blood they needed, whether they had learned where Freya was being held prisoner. But something in his aura held me back, so we listened to an album by Draconian in silence.

When I returned to the Thaden house, I found that four adults had taken my SUV in a quest for groceries. I rolled my eyes when Sango told me and said that was just asking for trouble. Usually Lise and I shopped together, once per week. "I think a lot of our guests are getting sick of being cooped up here," Sango said, his brow wrinkled as he adjusted a new camera above the front door. "Hopefully Max and his buddies learned something useful last night."

"You haven't talked to him yet?"

"I haven't seen him this morning."

I sighed and entered the vestibule, closing the front door behind me and using my ice to do a quick sweep of the grounds. Max and my husband were in their respective bedrooms. I sensed Stefan's Föhn in the gable he shared with Vreni; his spirit felt as peaceful as my son's, asleep. The vibrant glimmers of their children hummed from the second-floor conference room, where they did their schoolwork each day along with their tutor, an outsider. I sensed no one else in the house, but it was a lovely morning. Üwe and Eva likely enjoyed a stroll through the gardens, a tradition they recently established.

I ended up ascending the front stairs and returning to my private chambers to check on Hans. I found him sitting on the edge of his bed, rubbing his forehead. "Headache?" I asked, my feet moving automatically toward the medical cart that housed his many pills.

"It's been pretty constant for a week now," Hans answered, setting his feet on the floor and looking around for his walker. I retrieved it from its place beside the head of the bed and brought it to him, ready to help him move around.

"A bunch of our guests decided it was a good idea to go shopping in a giant caravan. Without me," I reported as we made our way to the bathroom one step at a time.

Once I helped him position himself on the toilet, he gave a quiet groan and met my gaze. "Not very wise of them, but I tend to understand. I'm still in here, Swanie.

All of me." He touched his chest with one withered hand. "But every day it's harder . . . to find my way out."

I turned my attention to the mirror and tried to choke back the lump of tears his words invoked. Was that how my little brother Dane had felt in his final days? Like he was trapped inside a failing body, unable to get out? I reached for a brush to tame my hair, its straight black locks sprinkled with strands of silver. "Honestly, I'm surprised my hair hasn't gone entirely gray, with everything that's happened these past two years," I said.

After helping my husband shave his face and brush his teeth, I got him settled on the couch in our private parlor. His hospice nurse—a Teuton woman in her fifties with a gentle heart—would come by in the afternoon to check him over. She told me just yesterday that within a few days or weeks, Hans would no longer be able to get out of bed, that we must make the transition to the stage of actively dying. It was difficult to give off the impression of tranquility while I watched my faithful Keyholder slowly fade.

I loaded a Nightwish album into the stereo and sat on the floor with my back to the couch, using my laptop to check through Beth's author platforms. Sales of her novels had begun to decline, the natural result of product depreciation and audience saturation. Since she would produce no new works, I was in the process of establishing a system to collect her royalties as residual income for her children until her books passed into the public domain.

Not long after I sat down to work, a wretched scream pierced my ears, and I leapt to my feet. I looked at my husband, who had stiffened, his eyes narrowing toward the hallway. "Was that . . . Max?" His tone was saturated with alarm.

I had not heard my son scream like that in ages. Ice shot through my veins, and I barely remembered to set my laptop onto the floor before fleeing the parlor. I jammed my glasses into the pocket of my jeans as ice veiled my vision, and I raced with the speed of my element to the front staircase. At the bottom I could hear my son's cries— howls of rage, of heartbreak, of despair.

Darkness blinded me midway down the stairs, a shade so thick that even my ice-heightened vision could not cut it. I groped my way down, clinging to the railing as I stumbled a few times. "Max?" I called out. "Pull your element back. I can't help you if I can't see."

The shadows gradually lifted. I reached the ground floor just in time to meet Max's eyes, so filled with anguish, his tears pouring onto the floor in streams of solid black. He knelt before a half-wrapped package; I had not noticed its arrival. The box was less than a meter long and appeared to be made of treated wood, its lid cast into the far corner, near one of my grandmother's antique vases.

My body froze, and I slumped upon the carved post of the railing, unable to order my feet to move—for the acrid scent of formaldehyde had accosted my nose, along with the safer aroma of packing dust. I stared into my son's eyes as his face screwed up in infernal anger, his jaw quivering to reveal his bared teeth—and there, in his clenched fists, I saw thick, tangled strands of black. Unmistakably human hair.

My stomach twisted as I smelled the formaldehyde again, and I crumpled to the floor, the remnants of my breakfast staining the hardwood. Tears clouded my eyes while I expelled everything in my stomach, and my ears began to ring, the nauseating image of hair clutched in Max's hands prompting me to moan. Sango came into the entryway—I sensed his energy—and I heard him say something, felt his hands upon my arms, but I could not see.

Then my son cut loose, hollering curses in both German and Bayerisch. I opened my streaming eyes in time to see him quit the room, the black hair still wrapped around his hands as he sprinted for privacy. Sango muttered a few choice words himself, leaving my side to slide the lid back onto that wretched box. He scooped something off of the floor before returning to me and helping me to my feet, his energy steadying me as he led me into the front parlor.

For a long time I sat mute on one of the nicer sofas, my gray eyes dazed, my ice evaporated entirely from my system. In my hands I held the paper Sango had given me, a note that had accompanied that awful package. It was addressed to me directly and read something along the lines of, *ran out of patience with your whiny daughter . . . suspected you wouldn't come to your senses . . . dismembered her slowly, piece by piece . . . sealed the remains in plastic and formaldehyde, for your edification . . . an electronic file of the entire process . . . next will be your son.* But my ice, in the process of melting, had blurred the ink. Finally my hands tore the paper into bits, littering the floor.

I cannot explain exactly what I felt, while I sat in shock upon that couch. I remember studying its upholstery more carefully than ever before, noticing an old stain of red wine tainting the lilac lines and helices on their whitish background. I envisioned Freya's face in the patterns, saw the tears in her eyes, the cries for help, for me . . . the incomprehension of this cruelty that had befallen her . . . and that final moment, as blood loss drained her consciousness . . . when she closed her dark blue eyes in death, memories of pain all erased forevermore.

Oh, my darling child . . . I wish it could have been a merciful crossing, from this world to the next. But now you're with your Opa, the man you love so dearly . . . and your Oma and Uncle Dane . . . your good friend Selina . . . and your half-siblings from a time long past. Oh Freya, could you ever forgive your Mutti?

I sensed the black fire sitting down at my side long before my eyes caught sight of my husband. His presence in the parlor jolted me out of my reverie, for he had not come downstairs since lunch on Sunday. He draped one weary arm around my shoulders and guided my head into his lap, his fingers curling around mine with the keys of Muniche in between. My lips quivered, and when our eyes met I asked him in a whisper, "You saw?"

His wan face was drawn with grief, and he did not need to reply. His sorrow exploded upon our bond, linking with mine; and we wept bitterly, our tears all of simple salt water, a mourning too profound for elemental displays. I wished he could have been spared the sight of his beloved daughter's remains, but he would see her again at the crossing that loomed on his horizon.

After a time, Sango and Stefan came to Hans, offering to help him return to our bedroom before the last of his strength burnt out. They helped him to his feet, and I let him go as they directed his hands to grip his walker. I promised him in a whisper that I would come as soon as I could, once I had passed on the sad news to the rest of our household.

Thankfully, everyone had left us alone long enough to weep out the initial pain. Now, as I tried to compose myself, my thoughts drifted toward the future, the internment of my daughter's remains, the possibility of holding a private funeral here on Thaden property, and the threat directed at my son.

He came to me shortly thereafter, his clothing and hands filthy, as if he had spent the last hour writhing in the dirt outside. But his countenance was set, his jaw firm as his eyes appraised me, seeing instantly that I had cried until I had no tears left. "I've had enough of this, Mutti," Max stated, his words thick with grim resolution. "I was supposed to protect Freya, and I failed."

"This isn't your fault. I've told you that a thousand times!" I interjected, grieved by the darkness in his eyes, his carefully restrained outrage.

"All I have left now is you," he went on as if he had not heard, holding my eyes solemnly with his. "To keep you safe, I have to be beyond the claws of death. Mutti, I have to become like Augustin. I have to be a Cursed One."

Chapter Thirty-two:
An Appalling Choice

I froze on the violet-patterned sofa, my ice reawakened at my son's horrid words—impossible words. The absurdity of his declaration drew a hollow-sounding laugh from the pit of my stomach. I closed my eyes, erasing Max's youthful face from my sight. *No. No. He can't honestly mean that.*

"No one," I breathed, shaking my head slowly at this folly, "no one . . . *wants* to be cursed in such an irrevocable manner. *No one.*"

"It's not a matter of wanting it," Max replied, sitting beside me on the couch, leaving one cushion between us— a safe distance? "It's a matter of necessity. I have no choice, unless I want to lose myself or you to the—"

"But you're talking about the *filial* curse, Max!" I exclaimed, my eyelids springing open as I rounded on him with the parental glare. "Don't you know the definition of the word filial? If you were cursed you would lose me! We would never be allowed to meet again in public, and do you seriously believe the next Keyholder would *permit* his Lady to have contact with a Cursed One? And think of your own life. You know what the curse means, more than any other young priest—you know it would cost you your *life!*"

"That's the point, Mutti. I have to be beyond death to protect you and the Torstein—"

"You want your free will to be chained to a *demon?*" I persisted, ignoring his comment for the moment. I was ranting, but my son would have to listen after proposing such madness. "And do you honestly think Wuotan would *let* you return to the earth, once he finds out you're a Christian and bound for heaven? I don't think he has any authority over such things. You probably wouldn't survive the final act of the curse, because you'd go straight to heaven, not to some intermediate level of devilish fire. Besides, even if it *did* work, I doubt Wuotan would let you use his gifts to help me. He hates me, Max. Augustin told me that centuries ago, and I doubt his opinion has improved much!"

"Mutti, please! Can't you just look at it from my perspective for a minute?" Max sighed in frustration, running his dirtied hands through his hair. I had expended my remonstrations for the moment—though many more loomed on the horizon—but I held my peace so my son could explain himself. I watched him minutely while he spoke, my icy eyes reading the depths of his heart.

Max saw that I had calmed myself, and he nodded, holding a hand out toward me as he spoke in a guarded but passionate tone. "Okay. I know you're not a man . . . and women don't have the same reactions as men have when they're faced with these kinds of threats. But . . . just try to understand. This madness is never going to stop, not with Freya's death, or with Pappi's. The NVH won't stop hunting for the Torstein until they get it, since they think it holds incredible power."

He broke off for a moment, his silvery eyes glittering with emotion. "Even if you protect the Torstein for the rest of your life, one day you *will* die, and so will I. And when that day comes, what are we going to do with the Torstein? No Teuton I know, priest or otherwise, really appreciates how devastating it can be. No one comprehends it but you and me, because I've seen the scars it left upon you, the destiny it destroyed. If we're both in heaven, how are we supposed to keep the rock safe from our enemies?"

Max paused for breath, and I shied away from him, plunging my spine into the fibers of the couch's armrest. *This is bad,* I realized. *He's really thought about this, and not just for the past hour. I've had similar thoughts, too, though I've always imagined I'd have to bring Augustin here to solve this. What have I done, speaking of him so freely before my child . . . and now he wants to be like him. He wants to be Wuotan's slave.*

"So that's where the filial curse comes into play," Max continued as I stared at him in silent horror. "If I were cursed, and dead, I would be beyond their power, and beyond time. I could plan the perfect retribution, punishing only the ones directly responsible for all of the deaths—Opa's, your cousins', our friends' . . . and . . . my sister."

He broke off again, wiping away a single tear. "You see what I'm saying. If I were a Black Priest, I could avenge *all* of the spilled blood and protect you, make sure your next Keyholder treats you respectfully. And after you've grown old, you could give the Torstein to me, for you know I'd never use it for evil. I'd probably never use it at all. It made a mess of your life, and I'd rather not have that happen to mine." He laughed bleakly.

When my son had finished, traces of darkness enriched his eyes. "Is this why you wanted to become a priest so early?" I asked in a grave voice.

Max looked taken aback. "No, it was mainly because I thought I needed to know all of the mysticism in order to try to rescue my sister . . . and to keep you safe. It's a power that the Saxons don't understand, and I've always believed we can't defeat them without magic. But . . . you're right, Mutti. I've been thinking of it for a while. It's been in the back of my mind since you told me that Augustin was a Cursed One."

"Then I am what drove you to this!" I moaned, dropping my head into my hands. "And I've tried so hard to present it in the proper light, never to make it seem like a shortcut to power and immortality. Oh, Max! How could I stand to look at myself in the mirror if I allowed my *son* to be cursed? How could I look Augustin in the face ever again, on earth or in eternity?" I rubbed at my eyes.

"Mutti," Max murmured, placing a hand gently upon my back, "you've never portrayed the fate of the Cursed Ones as glorious. You made it clear in your classes that being cursed is a terrible fate, something the Teuton people should never have created in the first place. But you also told me that your love saved Augustin from losing his humanity.

"See, I think that if a Black Priest has purpose, he doesn't have to grovel or give up hope. Guarding the Torstein would be my purpose, for with it are all my memories of you. And I'd be staying in the Black Castle, the place where Augustin's old tomes are kept. I could read them all, everything the world has forgotten!"

"But you'd be staying there for years and years, maybe even centuries," I reminded him, lifting my head and turning a little to the left, so I could take his hand. "You'd be barred from heaven, trapped on earth until another man survives the filial curse. And the entire time, Wuotan will be raking his claws through your heart, dragging you into bitterness and despair, punishing you anytime you do something good."

Max smiled sadly at me, his darkness meeting my ice through our fingers. "I'll take all of the consequences. Glory can't be had without sacrifice. I'll admit, though, that I don't like the idea of meeting Wuotan again." He shuddered, a faraway look in his eyes. "The initiation was bad enough. But I would do it, for our people. For you. For our future."

"You'll have to take this up with your Pappi," I told my son, washing my hands of his schemes for the moment—though it would be only a moment. "I'm not the head of this family, so I don't have the authority to curse you."

"That's true," Max allowed, looking somewhat disappointed. But as he rose to exit the parlor, he met my eyes one last time and noted, "It won't be long until you *are* the head of the family."

When Vreni, her security guard, Lise, and Alison returned with their load of groceries, I joined the women in the pantry to put everything away and tell them of my daughter's passing. Lise broke down in tears at the news, and Vreni drew me into a fiery embrace while Alison stood off to the side, shaking her head. "These people are just freaks," she said, dabbing at her eyes. "Serial killers who get off on torturing people."

I could not disagree with her. Pulling away from Vreni, I murmured, "We're going to try a few new things." But I kept the truth of the matter to myself, as the dark recesses of my brain fabricated images of my son's pale arm stained black, his blood pouring into a bowl, the irrevocable spell that would take his life: *Cursed for all of time.*

Günter might get his successor after all.

Sango called the authorities to have Freya's remains taken for forensic work, and he handled our family's official statement about this latest crime. He believed that they may be able to trace Ostermann and the other brutes who had raped her. Sango was frustrated because the new cameras he set up to record the porch caught no signs of who delivered the box. He had not yet activated them when it arrived, but his shield had caught no trespassers. That told me that a Teuton in spirit form delivered Freya's remains and vanished immediately thereafter.

Max pulled me aside in the laundry room after dinner to say that he knew the location of our enemies' lair—those two men's blood had revealed a few things after all. He said that their security measures were very intense, so he must plan out his attack carefully.

Hans' exertions that day drained him to a shell. Somehow, he still carried my spirit into our dream world once I managed to fall into slumber, and we spent the night resting at the stream with our feet in its waters. I noticed that his spirit appeared paler than usual, his radiant glimmer diminished.

"I fear I have only a few weeks left," he said after we sat in silence for at least an hour. He gazed at the moon high above as he added, "Once the time comes for stronger sedatives, I don't think we'll be able to meet here any-more."

That had occurred to me already, and it was not a pleasant prospect. Since our Teutonic marriage in December of 2001, Hans and I had dreamed together almost every night. When circumstances held us apart, my Keyholder still guided my spirit into the ethereal realm while I slept, so no nightmares could haunt me. Once he left this world, I would have to dream alone. I suspected that I might have to return to my eleventh century habits—spend half the night with my body coated in ice, foregoing sleep for a breath of peace.

"I'm still not sure . . . what I should do . . . after you're gone," I said, choosing not to address the subject of my nightmares. "I'm not interested in submitting my will to Herr Brennemann or any other Teuton priest. The next Keyholder might want me to have more kids." I cringed.

"You did have another life, long ago."

I drew my knees up and laid my cheek upon them, studying my husband's visage as he gazed at the night sky. "If I go back there, Muniche's bonds will make me believe I want Prince Otto. And I don't. Sometimes I think Max was right, when I first told him what was going on with the NVH. He said I should bring Augustin here and ask him to take the keys."

Hans looked troubled, and he shifted position to look directly into my eyes. "Bring him here so you could grow old and leave him within five or six decades? Seems a bit selfish."

"Yeah," I sighed, sitting up a little and looking toward the silver oak I had planted beside the stream just over a decade ago. Its bark seemed to sparkle in the moonlight, a mystical wonder. "Augustin wouldn't take Muniche's keys, anyway. He told me he never wanted to give up control of his heart."

"Not every man is bold enough to make that choice."

I fingered my icy robes, their crisp chill refreshing me as I considered my husband's words. My thoughts drifted toward the choice our son wished to make, one much more onerous than taking on the responsibility of a Teuton city. "Did Max talk to you . . . about how he wants to protect the Torstein?"

"I have no plans to curse my only son, despite his wishes. Wuotan has punished our family enough," Hans responded, closing the subject.

The subsequent weeks dragged in a sludge of melancholy. As the hospice nurse had predicted, Hans found himself unable to summon the strength to get out of bed after that sorrowful Tuesday. His awareness faded with each passing day, and I spent most of my time with him, prepared to offer any support he needed. We held a private funeral for Freya after the forensic unit finished with her body. Her urn, violet-flecked obsidian to match her element, was placed in the Thaden family vault, an event that made her absence feel real, the final door closed.

I began to seriously ponder my next move during those weeks, as I watched my loyal husband slip further and further away. No matter what, I would *not* allow Helge Brennemann or some other priest to reshape my heart's yearnings using Muniche's bonds. I had permitted it at the start of all this, when I left the eleventh century behind after one of my happiest moments—my marriage to Augustin. Then Prince Otto had cursed his city as her enemies destroyed her, and since then I had shouldered her burdens along with my own. Nearly twenty years now, and that was long enough. At least when I learned that Hans was my Keyholder, I already trusted him, respected him. I felt no similar regard for any other priest in München.

My intuition urged me to make good on my darkest desires—to flee to some medieval era and join Augustin for a few fleeting decades of bliss. If I did that, I must ensure that my present day legacy could shine on without me. While sitting at Hans' bedside, I worked toward that very thing, making adjustments to our family's accounts, files, and contacts. I willed the Thaden house and property to my son, along with all of our investments, under Üwe's charge until Max came of age. I finished establishing

Beth's fortune as residual income for her sons Connor and Logan, discussing the particulars with Onkel Jens and Aunt Linda.

I also considered Max's plea more seriously, though I did not share it with anyone except my husband. Although it sickened me to imagine myself cursing my own child, I began to recognize that Max had a keen grasp on our situation. A Black Priest could certainly shield the Torstein from misuse and eliminate the NVH's threat to our people. Günter would not help us without payment, and the specter who saved me in the Leutasch Gorge preferred to skulk on the sidelines. Augustin could do it, and would do it if he cherished his love for me; but it would be cruel to bring him to a time so different from his own and demand that he stay indefinitely.

Maybe after Hans passes, Max and I can pack our things and scurry away to the Black Castle. Then I could curse my son there and order Günter to make good on his promise. With two Cursed Ones on the hunt, the NVH won't last very long. While they eradicate these terrorists, I can use the Song of Time to return to the man who loves me without reservations, without needing a city's keys to inspire his devotion. And I'll have to do it quick, before the next Keyholder decides to track me down and force me to yield.

On the first Saturday in March, the 7th, Hans remained aware for most of the afternoon. His dark blue eyes glassy, he requested that I bring each member of the Thaden household before him, so they could all speak their separate farewells. He seemed sure that this was his last chance to appreciate such things, for he told me that those who had gone before him lingered at the edges of his dreams. He had seen his mother Johanna, as well as his father and Freya.

I remained on the outskirts while our friends came and went. Situating myself on one of the lounge chairs outside on the balcony for the majority of the afternoon, I checked a few business-related things on my laptop, the crisp air swirling around my body, speaking softly to my ice. I wanted to lock everyone out of our bedroom so I could start packing a bag or two; I would have to do that tonight when Hans slept. It felt unreal to gaze out over the gardens and the trees beyond, the curved stone walls that bordered Thaden property. This had been my home since I was twelve—twenty-eight years—and soon I would leave for good.

At one point I laid my laptop aside and wandered to the railing of the balcony, leaning down upon it with my eyes fixed on the backyard's tiny forest. With ice enhancing my vision, I could see the silver glint of that stately oak that claimed these grounds long before my father did. Its fairy had offered me occasional guidance throughout my life. I wondered what it would think if it knew I intended to flee to the past and renounce my responsibility forever.

The *Eihalbe* once told me that Augustin's path was murky, treacherous, and infinite. I was about to walk that path no matter the consequences. It could be no worse than what I had faced here. With our shared devotion as our strength, we should be able to counter Wuotan's wiles. I still believed that love was stronger than death.

Concentrating more deeply upon my ice magic, I fashioned a swirling set of crystals, casting them in the direction of that silver oak tree. They carried my message along to its fairy—gratitude, respect, farewell.

"Please guide my son toward the path of light," I whispered in Teutonica as the breeze swept my elemental offering to the forest. "His course is about to become like Augustin's . . . and he'll need nature's counsel."

Chapter Thirty-three:
The Filial Curse

That night while Hans slept under morphine's shroud, I slipped upstairs to Max's bedroom to inform him of my plans. His irises went completely black as I explained that we would need to leave the house as soon as his father died. "When he wakes again, he's going to ask me to call Herr Brennemann so he can pass on the keys. I'll stay by his bedside until he passes, but after that we have to go. Right away. Tonight I need you to pack the essentials, and I'll do the same."

Max nodded, his darkened eyes earnest. "Where are we going to go to hide from Herr Brennemann?"

I chewed on my lower lip and summoned the courage to say, "We're going to the Black Castle. And if you still think you need to give your life in order to stop the NVH, I can curse you there and let Günter do what must be done."

Tears welled in my eyes as I agreed to perform the vilest act against my son, the one that would taint his legacy forever. But he stepped forward to take hold of my right arm, his darkness reaching out to reassure my anguished spirit. "We can do this, Mutti," he declared in a quiet voice. "For Freya. For our people."

Once I returned to my bedroom, I threw a couple extra outfits into a duffle bag, including one long dress of flowing sapphire. Not quite eleventh century style—I had nothing that hinted at such an epoch—but if I traveled straight to Augustin's cottage beside the Rhine, he could find me more appropriate clothing later. Aside from my most comfortable pair of sneakers for the flight itself, I packed a pair of leather shoes I had not worn since my days at Süddeutsche Getriebe. Luckily they were still in decent shape.

After midnight I spent some time in the kitchen and pantry, snagging what seemed suitable to add to my bag. Dried Landjäger, mixed nuts, raisins, granola bars, a bottle of multivitamins, a metal thermos for water. Just for kicks, I grabbed a fork—the utensil I had missed during my twenty-two years in medieval Bavaria. Maybe Augustin could make a few more of those if I brought him one as a sample.

Back in the bedroom, I retrieved a camping blanket from my closet and a small neck pillow, deciding that I wanted to be at least somewhat comfortable before I departed the modern era. Who knew whether Günter had any extra beds in his ghastly castle? He had mentioned it was not fit for company, so I expected naught but bare bones. I could always set up shop in that chamber with the scarlet couches; those were comfy enough.

While in the closet, I thought back to the items I had packed for my "grand excursion" into eleventh century Bavaria. No point in bringing a camera since I had no plans to return to the future. No need for contact lenses, either; I could just use my element to perfect my vision if I had to really look at something. Toiletries, though? Günter may not have any of those, either, aside from whatever his windy female partner used. I laughed at the idea of carrying a twelve-pack of toilet paper through the gates of time as I headed for the bathroom. *Ah, the super sanitary rags. How I've missed them.*

After adding my shower bag, hairbrush, toothbrush, and toothpaste to my duffle bag, I stepped through the private parlor, where Hans' hospice nurse slept lightly upon the couch. An inspiration had struck me, and my feet automatically carried me to the library, the room that had once been my stronghold against reality's sorrows. My Latin-German Bible stood there among other religious works, and I knew that I ought to bring it along to brush up on my Latin.

I pulled it out from between my father's old Bible and a commentary by Oehler. My fingers traced the cross inlaid upon its leather cover, and I remembered how Freia had sought God's comfort among these pages when the two of us shared a room at the Meldorf estate. I would have to visit her and Heinrich, and maybe even my children. My five medieval children who had no Saxon terrorists hunting them with the intent to kill.

But will they even recognize me? The Mutti they remember was disabled, overweight, and ill. It might be better to just observe their lives while in spirit form, protect them from the insanity that permeates my world. I wonder whether Cammie and Alger got married . . . or Max and Katchen Denlinger. Did all of my kids manage to build families of their own?

Eventually I fell asleep on my bed with Augustin's last letter lying beside me. My hands had creased it often over the years, and some of the ink had blurred, the edges crumbled away. He had come for me once, to save me from his irate peer, and now it was time for me to repay the favor. Max could handle everything here, and I would return to the man who loved me unconditionally, even if Muniche's soul punished my heart every minute of every day. It was a small price to pay to taste Augustin's devotion again.

I awoke suddenly, yanked from a dream that left a strange distaste in my mouth, its themes escaping me. Pushing myself into a sitting position, I realized that I had not changed into my pajamas—I wore an old Ocean City sweatshirt and leggings. My eyes caught sight of the page adorned with Carolingian miniscule, lying forgotten beside my pillow. *I stayed up too late.*

Stretching my arms with a groan, I turned to peek through the curtain at the left door to my balcony; my temporary bed was positioned to block that door. Gray dawn greeted me beyond the tinted glass. As I blinked sleepily at the low clouds, I heard my husband give a rattling gasp. I sensed his frailty through our bond and pivoted my focus toward him instead. His last day.

I climbed to my feet and made my way to his bedside. Hans' eyes were open wide, moving away from the ceiling above to rest upon my face. I bent to kiss his hollow cheek and glanced at the tray that held his medicines. "Do you need some water or more morphine? I don't want you to be in pain."

Hans had barely managed to swallow a few sips of water yesterday, but I had no wish for him to feel as parched as a desert in his last moments. That would be simpler than offering morphine, which his nurse had taught me to administer through the rectal route ever since he lost the strength to leave his bed. I found a half-full jar of mineral water and looked around for a cup, but Hans' cracked voice seized my attention. "Swanie . . . you . . . you're . . . afraid."

I looked back at his countenance as I felt his spiritual hands brush my heart as though from a distance. He still sensed my emotions; he knew I did not want to perform the required duty: *Call Helge Brennemann. I must pass these keys to a noble recipient, one who will honor both our city and you, her Lady.*

I set the bottle back onto the tray and sidled closer to my husband. I saw the keys of Muniche lying before my glitter lamp on the bedside table opposite where I stood. Uncertainties boiled over within me, and I blurted the truth before I could think better of it. "I don't want Helge Brennemann to be my new master. I know you have to do it, but after that, Max and I are leaving."

Hans' glassy eyes drifted toward the curtains draping the balcony doors. "Your . . . bag."

My eyes opened wider as I noticed the duffle bag discarded at the foot of my bed, right up against the deep blue curtains. "Right. I need to hide that so no one figures out what Max and I are going to do."

In a flash, I swept it into my walk-in closet, then shoved my laptop into its case. If I waited around long enough after cursing my son, I could show him everything he needed to know to handle the Thaden family's accounts and investments. An immortal memory never forgot any details.

"Swanie." Hans' voice sounded as vacant as his stare. I saw that he looked toward the corner of the room where my desk once sat—toward Üwe's paintings that portrayed my heart's eternal struggle. *Muniche and Her Keyholder*. And *Augustin*.

As I came to Hans' side, he began to cough, his chest rattling as he struggled for breath. The hospice nurse entered the bedroom within seconds, tending to him until the spell had passed. She checked his blood pressure and his heartbeat, then murmured that she would prepare his morning doses of medicine. Hans gasped again, and she met my gaze with a look that said, *We'd best ease him into slumber so he can pass peacefully, without pain.*

But while she added morphine to a syringe, Hans bit out the word, "No." His voice sounded stronger than before, and my forehead wrinkled at the hard look in his eyes. He needed to relinquish his position as Keyholder first; I knew that.

His nurse tried to soothe him into compliance, but he glared at her and told her to leave. She appeared affronted, but I laid a hand on her shoulder. "There are things the *Leitaeri* must do before the end. We have to accept that."

"He's suffering," she responded, her irises taking on the brown hue of earth.

I stood firm. "It's his choice." Ice cooled my blood, preparing me to defend my husband to the last.

The nurse heaved a sigh and grumbled, "I'll be in the parlor."

After she had gone, I forced myself to meet Hans' gaze. "I can call him now. Your successor. Just tell me I must." I endeavored to mask my distaste.

"Max," my husband croaked, his eyebrows slanted downward. "Call Max. Then bring . . . a bowl . . . paper . . . an iron pen"—my jaw dropped—"there's one in . . . my office . . . . And a knife."

Part of me wanted to scream, *No! Don't do* this *as your last act. Don't consign the son you love so dearly to the bowels of hell!* But the truth of the matter struck me right between the eyes. Hans would curse Max himself so our son would never face the temptation to kill the one who cursed him . . . and so I would not have to live with the guilt. I had not expected this.

Tears blurred my vision as I ran from the room. I blew by the hospice nurse on my path to the hallway, and ordered her to summon my son to his father's side immediately. Then I scampered in a mad daze from this chamber to that, retrieving all of the items my husband required. I had to do this without thinking, or I would fall at Hans' feet and beg him to reconsider.

When I stumbled into the kitchen in search of a bowl, my unsteady hands clinging to an iron pen and a sheathed knife, I found Üwe standing before the coffee pot, sipping from a Süddeutsche Getriebe mug. "He's about to level the curse."

I gasped as I tugged a bowl from an upper cabinet, nearly losing my grip on it in the process. "You *knew?*" Frantically, I tossed the knife and the pen into the bowl, then tore a blank page from the notepad on the counter. Good enough.

Üwe appeared at my right side and offered me a jarred three-wick candle decked with yellow flames. His eyes looked grim behind his thick glasses as he nodded at me. "To burn his name."

I blinked at Üwe in confusion before recognizing that Hans could not invoke the necessary flames himself, on the door of death. I swallowed hard and accepted the candle. "Thank you. Please . . . could you . . . could you keep everyone away from the bedroom . . . and the parlor, too? I don't want people to know what Hans is about to do. Not yet."

"You got it. I'll keep the hallway clear."

When I reentered our bedroom, I found myself looking at three people—Hans, the nurse, and Max. My son had been awake for some time already. He wore black jeans and a matching pullover with three stripes across the center, his hair slicked neatly, falling just past his shoulders. His silver eyes met mine the moment I stepped through the door, and then he saw the pot I held, the knife sticking out of it—and he gasped, abject terror flashing for an instant across his youthful face. But he controlled himself with the finesse of the seasoned priest. His boyish lips settled into a solemn line, his eyes veiled.

Hans ordered the nurse to leave and not return until I called her, no matter what sounds she may hear coming from the room. The nurse looked affronted all over again, but she complied. I heard Üwe's voice in the parlor, likely advising her to move into the hallway, to give our family the necessary privacy. I hoped she had no concept of why I held a bowl and a candle . . . and a knife and iron pen.

Summoning my nerve, I approached the tray at Hans' bedside and made a space for the candle and the bowl. My son stepped forward to remove the water jug and the blood pressure monitor, then gestured for me to place the paper and pen there. I did so, then stepped to my Keyholder's side, unsheathing the knife and manually wrapping the fingers of his right hand around its handle. I would likely have to help him make the cut, for his hand felt bloodless and cold.

Hans and I shared a look of understanding, and then he addressed his son in an uneven voice. "Max." The boy stepped forward, his lips trying and failing to form some sort of smile. Hans looked him straight in the eyes as he inquired, "Is this still what you want?"

"It is not something I want, Pappi," Max whispered, sounding as though he choked on tears. "But I see no other option . . . for our future."

"Then understand me . . . when I say . . . that I do this with my body . . . but not with my soul." Max nodded wordlessly, one tear trickling down his left cheek. He rolled up the right sleeve of his pullover and laid his hand onto the blanket beside Hans' feeble hand. Then he looked at me and at the knife in Hans' withered hand, his silver eyes asking me to take my required place.

I gritted my teeth as I set the bowl upon the blanket and Max balanced his arm overtop of it. I positioned myself between the father and the son, taking hold of Hans' right hand, prepared to help him direct the knife. And I shut my eyes in a mixture of horror and denial as my husband's tremulous lips began to speak those dreadful words in fluent Teutonica.

"In the Name . . . of the Most Holy God . . . on this Lord's Day . . . I curse your name . . . I cut off your life from mine . . . strip your name from you . . . casting you out from your people . . . until this earth perishes in fire . . . consigning your soul . . . to Wuotan . . . for all of eternity . . . that this fate may be . . . assigned to you with . . . all of its sorrows, you must write . . . your desecrated name . . . with your own blood . . . cursed for all of time."

I felt Hans' arm twitch beneath my grasp, and I opened my eyes, guiding his hand forward to make that unalterable slice upon our son's artery. When I saw the blood well crimson and fresh, I moaned and squeezed my eyes shut again, images from the past binding me in chains.

Augustin's hatred, his resignation as he met his brother's gaze. The flash of the blade, the coarse smell of blood. Paulus' indifference, Prince Otto's beatific smile, Lady Maria's cold triumph. She had merely held the bowl between the two hate-filled brothers, while I directed the blade itself. I was worse than she. Muniche's firstborn son, cursed a second time . . . Augustin Abelard Ulrich . . . and now Maximilian Johannes Meissner.

I opened my eyes as the stench of blood permeated the bedroom. My gaze fell automatically to the bowl upon the blanket, halfway filled with blood. My eyes strayed from there to Max's forearm, and I saw that he had clamped his left hand securely over the gash. I abruptly realized that I still clung to Hans' limp hand, and I dropped it, the knife slipping away from his grip. Why had I let this happen?

Stay focused, Swanie. We need to finish this. I reached my trembling hands out to take the bowl, to move it to a more stable position on the tray. Max took one step toward the tray, appearing calm as he lifted the iron pen and dipped it into his blood. I staggered backward, practically falling on top of my sick husband, for I saw the scab congealing there, on the tender skin of his forearm. *Black already. Black to match his darkness. Black to signify his demonic destiny.*

"Swanie . . . the . . . candle." Hans began to cough again, and I moved to support him as his face cracked in anguish. Max appeared with the water bottle, offering a few sips to the man who had just cursed him. The irony was not lost on me as I blotted the water and saliva from my husband's lips and chin. I attempted to send a bit of my own vitality into Hans' spirit through Muniche's bonds, though his grasp on my heart had nearly vanished. Angst twisted me in its grip.

Max brought the candle to Hans' bedside, its three yellow flames shooting upward in an unnatural manner. Üwe doubtless knew we had reached the tipping point and extended his magic to ensure we could finish the rite. Thankfully he kept the nurse away despite my husband's choking.

Hans' eyes met mine, and they shifted pointedly toward the tray, where that sheet of notebook paper lay with our son's name scrawled in blood: *Maximilian Johannes Meissner von Thaden.* I caught his silent message and brought him the paper, placing it between his inert fingers before stretching his right hand over the candle myself.

My husband gave a wheezing rattle, and I allowed the paper to fall upon the candle's flames as he gasped, "May the name . . . of Maximilian . . . Johannes Meissner . . . von Thaden be . . . burned . . . and may it . . . never . . . be spoken . . . again."

I saw the yellow fire change color, its tongues bursting with red and a bit of bluish-green. And I saw Augustin walk away, into the forest . . . and I heard myself call his name, tearing the laws of the Teutons to shreds . . . *Augustin!*

I did not notice that I had moved away from the bed until I bruised my fingers upon the edge of the door to our parlor. But I knew that I could not stay in the room, not now. Reason had left me, and I needed to crawl away somewhere and weep. I had to beg for Augustin to hear me, from heaven or hell, and forgive my greatest sin.

I heard Max's footsteps trailing me as I entered the parlor. I hoped he had packed his things last night, that he was prepared to drive to the mountains with me to face our separate destinies. But my husband's voice called him back, and my eyes passed absently over Üwe standing beside the door to the hallway. He opened it for me without speaking, seeming to sense my loss. I sincerely hoped that Üwe would not be the one to destroy all record of my son's name.

The nurse stood in the hallway tapping one foot. When I passed through the doorway, she opened her mouth—likely to demand that she be permitted to tend to her patient—but Üwe ordered her to go to the kitchen and find herself something to eat. We had the situation under control, and Hans wanted privacy. Vaguely, I heard her retort as I sank onto the floor with my back to the wall. I could not speak, nor could I think.

I know not how long I sat there with my arms wrapped around my knees, my ice-veiled eyes blinking at the hardwood floor. I felt as though I drifted rudderless in the ocean. My faithful master was dying, our bond dissipating further each moment . . . and my dearest son had been cursed at his hands. Max had no choice but to die, and he was a Christian. Would God allow him to take a demon's hand and return to earth, or had Hans leveled the terrible spell for naught? Was it possible for a Christian to complete the curse, or would my son be doomed to a fate unknown to our people?

A hand of darkness touched my shoulder, and a familiar voice quietly asked me to stand. As I climbed to my feet, I raised my head to meet Max's gaze and saw that his eyes were full of shadows, astonishment having mastered his composure. I forced a smile in spite of everything and asked, half in jest, "Did he give you an ultimatum to leave the house before the hour is up?"

Max shook his head. He lifted his right arm from where it hung at his side, his sleeve rolled down to hide the forming scar—and I choked on my own breath, bumping hard into the wall behind me. "He gave me *these*." To my astonishment, I saw München's keys dangling from my son's fingers.

Chapter Thirty-four

A Deathbed Confession

I threw my hands back against the wall as the hallway seemed to spin, its shapes and colors all revolving around those five brass keys held in the fingers of a Cursed One—*of my son.* I sensed the turmoil in my heart, the confusion warring with a new and alien devotion, solidifying the maternal love I had always felt for this young priest standing before me, altering it, molding it, *completing it.* My heart throbbed, my bond with Hans fading, disintegrating gradually into a mere thread of evaporating life. And just several steps away from me stood this boy who was about to become a dead man, a slave bound to earth, a sycophant forced to bow before Wuotan—*Muniche's master guardian.*

I had imagined this, toyed with the concept of a Black Priest becoming the Keyholder of Muniche. But I had envisioned it being Augustin, or maybe Günter if he did not already have his windy partner. Never had I ever expected my cursed son to hold the keys, harkening back to the days of old, the duty passed from father to son. From a father to the son he had just cast out, disowned.

Max stood frozen, his black eyes as round as the full moon, observing my reaction with a look of contrition. At last I forced myself to speak, though I hardly recognized my own voice. "How . . . could he . . . have done such a thing?" Hans did not view the filial curse like I did—a terrible but meaningless spell that could not cast its victim to hell. He had always referred to Augustin by his cursed name of Wolfgang, but now he had given our city a nameless Keyholder.

"He told me . . . that I'm the master guardian Muniche needs," Max murmured, his jawbone quivering in restrained passion. His gaze fell from my face to the keys in his hand. He drew them back against his chest, his fingers winding around them, his black eyes aglow with reverence. "He says I need to avenge you . . . protect our people . . . challenge Wuotan's plans to destroy us."

I took one step toward him, lifting my left hand from the wall. My son had taken on a vast responsibility, one that outweighed that of any Keyholder before him. My lips parted to say something, though I knew not what would suffice—for my spirit seethed, utterly mystified. The youthful priest met my eyes and nodded, his expression morose as he said, "I have to go."

"Wait." I took another step forward, stretching my hand out toward him. "We planned to leave together. I packed a bag last night."

Max withdrew, his element drawing shadows down upon the hallway. "I'd rather . . . do this part myself. I don't want you to see . . . what I must face."

Latent fear lurked deep in his eyes, and I understood that he did not want me to watch him die—to watch Günter slay his successor on the heathen altar, to see my beloved son's mortal body incinerated by Wuotan's flames. But what would become of him afterward, when his soul departed an irreparable shell? Had a Christian ever been cursed before? Would Max be allowed to return to earth?

I could not form the unanswerable questions, though they solidified into a lump in my throat. But I did manage to choke out the plea, "You . . . you'll come back . . . right?" I knew not what I asked.

He came to my side in an instant, taking my trembling hand in both of his. I felt his darkness seeping into my spirit while my mortal senses detected the touch of brass between our fingers. "Don't worry," he whispered, bringing my hand to his lips, his eyes laden with a profound fidelity. "I'll return as soon as I can, and take you away from here. I promise . . . *Leitalra.*"

He spoke the phrase as an ancient endearment that stemmed from a Keyholder's soul. My body quivered from head to toe, and my son's eyes drifted toward the door to the parlor we had just quitted. "He wants to talk to you," he informed me quietly, releasing my hand and turning away.

I remained in the hallway just one second more, watching the young priest head for the staircase, to retrieve his things from the room that was technically no longer his. My heart pattered anxiously in my chest, my earlier plans slipping away from me piece by piece. Uncertainty reigned once more as I reentered the private parlor, my gaze locking upon Üwe's face. He said nothing but gestured toward the bedroom doorway, where my dying husband waited.

When I reached Hans' bedside, I found his breathing sporadic, his vacant eyes shifting here and there along the ceiling and upper walls. He had finished his final tasks, and I wondered whether he preferred to drift away peacefully now. I took his right hand in mine, though I doubt he felt it. "I'm here, like you asked. Do you want me to give you some medicine?"

Hans' eyes widened at my voice, but his gaze remained fixed in place above the bedroom doorway. "Tell . . . her." The words rattled their way out of his throat. "But . . . how."

I watched my husband's face, strongly suspecting that he spoke to a spiritual apparition and not to me. Which saint was in the room with us now? His mother? Freya? Someone else entirely?

"Hans . . . tell who?" I whispered.

"Swanie . . . ." His dark blue irises shifted to mine, and they seemed to burn me, though they held no fire. "Words aren't . . . enough . . . you must . . . bleed me."

I could not hold back my shock. "Bleed you? But master, you can't mean that. Not now."

I felt his spiritual hand grasp my heart, a feeble attempt to rebuke my lack of compliance with his dying wish. "You . . . must." His eyes clouded over.

I shook my head at him, but I saw how greatly it cost him to clutch the heart of my soul when he barely had the strength to speak. "Okay," I surrendered, though my stomach roiled at the idea of drinking blood, for the first time since . . . .

"But Hans," I said, reaching my free hand out to smooth his brow, "you know I'm not very . . . skilled . . . at bleeding people. I've only done it once, and I almost *killed* Augustin because I couldn't stop."

His gaze became so ironic that it almost prompted me to laugh. I could hear his response in my mind, though he did not speak it aloud: *What does it matter if you bleed me to death? I'm dying already.*

So I knelt at his bedside and stared down at his withered neck, recalling the countless times I had kissed him there, as I traced my fingers along his veins. The tiniest of smiles passed like a ghost across his lips. I groaned, unsure whether I could really accomplish his last request. How could I manage to *bleed* this dying priest, this compassionate master of mine, when he looked as though the slightest breeze might snuff his flame forever?

But he smiled again, just as briefly, and endeavored to tilt his head back upon the pillow, baring his neck, its veins evident even to the untrained eye. *I can't believe I'm about to do this.* I reached one hand forward, laying it gently upon his artery, feeling his pulse—already so weak—and I spoke my final hesitation. "How will I know . . . what to look for?"

"This . . . secret . . . my worst . . . secret. Swanie . . . we are . . . the same." Hans' eyes seemed to burn me again, though my element sensed no fire in his blood at all. I broke away from his gaze to stare at his artery, suddenly afraid of what I was about to see. *Hans' worst secret.*

I gritted my teeth, steeling myself, then brought my head close to his neck, smelling his sweat, his wasted flesh. Nothing there seemed to invite me in, as the scent of Augustin's skin had done in the glade by the stream. I abruptly wondered whether Hans' blood may taste like drugs, like those wraiths at the Black Castle said about Günter's sacrifices.

"Hans," I breathed, my lips hovering a centimeter from his neck, "if . . . if I . . . kill you . . . just remember that I love you . . . always." I did not look at his face again, for fear of seeing that pained expression, the unspoken phrase in his eyes: *You may not say that after you've seen the truth in my blood.*

I took a deep breath, squeezed my eyes shut, and sank my teeth into my husband's artery. The blood, thick and slow, drained into my mouth. I almost backed away, almost vomited at the taste—just as repulsive as Augustin's blood had been. But I forced myself to swallow just a sample, as my husband had asked, seeking his secret, his confession.

. . . And I was a young man, thirty, a Teuton priest and the Keyholder of Muniche, sitting at a desk strewn with books, on a bench in a park, standing at the banks of a frozen lake, always with a woman, a young woman, nineteen, hair like the ravens' wings, eyes azure like the sea. She gazed into my eyes on a wintry night, confessed that she loved me, that I had taught her so much about our people, about her magic, about her ice. My heart rebelled, chained to a matron, though another corner of it blazed with desire, with adoration. I wept, torn in two, as I told her, "Camilla . . . we can't. My duty lies with Muniche. I'm not free . . . and never shall be. Forgive me." Her icy tears dampened the snow.

. . . I introduced her to my employer Maximilian, a Teuton of strong blood, a businessman destined for success. Anything to distract her from me, to quell that fire that raged in my veins whenever I saw her at church,

from where I sat at the organ, playing the songs of God. She seemed to fall for him, to enjoy his company, to look into his eyes with signs of love. And she told me solemnly one day after church, "Hans, I'm going to marry Max. And I'd like you to officiate our Teutonic wedding, if you are able." I saw how dearly she longed for my blessing on her future, since we could never be together, secret lovers held apart by an ancient bond. So I consented to wed them.

. . . She moved into my employer's house, and I tried to put space between us, to complete my duties at the office, never attend any parties. But I still saw them at church, Camilla and Maximilian, and in due course their infant daughter Swanhilde, a tiny copy of her mother but with her father's eyes. Camilla's smile, forever brilliant, gave me a small taste of pleasure. I had not done everything wrong, bringing two Teutons together, forming this family that reflected the glories I could never have, as Muniche's Keyholder. But a few years passed, and Camilla's delight faded, her smile suddenly a façade. It pricked my soul, every time I met her eyes, seeing her hypocrisy, her unhappiness.

. . . I was thirty-seven, alone at my apartment on a wintry night, my solitude interrupted by a knock on the door. I answered it, found myself staring at Camilla, wrapped in a pricey wool coat that trailed the ground, tears in her eyes, lips trembling, hands uncovered, coated with ice. I urged her inside, out of the cold, asked what troubled her, and she cried out, "Oh, Hans, I don't love him! I tried, I really tried! And Max is a good man . . . a good man . . . but I'm not suited for his world, for a husband who isn't a priest. Hans, it is you I love!" I backed away from her, horrified, wishing I had not let her in the door, begging her to go, to return to her husband. She said he was away on a business trip, and she did not want to sleep alone, with her dreams. The fire ignited in my veins, I roared, "Camilla, NO! We can't!" But she advanced on me, casting her coat to the floor, revealing black lingerie underneath. I gasped, knowing it would be

inevitable now, and she cried, "All I want is you!" No further invitation needed, I put my hands on her, peeling the silk away as her hands removed my sweater, unbuckled my belt, and I threw her down upon the sofa, aroused past the point of no return. My flaming lips met her frozen ones, my teeth sank deeply into her neck, as deeply as my body sank into hers, and I felt her icy arms imprisoning my shoulders, her moans inflaming me further. The ice princess was mine.

. . . It went on for almost two years. She came to me whenever her husband was away on business, sharing my bed, enticing my lust, gratifying my darkest desires. She was enchanted, a slave to a priest, and I could not resist her charms, that impractical communion of fire and ice. Then our world shattered in a single instant, she came to me in broad daylight, terrified, horrid words spilling from her lips, "Oh, Hans! I'm pregnant . . . and I haven't slept with Max in over four months!" My sin struck me between the eyes, and I ordered her to leave, to never return, to get in bed with her husband at once, NOW!

. . . The months crept by so slowly as I tried to distance myself from this ice princess again, as our child grew inside of her. Then one afternoon a perversion came over me, two hearts connected with Muniche, with my responsibility, one that led to an icy siren, an aberration. I had never read of such a thing, this could not be, a devil to torment me, to make me fall again. And Camilla was there when I went to confront this witch who falsified Muniche's bonds. She tried to hold me back, tried to fight me with her ice, but her vitality was nothing to mine, her pregnancy having weakened her. I pushed past her, into the snowy forest, where the witch died in front of me, her blood staining the snow, her eyes gazing past me at something I could not see. Camilla told me, after the witch's body vanished, "That was my daughter, Swanie. She's destined to be your Leitalra, and she'll need someone to teach her, to train her, to be what I should have been . . . to you."

. . . So I honored my lover's final wish, and her icy daughter Swanie became my Lady, my wife, my ice princess, my Camilla . . . in her dances . . . in her touches . . . in her body . . . in her spirit . . . in everything . . . I always see . . . Camilla.

I broke away from my husband's neck of my own free will, hardly recalling to stem the flow of blood, for my brain was flooded, overflowing, suffused with a whirl of emotion: horror, anger, betrayal, hurt. I blinked once, twice, more times than I can count, pressing my hands to my temples as I saw my own face before me, then Camilla's face, blurring together, becoming one and the same, seduced by a black-fired priest.

My stomach twisted rather belatedly, and I brought my hands to my mouth, my legs wobbling as I staggered for the bathroom. I might have heard a gasping thread of a voice trailing after me, whispering a dying prayer for forgiveness; but I barely made it to the bathroom sink before my stomach rebelled, Hans' blood spewing from my mouth in clotted clumps, almost cutting off my airways. I choked, pressing one hand to my stomach as the other reached erratically for the faucet, switching on the cold water, rinsing away that mass of blood, staining the porcelain with rust. And when I found that nothing more remained in my sickened stomach, I splashed my face over and over with frigid water, gawking at my reflection in the mirror, breathing shallowly, attempting to sort out this startling truth.

So he loved Camilla, the whole time. He was the reason my parents met . . . that unusual blending of middle-class with riches. But it wasn't enough, for Camilla or for him, and their adultery ruined my family.

My first reaction was fury, plain and simple. I could hardly believe that my husband—the man I had trusted so naïvely with my heart, the man I had believed loved me more than any other woman—*Hans* had kept this from me for almost eighteen years of marriage. No, longer than that, I corrected myself. I had known him since the age of twelve, when he moved into one of the cottages on Thaden property to manage my father's finances and house business. Twenty-nine years.

For decades this man had made love to me, caressed me, fondled me, spoken sensuous avowals of eternal devotion, called me ice princess—and the entire time, he imagined me as Camilla. It was not a tough comparison. I looked very similar to my mother, though her eyes had been blue rather than gray, and she had stood several centimeters taller than me.

That man ruined my entire world, burning everything to cinders. I saw it all now, how my childhood had shattered due to this husband of mine and his inability to resist temptation. Camilla had met him at church and gravitated toward his fire, asking him to teach her more about her magic, about Teutonic lore. So he taught her, an ignorant maiden some ten years his junior, and she fell for him, just as I had. She relinquished her freedom to the mystery of the Teuton priest—and like Augustin once told me, those women who fall under such a spell can never be satisfied with a lesser man. Not even with my father.

My father had been an affluent man, a popular man, and a good man. He had even studied for the priesthood at one point in his life. But it was not enough for Camilla, for she had been seduced by Hans Meissner, the most powerful priest in München—*the Keyholder*. Had my father known of their affair? Was that why he assumed I had cheated on Joel with a Teuton priest during my stint in the past . . . because his wife had done exactly that?

Dane had been only my *half*-brother. It seemed like a sick joke, but now I realized that his smile had looked very much like Hans'. My mother and Hans had carried the mutated genes that disabled him, that took his life far too early. Their sin had slain an innocent child, hurt a decent man, doubtless broke Bertha Lohr's heart as she sensed her young Keyholder's lust for an icy maiden.

I recognized that their relationship would never have stopped if Camilla had not died in childbirth. Hans' memories of her were charged with passion and desire, even after thirty-five years apart. The bond of the keys was not strong enough to hold them back from each other. Camilla's and Dane's deaths were Hans' penance. During our marriage he had to smile fallaciously at his father-in-law, knowing he had stolen everything from that man—his wife, and now his daughter.

And I was Camilla to him, the one he should have married, the one Muniche had kept from him . . . the true love chained . . . unattainable.

Then I saw it, as plain as the water trickling down my face: *We were exactly the same.*

Both of us had found our chosen love, though circumstances held us apart. That was why my mother spoke those words to me, when I told her about Augustin in that cozy restaurant as we hid from the Keyholder: *Sometimes people find their one true love here in this life, but they can't be together until the next.* She spoke of Augustin and me, of Hans and her. She was the spirit Hans gazed at while lying upon his deathbed . . . she was the one who asked him to tell me the truth.

That was the difference between us. I had been upfront about my loyalty to Augustin from the start, even before I recognized Hans as my fated mate. But he was too cowardly to tell me the truth, fearing that I would despise him, reject his place as my Keyholder, my master, my destiny. No one could fight a Teuton city's bonds forever. I had submitted . . . and Hans had gotten his ice princess, though not the one he longed for.

The epiphany that Muniche's bonds had endeavored to blur from my heart arose before me as I stared at my reflection. *Augustin loved me of his own free will. There were no ghosts in our bed, no Keyholder, no husband, no working women, no sirens. He wanted me first, me alone. And it's time for me to return to him and defy Muniche's influence for the rest of my life.*

I ran a damp cloth over my face and dried it, tugging a comb through my tangled hair, looking calmly at my reflection now, knowing the whole truth of the matter. I had to forgive Hans, because he had forgiven me. We had each made our own awful mistakes, but it was time to move on, to embrace the future.

When I reentered the bedroom, Hans lay unmoving upon the bed, his eyes closed, his face whiter than snow. But I still felt the fragile connection between us, so I knew he was yet alive. "Hans," I whispered, leaning close to his face, "I forgive you. And I love you still . . . always." His eyes twitched behind his lids; he exhaled once, and then died with a faint smile on his lips.

Chapter Thirty-five:
Settling My Affairs

The next few days progressed in a flurry of activity. I felt as though I would never get the chance to sit down, let alone sleep. I could not hold a private funeral for my late husband, since he held the keys of Muniche, even if such an event may draw our enemies' attention. Üwe helped me plan the ceremony, which would take place on Friday afternoon at the Theatinerkirche. He sent out a message to the Teuton community as a whole, announcing that Hans Meissner had passed away and that everyone was invited to celebrate his life on Friday, the 13th of March.

Max departed the house before I finished making up my own mind about my Keyholder's affair. Sango had sensed him exiting the energy shield through the side gate—he reported that fact to Üwe while I spoke my final words to Hans. Thus far, Üwe and I were the only ones who knew that Hans had cursed his son and offered him the keys. I decided to keep Max's fate under wraps for the time being, since most Teutons were taught to fear Cursed Ones. It was my son's prerogative to make the truth known when he was ready.

During that hectic week, I did my best to settle my own business and ensure that my legacy would carry on without me. I sat down with Vreni and Alison—who studied psychology with the intent of helping others heal from trauma—showing them what they needed to know to help *Selakerza* thrive in my absence. I urged them to hire both Teutons and outsiders, so survivors of every type could find support there, and I passed a list of my father's contacts to Vreni so she could tap them for donations and further connections.

I sat down with my lawyer and Üwe to notarize my will, editing it so all of my financial assets and the Thaden property would go to my son under whatever name he chose for himself. Although Üwe was the only Teuton priest who knew of my son's curse for now, word would eventually spread, and all records of Max's existence would be destroyed. That task would doubtless fall to the other council members and priests in the city, once he came forward as a Black Priest, Günter's successor.

On the evening before Hans' funeral, I invited all of the adults occupying the Thaden house to the dining room table for an official discussion on the future. I claimed my late husband's chair at the head of the table, with Üwe seated to my right and Vreni to my left.

We enjoyed a meal of sandwiches and potato salad first, and I allowed my eyes to roam over every face at the table. Vreni and her priestly husband Stefan, manager in her father's pharmaceutical empire. Fonsi, his radiant element still dimmed by a longing for revenge, and his stepdaughter Alison with her youthful desire to make the world a better place. Siggi and Lise, who had worked under my father for over two decades, outsiders with unwavering allegiance. Sango, whose expertise had sealed Thaden property off from intruders. And Eva Peninger, sitting silently at Üwe's side, her heart gradually crawling its way out of her late husband's suppression.

Vreni's security guard watched over her sons in the kitchen. It was time for me to give the rest of the household an inkling of my plans. So after I finished my salad, I laid my fork down and informed everyone that I intended to go away for a while. I said that Max and I would explore some options that my former Keyholder had not. "I'm not going to give the NVH what they want. Max will be handling that going forward, so the rest of you will need to consult with him about any new developments. I predict that the threat will be quashed by summer, so it'll be safe for all of you to return to your homes and your jobs."

I paused to give everyone time to consider, but the only one who raised a question was Eva. "What about this new virus? Italy is in a lockdown, and for all we know, Germany may do the same. Would it be better for some of us to stay here until it's contained?"

Fonsi muttered something to Stefan, and I saw Lise's face crease with worry. "So far, it looks like the greatest danger is to the elderly," I noted, glancing at Üwe. "As long as Max agrees, this house is open to any of you who prefer to stay away from the public. Those who stay should continue to help with the housework and yardwork, since this property requires a lot of upkeep."

Eva and Vreni nodded, and Alison declared, "I'm planning on spending a semester or two in the dorms, starting this fall. So I won't be in the way for much longer."

"You're not in the way," Fonsi assured her, jostling her shoulder.

Stefan cleared his throat and addressed me, his expression inquisitive. "From what you've said, Swanie, it seems that you know where Max has gone. He hasn't been seen by anyone, including Matthias and Jan, since last Sunday."

"I'm aware, and what he's doing is his concern. I expect him to return within a few weeks, and he might share his accomplishments then."

"He's infiltrating the NVH's lair, isn't he?" Fonsi queried, his gray eyes alight with anticipation. I wondered whether he, too, had drunk some blood on the night when he, Max, Stefan, and Matthias visited that office in Leipzig.

"It wouldn't surprise me," I said, though I knew Max had darker things to finish first.

"I'm behind whatever he does, come what may," Fonsi stated.

"Same," Sango said, exchanging a grim nod with his brown-haired peer.

Scores of mourners filled the nave of the Theatiner-kirche on Friday, mostly Teutons from München and the surrounding area, though five Keyholders and Ladies came to take part in the ceremony. Some of Hans' extended family attended his funeral, most of whom I had met only once before, at our wedding. Everyone from our church came to pay their last respects, along with a number of business contacts Hans made during his years of organiz-ing the affairs of the Thaden house.

Whether our son managed to attend or not, I could not be certain, for so many Teutons packed the sanctuary that I would have had trouble identifying Max's darkness amid the crowd of elements. I sat with Sango, Lise, and Siggi, gaining most of my composure from the strength of Sango's energy. Thankfully, I was not required to speak some sort of eulogy on Hans' behalf, since the Teuton community expected me to be too grief-stricken to address the public.

During the ceremony, I immersed myself in a sea of reminisces, thinking of all of the wondrous moments I had shared with Hans, my caring Keyholder. He had been a good man despite his past failures, loving me tenderly in spite of mine. It surprised me that I did not feel incredibly despondent at the severing of our bond. Üwe had come to my side shortly after Hans had passed, sharing in my grief while I wept tears of ice. His companionship gave me the strength I needed to move forward, to tackle the tasks I needed to accomplish.

After the funeral, I told Sango and Üwe that I planned to depart on Sunday at the latest, whether Max made an appearance by then or not. I loaded the duffle bag I had packed a week ago into my M-Class, along with some things I thought my son might want. With Üwe's help, I collected a stash of books from the library, and he wrapped several of his paintings for my son to display at his Alpine castle. *Augustin*, the Cursed One searching the dark forest for his one true love; *A Priest Embraces the Grandeur of Redemption*, Hans standing before a cathedral's altar with organ pipes rising in the background; and *Ice Maiden*, the rendering of my mother caught in a spectacular elemental dance.

I refrained from packing the likeness of Muniche and her Keyholder into my SUV. Instead, I entrusted it to Üwe with the request that he present it to my successor, whoever she turned out to be. "I'm sure she'll have a lot of doubts and fears in the beginning, like I did, but maybe the artistic beauty of your painting will reassure her, along with my note," I told him.

In response, Üwe unfolded the brief note I had written to the young lady who would become Muniche's next *Leitalra*, reading it aloud. "'My dear girl, may this never be true of you. Don't fear your fate, or the darkness. I'd have married the man myself, if he wasn't my son.'"

Üwe raised his eyebrows and met my gaze, his blue-gray eyes radiating approval. "I'll definitely pass it along," he promised as he set the painting among the others he had brought from his studio. *Muniche and Her Keyholder: Unending Faithfulness at Indescribable Cost.*

On Saturday morning, Üwe caught me on the back staircase on my way to the kitchen in search of a quick bite to eat. "All the priests on the Teuton Council of München will be stopping by this afternoon," he said, not looking particularly pleased. "I know you'd rather let your new Keyholder come forward of his own volition, but your guardians are getting a bit impatient."

I halted four steps from the bottom. "They want to interrogate me?"

"You, and probably Stefan and myself. Since we live here, they likely think we have 'insider information.'" Üwe's eyes traveled toward the ceiling.

"Stefan doesn't know. Unless you've told him."

"I haven't."

I sighed and waved for Üwe to accompany me to the kitchen. Stefan and Fonsi sat at the table with mugs of coffee and plates of farina, the newspaper spread between them. I greeted them vaguely and poured myself a glass of orange juice. After fishing a granola bar from a box in the pantry, I beckoned my companion to follow me out the side door into the gardens.

It was chilly outside, so I summoned a trace of my element into my blood to protect me. I wandered toward the back deck and sat on the steps, taking a bite of granola before raising my eyes to Üwe's. "Maybe the other three priests on the council think *you're* the Keyholder."

Üwe gave a caustic snort and crossed his arms, fiery heat radiating from his body. "Old One, yes. Keyholder, no. If they believe that, then my . . . reputation has forsaken me."

That reminded me of something, and I cocked my head at my friend. "What exactly . . . are you planning to do . . . about Eva?" I inquired, trying to word the query respect-fully.

Üwe averted his gaze to the manor behind me, and I chewed on my granola bar, watching conflicting emotions stencil their lines upon his countenance. At length he cleared his throat and said, "I've been asking myself that for quite a few years now."

"But if you prefer men . . . ." I sipped from my cup of orange juice, unsure what to make of this elderly priest standing before me. My mother had called him 'gay.' Üwe had not rejected that label. Yet he harbored an attraction to Eva, a woman of light, one whose heart had been crushed by a sadistic priest.

A chuckle broke the morning's stillness, and Üwe's arms dropped to his sides. "See, that's one of my least favorite things about humanity. Always trying to label others, to squeeze them into a box, into a category. If I'm gay, I'm only allowed to date men. If I'm straight, I'm only allowed to date women. But what if . . . what if I feel a camaraderie that goes beyond all that . . . a soul that speaks to my soul, that loves me for who and what I am?"

Warmth bloomed within me as I grasped what Üwe meant. "That's exactly how I always felt . . . about Augustin.

It's always been there, in spite of the city's influence, in spite of the bond I can't control."

Üwe smiled down at me with yellow flames dancing in his eyes. "You need not fear for me or for Eva. I'll support her in any way that she asks. My heart has belonged to her for ages now, and no circumstances or preconceived notions can change that."

When I rose from the steps, he placed an arm around my waist as we headed for the house. "And Swanie, I think your future plans are sound," Üwe murmured in my ear just before we reached the glass doors to the dining room. I met his gaze as he explained, "It'd be best for you to vanish into the past for good, before the city bond alters your maternal love into something else."

I shuddered at that idea, for I had occasionally thought about Lady Maria throughout the past week, drawing parallels between her and me. At least Prince Otto was not her biological son. How had past Teuton Ladies handled the city bond, in the days when Keyholders traditionally passed the keys to their sons? Did they simply leave the connection incomplete until death?

Eva helped me prepare herbal tea and a dish of scones for our priestly guests. They arrived in a single car just before two p.m., and when Sango informed me of their presence, I asked him to linger nearby in case things got tense. "They've come to find out who the new Keyholder is," I told him as I carried the teapot and cups toward the front parlor. "I'm not sure how they're going to react to the truth."

Sango did not yet know the Keyholder's identity, either, but he gave me a determined nod. "I've got your back, Swanie. If they try anything against you, I'll use my energy to bridle their magic."

Fonsi overheard Sango's declaration, for he stood in the vestibule with his eyes narrowed toward the front parlor. He met my gaze and sauntered to Sango's side, his irises flaring with light. Eva and I left our protectors behind, entering the parlor and setting our wares onto the mahogany table standing before the lavender-patterned couch. Eva brushed my sleeve and took her leave, her eyes lingering on Üwe for a moment—he sat in the armchair that faced the vestibule, his visage stern.

All of the council members wore their black robes, prepared for a formal gathering, it seemed. My son's friend Matthias sat on the couch with the snowy weatherman, Helge Brennemann; the younger man took the initiative to pour a cup of tea for his companion as well as himself. Herr Brennemann sported slicked black hair with a matching beard and wide gray eyes—a face I recognized from the evening weather reports. Matthias appeared more relaxed than his older peer, his dark brown hair just a bit frizzy, his blue eyes turned downward whenever I looked his direction, in respect of my age and position.

Josef Fehr sat formally in the armchair that matched Üwe's. A man in his mid-fifties, his thinning hair appeared more gray than brown, his hazel eyes nigh hidden beneath bushy brows. He was the true unknown of this bunch, and I offered him a cup of tea and a scone, wanting to give the impression of gentility. He took both with a polite nod, his eyes remaining on Üwe more often than not. He likely believed him to be the new Keyholder, Hans' trusted comrade.

I moved to prepare a cup for Üwe, but he waved me off and rose from the armchair. "Don't worry about me, Swanie. And please, sit. I perched myself on this chair for the sole purpose of saving it for you."

I felt myself blushing, a ridiculous reaction. "I appreciate that. Would you like some tea, Stefan?" I turned toward where he stood at the doorway to the music room, trying to hide my flushed cheeks from the other priests.

Stefan shook his head and maintained his position, wind lurking in his irises as they shifted from me to the other priests to the window with its view of the front porch. He was on guard, just like Üwe, who stood to the right of the armchair as I settled myself upon it, teacup in hand. *This is going to be interesting.*

We exchanged a few basic discussions on the subject of settling my affairs, and Matthias offered his services if I needed help moving heavy objects. He and Üwe put in a few comments regarding their ongoing hunt for the NVH; this topic inspired loaded looks from Herr Brennemann and Herr Fehr. Meanwhile, I shifted my feet beneath the skirt I had donned for the occasion, awaiting the questions that hung heavily in the air. A slight frost coursed through my veins.

"We assume, my Lady Muniche," Herr Fehr said at length in his tenor voice, straightening in his armchair, "that you were present at Herr Meissner's deathbed, and therefore know the priest to whom he granted the keys."

Finally. I nodded, sensing Üwe's disquiet, then took a sip from my cup. "Since the man has not yet come forward," Herr Fehr went on, sounding perturbed, "would you mind telling us his name?"

I almost spluttered into my cup. I heard Üwe take a breath, but I held a hand out to him before he could respond. "I could not do that, Herr Fehr, for I do not know his name."

"But you saw the priest to whom your husband gave the keys?"

"I know him well," I answered. I had better just come out with it before I confused them enough to transform the parlor into a den of elemental attrition. I cast my gaze toward the two younger priests on the couch as I admitted, "The new Keyholder was my son, but I do not know his name." I looked down at the teacup I held in my lap. Üwe placed a supportive hand upon my right shoulder.

There was a short and frantic silence, and then Herr Brennemann grunted, handing his now-snowy teacup to Matthias. The young priest who had long been Max's good friend stared at me, agape, his eyes flames of yellow-orange; the tea in the weatherman's cup thawed instantly at the touch of his fingers. I heard Stefan make a noise that sounded like abrupt comprehension, and then Herr Fehr rose to his feet, his hands balling into fists. "Are you implying that Herr Meissner *cursed* his son . . . and then offered him the *keys?*" He was baffled and angry, his fists hardening into burning stone beneath his sleeves.

"It was an unavoidable fate," I said, addressing all of them, my ice detecting the tension in the room. "While I have no desire to fully explain everything now, for the sake of your safety, I will say with complete confidence that my husband made the right decision. The young priest who was once my son has no evil designs upon any of you, or upon this city or her people. I can assure you that he'll prove the most capable—"

"But *Leitalra!*" Herr Brennemann interpolated, his beard peppered with flurries, "good intentions aside, *how* could your husband dare to hand München over to a *Black Priest?* It goes against *all* customs!" He looked exceedingly distraught. The poor snowman likely expected to be the next Keyholder himself.

"What did he do . . . to deserve the curse?" Matthias asked.

I answered my son's friend with a sad smile, "He chose it. The enemies my family has been battling can't be beaten, except by one who is beyond death, one who can avenge Muniche properly."

Herr Fehr looked upset. He rubbed his sizzling hands together and moaned, "This is . . . very . . . unorthodox. Was Herr Meissner in his right mind?"

"He was sane, without question," I answered immediately, remembering the clear thoughts I had read in his blood just minutes after he performed the curse and passed the keys to his lost son.

Several of the priests began speaking at once, the tea and scones forgotten, their elements churning palpably in the room. Üwe stepped forward to rebuke their impertinence, and my ice sensed Stefan's warm wind sliding closer to me, a silent shield. "Everything you told us at dinner makes sense now," he whispered to me, sounding thoughtful. He did not appear utterly disgusted by my son's chosen fate.

As Üwe, Herr Fehr, and Herr Brennemann exchanged barbs, a dark voice cut into the parlor. "There is no point in all of these objections. Herr Meissner did what he believed was right, and it cannot be undone."

I gasped one short, icy breath, rising from the armchair as my son entered the parlor, clad in a majestic robe with the raised hood shadowing his face, along with his darkness. He wore the keys of Muniche around his neck on a silver chain, blatantly exhibiting his position before this gathering of priests bound by tradition, all of whom had fallen quite silent now. They probably gaped at this striking Black Priest in some sort of horror, but I did not look at any of them. My eyes were only for my new Keyholder, who approached me with a respectful gait, his gaze locked with mine, his gloved hands extended.

I could not move. I stood like an iceberg beside the armchair, trembling, my hands rising of their own accord to touch his fingers. He kissed each of my palms, his eyes never leaving mine. "My precious Muniche," he murmured, "did you fear I'd never come for you? You tremble."

"No," I whispered, the sound practically inaudible. "I've already packed the SUV. I've been waiting for you . . . *Leitaeri*."

He smiled a slow, enigmatic smile, brushing a hand across my hair. "That is good, *Leitalra*. I have prepared a chamber for you, but I'm afraid the castle isn't exactly furnished for human company."

"It's fine. I've been there before." I hardly knew what I was saying. I studied my Keyholder's countenance, seeking something there that reminded me of my son. His youthful cheeks had thinned, his eyes and mouth appearing matured and solemn, and he stood over a head taller than me. "You look like you aged about ten years," I said in an undertone, squinting at his features.

The Black Priest laughed, letting down his hood to reveal his black hair, thick and long locks of ebony. "Age fifteen was not what perfection my body could attain on this earth, apparently," he said, loud enough for the other priests to hear. Then he laughed again and pulled me to his chest, protectively.

"I've come to take my Lady home to my castle, of which all of you know, I am certain." I finally looked at the others as my Keyholder held me securely in his arms, seeing their separate expressions of alarm, repulsion, disbelief. Even Stefan looked uncertain; only Üwe gave me a knowing nod.

"I realize that most of you are in shock, with this unexpected turn of events. Therefore I propose that I take my Lady and go, so you can debate without my intrusion. I invite all of you to visit the Black Castle at any time, for you are the guardians of my precious Muniche, and I have no desire to hurt or kill any of you, rest assured." My son chuckled darkly.

I had a thousand questions for my new Keyholder, though most could wait until we left the Thaden house behind. Fortunately, Matthias gathered the courage to ask what would have been my first query.

"*Leitaeri* . . . what . . . are we . . . to call you?" He stared at his friend with a look of wonder.

The Cursed One met Matthias' gaze with a paradoxical expression, taking my left hand in his right as he replied, "I've taken the name of my greatest predecessor, hoping that I may follow his example as I avenge my city and my Lady."

I started as my eyes swept over my Keyholder's form from head to toe—his strong stance, the obsidian locks of his hair. "I am Augustin Abelard Ulrich von Bayern. My friends may call me 'Gust' in honor of the life-giving element. But I know that you will always call me 'Max,'" he appended, looking at me with eyes of unfathomable black.

Chapter Thirty-six:
Eternal Life

Before we departed the Thaden house, Max spoke to all of the adults who lived therein, informing them that he would be in and out and that he expected them to keep things running smoothly in his absence. While he made his rounds, I packed a few extra bags of groceries from the pantry and kitchen. I knew not whether the Black Castle's kitchen was prepared to take on another living human, nor did I know whether Günter and his windy partner still resided there. Maybe Günter had asked Max to kill them both.

Later, as I guided my M-Class down the driveway, I shot a glance toward my son, who flipped through my CD collection. His decision to name himself *Augustin* had upended my emotions, as I felt Muniche's bonds at work upon my heart, urging me to embrace my new master. *He's still my son. All the more reason to leave.*

"Need me to make any side trips before we head for your place?" I asked him, trying to put forth the impression of indifference.

Max shook his head, having retrieved my old Epica albums to load into the stereo. "No, but we'll be getting off the Autobahn at a different exit."

That meant there was a secret entrance to the Black Castle, and I was about to discover it. "Sounds good to me."

We sat in relative silence as I drove south toward the mountains, with Max growling alongside Mark Jansen as symphonic metal filled the car. I suspected my son felt just as awkward as I did—he was fifteen, after all, grappling with the standard teenage struggles on top of everything else. The many questions I had for him chugged away in my mind, and at length I broached a safer topic first.

"So did Günter ask you to stop his heart?"

"What? No!" I caught Max's horrified look.

I smiled, feeling a small touch of relief. "The man demanded a successor for some fifty years, and he found a girlfriend first."

"She's his wife. Her name is Zorina. They went off on a sort of honeymoon after I . . . completed the curse."

"So he's going to show her the world's beauty. Good for him. It must have gotten boring being stuck in that castle for so long."

My son laughed through his nose. "Günter got around, but this is all new for her. I think they were going to the beaches of Thailand first."

I sighed quietly as I passed a semi, my gaze returning to the peaks ahead more often than not. It would be wonderful to share a similar holiday with the man I loved so dearly. Maybe I could convince Augustin to show me the many places he had traveled in his youth, introduce me to his teachers in Salerno. I had not yet decided in which year I planned to return, but it would be after Prince Otto's death in 1074. No part of me wished to deal with Muniche's soul pining for a traitorous Keyholder.

"Was Zorina . . . one of the young women Günter used to breed children?" I winced as I asked the question, giving my son a side-eye. Hopefully her love for him had grown out of something deeper than Stockholm syndrome.

"She was. But that's her story to tell, not mine. Günter stopped doing that because she opened his eyes to how oppressive it was. He'd convinced himself he worked for the good of the Teuton people, ignoring the fact that he enslaved women in the process." Max tapped his fingers against the armrest.

"Wuotan clouds one's judgment," I noted, having had enough experience with that over the years. I heard my son's intake of breath when I spoke the demon's name, so I steeled myself to face the truth. "When exactly . . . did you complete the curse?" My heart pattered within me at the subject.

"Tuesday."

He had been dead for four days now. "So God allowed you to return."

"That's . . . ." I sensed Max's distress through our tenuous connection, and my forehead wrinkled as I shifted my eyes to the right. The keys of Muniche stood out starkly against the black cloth of his robe, drawing my spirit toward this man who was about to splinter my long-held perceptions.

"As it turns out, I wasn't actually a Christian. Before," my son confessed in a repentant tone. I gasped sharply, and my right hand shook where it gripped the steering wheel. Quickly, I steadied it with my other hand.

"Of course you were a Christian," I said, denial sweeping me into its ocean. "I remember when you put your faith in God at a summer Bible club. You've been walking the path of light ever since."

"Not really. I was just following the other kids that day. A bunch of them went to the front to 'give their hearts to Christ.' I repeated the prayer, but it didn't mean anything to me. It didn't change my soul, and I didn't repent of my sins. When Wuotan dragged me into darkness and showed me hell's gates . . . that was when I realized it was true. Hell and heaven. God and Satan . . . and his minions. I never really believed until that moment."

"Oh, Max," I groaned, his confession bringing tears to my eyes. "How could you have *asked* to be cursed if you hadn't put your faith in God? Wuotan enslaves his servants, just like Günter enslaved the women he bred. Oh my son . . . ."

"I understand it now, *Leitalra*," he assured me. "The truth struck me when the demon offered me a delay of judgment—a return to earth until I chose to face hell. That's the best he could offer, while God offers eternal life in paradise. As soon as Günter and I returned to the castle, I seized his robes and asked him whether it was too late for me now, whether my death meant that God would no longer hear my cries."

I could hardly concentrate on the highway before me. Thankfully traffic was light. My son paused in his discourse, and I felt as though all of my beliefs hung by a thread. "Well? What did Günter say?" I prompted.

"Heaven's gates don't close until a person leaves the mortal world for good," Max responded, and a shout of triumph burst from my heart. "Günter's been studying it for a while. Zorina put her faith in God before she became his wife, and she prayed hard that her master could join her in eternity. He certainly will, and he told me Wuotan hasn't been able to torment his heart ever since he granted it to God. Something restrains the demon anytime he tries to punish him."

"I knew it. I *knew* it!" I interjected, joy rending my uncertainties away. "I told Augustin that years ago, that if he put his faith in God, he'd be protected from Wuotan's wiles. But he just kept insisting that Wuotan would torture him if he repented of his sins. Oh, he's got another thing coming now!"

"It's true freedom, handing one's destiny to the Creator," Max murmured, his own joy uniting with mine, darkness and ice as one.

After we had driven along a succession of back roads, my Keyholder directed me to an almost-invisible turnoff at the base of his mountain, long before the road to the trail I used the previous October. The unfamiliar gravel drive plunged into the forest itself, branches of fir bending down to conceal my SUV's course. Some ten minutes later, the drive ended at what appeared to be a decaying shack made of aged timber, built against a solid crag of grayish stone.

"This is where Günter stores his cars," my son said, opening the passenger door and gesturing for me to get out, myself. "No curious hikers would suspect such a thing —a garage cleared out of the rock, hidden by an 'abandoned' shack."

"Wait a minute," I implored, stepping onto the bed of pine needles. My eyes followed my Keyholder's dark form as he approached the overhead door, rolling it up in one fluid motion, revealing the superhuman strength he had gained as a Cursed One. "Are you saying this shack leads into the rock face?" I removed my glasses and cast my vision in a sheen of ice, trying to see beyond the doorway.

A flashlight beam suddenly broke the darkness. My son advanced toward me, his priestly robe coupled with the forest's shade bringing an image of the Grim Reaper to mind. "This shack shields one of many entrances to the Black Castle," he told me, coming near to where I stood next to my SUV, the driver's door still open.

He placed one arm around my shoulders, likely sensing my uneasiness, his gloved fingers gently stroking my arm. "Günter constructed this with help from his predecessor Konstantin, who claimed the power over stone. Inside there's a freight elevator that leads into the fortress' lowest cellar."

Impressed by the concept of modern conveniences in an ancient stronghold, the truth of the matter made me chuckle. "Günter was lightning, so he must have designed the castle's electrical systems."

"The castle's power runs on a substation he created," Max murmured, his gloved fingers cupping my throat as his lips brushed my hair. "And I, of course, have plans that should protect this place forever from human interference —a gloom that even the strongest light can't pierce." He released me and directed his flashlight toward the pine needles at his feet. I saw, to my astonishment, that its beam stopped short about ten centimeters from the forest floor, hitting a wall of solid black.

"If you unleash your darkness upon the trail, too, any meddlers would be unable to find your tire tracks," I observed. Max laughed heartily and waved me to the driver's seat so I could park inside.

My Keyholder preceded me into the shack, its electric lights disclosing a well-fitted garage complete with all the necessary mechanic's tools. But my eyes fell upon the three vehicles that apparently belonged to Günter: an ice-blue Ferrari, a silver Porsche, and a sizeable box truck. *Good grief, that cursed doctor has a few things in common with my Pappi. I bet he uses that truck to transport raw materials or furniture . . . or a huge group of sacrifices.*

I parked my SUV beside the Ferrari, wondering if Günter planned on teaching my son how to drive, when he and his wife returned from their holiday. Max opened my door for me after sealing the garage's entrance. Then he proceeded to unload the entirety of the goods I had packed, carting it all in huge piles to the freight elevator, steel and spacious.

When we reached the castle cellar after Günter's elevator embarked on what seemed to be an interminable climb, my Keyholder proposed that we leave all but the most needful items behind temporarily, so he could lead me to my chamber. I agreed, and Max took up my duffle bag while I carried just my purse. My son led me down a central hallway with numerous branches, gesturing here and there to point out dungeon cells, torture chambers, and storerooms.

We entered a standard elevator at the center of the cellar and rode it to the ground floor. During the ride, Max mentioned several chambers that held stacks of currency and bars of gold, silver, and platinum. He had not yet had a chance to fully explore the fortress, but Günter had told him it was stuffed with a wide range of endeavors with which Cursed Ones had passed the hours. "He calls it a 'place rife with neglected genius,'" Max said.

"Konrad and Kasimir were hardly geniuses, since they made me take the stairs to the sacrificial chamber on

Halloween," I joked as we exited the elevator. "Günter did the same and made me walk halfway up a turret to boot."

"It's easy for the dead to forget that the living have limits to their stamina," Max reminded me with a sly smile. I suspected that he slowed his stride solely for my comfort as we ascended the northeastern turret—the one with the parlor where Günter and I had spoken.

We left the staircase at the level below the parlor, and Max led me to an aged wooden door, where he paused with his left hand upon its knob. "The room's not much," he said, a hint of a blush coloring his cheeks, "and I don't think it's seen a lot of use in the past century, considering how much dust I had to remove. But it has its own bathroom and a window seat with a view of the mountains." He broke off, his eyes trained on the stone floor beneath us, then turned the knob.

It was a lovely room, about the size of the parlor I had shared with Hans throughout our marriage. The walls were hung with tapestries of indigo and a deep maroon, garnished with coiled patterns of sable. A wine-colored rug adorned the floor, protecting the feet of a human occupant from the stone's chill. A canopied queen-sized bed stood with its headboard against the wall across from the entry, its curtains and blankets complementing the indigo upon the tapestries.

Right beside the bed, across from the doorway where we stood, I saw the cushioned sill Max had mentioned, perfect for gazing out at the peaks. A mirror and sink ornamented the wall on the other side of the window, and at the right corner I saw another wooden door, half-open, the outline of a toilet visible beyond. For a moment I ruminated on which past Black Priest had installed the fortress' plumbing; then I glanced over the other contents of the chamber. A bureau and wardrobe made of wood with a cherry finish, a luxurious-looking couch of a black fabric that matched the trim of the tapestries, and, suspended from the ceiling, a chandelier illuminated by a decent number of bulbs, casting the room in a vibrant light.

I stepped forward to lay my purse upon the bureau, recognizing that it was time to address the elephant in the room. I had not yet told my son about my plans to forsake the modern era. "This room is perfect, *Leitaeri*," I said, strolling toward the bed to sit upon its edge. "But I think you might be under the impression that I wish to stay with you here, as your wife. You know that's not possible."

Max trailed me into the chamber and set my duffle bag beside my purse, his silver eyes veiled by his darkness as he turned to face me. He chewed on his bottom lip for a second before saying, "I know. I've felt Muniche's bonds urging me to claim you . . . but I can't. The curse didn't change our relationship. Not really." His fingers touched the keys hanging at his chest.

"It changed nothing," I confirmed. "And that means you're free to call me 'Mutti,' while I can call you 'Max,' or my son." The fact that he had referred to me solely as *Leitalra* or *Muniche* since our reunion gnawed at my peace.

My son's shoulders sagged, and he ran a hand over his face, his eyes closed in what may have been anguish. "I'm nervous. Nervous about . . . the woman our city will choose . . . to take your place. How am I supposed to convince her I'm good, that I follow God . . . with this death clinging to me, and this black line scarring my skin?" His wide sleeves slid down as he rumpled his hair, and he glared at the cursed mark on his right forearm.

"It'll take time. You'll need to be patient and gentle with her, especially while you're in the midst of punishing our enemies. Guard your heart carefully and make sure it doesn't blacken with vengeance."

"I don't know how to do anything romantic," my son groaned, wandering to the window and laying his left hand upon its frame. "And the city bond is meant to be permanent. What if I mess everything up?"

"Muniche will choose the Lady you need." I repeated the platitude often heard in Teuton circles—one I did not wholly believe. "And I expect you to honor her as you've honored me. I won't be staying here very long, actually.

I've thought long and hard about my destiny, ever since your father"—Max winced at that term—"learned that his time was short. When you took the keys, that confirmed it in my heart. I'm going to return to Augustin, the man Muniche tore from me."

Max's body shuddered, and he favored me with an unreadable expression. "There's something you might want to check . . . before you go. Günter told me that your encounter last October made him curious about your past, and that he found some . . . interesting information amid the writings of Wolfgang. Information about your death."

Chapter Thirty-seven:
Prophecies from the Past

Early Sunday afternoon, Max led me to the northwestern turret, the contents of which had been neglected by his recent predecessors. We prepared scrambled eggs for lunch—I learned that Günter kept chickens and goats in a hidden meadow—and my son simply watched me eat, seated across from me at the table in the castle's expansive kitchen. I offered him a sample more than once, but he finally admitted that the taste of food no longer enticed him. "The eggs are dead, as is that granola bar," he explained in an apologetic tone. "I've got enough death inside of me. The life exuding from your blood and spirit appeals to me, though."

That admission prompted me to chuckle, and I stated that he must resist the urge to bleed me. "That sort of thing tends to stimulate other attractions, ones we don't want to act upon," I told him with a wink.

My son agreed, and after we cleaned up we struck out for the chamber that held Augustin's encyclopedias. A windowless room on the third level of the northwestern turret, it boasted no electricity and therefore no heat. Max advised me to dress warmly before I departed the bedroom that morning, so I had clad myself in my Ocean City sweatshirt, jeans, and thick socks beneath my sneakers.

When we reached the chamber, its iron door sealed against the elements, I lifted my gaze to the lintel while my son undid the latch. Etched into the stone with the power of fire in the elegant handwriting of a medieval chronicler, I saw the following words in Teutonica: *Official Records. MXLV-MCDXCIII.*

The chamber itself was rather confining, just seven paces from the door to the opposite wall, the width narrower still. A simple chandelier hung at the center of the ceiling, its candles ancient and dusty. Max brought a torch to light it with flames of natural fire before setting the torch into a notch outside the door, his actions awakening hazy memories of my days in medieval Muniche. The contents of the chamber—two six-shelved bookcases running the length of the left and right walls, and one three-legged stool that looked as primeval as the castle itself—were riddled with cobwebs, mildew spoiling some of the leather covers.

"You'll need to do a better job at preserving this place," I commented to my son as I looked around, wishing I had brought a dust rag. "It's a treasure trove of the history our people choose to forget. Since you've taken Augustin's name for yourself, I expect you to honor any legacy he's left behind."

Max bowed his head and pointed toward a shelf on the left, to where a tome bearing a brass placard on its spine that read *1074* rested. All of the volumes filling the shelves were bound in leather, their covers bare aside from the labels on the spines. Although previous Cursed Ones had little interest in my medieval lover's records, I felt certain that I could spend at least a year in this chamber, reading what Augustin had set down in his Carolingian miniscule.

The cover of the *1074* tome showed evidence of recent handling—fingerprints upon the dust. The second thing I noticed that set it off from its counterparts was the absence of three pages just past its midpoint. *So this must be the one Hans consulted twenty-one years ago, when we first researched this stupid rock that messed up my life.*

My son manipulated the air in the chamber to clean the stool of dust, then handed me a pair of white gloves. "Günter says you should start in Chapter Six, page 235," he told me.

The book opened naturally to the scar from the torn pages as I plopped down upon the stool. I smiled wistfully at the familiar handwriting, tracing my fingers down the left page, my eyes running over a few phrases: *dire situation for trade . . . spread eastward . . . pestilence had run its course.* But I shook myself before I could get lost in the paragraphs before me, flipping backward in a search for chapter headings.

I discovered that each chapter denoted one month, and some were lengthier than others; therefore, Chapter VI referred to June. I also noticed, when I came to the correct page, that the numbers decking the upper corners of each leaf did not follow the standard Roman pattern of that era. They were all Arabic numerals, styled in the way *I* would shape them.

Interesting. I don't remember discussing mathematics with Augustin. Maybe he learned it from medical terminology, since he studied Arabic remedies in Salerno, I thought. Before I had a chance to reason out this mystery, I started reading the contents of page 235, and all other thoughts evaporated from my mind.

I remained riveted to the sheets of parchment before me for a solid hour, barely a breath escaping my lips. My son hovered nearby in silence, and I got the impression that he had read this account already. When I closed the volume and looked toward the blank wall dividing the shelves, I could almost *see* Augustin's words written on the stones in a fiery hand . . . spelling out my latest destiny, a prophecy I could not disregard. My lips quivered at last, a whispered voice in the forgotten storeroom of history: "Well . . . that's just shit."

The page to which Günter had directed me contained a few lines describing some sort of plague that had crept slowly along the Rhine River, spread by the traders, ravaging each riverside settlement in turn. These sentences spoke of fever and disorientation, a victim's lapse into insensibility and death. Even Augustin, with his above-average medical knowledge, had been unable to halt the plague's course. While he did not mention his own role in the matter—like a good Teuton chronicler, he refrained from referencing the Cursed One—this section ended with the statement, *Some have considered barring all southbound crafts from entering Eisenwald and closing the eastern roads in an attempt to isolate the pestilence so it may run its course.*

Right after this repugnant segment—obviously a continuation of the topics discussed on previous pages—there was a break in the text, and the subsequent section bore the disquieting heading, *Muniche's Prince and Lady: Their Unlikely Reunion in Death.*

Augustin had devoted two whole pages, front and back, to this tragic tale, beginning with an introductory note that answered the question that bothered me whenever I thought of Prince Otto: *At the destruction of Muniche in 1066, her Lady escaped into the future using her Keyholder's last gift, his Song of Time. This left him without a female counterpart for eight years, a fitting retribution for his final act toward her, cursing the very city he swore by his blood to protect.*

I thought I detected a bit of that old resentment in Augustin's choice of words. The next sentence confirmed it. *Nonetheless, fate wished to smile upon the shamed Prince one final time, sending his Lady back to him as a comfort in his final days, a companion in death.*

Augustin's record explained that I—he did indeed identify Muniche's Lady as 'Swanhilde von Thaden'—had returned to the eleventh century after spending some twenty years leading Muniche faithfully in my own era. However, my destiny in the twenty-first century had proven grievous, so I had played Prince Otto's song for one final encore, coming to die with the man whose wizardry had shaped my entire life.

Augustin expounded on the parallels between the Prince's experience and mine, how Wuotan's sorcery had ruined our personal lives, yet the Teuton people would remember us for the good we had done. Each person plays a role in the grand scheme of history, Augustin asserted, and perhaps some eternal principle could be gained from the noble suicides of a broken Keyholder and his Lady, both realizing humility and forgiveness at the end.

The Prince and I spent ten days alone together in the forest outside of the plague-riddled Eisenwald. Of this Augustin wrote only one evasive statement: *They likely shared those glories that only the Keyholder of a Teuton city and his Lady can know.* My cheeks heated at the implications of such a thing.

He recounted the suicide in detail, pinpointing the date as the 27th of June, the night of the new moon. Apparently the Prince and I had found a raft somewhere, or fashioned one out of sticks and reeds, floating it out to the middle of the river just at Vigils—or, in modern terminology, midnight. We stood together, each wielding a stone knife—Augustin mentioned the starlight glinting off the blades, proving that he may have embellished this a bit. After exchanging a few unutterable phrases, we slit our wrists and then our throats, plunging together into the great German river that would serve as our grave.

Augustin's account of our suicide closed with the words, *Thus, Muniche's Keyholder and Lady were both dead, reflecting the unfortunate fate of that grand Teuton stronghold that lies as rubble along the Isar, awaiting life again.*

I rose from the stool and laid the volume upon it, my emotions in chaos. Placing my hands on my hips, I met my son's gaze. "How . . . *how* could Augustin . . . write . . . that I'm supposed to die . . . with Prince Otto? That's not why I want to go back there. That man cursed us both!" My jaw quivered as my heart throbbed defiantly against Muniche's bonds—against the cruel hand of fate.

Max stepped back to lean against the doorway, antagonism radiating from his aura. "I thought the same thing when Günter showed me. You love Augustin, not that awful Prince. All he did was ruin your life, fail his Lady, curse a man due to an inferiority complex. But that book says you died with him."

I shook my head, gazing out at the passageway and the flickering firelight from the torch. "I mean, it makes sense from a historical perspective. Ritual suicide means final death for time travelers. So I'm fated to kill myself with the man who invented the damn thing."

"Augustin watched you die," Max grated, his resentment dimming the candles above. "He watched you leave him alone on this earth for four hundred years."

I took the Lord's name in vain as I realized what my son was saying. Was I truly fated to break Augustin's heart in the starkest betrayal? I placed a hand to my forehead as my knees grew weak.

"Max, can you . . . can you . . . help me back to my room? I need some time . . . time to think this through." I choked on my tears and my son swept me into his arms, his voice soothing me as his darkness carried us back to the neighboring turret with inhuman speed.

When I ate dinner that night—a dish of leftover chicken stew I had brought from the Thaden house—my son sat in silence, his expression unhappy. I spoke a few pointless phrases on the weather, muses on whether Üwe and the other council members had come to a consensus about Max's status. He did not take up any of those subjects.

After I finished my last bite of stew, I wiped my mouth with a napkin and addressed something that needed to be resolved. "I guess Günter has some sort of medical lab in this castle?"

Max met my gaze with an uncomprehending look. "Yes."

"Well, you realize you're going to have to play surgeon on my hip before I leave." His eyes darkened, and I explained, "Since I don't plan on returning, I'll have to give you the Torstein first. I don't know what would happen to it if I just went . . . with it still inside of me." I had shared the Torstein's location with him the previous night.

My son shook his head at me and abruptly exploded. "How . . . I just don't see *how* you can do this." His voice was low and hoarse, and his irises appeared jet black as he stared me down. "*How* can you really go back to that place just to die with *him? And* how can you do it while Augustin watches you abandon him for the man who cursed him?" He broke off with a groan and rubbed his temple.

"Max, it's probably better that we don't discuss this." I rose from my seat and headed for the sink to clean the dishes. "I don't know yet if I'll actually do what that tome described. It may be what's 'supposed' to happen, but that was just Augustin's official record. He probably wrote a more detailed account elsewhere, about meeting me again."

I could say no more, for now my hands had frozen right beneath the scalding spigot, my element protecting my skin from harm as I saw his face before my eyes, heard my voice telling him, *I didn't come here for you. I came for the Prince.* I could not hurt him so cruelly, no matter what his encyclopedia claimed.

Hands of darkness locked upon my wrists, pulling them away from the hot water, swathing them in the fabric of a towel. "That's just it, Mutti," Max said while I dried my hands; he took charge of cleaning the dishes in my stead. "There must be more to the story, something we don't know. You've always said the Torstein and the Song of Time are gateways to the past, not to the future. And how can one really *know* her own future? Isn't divination against the will of God?"

His words troubled me, and I remained silent while he finished scrubbing the dishes, tossing him my towel when he needed it. Once he had turned the water off and given me his full attention, I met his gaze and reminded him, "What we saw in that book was from the *past.*"

"But it was *your* future . . . *Leitalra.*" He smiled crookedly at me.

My son informed me, after I had showered and dressed for bed, that he intended to take action against the NVH that very night. He said he would go alone and collect hostages to bleed for further information on our enemies. "I'll give the other priests a report once I've finished," he said. "But I wanted to make sure you'll be okay here by yourself all night."

"Is there any chance someone might stage an attack?" I asked, raising my eyebrows at him playfully. Such an enterprise would prove utterly insane; the Black Castle was sealed tightly against any intruders.

A crease appeared between Max's eyebrows as he replied, "If anyone shows up unannounced, Teuton or not, cry out to me through our bond. And do it if you need support of any kind, please. Your distress has troubled me all day."

I sensed Max's element reaching cautiously toward my spirit, offering what comfort he had to give. I shut my eyes for a moment to bask in the certainty of his care, his immortal power seeking to restore my vigor. That was a privilege I had greatly missed in Augustin's absence.

"I think I can make it through one night by myself," I assured him, opening my eyes to look into his. "I'm still trying to decide how to interpret what Augustin's tome said. There has to be more to the death tale of the Prince and his Lady . . . something not fit for an official record."

"I hope you're right," Max murmured, drawing me into an embrace.

My dreams brought me to a dark forest like the one in Üwe's painting, and I spent the night calling for Augustin in a landscape of mist and shadows. Every now and then I would hear his voice, but the only man I found was Prince Otto, his eyes boiling with red fire, the keys of Muniche hanging around his neck. Somehow she stabbed me even in sleep, rebuking my yearning for a wraith who refused the sacred duty. By morning's light I remained undecided. Must I go to the year 1074 and die with Prince Otto, the man for whom I felt no love?

I put on the same outfit from the previous day before making my way to the kitchen in search of breakfast. Though I had not yet seen my son, I sent my element in a wide arc while I descended the turret's uneven staircase.

My ice sensed Max's darkness somewhere amid the lower levels, which likely meant he had succeeded in his endeavor, captured some prisoners.

He came to me as I savored an omelet stuffed with bacon and onions, rage cloaking him in a shroud of death. "Mutti, you need to come with me right away," he spat, gritting his teeth. "I found more than we bargained for last night."

Leaving my half-eaten omelet behind, I followed him to the elevator, which carried us to the level with the dungeon cells. A male voice moaned pitifully as we walked down a forbidding passage lit by bare electric bulbs. But when I recognized the occupant of the cell Max opened, my element froze me into an iceberg.

Chapter Thirty-eight:
Outright Treachery

The cell looked like something out of the Middle Ages, hooks for shackles welded into the stone walls, a single drain at the center of the floor. One blanket was bunched in the far corner, and a waste bucket sat to the right of the door. The cell had no windows, the sole light coming from a buzzing bulb over the door. A stocky woman with a mop of brown curls sat against the far wall, clad in a pair of ripped skinny jeans and a purple blouse with stains under the armpits. Fetters that gave off an otherworldly shimmer clamped her bare ankles, restraining her elemental magic.

But when Max opened the cell's door, the woman scrambled forward, wide blue eyes fixating upon me like those of an animal. "Swanie! Get me out of here!"

She charged headlong into an energy shield of some sort; I had not sensed its presence, but it stopped her centimeters from the hallway. My ice had overtaken me to the point where I could neither move nor speak, my brain not wanting to put two and two together. The woman cried out and rubbed at her forehead, her wails echoed by the male prisoner somewhere further down the passage.

"Quiet, you fucking swine!" my son roared toward the second voice, hatred rolling off of him in solid waves of darkness. "If you keep that up, I'll see to it that you never speak again! It's not like you need to, after all."

"Swanie." The woman in the cell had plunked back onto her buttocks, her shuddering hands batting hair away from her face. "That man is mad! Did he bring you here, too?" Her terrified eyes drifted from me to my son.

My son's hand fell upon my shoulder, pulling me close to him, effectively breaking shock's hold on me. "She's convinced herself that she's done no wrong. Disgusting," he growled in my ear.

"Marga?" Her name made its way out of my lips at last, my voice cracking with a mixture of confusion and hurt.

"Don't listen to him. He tells lies!" Marga shrieked, crawling back to her former position against the far wall. She crossed her arms and glared at Max with a pouting expression.

"My son would never lie to me." My willpower had reasserted itself.

"Your son?!" Marga cried out, her torso shaking with mocking laughter. "Your son's a madman! That makes you just as guilty as him." She pointed one trembling finger at us and cackled.

"What has become of you?" I whispered, shaking my head at the woman I had once considered a friend. A friend so trusted that I told her of my eleventh century journey. A friend I had helped hone her elemental gifts.

"Tell her what you've done," Max ordered, raising his voice to address the woman in the cell. "Tell her how you've betrayed your own people. Tell her how you've betrayed your own *friend*."

Marga babbled something about lies and how I had chosen to walk the dark path, collaborating with a priest who would lock her in a cell so primitive. "At least Freya's room had a bed and a toilet. She even had a TV!" Marga shouted.

My lips parted in horror when she spoke my daughter's name, Max's arms the only thing keeping me on my feet.

"Freya?" I repeated, the name scraping my throat with sandpaper. "You . . . you played a part . . . in murdering my *daughter?*"

"I took care of her!" Marga hollered, as if some foolish part of her believed she could redeem herself in my eyes. "She loved me, called me 'Mutti.' She told me how mean you were to her, not letting her fight back against the bullies at school, calling her stupid since she couldn't write well, putting her brother on a pedestal since he was smart, talented, a *boy*." Her eyes narrowed at the Black Priest holding me in his arms.

I gawked at Marga, her accusations finding no purchase. "Oh, you'll pay for that one, bitch," my son threw at her, his anger sizzling along our incomplete bond. "You're the stupid one, thinking it'll help you to cast the blame on the only woman I love."

"Did you . . . help them kill her? Help them . . . rape her?" I could barely shape the word. My anus clenched at the memory of what that audio file contained.

"I protected you!" Marga blurted, her cheeks flaming. "When they found out you had the Torstein, they wanted to go after you first. I convinced them to offer you money instead!"

"And slaughter eighteen of your own people and ten outsiders? Never realized my Mutti was friends with a heartless serial killer," my son interpolated with a caustic snort.

Marga sneered at my son, and I gnawed on the inside of my cheek, trying to gather the courage to speak the most pressing questions. She would probably lie, but I needed to hear her excuses. "How did the NVH find out about the Torstein? Did you offer them your blood to bargain with Wuotan? Or did you betray my secret yourself?"

Something strange passed across Marga's face, and she took up the blanket to wring it in her hands. "It was him. It was always him. He promised we could live in luxury once they got the Torstein. They'd pay us millions for our help."

I blinked, not following her narrative. "He?" I directed the query to my son.

"She's talking about Mary," he said in an insolent tone.

"His name is *Marinus!*" Marga shrieked, her cheeks growing redder. "And he's got bigger balls than *you*, with your—"

"Really? Sounds like a girl to me." Max chuckled and glanced toward the piteous moans pealing occasionally from further down the passageway.

Marga hurled several insults at my son, her hands having wrung the blanket into a ball. I sighed at Max's attitude; name-calling would get us nowhere. A friend I had trusted had cast her lot with a cabal of Saxon terrorists, had ingratiated herself with my captive daughter, had called me two summers ago to say that my father and Beth had met a terrible fate.

"Was it you . . . who poisoned my Pappi and his wife?" I asked, forcing the words through my teeth, my hurt gradually shifting into resentment. "My Pappi, the one who welcomed you to stay in his house after Ivo—"

"It's all *your* fault none of the Teuton guys wanted me!" Marga burst out, giant tears working their way out of her eyes. "You're the *Leitalra* of Muniche, and it never once occurred to you to defend me, to *tell* our people Ivo was wrong about my blood! You went on and on about Teutons having kids with Teutonic people but never mentioned my name! Marinus gave me everything *you* wouldn't. Nobody can judge my blood status anymore, and I can open cracks in the earth now."

She sniffed loudly and plopped her palms upon the stone beneath her, as if expecting it to heed her call. The shackles on her ankles stifled her magic inside—the olden method of restraining a Teuton by force rather than drugs. My son gave a quiet snarl and said, "How much good has it done you now, when the earth will never respond to you again?"

"Then . . . you betrayed me . . . betrayed our people . . . because they believed Ivo over you? Because they discriminated against you?" I looked at Marga but saw the Teuton traitors from the eleventh century—the ones who collaborated with the Saxons to avenge themselves against those who held blood purity above elemental magic in general.

Marga's blood had been eighty-five percent Teutonic at birth, the lowest level at which elemental control was possible. But her ex-boyfriend Ivo had spread the word that her blood was tainted since she had trouble wielding her earth magic. Apparently she had never made peace with his defamations.

Marga stared at me and began to sob, likely another attempt to garner my sympathy. But she had admitted to grooming my daughter, to sharing my secrets with her boyfriend, to inciting the NVH's actions against us in hopes of gaining a profit. I found that I felt no pity for her. I stepped away from my son's arms as the collective soul of Muniche united with my icy spirit to look down upon the woman who brought destruction to her people. To her sons and daughters.

Their souls cried out to me from the grave. My father. Lena and Beni, Traudl and Mane, Selina. Ina. Rudi, Oskar, Warren, Jürgen. My daughter Freya. Muniche's offspring demanded vengeance.

"She's not telling you the whole story," my son stated at length, standing behind me with his arms crossed beneath his robe. "Jealousy has stoked her fires since the day she first met you and learned you were ninety-five percent Teutonic. Blood high enough to never be questioned. A Thaden, destined for success. Mother of eight children in the past. Fertile. Mother of two children in the present day.

"While this one couldn't have children at all. She tried it with Ivo. She tried it with Derek. She tried it with the outsiders in between. And she tried it with Mary. Nothing could give her what she wanted.

"And she looked at you, a happy mother of a son and daughter. Mother of Muniche as a whole. Prosperous. Popular. Everything she wanted. She murdered her own city's Lady hoping Freising's soul would choose her next. She didn't."

Marga wailed at my son's words, tearing her hands through her curls as she screamed that it was not fair, that everyone had misjudged her. But I knew that blood cannot lie, and my son had bled both her and her pitiful boyfriend Marinus. "You killed your best friend in that bathroom, didn't you?" I questioned in a dead voice, Ina's spirit crying out to Muniche's soul within me. "You shot her up with fentanyl because she had a daughter, a husband, a job. The life you always wanted."

Marga yammered something unintelligible about Ina, and I turned my head to the right to meet my son's gaze. I had heard enough of this. The NVH's empire was crumbling, their spies' influence dissipating into smoke.

"*Leitalra,*" Max said, the Keyholder's authority weaving through his voice. "Has she earned justice or mercy?"

For a moment I wavered, as I looked down upon this woman I once trusted as deeply as my other girlfriends. What had become of the cheerful girl who danced around the Maypole, swayed to the music at festivals, chatted on ICQ about the fun things in life? Somehow, she had drifted away from me, away from her people, into a vat of distaste that transformed her into a criminal.

As her wide blue eyes met mine, I allowed Muniche's power to speak through me. "Justice."

"So be it." My Keyholder spoke in Teutonica, and Marga threw herself at the energy shield that held her, clawing at it with her fingers and cursing me, cursing my son, cursing the city of München. I turned away, heading for the distant elevator without a backward glance. I never wanted to see her face again.

My son joined me when I stepped through the sliding doors, his fingers casually hitting the button for the castle's ground floor. "Same fate for the boyfriend?" he inquired in Bayerisch, leaning against a wall as the elevator started its climb.

I nodded, disgusted by my former friend's treachery. "They're the ones responsible for this whole thing. I don't think rehab or prison would cut it."

Max chuckled quietly. "Marinus is an ex-convict. Spent ten years in our people's dungeon because he used his dark energy to kill an outsider. Obviously didn't learn a thing then, won't learn anything now. Except pain."

"So be it," I murmured in Teutonica, a sense of relief clasping my heart.

"I'm going to wait until Günter comes back before finishing this. He has . . . a lot more experience with torture than I do." My son cleared his throat and shot me an apologetic look. I simply shrugged as we stepped onto the ground floor, and my son went on as we pointed our feet toward the kitchen.

"And I'm going to invite Fonsi to do what he wants with Marga. She killed his wife, and she's the one who lured Freya out of her school. Marinus poisoned Opa and Oma and dropped off the box . . . with my sister's remains." He took a deep breath and finished, "And they were both responsible for the explosion that killed the four council members."

"Sounds like a perfect plan to me," I said. "What about Ostermann?"

My son's face grew hard once more. "I know where he hides, and I'm going to bring him here tomorrow night. He made the call for each killing."

I nodded, Muniche's power stirring my soul. "Sacrifice him, *Leitaeri*," I said in Teutonica, my departed children demanding the ancient reckoning.

"It would be my pleasure, *Leitalra*," Max responded in kind. The two of us entered the kitchen a second later, and I retrieved what remained of my omelet and carried it to the microwave. This day had started off with a bang.

Max showed me around the entirety of the castle that day. Günter had used the southeastern tower primarily; his medical labs and the bedrooms where he once housed his female slaves were there, along with an overabundance of baby-related equipment. The upper floor of that turret contained the chambers he shared with his wife Zorina. My son and I left those alone, respecting the couple's privacy.

One of the upper floors of the northeastern turret held enormous collections of fabrics and clothing in styles from centuries past, some of it moth-eaten, all hung now with dust and cobwebs. I had a notion to grab a couple of the dresses that were in fair shape, to clean and bring along on my journey to the eleventh century. The top floor had once been used as an observatory, comprised of one domed chamber with several portals opening to the sky. My son and I studied the antiquated stargazing equipment resting here and there, the walls bearing a plethora of etched symbols, some scientific and others pure astrology.

Max showed me the inner gardens with their tunneled pathway to a meadow further down the mountain. There, I found that Günter kept two greenhouses of edible plants and flowers, along with his collection of chickens and goats. Though I had no wish to think about the two Teuton criminals my son held in the cellars, I reminded him that they would need to be fed and their waste buckets cleaned. "I'd say the milk and eggs will do," I told him, for I noticed that two of the goats were lactating. "Maybe an occasional leaf of lettuce. Don't forget to milk them every morning." I gestured at the goats, and Max promised to do so.

In the main portion of the castle, my son brought me through an archway into a room that appeared to be a chapel. Large and open, ringed with columns and balconies, stained glass windows adorned the right wall, sending multicolored rays of light into the vast space before us. The floor was of marble, and some distance away from the entrance stood a grand staircase leading to what could have been considered a stage, with two smaller stairwells ascending on either side of it toward the balconies.

Two marble fountains flanked the staircase at the base of the stage. While they sported no water, the viewer could still appreciate their intrinsic beauty, their spouts carved in the likeness of musical instruments—I recognized a lute, fiddle, harp, flute, and trumpet. But just a small part of my brain bothered to appreciate the artistic genius in the chamber's design, the majority of my attention snared by the iron pipes that rose in clusters to the ceiling, small and great, all leading back to that grand instrument that had forever entranced my soul, its console visible upon a loft to my left—*the organ.*

"If it's your plan to do as Augustin's tome says, and use the Prince's song to open your final portal through time, this is where you can do it," Max said, his gaze also upon the organ pipes.

"It's been too long since I've played a majestic organ like this one," I mused, my feet moving automatically toward the loft. I glanced back at my son as I walked and said, "Let's see if there's any music lying around up there."

When we reached the loft, I saw that the organ console appeared quite old, a precursor to the days of electricity—and yet the instrument had an *on* switch and bulbs that illuminated the keyboards and stops. "Günter's an organist," I gathered, prompting Max to shrug; that subject had apparently not come up between them. My eyes raced over the four keyboards, the full pedalboard, and the large selection of stops before resting upon a pair of shiny organ shoes lying near the console. I gestured at them while I climbed onto the bench. "Told you so."

A rack bearing a vast selection of scores stood against the wall to the right of the console. "I'm going to need you to snag my pair of organ shoes next time you visit the Thaden house," I said to Max as I hit the *on* switch, the powerful sound of a generator kicking to life somewhere behind the pipes. "I'll need those to play the Song of Time properly. Don't want to break my feet this time around."

"I'll get them tomorrow night," my son promised.

I played two pieces by Bach and one by Mendelssohn, fumbling over the pedalwork thanks to my sneakers. The chapel's acoustics proved magnificent. When I hit the lowest notes of one of Bach's fugues, I almost believed I could feel the whole fortress reverberating around me. My fingers did not stumble, and when I finished I murmured, "This'll be perfect, if I can just figure out whether or not I can really *do* what Augustin's tome described. Maybe I don't really have to die with the Prince. Maybe we decided to write that together, to give history a romantic view of ritual suicide."

"Romantic suicide." My son rolled his eyes, and I offered a half-smile, still unhappy about the destiny that loomed before me. I was sick of having no control over my fate, whether Muniche's bonds or Augustin's records directed otherwise.

That evening Max removed the Torstein from my hip, using one of Günter's potions to knock me out for the procedure. Once I had regained my senses—it took some doing after the shot he gave me—I studied the blood-red rock where it lay on a medical table beside the chair where my son had placed me. He had already cleaned my flesh off of it. It glowed a muted ruby under the fluorescent lighting of Günter's laboratory, lying still like a sleeping giant, waiting for some unsuspecting soul to awaken its terrible power.

I looked down at my right hip, seeing little obvious change aside from a thin scar left by the blood control of a cursed priest. "You must protect it at all costs, Max," I reminded him when he came to my side to see how I was faring. "It can make or break a people."

"No one will ever use it for evil under my watch," my son pledged, eyeing the stone with a look of respect. "I've learned a few protection spells to place over it once it's hidden. No one will know its location unless they bleed me, and that's not a privilege I tend to offer." He grinned rather wickedly at me.

I took a long shower that night, my muses drifting from the jarring account Augustin had written about my fate to Marga's betrayal. Although I felt no guilt for defaulting to justice rather than mercy, her convoluted excuses troubled me. She seemed to acknowledge that she had done wrong, yet she contended that she was not at fault.

I still remembered how amiable Marga had been while she stayed at my house during the summer of 2001. We had shared so many girlie conversations—laughing about boys, commenting on recent movies, on music and trends. With my help she had learned to invoke earth from her

Teuton blood, growing ever closer to giving its magic full control to free her spirit from her body. She had exulted about the opportunity to visit her best friend Ina in spirit form, beyond the reach of prying eyes.

She never once told me of her struggles to conceive. I knew that her blood status upset her, but I expected her magical proficiencies to supplant that. Instead Marga had allowed her sense of inferiority to drag her into crime, to murder her best friend and so many others.

I should have taken the effort to stay in contact with her over the years. Jealousy had consumed her, transforming her into someone I did not recognize. I prayed for her soul that night as I lay in bed. Marga's family had never been religious, but she would soon look death in the eye.

On Tuesday, Max departed after lunch in a quest for my organ shoes and the nefarious leader of the NVH. He said he would summon me in the morning to mock Ostermann once he chained him in the dungeon. After he left, I spent an hour browsing through the clothing on the fifth floor of my turret, retrieving two dresses that appeared salvageable. One of light green linen, the other of vibrant red, they would be appropriate for the summer months.

While the dresses lay soaking in my bedroom in a washtub I had unearthed, most of the grime and mildew scrubbed away, the unexpected arrival of two men jolted me from my tranquility. Both had braved the precipitous trail to reach the Black Castle's front entrance.

Chapter Thirty-nine:
No Blissful Life

The pealing of the castle's chimes lured me away from my reading; I had nearly finished a final book in a fantasy romance series—the last I intended to read before leaving this era. I likely would have ignored my guests had my ice not recognized Sango's energy. Glancing up from my e-reader, I looked out the window to see him standing between the stone angels that guarded the front portico, holding the chain for the fortress' carillon. *Oh. That must be the doorbell.*

I could think of no reason for Sango to visit my spectral domain, especially since the master of the castle was away on business. He had likely missed my son, who had struck out for the Thaden house shortly after lunch, traveling through the magic of his immortal darkness. Maybe Sango brought news about the others in my former household. Hopefully none of them had run afoul of the NVH. Either way, this visitor constituted no threat, so I descended the twisted staircases of the northeastern tower to invite him in.

When I pulled the main door open and stepped forward to welcome Sango to a place he had likely never expected to visit, my eyes widened, and my hand fell off of the doorknob, my greeting vanishing from my mind. Sango, attired in sturdy hiking pants and navy blue parka, his customary smile spread across his face, was not alone on the veranda. Standing some distance behind him, his eyes studying one of the grim angels, was a man whose outfit—faded blue jeans, gray hoodie, white sneakers, and L.L. Bean backpack—labeled him instantly as a foreigner.

Before I had the opportunity to recover from my initial heart attack at the fact that Sango had brought someone with him, the interloper turned to look at me, his hazel eyes full of unhappiness. I gasped as my element flooded my veins, reaching out to touch this mournful soul before me, this man I had never expected to meet again on earth, let alone at the lair of the Cursed Ones. A name escaped my lips, expelled in a wintry breath: "Joel!"

"He came to the Thaden house this morning, seeking you," Sango explained, appearing almost as confused as I felt. "He has some business to discuss with you, he says, urgent enough to lead him here." He raised his eyebrows at me, looking contrite.

"I have little business left to complete. My time here is short."

"So is his, apparently." That caught me off guard. I sneaked another glance at Joel, who loitered near the angels, kicking at a loose stone. He really did appear quite haggard, from the dark circles under his eyes to his disheveled hair and the way he fidgeted, his wind retreating from my attempts to reach him. None of those characteristics fit with my vague memories of this man—the medieval lord who had pressed on doggedly after his children's deaths, after horrific battles, after learning his wife never loved him.

I invited both of them inside for a chat, but Sango declined, citing a prior engagement involving the police, who were seeking me due to allegations of fraud surrounding Süddeutsche Getriebe. "I have no plans to disclose your current location," he assured me when I frowned at the news, "but I would suggest that you don't waste your time getting on your way. The NVH is going after Leon and Lothar now, and the situation is about to burst wide open. Especially with your Keyholder—" he gave a discreet cough "—slinking around with vindictive plans."

I nodded once, recognizing that Max must have passed his intentions along to the Thaden household earlier, probably on the day he captured the two Teuton traitors. "You can make my will public on Friday," I told him quietly. "My course is set. I won't be coming back here anymore."

He ducked his head at me, and we spoke our farewells. Sango promised to always accept my son despite his curse, to advise him in the trials to come. Both Üwe and Stefan had accepted my son's choice and intended to help when needed with his revenge, along with Fonsi. "Siggi, Lise, and I will keep the house running for him," Sango pledged.

Soon afterward, I brought Joel to the parlor in the northeastern turret, the place I deemed a fitting venue for us to talk. When we entered, I switched on the electric lamps while Joel set himself with a heavy sigh upon one of the scarlet sofas, tossing his backpack at the far end. My mouth felt dry as I glanced at him, then at the maroon curtains framing the patterned doors to the balcony. I moved to the opposite couch, the hearth beside me. Joel remained silent, the cuckoo clock ticking off seconds as I counted them in my head.

Five minutes later, his hazel eyes shifted to my face. "So you're planning on dying this weekend?" he asked, his English carrying the familiar South Jersey lilt.

"Not exactly. But my life didn't turn out all wonderful like you apparently assumed," I shot back, his detached tone irritating me. He lounged far too casually upon the sofa where I had sat with Günter, his eyes darting away from me to the maroon curtains that framed the balcony doors.

He snickered rather acerbically, draping his right arm along the back of his sofa with the remark, "Well, that makes two of us."

That comment gave me pause. I sensed the mockery in his inflection, a mordant sarcasm that reflected the misery

I had seen when our eyes first met. So I reined in my own exasperation to say, "I always figured you graduated and took over your father's real estate business, married a woman who loved you, one who appreciated you for who you are."

"Maybe I did all of that," Joel responded, his face darkening, his gaze still upon the curtains, away from me. When he went on, his voice grew so strained that I had to lean closer to hear him. "And maybe it was all taken away from me because of that damn rock."

His lips curled into a sneer, and he shot me a sidelong glance as I froze, ashamed of my earlier assumptions. "Unlike you, I don't have some ghastly castle to run to when I've lost everything."

"This isn't my castle," I said, an instinctive response to defend myself. "It belongs to my son—or rather, the priest who was once my son, depending on how you regard the filial curse." I gave a humorless chuckle, figuring it would be best to divulge the worst of my circumstances to Joel right away, before he condemned me for living a great life while he suffered.

I focused my gaze on the hearth as I went on, studying the cinders that had long remained undisturbed. "I've lost my entire family because I wouldn't give up that 'damn rock,' as you call it. My Pappi and Beth, my closest friends, and my only daughter." My voice broke, but I cleared my throat, ordering myself to keep calm. "I guess I can blame my son's fate on them, since he chose to become a Black Priest in order to defeat them . . . a ruthless group of power-hungry Saxons."

"The NVH," Joel supplied. When I averted my eyes from the fireplace I saw that he looked at me now, sympathy glinting in his hazel eyes. "Yeah, I faced them too. Not until after I'd built a comfortable life for myself and my family, thanks to Hudson Real Estate. I enjoyed making sales, developing new land, seeing the relief on customers' faces when they finalized a lease on a home."

He sighed with a ghost of a smile, his fingers tapping the back of his sofa. "I did get married, too, to a beautiful woman who loved me dearly. Pretty sure we ran into you and Beth when we collected our caps and gowns."

He looked at me for confirmation. I nodded mutely, an old memory running through my mind of a youthful Joel leading a vibrant girl with blond curls. "Her name was Melody, and she was everything I could have hoped for," he went on. "More wonderful than I had ever dreamed." Tears welled in his eyes, and he spun toward the curtains again, struggling to compose himself.

Though it is rather dreadful to admit it, my first thoughts as I listened to Joel's sorrowful reminisces ran along the lines of, *Everything you could have hoped for . . . so she wanted to have sex every night, did she? Five or six kids at that? Did she mind cleaning up afterward, when your wind whirled amid the contents of the bedroom? Did you tell her what it meant to be a Teuton? And what about those scars on your chest?*

But when he met my gaze once more, I clearly saw the effort it took him—the trembling in his jaw, the lingering moisture in his eyes. All of my criticisms went up in smoke. Here before me sat a broken man, one who had gained and lost what pleasures this world can offer. We had too much in common for me to ridicule him now. "The NVH killed her?" I queried in a soft voice, guessing the truth but needing to hear it confirmed.

"They sent me a recording of it," Joel answered, his face screwed up in pain, "along with her hair and a vial of blood. They must have a sick sense of humor, I guess." His voice trailed off, and he ran his hands through his blond hair, which was flecked with gray, cropped short with the bangs disheveled.

"They sent me a recording of my daughter's death, too," I noted, thinking of the letter I had torn to bits while I wept for my lost baby. "But I never did find the actual file. I think Max swiped it. It was bad enough seeing that box with her body parts preserved in formaldehyde and plastic." I broke off, for I saw the disgusted expression on Joel's face and knew I should go no further. He had seen enough pain himself. I need not prattle about mine.

He told me a little more about his recent experiences, the messages he had received out of nowhere regarding the Torstein, the threats directed at his family, the sudden deaths of his parents, his sister Gloria, his own four sons, and finally his beloved wife Melody. This last murder had driven him to the point of despair, for Joel had no clue where I had hidden the Torstein. His inability to halt the NVH's slaughter had erased all color from his world. "I think they're insane, a bunch of blood-glutted madmen. I doubt this deranged killing would stop if they actually *had* the Torstein."

"They'd just take it to the next level, like the Holy Roman Empire did in its lust for power and control," I surmised, shuddering at the prospect of another 1066, another repeated history. "It all boils down to jealousy about Teutonic magic, the blood sorcery and the elemental gifts. Our people are a threat to the grand scheme of things, since humans aren't meant to wield such power. No one but Wuotan's children—"

"But that's what threw me for a loop," Joel interrupted, breaking my train of thought. "I figured all of that happened to me because I actively ignored the commands of the Torstein—the warning that time travelers must learn from their journeys and put that knowledge into practice. I chose to forget that part of my past, to pretend it was all a dream, even to the point where I almost believed that the scars on my chest were the result of a childhood accident. I could never really disregard the wind in my spirit, but I learned to control it strictly, releasing it only when no one would notice.

"But see, I expected to come to München and find you living happily ever after, managing Süddeutsche Getriebe, raising a virtuous Teuton family like the Keyholder and Lady should. I planned to come and see it, to remind myself of my failure. Then I'd jump off a cliff somewhere, maybe off this mountain. But instead . . . ." He bit his lip and lifted his downcast eyes to meet mine, pure bewilderment on his face.

"It's not because of the Torstein," I said, rising from my sofa and crossing the floor to stand by the balcony doors, tracing their intricate patterns with my right hand. "This all happened because of Wuotan. He brewed jealousy in the heart of one of my former friends, incited her to tell our enemies about the stone. Wuotan holds some sort of grudge against me personally, and probably against you, since we're both Christians who tampered with his devices without pledging service."

Joel gave me a long look. I could tell he accepted my rationalization. But when he spoke again, he caught me completely off guard. "Augustin told you that, didn't he?"

I froze beside the doors, my fingers leaving a trail of moisture upon their wood. "He . . . cautioned me about it," I admitted, shocked that Joel had actually brought up the subject of the man with whom I had committed spiritual adultery throughout our fifteen years of marriage. And he appeared so calm in doing it, his posture casual on the sofa, his ankles crossed, his hands idle in his lap, his eyes measuring me.

I shook myself and added, "But I never thought it would end up *this* bad. My Pappi told me about Wuotan's vendetta right after we got back from the past. I never thought he'd use one of my friends to kill so many people, to saddle me with guilt. But my son Max has the Torstein now, and he'll make sure no one misuses it. He's going to bring the murderers to justice, one by one."

"He's the one who owns this castle?" Joel raised his eyebrows at me.

"He inherited it when Hans cursed his blood," I answered, leaning against the doors as I appended, "and he holds the keys of Muniche."

Joel swore, his eyes bulging. "*Please* tell me you two haven't become like Prince Otto and Lady Maria!"

"Heck, no! Max is my biological son. The curse didn't change that; neither do Muniche's bonds. That's the main reason I'm about to leave, actually. That and . . . well . . . we found some information that implies I go to the past one more time." I winced as I said it, thrusting my hands into the pockets of my jeans. I would go to the year 1074, and then I would fight like mad against my foretold destiny.

"So that's what you meant when you asked Sango to make your will public. I thought you were going to commit suicide." Joel wrinkled his brow at me.

Might as well keep on spilling my guts. It's not like he has any right to stop me. "According to Augustin's official history, I *am* going to commit suicide. With the freaking Prince." I told Joel a little about what I read in the tome, but I kept my plans for defiance to myself.

"Ritual suicide is when you cut your wrists and throat and jump into the Rhine River, correct?" Joel queried when I fell silent, looking pensive.

"On the night of the new moon," I said.

"On the night of the new moon," he repeated, leaning forward and placing his hands between his knees. I had no idea where he was going with this, so I just remained against the balcony doors with my hands in my pockets.

"We raised five children in the past, and we know they must have succeeded . . . become prosperous and happy . . . or else you wouldn't be here, right? We were the ones who started the Thaden line."

He glanced at me out of the corner of his eye, and I nodded, adding a few comments on the genealogy book Hans had shown me years ago. Joel's eyes gleamed with fascination.

"You sent them to Eisenwald on the Rhine, where Heinrich and Freia would have reunited . . . after Muniche fell," he clarified, rehearsing the plans we had laid out to protect our medieval family. "It'd be nice to see all of them again, even from afar, to know that one of my families survived, even thrived."

I smiled at a rush of bygone memories—an icy daughter with blond hair, a dark-haired son who resembled the Max I had borne here, a best friend and her husband frolicking in a dance. Joel must have been remembering the same things, for a moment later he asked, "Do you mind having company on your last trip back?"

"Augustin's record didn't mention you," I blurted, not thinking.

"Why would it? I'd just be some random Teuton leaping into the Rhine out of desperation, not because of some mystical romance with a defeated Prince. If we go one month ahead of time, say the day of the new moon in May, I could do my suicide first, then leave you to meet your Keyholder." Joel raised one eyebrow at me, his expression resolute.

Chapter Forty:
The Fallen Criminal

I found that I had no argument against what my ex-husband wished to do. He had lost his family—the most important aspect of his life. His urge to die was a rational choice, not insanity or selfishness as our culture tended to label such finality. I talked through it with him to clarify this and learned that he had not set foot in his real estate office since his first son had been kidnapped back in February of 2019. He had wasted a slew of funds on private investigators and offered rewards, gaining nothing in return.

"My sister had a husband and two kids," he mentioned at one point. "And to be honest, I'm afraid that if I keep hanging around, the NVH may take them out next. Or go after my employees."

We shared the same fears. I told him how I had gathered my remaining close friends into the Thaden house, hiding away from the world in an effort to thwart our enemies' machinations. Even though I had a Cursed One working to bring them to justice, there was no telling whether they might bump off a few extra people before Max got them all.

Eventually the conversation transitioned to my—our—plans to escape into the eleventh century. "I feel like we always do this stuff at the last second without thinking through what we need to bring," Joel said in jest.

"Maybe *you* do," I rejoined with a smirk. "But it's not like you'll have to worry too much about supplies if you're going to die the night we get there. There's a bunch of medieval clothing a couple floors above this one, if you want to look for a tunic and pants for yourself. I've got two dresses soaking in my bedroom."

I showed him the rooms with the clothing, then made my way downstairs to the kitchen, wanting to prepare some sort of meal for the two of us. My son would not return until late tonight or tomorrow morning, and I suspected that Joel might appreciate the chance to deride Herr Ostermann before we left. Hopefully Max had no trouble corralling the NVH mastermind.

We shared a meal of goat cheese, tuna from a few pouches I brought from the Thaden house, and hard pretzels, washing it down with a bottle of Apfelschorle. Joel remarked that he had missed the taste of the sparkling apple juice, something difficult to obtain in New Jersey. He had managed to find a tunic and pants that fit him and bore no trace of mold or mildew, which impressed me. "Did you use your wind to sniff for mold?" I asked him as we ate.

His cheeks reddened bashfully as he answered, "Yep. I'm back among the Teutons now, so there's no point in keeping my element on the down low."

Joel had also come across a pair of leather bags amid the clothing, which he carried down to my bedroom after we ate. He took it upon himself to dry my two dresses with a hot blast of wind, and I hung them in the empty wardrobe, planning to don the red one for our trip. I intended to bring the blue one I packed at home as well, even though its style did not quite fit our destination.

I let Joel use my bathroom to shower before bed. Thereafter he returned to the floor below, intending to sleep on one of the scarlet sofas. Grateful that he harbored no notions of an elemental one-night stand with ice—something I had no desire to arrange—I closed the bedroom door behind him, then curled up on the canopied bed with my e-reader, prepared to finish the series at last. Tomorrow would be a full day. I could hardly wait to view those labradorite gates again, to return to the priest I had chosen to love.

Our arrival date was to be May 27th, 1074—the night before the new moon. That would give Joel time to check on all of our children and shoot the breeze with Heinrich, his good friend. Once Joel offered his body to the Rhine River, I would have twenty-eight days before my own foretold suicide. Ten of which I must spend with Prince Otto, if I obeyed history's prophecy.

But the other eighteen days belonged to Augustin and me. That should be long enough for us to work out a viable alternative . . . or at least long enough for me to beg him to discard Wuotan's chains, to put his faith in God.

On Wednesday morning, my son met Joel and me in the kitchen, where he was in the process of cooking a pair of omelets. Clad in the standard priestly robe with the keys of Muniche hanging from his neck, Max greeted us warmly. He said Sango had told him of Joel's visit, and introduced himself to him as Gust.

"I stopped by the Thaden house after dumping the garbage in the cellar," he reported in a buoyant tone, grinning at me as he flipped the omelets. "Picked up your organ shoes and found out the government has closed Germany's borders. You got here just in time." He nodded at Joel.

"Is this virus *really* all that?" Joel muttered tiredly as he sat across from me at the kitchen table. "And have you got any coffee?"

Once we finished our breakfast and washed the dishes, my son led us to the elevator on a course for the dungeons. He conversed with Joel while the elevator descended, discussing what had happened to his family in New Jersey. Max said he had seen Ostermann's decision to extend his cabal's reach into the U.S. for the sole purpose of tormenting Joel.

"You'll be pleased to see him in his current place," my son declared as we stepped into the cellar. He wrapped a supportive arm around my waist and turned in the direction of the twisted staircases near the freight elevator—away from the cells where Marga and Marinus languished.

Joel trailed behind us without speaking as my son continued. "Ostermann's body is yours to do with as you will. Just leave enough blood in him for tonight."

I shuddered a bit in Max's grasp when he spoke those words. Joel made a sound in his throat and asked tentatively, "What exactly . . . happens tonight?"

"Muniche's *Leitaeri* and *Leitalra* have decreed he be sacrificed to the demon he serves," my son answered in an imperious tone, speaking Teutonica.

I heard Joel's intake of breath, and he murmured, "It's been a *long* time . . . since I've heard anyone speak that language. Wow."

"You remember enough of it to hold a conversation with Heinrich?" I asked in Teutonica. Thus far, Joel had spoken only English since his arrival. My son's English sounded almost exactly like Joel's, since Beth and I had shaped his dialect.

Joel met my gaze as I looked back at him, and a slow smile spread across his face. "I hope so?" he responded in Teutonica, inflecting it as a question.

"Perfect." Max and I spoke the word simultaneously, and we both started laughing. But a few steps later, he guided me beneath an archway into a circular compartment I recognized.

This was where Günter and the Cursed Ones from hell had celebrated All Hallows Eve, with the cauldrons flaring and a drugged woman upon the stone altar at the center, serving as their blood sacrifice to Wuotan. Now the cauldrons burned with natural flames of yellow-orange, smoke rising to the vent at the center of the ceiling. At first my brain could not make sense of what lay upon the altar. But my son eased me a few steps forward, both of his hands upon my shoulders, his voice soothing me—and then I recognized him. Naked and spread eagle upon the stone, his wrists and ankles shackled to its corners, lay Markus Ostermann, the head of the NVH.

I heard myself gasp, and my son guided my unsteady feet to the foot of the altar, where the humiliated thug could not help but see me. His ugly head turned to the right, and his blue-green eyes locked with mine, widening in horror as they traveled to the man standing beside me—Joel, his expression murderous.

"You see, Markus?" my son addressed him in German, his tone laden with ridicule as he drew me close to his chest. "Today marks the downfall of the one who scorned the loyalties of the Cursed Ones. You will die here, sacrificed to Wuotan, the demon you trusted to protect you from a Teuton's wrath. The innocents you murdered look down on you from the walls of this chamber, their voices crying for your blood."

Sensing Muniche's collective soul throbbing around my heart, reacting to her master guardian's words, I drew a shuddering breath and closed my eyes. Did I really want to welcome those slain souls to scream within me afresh, rousing me to wield justice's sword again? Or should I let my Keyholder shoulder it this time, allow the men to unleash their vengeance upon the one who crushed our hearts?

"So speak now," my son commanded, stepping away from me to take hold of Ostermann's forehead, his claws sinking into the flesh beneath the Saxon's auburn hair. "Confess your crimes to them, as you would to a priest. Let them see the depravity of your heart, and rejoice in your punishment!"

Max's hands tightened on his prisoner's head, his fingernails sharpened into points that extended several centimeters beyond his fingertips—a sign of a Black Priest's death. Ostermann moaned, his eyes darting from my face to Joel's, perhaps seeking sympathy. But I felt nothing when I stared back at him, nothing but a strange apathy and a growing dread.

Joel slipped his hand through mine as Ostermann began his confession—grudgingly, it seemed, but I knew

Max would not allow him a reprieve. He mocked his prisoner intermittently as the Saxon choked out his apologies, promising him greater pain if he skipped over anything, sinking his claws into his skull until his blood stained the altar red.

Max already knew everything Ostermann had done, down to the last detail . . . the name of every accomplice . . . their roles, their level of guilt . . . and he knew it because he had bled the man already. He glared down at his prey with pitch black eyes, his sharp teeth bared in anticipation —a stance I recognized. I had seen Augustin's thirst for blood and death long ago, that night in the forest when his demon lord had possessed him.

Suddenly I felt Joel's arms holding me up, steadying me against a wash of dizziness. While I heard the sentences Ostermann spoke, my eyes blinked fitfully against an appalling memory of a Black Priest bending over my body broken on the ground, his eyes bright with vindictive fire as his lips formed the words, *Would you like to know . . . what I plan . . . to do to you?*

To this day I do not know how I managed to stand there and listen to that naked man's words, his voice breaking more often than not. He admitting to having found a way to call on Wuotan himself though he had no Teuton blood, how the demon lured him into a pact to collect the Torstein, to erase the Teuton people from the pages of history. Wuotan had offered him a throne in hell for his efforts, along with an infinite supply of wealth on earth.

The demon gave Ostermann the charisma to persuade the other members of the NVH to focus their research on time travel rather than Germanic history, to convince them that the Torstein was their gateway to fortune. Marga and Marinus gladly joined his enclave, granting the NVH what they needed most—Teutonic magic, methods to commit their crimes without leaving evidence behind.

Ostermann made his way through each death one by one, crocodile tears draining from his eyes just as the blood dripped from where Max's claws sank into his skull. When he mentioned that he paid a special team in the U.S.

to kill Joel's loved ones in despicable ways, I felt his arms grow taut around me. Joel's chest began to heave, and I saw the flames flicker at the breeze that sprang up in the chamber. At this rate, he might insist that we wait until tomorrow to open time's gateway, just for the privilege of witnessing the sacrifice.

When Ostermann began speaking of Freya's and Melody's fates, I fixed my gaze on the cauldrons, ordering myself not to think about what I must hear. Max growled at his prisoner, demanding that he admit every part of his sins with the last two victims.

Tears poured down my cheeks as the fiend spoke so indifferently about my daughter, how Marga used her motherly charms to soothe her after each beating and rape—there had been many. He and his cronies had taken her clothes away from the start, leaving her naked in her confinement, shooting videos of her humiliation. My son cut him off before he could describe the process of her dismemberment, snapping that it was time to move on. I sensed the black knives of his anger stabbing at the atmosphere.

I hardly heard any of what Ostermann said about Joel's wife. Now I saw carnage in the fiery cauldrons—images from the fall of Muniche, memories of the dying city's agony settling eternally onto my heart, tearing my very body to pieces, inflamed by the hatred of Saxons and the demon who drove them to punish us. It was too much. Did this murderer not realize what he had done, throwing in his lot with a devil who knew the past by heart, who knew full well that retribution would come, swift and sure?

I abruptly noticed that Ostermann had fallen silent. I forced myself to look at his face again as Max bent over him dangerously. "And are you sorry, Markus, for putting your fellow human beings through such torture?" he snarled in a voice much older than his fifteen years.

The fiend lost what composure he must have had, for he began to wail, sobs shaking his naked frame. Pitiful phrases spilled from his lips, pleas for mercy, for a second chance, insistence that he had been compelled to do it all, that it had not been of his own free will. I saw my son's face darken at Ostermann's words, and for a second his black eyes met mine.

"Did Wuotan possess him . . . during any part of this?" I whispered, hardly able to summon my voice from deep inside. There seemed to be no blank spots in the man's confessions, but I wanted to be sure.

Max scowled and sank his claws deeper into Ostermann's head. He cried out in pain as my son said, "Only once, when the fool first summoned him. His heart was black enough already, caught up in racist drivel about blond-haired people. He clung to Wuotan's lies like they were divine proclamations."

I grimaced at the blubbering fiend and gave a single nod. "Then he deserves to grovel before his demon lord in hell."

Max smacked the Saxon powerfully across the face, jerking his head to the side, leaving bloody streaks upon his cheek. "I fear we have no patience for your lies. Tonight you'll meet your master, and this day you'll learn the full meaning of pain and humiliation. Your wasted life is over. Only God can grant you mercy." He pulled a dagger from beneath his robe and turned to the adjacent cauldron to heat the blade.

Joel loosened his grip on me and addressed the Black Priest in a singular tone. "Pretty sure I'd like a blade or two, Gust."

Max's eyes focused on Joel, and he chuckled, an insidious sound. "You have every right to help me, Mr. Hudson. Would you accompany me to the armory?"

Joel nodded, stepping away from me and trotting to my son's side, his eyes livid with fury and expectation. Meanwhile, I stood rooted to the floor, my gaze drifting from the two vengeful Teutons to the doomed Saxon chained to the altar. I thought about what my son had said, about God granting mercy. Was Ostermann worthy of redemption?

Max placed an arm around my shoulders. "Would you like to come with us, Mutti?" he inquired in a low voice. I shook my head, preferring to remain with the shackled prisoner, to exchange a few words with him privately. My son promised to return soon, and he and Joel slipped out.

In their absence, I gathered my courage and stepped closer to Ostermann's prone form, studying his torn skull as he whimpered. Looking from the gashes staining his hair to the scratch marks where my son had slapped his cheek, I pursed my lips. Long ago I had felt similar pains at the hands of a Cursed One possessed by his master. They would ache and throb, remaining open unless a Teuton felt generous enough to seal them through magic.

I felt no such generosity.

I bent down on one knee, thankful that the altar had grooves cut along its base to catch the blood that trickled from Ostermann's skull. At least I need not tarnish my jeans with his fluids, for I wanted no part of him clinging to my clothing. But I called my ice forth, freezing my fingers and laying them upon his swollen cheek, one tiny offering of relief to my condemned enemy. His skin felt fevered, and he expelled a strained gasp at the touch of my frozen fingers.

"The situation is in my son's hands now," I murmured to him in Sächsisch, the skin of his face twitching beneath my fingers. "He won't stop his vengeance until everyone who had any part in these slayings has paid their dues. Thankfully, Max has the decency to avoid attacking their families. But all of your comrades will fill these dungeons in the coming months."

Ostermann did not reply, but he ceased his moaning, his blue-green eyes betraying pain and confusion now, no hatred. "I warned you about the Cursed Ones," I reminded him. "Max knows about the one I mentioned in the beer garden last October. My husband from the past. He wants to be like him."

The Saxon still said nothing, though I saw dull horror appear in his eyes at the prospect of an avenging Black Priest ripping through his comrades like a knife through butter. I rose to my feet and lifted my hand from his face, frowning at the blood that spotted my icy fingers. Since the chamber contained no towel or water faucet, I stepped forward to wipe the blood onto Ostermann's chest hair. He had a lot of it. His cock was diminutive, the length of a travel-sized body wash.

When I looked back at his face, his eyes finally glittered with repulsion, as if his chest hair was important to him. He still pressed his lips tightly closed, so I shrugged and turned to go. But my conscience pricked me as my son's statement resurfaced in my mind: *Only God can grant you mercy.*

"Max spoke the truth earlier, when he said that you could ask God for mercy, even now," I heard myself telling the Saxon as I paused beneath the archway. "He has forgiven worse sinners than you. Since you're about to enter eternity, you ought to consider repenting."

Ostermann huffed, appearing quite annoyed. "God's not the one who offered me a throne, you bitch," he spat in Sächsisch dialect.

I blinked at him, marveling that the man actually believed a demon's lies. *Just like Eve in the Garden,* I thought. *She believed eating the fruit would make her a goddess.*

"So easily misled," I murmured, more to myself than to the fiend on the altar. "I hope you find hell more pleasant than this dungeon."

On my way to the elevator, I encountered Max and Joel, the latter armed with a bow and arrows, the former sporting just the dagger. Both of them wore expressions that reminded me of Augustin's when he played the role of Muniche's executioner.

"Not staying to witness his punishment?" Max tilted his head at me, then gestured at Joel. "He's going to shoot an arrow into each of his feet and hands, and I'm going to—"

"You don't need to give me the gory details," I cut him off. "I'm going to go pack the leather bags Joel found so we can get out of here. You two can catch up with me when you're finished."

I looked pointedly toward the archway from whence I had come, and the two men nodded, seeming to accept my unwillingness to watch their triumph. Joel admitted that he might be interested in some lunch afterward and said there was a compass in his backpack. "Might not be a bad idea to bring that along, in case you decide to evade your fated master," he said.

I waved them away and headed for the elevator, Joel's suggestion stoking the flames deep inside my heart. But as I rode back toward the main floor, my thoughts shifted to my son's urge for vengeance.

I recognized that I ought to write one final letter to Max before we departed. There were a few rules I needed to ensure he would follow while he meted out his justice. Each criminal, no matter how depraved, must be offered the chance to repent—and after, they must pay for the blood they spilled.

Chapter Forty-one:
One Last Journey

Back in the northwestern turret, I turned my attention to the pair of leather bags Joel had scrounged from the upper floor, undoing their flaps and shaking them out. I stuffed the camp blanket and neck pillow into the larger bag that I would carry, tucking my Latin-German Bible beneath the modern blue dress and the medieval light green dress. I added extra underwear and socks, along with the fork from home and a sharp knife from the Black Castle's kitchen. That pretty much stuffed the first bag to the brim—these were not as large as the packs we had taken on our initial trip to the eleventh century.

I packed all of the food into Joel's bag before carrying it up to the parlor with the sofas. His backpack sat open on the one across from the fireplace, but I decided I did not wish to paw through his private things. I laid the leather bag beside Joel's backpack for him to load it as he wished. Then I returned to my bedroom and settled myself onto the cushioned window seat with a pen and pad of paper in hand.

When Max entered my chamber, I was just folding my letter and placing it atop the bureau. He chuckled as he

405

shut the door behind him, still appearing quite formidable in the hooded robe of the Teuton priest, though his eyes were a serene silver. "A mother's final admonitions to her poor lost son, begging him not to sacrifice his humanity on the altar of revenge." He gestured at the letter with a smirk, then met me in the center of the rug, imprisoning my hands in his and lifting them to his lips.

I smiled, shutting my eyes to focus on his darkness seeping into my spirit. "That, and some motherly advice on my successor." I winked at him coquettishly and glided to the bed, Max just a step behind.

His face grew petulant at the subject of Muniche's new Lady. "Mutti, it really worries me, the idea of being bound to some girl I barely know. Muniche will probably choose one of the girls you taught, but . . . I don't know. By the time I actually started *thinking* about girls that way, you'd stopped your classes."

A sigh passed through my lips as I sat down on the bed, beckoning him to join me. "Did you enjoy talking with any of them, trying out your elemental magic when we gathered by the gazebo?" I asked.

Max sat beside me, his strong shoulders slumping a bit. He rubbed his hands through his hair and stared straight ahead, at the now-empty wardrobe. "I don't know. A lot of the other guys got interested in girls before I did, even the ones in my class at school. Sophia's okay, but she probably won't get chosen since she's up in Finland right now."

"That reminds me, please make sure you check in with Erika's family once they come back home," I urged my son, studying his profile. "They should be back sometime in April or May, but if not, Rudi knew their address. You might be able to dig it up somehow and let them know when it's safe."

"I'll take care of it," Max said, running his fingers along the indigo blanket beneath us. "There was one girl who used to flirt with me during your classes," he went on, an unhappy expression creasing his face. "I think her name was Jasmin. Something like that. But pretty sure she was just interested in me because she knew our family was wealthy."

"Hmm. My Pappi dealt with that a lot," I noted, disappointed that my son had already experienced the pointlessness of shallow interest. "I did a few times, too, although it was usually just outsiders. I think Muniche chose me at birth and kept the unworthy Teuton men at bay."

"Unworthy," Max repeated with a mordant snicker, his eyes meeting mine for a second before darting away. "I guess that's why only the Keyholder interested you, even before the city chose you. And why you couldn't force yourself to feel anything for the other priests in München." I made a sound of agreement, and then my son brought up the question that had haunted me for too many years.

"But why Augustin? Why him when he refused the keys?" Max shifted on the bed to face me at last, his right hand reaching to grasp the mortal symbol of his responsibility.

I sighed, his fingers seeming to reach for my heart but falling short, since our bond remained incomplete. "Maybe I'll figure that out when I go back."

"I wish you could come back here just for a second. Just long enough to tell me you made peace with my greatest predecessor."

Raising my eyebrows at Max, I said, "Maybe I *will* tell you. Maybe there's a hidden alcove somewhere in this castle that holds the true story of Swanhilde von Thaden and Augustin von Bayern. A fantasy romance with a happy ending. I'm not going to commit suicide with the Prince unless I have no other choice."

Max groaned quietly and gathered me into an embrace, his nervousness about my fate bolstering my resolve. I refused to accept that I was destined for the worst fated mate in the history of the Teuton people—the one who cursed his city with his own blood. The fallen Prince could not earn my devotion, not while Augustin stood in the wings, slaying my enemies with his death.

When my son released me, I rose from the bed and returned to the cushioned seat at the window. Glancing toward where my purse sat upon the bureau, I said, "While technically, everything I brought with me to this castle belongs to you, I'm especially entrusting you with the gold locket your Pappi gave me on my nineteenth birthday. I've kept a magnificent picture of him in there since the days of old. I expect you to preserve it well, as a physical memory of your predecessor." I nodded toward the five brass keys resting upon my son's chest.

One side of Max's mouth twitched. "I'll never forget Hans Meissner. I carry two physical memories of him with me always." His silver eyes drifted from the keys of Muniche to the tip of the black scar on his right forearm, peeking out from under his sleeve.

"I think that locket will serve as a more pleasant reminder of your Pappi," I told him, not pleased that he had referred to his father by his name. "You shouldn't hold the curse against him. Remember, you chose it."

"I know," Max sighed, his clawed fingers tracing the scar as he gave me a wavering smile. "And I've been thinking about paying a visit to the family vault so I can bring Freya's urn here. I'd rather it be with me instead of sealed in darkness, forgotten."

"I like that plan," I said. "A physical memory of your Pappi and your sister."

"And what do I have from you?" he queried in a pained tone. When I met his gaze, I saw black tears trembling on his eyelashes. Before I could move to console him, he climbed to his feet and approached me at the windowsill, casting me in his thick shadow. "I've thought of something, actually," he whispered, his hands plucking uncertainly at the black fabric of his robe. "You might think it's barbaric. But for one in my position, it's the ideal memento."

I smiled at him demurely. "My blood?"

He smirked and lifted his eyes from the floor. "You're quick."

"I know how dead men are," I responded. Max laughed, pulling a syringe from beneath his cloak. I eyed it, knowing he had found it amongst Günter's old medical equipment. Then I rolled up my right sleeve and said, "You can take as much as you want. All of it if that suits you."

Max gave me a fond smile, stooping down to finger the vein at the crease of my elbow. "Ah, my dear *Leitalra*, I require only two vials."

I winced as the needle pricked my skin. But my son's hands were steady, so I watched the first vial collect my blood, watched his fingers deftly replace it when it filled. Afterward, he closed the wound expertly, breaking the needle in his hands and placing the two vials with my blood in one of his pockets.

"Now I'll always have a physical memory of my beautiful mother, Muniche's greatest Lady," he declared, looking satisfied.

I glanced upward at the ceiling as I folded my sleeve back down. "Do you know if Joel's finished with Ostermann? I seem to recall him saying something about lunch."

Max lifted his eyes to the ceiling and responded, "He's up there now, and it sounds like he's packing. I can go prepare some food for you, if you'd like to change. I thawed some chicken from Günter's freezer yesterday, and I know how to make a stew."

"You're going to have to learn to make a lot more than that if you want to impress your new Lady," I called after him as he exited the room. He muttered a word or two before closing the door behind him, and I grinned. I trusted that my successor would be a young woman with an open heart and an open mind, one who could complement my son effectively as Muniche's Lady.

After using the toilet for possibly the last time ever, I clad myself in the red linen dress, slipping my feet into my pair of leather shoes. I looked at myself in the mirror over the sink as I adjusted the dress, then tugged a brush through my hair, realizing belatedly that I had no head covering. I considered for a minute or two, then chose to simply braid my hair, securing it at the bottom with a black hair tie. I blinked at my face for a moment, knowing there was no point in makeup—I had not put on any today, and my visage appeared tired and coarse, that of a woman who had seen too much grief in recent years.

I brushed my teeth one last time, then stuffed my hairbrush into the top of my bag. Just before I set out for the kitchen, my mind traveled to Augustin's last letter to me, lying in my purse's hidden pocket. So I fished it out of my purse, along with the three parchments torn from his *1074* tome; my son could put those back where they belonged.

I laid the parchments onto the bureau beside the letter I had written to Max, then took up the sheet of computer paper and read Augustin's final lines again. Pangs of sorrow struck my heart, mingling with the ever-present admonition of Muniche's soul. *I shall devote all of my resources and intellect to solve the conundrum of that cord that shackles you apart from me. And if . . . I discern a solution . . . I shall come back for you. You will always be everything to me.*

The paper crumpled in my hands. I shook my head slowly, knowing that I needed to dispose of that letter before Max found it. So I trudged to the bathroom, falling to my knees before the toilet, my hands ripping the paper to shreds while my heart wailed inside of me. "Did you find that way, Augustin?" I whispered to the mirror after I had flushed the toilet twice. "And if you did, why didn't you come? Now I have to come to you, with a far heavier cord to break."

When I entered the kitchen some time later, Max had just begun to dish out the chicken stew. He and Joel were chatting like old buddies about Ostermann's fate, and I saw that Joel had brought his smaller bag with him to the kitchen, lying on the floor beside his chair. He wore a deep blue scoop-neck tunic and dark brown trousers; that coupled with the slight growth of fuzz on his face sent me a thousand years into the past. I blinked and imagined him sitting at the long table in the great hall, gnawing on a chicken leg while wearing similar attire, our children climbing onto his lap, begging for a game using his wind, their ebullience making him laugh heartily, content.

"Welcome to the Rhineland, weary time travelers." Joel spoke the phrase in Teutonica, half of his mouth curled into a smile as he took in my outfit. I curtsied with a grin, playing along, and joined the men at the table, summarily commencing a conversation in Teutonica regarding our upcoming journey. The mood around the table seemed surprisingly upbeat, considering the fact that Joel was about to step into the abyss of death, with a brief detour to the past.

"By the way, Gust, your Mutti's trying to kill me prematurely," Joel remarked at one point, a smirk belying his words as his hazel eyes slid to mine.

"What?" I had no clue what he was talking about.

He pushed at his bag with one shoe—a white sneaker, hardly appropriate—and said, "You packed mixed nuts with a bunch of almonds."

I rolled my eyes at Joel's attempt at humor and swallowed a bite of stew. "I had no clue you were going to show up out of nowhere when I packed food for this trip. You can have the raisins and jerky."

"How in the world did you survive in the Middle Ages with a nut allergy?" Max inquired from where he washed the pot at the sink.

"Very carefully," Joel answered through a mouthful of stew, and I rolled my eyes again. He told me an instant later that my son had given him a few bits of gold from one of the cellars in case we needed to trade for something. That prompted me to roll my eyes at myself, for I had completely overlooked valuables this time. "Got some twine, my compass, a nice blade from the armory, and an extra pair of socks and underwear," he added.

"And he's bringing along that bow he used on Ostermann," Max said. "Have to admit, the man's a good shot."

Joel thanked him, and they spent a few minutes yapping about archery and the differences between a longbow and a crossbow. I tuned them out as I savored the stew, my feelings still tenuous at the notion of returning to that riverside village with the intent of finding Augustin . . . and his awful ex-brother. What exactly were the Prince and I supposed to *do* in the forest for ten days? Bemoan our condition or have a whole bunch of sex?

Sex with Prince Otto was a strange concept. I thought back to how I recalled him looking the last time I saw him up close—in the winter of 1060 when he came to interrogate me about his brother Paulus' fate. Decked in royal splendor with all sorts of jewelry, his short hair and thick beard as black as the winter night, his blue eyes judging every emotion that ran across my face. Was the man any good at sex, or was he like Joel—the type who pleased only himself? Had he knocked up any maidens during his eight years of wandering . . . and if so, did he have any diseases?

That thought sent a twinge to my stomach. Despite Augustin's promiscuity, he had been clean when we sealed our bond forever the night before his curse. At one point during our years of shared dreams, I had asked him about it; and he said he used to get the occasional lesions—likely herpes—but nothing worse. Thankfully he had not suffered an outbreak during our erotic night. A dead man could contract no infections, of course.

But the Prince? I shuddered at the idea of taking a tainted cock into my body. Maybe ritual suicide was inevitable for both of us.

I kept my muses to myself and followed my son and Joel to the chapel after we finished our lunch. The two of them seemed to get along far too well. It made me wonder exactly what Joel had told Max about our time together in the eleventh century. My son knew that my loyalty lay with Augustin, yet he had accepted Joel's part in this without judgment. Maybe Üwe and Sango had let him in on a few things when he went to collect my organ shoes.

Joel murmured a few accolades when we entered the chapel, marveling at the colorful hues adorning the columns and floor. He had his bow and arrows slung over his left shoulder while his right arm cradled his bag. "Whoever built this room must have believed in God," he commented.

"Augustin built this room." The statement spilled from my lips before I could think better of it. My son and Joel paused at the stairway to the organ loft to look at me, and Max's eyes glinted with approval. He believed I could restore Augustin's faith during this trip, and I hoped like mad he was right.

When we reached the loft, I set my bag beside the console and bent down to untie my leather shoes. My son produced my organ shoes from beneath his robe, handing them to me with a solemn expression. "I hope those gates stay open long enough for me to swap my shoes out, once I've finished that final scale," I joked as I tied the laces. I knew that they would indeed, for they had stood by stoically on the day I dragged Freia into the future . . . the day I bade my newlywed husband farewell.

Max said nothing to my joke, and Joel gave a vague snicker. The situation was far too serious for laughter now. I squared my shoulders and climbed onto the organ bench, flipping the switch and hitting the proper stops from memory. I paused with my fingers hovering above the keyboards, swinging my head around to face Joel. "May 27th, 1074, the hill above Eisenwald on the Rhine," I reminded him pointedly. "*Don't* send us twenty years back, or I might just kill you myself."

"May 27th, 1074, the hill above Eisenwald on the Rhine, adjacent to the trade route to the east," Joel confirmed with a nod. "In the morning."

"Got it." I turned back to the keyboards and began the Song of Time without further ado, hearing the harmonies reverberating around the chapel, singing to the peaks outside, resounding in our souls. I focused my thoughts on that specific day—in the morning like Joel suggested—that grassy hill above the Rhenisch town. I had stood there twice in the mortal world and countless times as a spirit, in dreams with a Black Priest, a specter of the forest. I could see it in my memory as plain as I saw the keyboards before me, the pedals moving beneath my feet.

We're coming, coming to the Rhineland . . . coming to see our children . . . to meet our closest friends . . . to die in the waters of Germany's greatest river. To die with the fallen Prince . . . the man who made all of this possible . . .

and to beg his cursed brother to uncover some solution . . . some way to defy this destiny of mine . . . these cruel bonds that seal my heart away from him . . . .

When I reached those final lines, I felt as though my feet were flying across the pedalboard, my fingers racing along two keyboards, tones of perfection pealing throughout the fortress. As that final note bounced off the chapel's stone walls, I heard that wretched crack splitting the air apart to the right of the organ. I chortled at the sight of those labradorite gates, creaking open ever so tediously to reveal the multihued obscurity beyond. *Here we go.*

I heard Max mutter something unintelligible, and I felt Joel's hand upon my back, silently urging me to come. I lifted my hands and feet from the console and leaped to the floor, bending down to rip the laces off of my shoes, my fingers stumbling. Steadier hands brushed mine aside, undoing the laces and removing the organ shoes, then sliding each of my feet into my brown leather shoes, tying their laces securely. And I raised my head to look into Max's eyes, smoldering pits of darkness boring into my soul. A thousand thoughts swirled through my mind, and my mouth went dry. "Max, I—"

He pulled me to his chest and covered my mouth with his, silencing me for the moment. My body quaked as his emotions swept into my spirit—pain, desire, resignation, devotion. Muniche's bonds sang within me at the caress of her master guardian. By the time my son released me, droplets of ice fell upon the floor of the balcony, rolling down my cheeks.

He held me at arm's length, his anguish nearly breaking my resolve to go. But I brushed my tears away and met his gaze as I whispered, "Please . . . be good to her . . . and read everything . . . all of the records here . . . even the ones no one else has found. Promise me, Max." I have no idea what made me ask such a thing, but suddenly it seemed just as essential as his gentle treatment of my successor.

"I will," he whispered back, his voice ragged, and he hugged me tightly one last time. "Now go. Go and find a way. Find a way to be with the man who loves you." The darkness in his eyes seemed as vast as the universe itself, renewing my resolve, granting me a portion of immortal tenacity.

I nodded at my son and lifted my bag from the floor, securing its strap over my left shoulder. Then I turned for the gateway, where Joel already waited. He held out his left hand, an invitation, his lips forming a wry smile, recognizing the irony of doing *this* again. Doing it not for adventure, but for death. And one final search for truth.

I locked the fingers of my right hand with those of his left, then used my own left hand to clamp my bag against my side. Right before we plunged into the void, Joel called over his shoulder, "Gust? Make all of them pay for driving us to this."

End of Book V

~*~

Turn the page and join Swanie for a wild ride through the currents of time—will it be her last?

His Name Was Augustin
Book VI excerpt
© C.L. Carhart

Chapter One:
Unexpected Discord

When Joel and I leapt into time's tornadic currents, I prepared myself for the usual experience. Loss of control, my body and spirit shoved violently into a tide that rushed contrary to the direction I traveled. Ghostly whispers spoken by Wuotan's sirens, his inhuman worshippers who mocked time travelers in a dialect understood only by the ancients. Eldritch moans slinking upward from the depths, from an unreachable abyss, horrors to frighten humans who dared to wield magic dissimilar to nature's progression.

In other words, I expected uncanniness that meant nothing in the grand scheme of things. Frights that I could brush off once we reached the gateway at the far end—May 27th, 1074.

But the ordinary escaped me this time.

As soon as I passed through those labradorite gates, my right hand linked with Joel's left, I felt my body upended. My wide eyes caught sight of the gates as they closed behind us and dissolved, leaving nothing but a tangled web of burning colors and obscurity in their wake. The standard sensation of advancement against a tide grabbed hold of me, but there was something else there, too. Something

416

more than the mere threads of history trying to block my path.

I heard a *scream.*

That should not have been possible. I recognized the voice as Joel's, and an instant later infernal blades sliced through my torso in a quest for my heart. Terror seized me, and I tried to move my arms to shield myself, to thrust my bag at the spectral entity that attacked me. In vain. The blades pressed deeper, and my eyes wheeled, my neck muscles refusing to shift my head's position. All I could see was the storm ripping at my braid, my clothing, my body.

"Swanie!"

Joel's tortured voice crying out my name snapped me from my confusion. I tried to answer him, but the sound my lips made was that of a dying animal. I *felt* my heart beating against the blades that held it—claws, I abruptly realized—my will infusing me with defiance. *The demon's trying to stop us both. He can't. I refuse to give him that power. We have to reach the past one last time!*

I sought the magic I claimed inside—my Teuton blood, my elemental ice, my eternal spirit. As my mortal lips screamed out in anguish, my soul recognized that it was time I take hold of the beliefs I had thrust at Augustin—a Black Priest bound in a demon's service. If Wuotan wanted to stop Joel and me from reaching the year 1074, only the divine Creator could defeat his plans.

"God!" I cried out, hardly able to force my lips to speak words in the midst of torment. "We belong to You! Bring us to . . . Your . . . ."

Foolish mortal! Wuotan's sinister thoughts washed over me from the inside out, his claws dragging me toward an infinite void. *Your Deity has no power here! He relinquished his hold on these currents millennia ago.*

Even in my agony, I knew the demon lied, trying to corrupt my faith as his liege lord had corrupted Eve. And now I heard the sirens whispering in my ears, calling me false, traitorous, a disappointment, a Teutonic Lady who allowed her children to die without remorse, who could not stand against a human antagonist, let alone a fallen angel. But I gritted my teeth and clung to my faith. In the sixty-two years I had walked in various timelines, God had not failed me yet.

"You're the one . . . with no power." I managed to shove the words between my teeth, the sting of the blades tapering off into the tossing of a storm, churning of the countless threads of time. A withering groan pricked my ears, and afterward Wuotan laughed, his scorn finding no purchase.

We shall see about that, Leitalra . . . .

The light of day sliced through the darkness, and I landed hard upon grass, Wuotan's frightening epithet ringing in my ears. I felt Joel's grip on my right hand, his fingers slick with sweat as he gave a choking gasp. Breaking my hold on him, I whirled to face the labradorite gates, poised behind us atop the hill where we stood. The violent currents within seemed to reach forward to grasp for me, and I raised my left arm in a silent command.

Be gone! Leave us to greet the past in peace.

A few threads of laughter trickled outward as the portal vanished. I breathed a huge sigh of relief, clutching my right hand to my throat. My leather bag bumped my hip as I shifted my feet and glanced down at the red fabric of my bodice. Had those invisible blades *actually* injured my body?

Before I found the wherewithal to slip a hand beneath my neckline to check, Joel yanked me into his arms, crushing me against his chest. His actions prompted my ice to freeze my blood, my eyes widening in shock as his fingers clutched me in a desperate hold. "Swanie? What . . . the hell . . . was that?"

Joel wheezed, and my own heartrate sped in the aftermath of what we had experienced. Despite the horrors I sensed breathing down my neck, I had no wish to seek comfort in my ex-husband's embrace. "Can you . . . let me go?"

He stepped away from me, his expression stricken. His graying blond hair appeared somewhat disheveled, and he placed a hand over his dark blue tunic. His hazel eyes shifted from my face to his hand, and he said, "I guess . . . we didn't really get stabbed in there? It sure *felt* like that's what happened!"

"I don't know what happened," I answered honestly, taking a few seconds to look around at the landscape. I recognized the Rhine's waters glinting gold in the sunlight opposite the village below us, farmland extending to the north while dense forests stretched to the south and west. This was indeed the hill beside the eastern trade route, with the medieval village of Eisenwald tucked away under the early morning mist. "It looks like we're in the right place," I remarked.

"Thank God," Joel murmured, sounding distressed. "I was praying the entire time we were caught in those currents. It felt like Wuotan tried to tear me apart."

"Same," I said, invoking my ice magic into my eyes to improve my vision. I saw no signs of stirring amid the houses below, so hopefully no villagers happened to notice the massive gates before they disappeared. "Did he say anything to you?" I shifted my attention to Joel, who stood with his hands on his hips, his chest still heaving.

"Wuotan *said* something to you?" His eyes widened.

"Mocked my faith, basically." Apparently the demon had not felt the need to do the same to Joel. I looked away, memories of my father's warning gnawing at my spirit: *Wuotan didn't say whether he wanted you dead . . . or something worse.*

"Pretty sure demons always do that," Joel said. He had set his things into the grass, bending down on one knee to sift through his quiver of arrows. "I read a story about some old preacher from the 1900s who called up a demon, and it told him he wasn't exuberant enough to keep the crowds entranced. After that he went all fire and brimstone."

A snort escaped my nostrils. "A preacher who called up a demon. Hypocrisy much?" I laid my own bag onto the ground to give my left shoulder a rest, moving to situate myself upon it. "Did all your arrows come through?"

"Looks like it. There are twelve in here." Joel took in my position and knelt into a more comfortable posture. "It really felt like something was trying to hold us back from coming here. That wasn't anything like our other trip, when it was just the whispers and the laughter."

"Makes me wonder if there's more to my destiny than meets the eye." I propped my chin up with one hand and gazed out at the river.

"You don't want to commit suicide with the Prince like Augustin's record said," Joel discerned.

"No. I don't. And I have only twenty-eight days to figure out why he'd write something so insane. Muniche's bonds or not, I *don't* feel some hopeless attraction to the man who cursed my city with his blood. Keyholder or not."

As soon as I put my feelings into words, though, I sensed Muniche's soul awakening inside of me, her countless departed children wrapping their essence around my heart in an unbreakable grip. *Muniche is lost, crumbled, cursed, forgotten,* her soul moaned within me. *Our master has forsaken us . . . the future holds no hope, no light . . . only heartbreak.*

Tears formed in the corners of my eyes, and I shook my head, working to maintain the willpower my individuality held dear. *Prince Otto doesn't matter. Muniche doesn't matter. The city will be reborn in the next century. I'm here for Augustin, the Teuton priest who loves me for who I am.*

"Swanie, I need to apologize." Joel cleared his throat, and I extracted myself from Muniche's reverie. His eyebrows curved upward as he said, "I shouldn't have grabbed you like that when we burst through the gates. I know you don't feel that way about me. I don't know what came over me."

"You were just in shock. It's okay," I told him.

"No. It's not. I felt you freeze, sensed your element coming to the fore. I'm sorry."

I sighed, my shoulders drooping a little. "I'm the one who should apologize to you," I confessed, guilt agitating my spirit. "I should have been honest when you tried to court me the first time we came here. I knew you weren't my type from the start, but I was too afraid to tell you."

"At least we both got to relish true love in the modern day," Joel mused, his fingers running the length of his bowstring.

I managed a half smile in response, for I had not told Joel about the bomb Hans dropped on his deathbed. My true love was here, south of Eisenwald, hidden in a woodland cabin apart from civilization—apart from the living.

"What made you fall for Augustin?"

Joel's question surprised me. "Is this the moment where we're supposed to spill our guts or something?" I raised an eyebrow at him, sensing the dew saturating the air around us. If we sat too long on this hill, we might need more than the spring's sun to dry our clothing.

"I'm just curious." Joel smiled and scratched at the slight growth along his jawline.

My gaze drifted toward the forests to our left as I replied, "It was mainly the fact that he treated me like a peer instead of like a brainless, emotional woman. You know we spent hours studying English and Ælte Teutonica before the Prince cursed him." I glanced at Joel, and he nodded. "He was smart, experienced, and unashamed of who he was. He had a reason for everything he did, even the terrible sins. And he was honest. He taught me things about Teutonic magic that no other priest would dare to unveil."

"Gust told me you had the heart-bond with him."

That threw me for another loop. I should not have left Joel alone with my twenty-first century son, apparently. There seemed to be no point in denying it, so I said, "Augustin held my heart for twenty-three years. And he didn't need a city's influence to inspire his devotion. We loved and respected each other."

"I think I might agree with what your son said before we leaped through the gates," Joel admitted, his forehead wrinkled. "'Find a way to be with the man who loves you.' Screw the Prince. If I were you, I'd run off with the Cursed One."

I chuckled at how he phrased it. "That's my plan as soon as you've made the Rhine your grave. We probably ought to decide how we're going to handle this . . . seeing our children again. Cammie and Max might recognize us."

Joel looked thoughtful. "Are you sure about that? Your hair was short back then." He nodded at my braid. "And you're in better shape now, for that matter."

I scowled at him. "Thanks a lot." It had taken a vast amount of effort to rein in my urge to soothe my unhappiness through overeating after the NVH had targeted my family. I had gained only five kilograms as a result of stress.

"I'm not sure if they'd recognize me, either," Joel went on. "I had a full beard in the eleventh century, and my hair was longer then, too. I probably should have dyed it before we left your son's castle."

"Too late now. I'm not going back through those gates for a do-over. Besides, I didn't bring the Torstein."

"Yeah, I know. We need to come up with a story either way, for why we're here, who we are." Joel rubbed his forehead.

"Teuton adventures seeking asylum from the Saxons," I supplied.

"What should our names be?"

That gave me pause. "Well, Heinrich and Freia will know who we are. But I guess if we want to keep our travels secret from our children, we'll have to ask them to call us something other than Swanie and Joel." I tried to think through the names of our noble peers from years past.

"I could be Otto. Or Paulus." Joel shot me a goofy look as he rose to his feet and stretched, shaking dew from his sleeves.

I scrunched my nose at him and stood up myself. "I'll be Hildegard and you can be Dominik." Those were the names of the husband and wife who occupied a neighboring estate to ours, back in Muniche.

"So we're the Kueglers. Fantastic." Joel shouldered his bag and quiver, then nocked a single arrow. "I might try to hit a squirrel on our way into town. So we'll look like true adventurers."

"I'm surprised you remember so much about a time you claimed to 'forget,'" I said as we descended the hill toward the trade route.

"The dreams never stopped," he muttered, his wind evident in his eyes as he scoured the grasses for unsuspecting prey.

Eisenwald lay still and quiet below the hill, the dirt path marking the eastern trade route curling off toward the main street. Joel and I set out for that familiar path, and he voiced a few reminisces about the last time we had come. I remained silent as we progressed, my thoughts in many directions. Part of me followed Joel's recollections—the children frolicking upon the grassy knoll, running into Freia's old nanny on the street, meeting Lord Edwin, Freia's gracious father.

But I also thought of meeting that phantom on the river, when I observed the Rhine snaking along its time-worn path. He had paddled us to his cottage, the bonds of the spirit loosened at last . . . the glory of our mutual love during that day we spent together . . . and the horror of the night, facing the demon who had conquered my lover's sanity.

Would I have to fear such a thing when I sought my immortal husband in several days? Wuotan had tried to slay me in time's currents. If he took charge of Augustin's hands, the demon could launch me back to my son in the twenty-first century—back to a place where Muniche's bonds lured me into a relationship I could never consummate.

I'll have to plant myself in this timeline, whether Wuotan likes it or not, I told myself, shoving aside the past that haunted me. *I don't think he possesses his Black Priests very often, only when he's aroused their anger. And Augustin shouldn't be angry to see me again . . . I hope.*

Joel shot an errant squirrel before we reached the edges of the village, his hands directing the arrow with ease. It struck the squirrel right through the nose, and Joel flopped its body over his shoulder with the remark that he could offer it to the cooking pot that afternoon. That reminded me that most people ate only two meals per day in this era—lunch and dinner. Lunch would be at Sext or noon, and dinner would be at Vespers or twilight. Eisenwald's church bells had not rung since our arrival; I judged the hour to be somewhere between Lauds and Terce.

I heard livestock stirring once we neared the first cottages, but overall the town appeared strangely quiet. We ran into no one on the path. When we reached the main street we saw just a few women headed for the well, a pair of boys herding a troop of goats. None of the townsfolk looked our way, and I noticed that the women all sported scarves tied about their noses—odd, for the weather was balmy for late May.

"So why is everyone scurrying around like they're expecting the apocalypse?" Joel muttered to me in English, casting doubtful glances toward those gathered at the main well.

The truth hit me in the face, for I realized that I had seen no boats parked at the wharf—an extremely rare occurrence at this Rhenisch town dependent on trade. "Augustin's record . . . mentioned a pestilence."

To be continued . . . .

Book VI comes out in June 2022
Order now from your preferred platform!

C.L. Carhart would be thrilled if you would leave a review for this book. Reviews help buoy an indie author's career, as well as her spirits. She appreciates your feedback!

Sign up for C.L. Carhart's newsletter for an inside look at her author undertakings, along with information on new releases and the occasional secret deal.
https://sendfox.com/clcarhart

Lurid Curse is available on library platforms! Ask your local library to order it in eBook and paperback so that C.L. can reach more readers.

Follow C.L. on social media:
https://www.facebook.com/CLCarhartAuthor
https://www.instagram.com/c.l.carhart.author
https://www.minds.com/clcarhart/
https://www.bookbub.com/profile/c-l-carhart

German Translations

ach - oh, ah

Alter Peter - St. Peter's Church in München

Bayerisch - Bavarian dialect

Eintopf - one pot stew: typically made with meat, green vegetables, potatoes, and herbs

Föhn - warm mountain breeze

Frau - Miss, Mrs.

Glühwein - spiced wine usually served around the winter holidays

Herr - Mr.

Jägerschnitzel - breaded veal with mushroom gravy

Käse - cheese

Kummervoll - sorrowful

Landjäger - semi-dried sausage popular as a snack

Leberkäse - finely ground meatloaf similar to bologna

Lebkuchen - honey-sweetened cookies usually served around the winter holidays

Norddeutscher Verein Historikers - North German Historical Society

Oma - grandma

Onkel - uncle

Opa - grandpa

Ostbahnhoff - east train station in München

Pappi - dad

Radler - beer mixed with lemon soda

S-Bahn - above-ground train system in larger German cities

Sächsisch - Saxon dialect

Sauerbraten - beef marinated in wine & herbs, served with heavy gravy

Spätzle - egg noodle pasta

Süddeutsche Getriebe - South German Gearboxes

Tante - aunt

U-Bahn/en - singular/plural, underground train system in larger German cities

Unmensch - monster, cruel person

Weißbier – wheat beer popular in Bavaria

Teutonica Translations

Aelte Teutonica – old Teutonica, used in the B.C.E. years
Der Weg Teutonisch – The Teutonic Way
Eihalbe/Eihalbae - singular/plural, fairy of silver oak
Gaestelort - spiritual realm
Gaestelort Troumerae - spiritual dream world
Leitaeri - Prince/keyholder of a Teuton city
Leitalra - Lady of a Teuton city
Selakerza - soul candle
Teutona/Teutonae - singular/plural, female Teuton
Teutonica - old Teuton dialect
Torstein - stone of the gate
Toteheri - dead army
Virstohran - ritual vengeance
Wuotan - demon lord of the Teuton people
Zoubaraera - witch

Pronunciation Guide
(for names and commonly used words)

Augustin – Au-GUS-tin
Bayerisch – BEYE-rish (eye is pronounced like eyeball)
Bayern – BEYE-urn (eye is pronounced like eyeball)
Dane – DAH-nuh
Der Weg – Dare Veg
Eihalbe – EYE-hahl-buh (eye is pronounced like eyeball)
Fonsi – FON-zee
Freia/Freya – FREYE-yuh (eye is pronounced like eyeball)
Ina – EE-nuh
Isar – EE-zahr
Ivo – EE-voh
Jan – Yahn
Jens – Yenz
Leitaeri – Leye-TARE-ee (eye is pronounced like eyeball)
Leitalra – Leye-TAHL-rah (eye is pronounced like eyeball)
Mane – MAH-nuh
Matthias – Muh-TEE-uhs
Miche – MIH-khuh
Muniche – MYOO-nih-khuh
Swanhilde – Swan-HIL-duh
Thaden – TODD-n
Torstein – TOR-stein (stein is pronounced like a beer
    stein)
Toteheri – TOH-tuh-hare-ee
Traudl – TROW-dool (trow is pronounced like cow)
Teutonica – Too-TAHN-ih-kuh
Üwe – EW-vuh
Vreni – FRAY-nee
Wuotan – VOH-tahn

About the Author

C.L. Carhart has been writing since the age of 4, dabbling in everything from children's books, to fantasy, to historical fiction. Eventually, her lifelong interest in European history inspired her to create a paranormal fantasy realm based on the Teutonic people groups. The *His Name Was Augustin* series provides a first glimpse at this other-world—a place rife with ancient mysteries and dark magic.

Born and raised in southern New Jersey, C.L. spends her free time hiking with her husband, enjoying metal music, snuggling her feline familiars, and dreaming of the wonders of Germany.

www.ingramcontent.com/pod-product-compliance
Lightning Source LLC
Chambersburg PA
CBHW060943190726
48286CB00005B/1405